PUTTERING ABOUT IN A SMALL LAND

Also by Philip K. Dick

Solar Lottery (1955)
The World Jones Made (1956)
The Man Who Japed (1956)
The Cosmic Puppets (1957)
Eye in the Sky (1957)
Dr. Futurity (1959)
Time Out of Joint (1959)
Vulcan's Hammer (1960)
The Man in the High Castle (1962)
The Game-Players of Titan (1963)
The Penultimate Truth (1964)
The Simulacra (1964)
Martian Time-Slip (1964)
Clans of the Alphane Moon (1964)
Dr Bloodmoney, or How We Got
   Along After the Bomb (1965)
The Three Stigmata of Palmer
   Eldritch (1965)
Now Wait for Last Year (1966)
The Crack in Space (1966)
The Ganymede Takeover (with Ray
   F. Nelson) (1967)
Counter-Clock World (1967)
Do Androids Dream of Electric
   Sheep? (1968)

Ubik (1969)
Galactic Pot-Healer (1969)
Our Friends From Frolix 8 (1970)
A Maze of Death (1970)
We Can Build You (1972)
Flow My Tears, The Policeman Said
   (1974)
Confessions of a Crap Artist (1975)
Deus Irae (with *Roger Zelazny*) (1976)
A Scanner Darkly (1977)
The Divine Invasion (1981)
Valis (1981)
The Transmigration of Timothy
   Archer (1982)
Lies, Inc (1984)
The Man Whose Teeth Were All
   Exactly Alike (1984)
Puttering About in a Small Land
   (1985)
In Milton Lumky Territory (1985)
Radio Free Albemuth (1985)
Humpty Dumpty in Oakland (1986)
Mary and the Giant (1987)
The Broken Bubble (1988)

SHORT-STORY COLLECTIONS

The Variable Man (1957)
A Handful of Darkness (1966)
The Turning Wheel (1977)
The Best of Philip K. Dick (1977)
The Golden Man (1980)
The Minority Report (2002)

THE COLLECTED STORIES OF
PHILIP K. DICK

1 Beyond Lies the Wub (1987)
2 Second Variety (1987)
3 The Father Thing (1987)
4 The Days of Perky Pat (1987)
5 We Can Remember it for You
   Wholesale (1987)

PUTTERING ABOUT IN A SMALL LAND

PHILIP K. DICK

This edition first published in Great Britain in 2014
by Gollancz
An imprint of the Orion Publishing Group
Orion House, 5 Upper St Martin's Lane, London WC2H 9EA
An Hachette UK Company

1 3 5 7 9 10 8 6 4 2

A CIP catalogue record for this book is available
from the British Library

ISBN 978 0 575 13206 1

Printed in Great Britain by
CPI Group (UK) Ltd, Croydon, CR0 4YY

The Orion Publishing Group's policy is to use papers that
are natural, renewable and recyclable products and made
from wood grown in sustainable forests. The logging and
manufacturing processes are expected to conform to the
environmental regulations of the country of origin.

www.orionbooks.co.uk
www.gollancz.co.uk

PUTTERING ABOUT IN A SMALL LAND

1

The trip was new to her. She had lived in Los Angeles for almost nine years but she had never started up Highway 99, the fast inland highway that people took to San Francisco, five hundred miles to the north. As soon as the last Chevron stations and cafés and tract houses had fallen behind, the highway made directly for the mountains; without warning, she found herself in a tight bunch of cars and trucks, traveling at immense speed—her speedometer told her it was between seventy and ninety miles an hour—in a cleft that had been cut into the first row of hills. Ahead of her were the mountains themselves and she thought to herself that they were so desolate. Nobody lived there, certainly. The diesel trucks passed her on both sides; far up in the cab the driver of each eyed her with that dull, aloof disdain that so infuriated her. And then the trucks went around the turn ahead and left her behind.

My Lord, she thought. Her hands, clutching the wheel, were white and damp. The racket of the trucks still beat in her ears, and she said to Gregg beside her, "Don't they go fast."

"Yes," he said, in a tone that matched her own. They both sensed their insignificance; they had been cut down to the stature of motes. Meanwhile, as they shared their anxiety, three more trucks roared past.

"I can't keep up with them," she said to Gregg. "I could, but I'm not. Good Lord, we're going seventy-five miles an hour. That isn't anything on this road. Those trucks are going ninety." Can you imagine, she thought, what it would look like if one of them turned a curve and found a car stalled in its path? The newspaper had accounts of such carnage, but she had never seen anything of that kind; the nearest had been an accident, happening ahead of her, in which a milk truck had sideswiped a taxi. Glass and milk had gone in all directions, and bits of taxi, too.

"It's unbelievable to think," she said to Gregg, "that people drive this every day of their lives."

Gregg said, "We don't have to go very far, do we?" His hands pressed together in his lap; the slow, nervous activity that his father gave way to under tension. On the boy's face a frown, a wrinkling of his brows, spread and consumed, got to his eyes and then his mouth, until he had been gathered up into a crimped little shape of concern. She let go of the wheel with her right hand to pat him reassuringly; his shoulder was as sharp and rigid as bone could be. Bone, she thought. Yes, he had hunched himself down into his bones, to peep out at passing things. Just a glance now and then, without any letting go.

"It's not far," she said. "We don't stay on this highway more than a few minutes. Then we turn off. Open up the map."

With a rustling, a stirring, he unfolded the map.

"Look at it," she said, her eyes fixed ahead, on the road. "Can you see where we are? I marked it in pencil, along Highway 99; do you see that? It's in red."

"Yes," he said.

"See that road turning off?" For an instant she glanced down. "Highway 126, I think it is."

"Yes," he said.

"Can you tell if there's a town there?"

After a long, long time, Gregg said, "I don't think there is."

A sports car, like a black raisin, passed them and left them behind. "I loathe those things," Virginia said.

"That's funny-looking," Gregg said, rousing himself to see. "Boy!" he said.

She knew, from having studied the map, that to make the turn-off she had to be in the extreme left lane, three lanes over. No signs were visible anywhere, and she began to fear the worst. To her left the traffic was heavy, unbroken; the cars and trucks seemed to gain speed constantly, as if they had decided to race her. She put on the left-turn signal, but the cars paid no attention. Or perhaps they did not want to pay attention; she saw the faces of the drivers and they were without excitement, painted on, faultless.

"They know I want to get over," she said to Gregg. "How can I get over if they don't let me?" The turn-off was probably around the next curve, unless she had passed it already. "Look on the map," she said. "See when the next turn-off is after that one."

Gregg began to rustle the map.

"Hurry!" she said.

"I can't tell," he said in his choked, apprehensive voice.

"Give it to me." Steadying the wheel with her left hand she glanced down at the map. But she could not keep her eyes on it long enough; a horn honked at her left and she swerved back into her lane. "Let it go," she said, pushing the map away. "I don't see why they don't let me over," she said.

Beside her, Gregg shrank down and paid no attention to the road. That maddened her; she felt isolated. Did nobody care? But then a space appeared in the traffic and she was able to get quickly into the next lane and from there over to the one she wanted. It was the fastest of the lanes, and at once, without volition, she found herself driving at the head-on traffic at a speed so great that she could scarcely keep from shutting her eyes.

"It just isn't worth it," she muttered.

Gregg said, "I think it's pretty soon. The turn-off." He sounded so humble, so timid, that she was ashamed.

"I'm not used to driving out on the highway," she said to him. The hills, she thought; they were so bleak, so lacking in life. Could a school really be set out in this wasteland? The hills in the East; before the present generation, other people had lived there, and before them, others. It was clear that someone had always lived there. Before the English the Indians. Before the Indians—nobody knew, but certainly some race, some form of life, intelligent, responsible. The animals, she thought; she had heard them in motion, active and alert. That kind of life was enough. Here, the hills were like refuse heaps, without color; the ground was only dirt, the plants were patches of weeds separated from one another, holding beer cans and paper that had blown down the canyons. This was a canyon, she realized; it was not a cleft. And the wind roared; she felt it lift the car.

So the city had gone as far as possible. One house might appear in a particular spot, a billboard would come, a gas station. But each would be set apart. No communication between them, she thought. Remote sparks at night, on the side of the highway.

"There it is," Gregg said.

Ahead of them was a construction, signs and a road; she saw signal lights and white markings on the pavement. Yellow flashed and she slowed the car, realizing, with relief, that nothing had gone wrong. "Thanks," she said. Before the light became red she turned left, and in an instant they had passed from the highway. The traffic continued in the other direction, and she thought to herself, Good riddance.

"We found it after all," Gregg said.

"Yes," she said. "Well, the second time we'd know where it was. We wouldn't have to worry."

He nodded.

The road, much narrower than the highway, entered an orchard of tall, peculiar-looking trees. Pleased, she pointed to them. "What are those?" she asked Gregg. "Those aren't fruit trees."

"I don't know," he said.

"Maybe they hold the soil," she said. "Or break up the wind." To their right a great far-off cliff of dry, reddish dirt stuck straight up, like the wall of a quarry. At the top a line of foliage grew, but the cliff itself was barren.

"Is it far now?" Gregg asked.

"I don't think so. We go through Santa Paula. You have the map; you can look at it and see how far it is."

He rattled the map, searching to find Ojai.

"It isn't far," she said. Now she saw smaller trees whose branches grew in tightly-wrapped heads. "Orange trees," she said, cheered up. The countryside was fertile; tractors had taken up residence in the middle of the fields. "This is farm country," she said. And the land, thank the Lord, was flat. "I guess we're up high," she said. "We're actually in the mountains."

Gregg watched the tractors and the men at work near them. "Hey," he said. "Those are Mexicans."

"Maybe they're wetbacks," she said.

The orange trees grew so short that she felt as if she had got into a play-world; she half-expected to come across candy cottages and tiny old men with white beards down to their turned-up shoes. Her gloom and nervousness evaporated and she thought that perhaps the school would work out after all.

Gregg said, "But what'll I do about school?"

Again she realized that he did not understand; he thought of it as summer camp. "Good grief," she said.

"And," he said, with agitation, "How about—" Squirming around on the car seat he said, "And how'll I get back home?"

"We'll come and pick you up," she said.

"When?"

"On the weekend. Friday night. Now you know that."

"What happens if I get sick?"

"There's a nurse there. Now listen to me," she said. "You're old enough now to be by yourself; you don't need me to be nearby every minute of the day and night."

Hearing that, he began to sniffle.

"Stop that," she said.

Sniffling, he said, "I want to go home."

"Now we've talked about it," she said. "You know it's so you won't have asthma. And you'll be in a much smaller class, only five or six children." Mrs. Alt, who owned the Los Padres Valley School, had stressed that in her letters.

"I want to go home," Gregg repeated, but they both knew it was no use; they both realized that she had made up her mind.

Their road, the one they wanted, cut off to the right and took them through a dense pack of trees, up a rise away from the farm country and orchards and fields. Tangled growth appeared; they entered an abandoned area that gave her the shivers. The road became narrow and tortuous and again she was aware of the desolation, the between-towns emptiness. Once, she and Gregg saw a hunter with a gun. Signs everywhere warned:

NO TRESPASSING.
PRIVATE PROPERTY.
NO HUNTING OR FISHING.

The hills had a hard, primitive vindictiveness, she thought. She noticed rusty barbed wire hanging from trees; it had been strung here and then—she supposed—cut away to make passage for some hunter.

"I see the stream," Gregg said.

The stream had been hidden by the drop and by the trees. As the car crossed a bridge, mostly logs nailed together, she saw for an instant a bunch of fishermen with their lines out. Their cars were parked off the road, and she had to slow almost to a stop to get by them. None of the fishermen looked up.

"Hey," Gregg said. "Look—fishing." For a long time he peered back. "Can I go fishing? Are we near the school?" Later, he said, "I never been fishing, but Patrick Dix went fishing with his Dad one day; I think that was up around some beach. And they caught this huge fish; it was really big. I think it was a shark."

The road turned suddenly to the left and rose so steeply that the car chugged and gears within the automatic transmission shifted and selected themselves. She put the lever into low range. Behind them two cars which had lined up fell back and became lost to sight.

"It's steep," she said, wishing she had been told about the mountains. "We're going up high."

They continued on up, turning constantly, until at last they reached the top of the mountain range. Below them lay the Ojai Valley; both she and Gregg let out a cry at the sight.

"It's flat!" Gregg yelled, standing up to see.

"Down we go," she said, gritting her teeth and holding onto the wheel. At each curve a sheer blank drop, unfenced, reminded her that she would have to come back on this road, perhaps at night. She thought, How can I drive this? Sixty or more miles each way . . .

"Look!" Gregg cried. "Here comes a bus!"

An obese, senile yellow school bus was working its way up the grades and curves toward her; in the bus children waved and leaped about. The road was barely wide enough for the bus, and already it had begun to honk at her. Is this your road? she wondered, not knowing what to do. The bus honked again and she brought the car off onto the shoulder so that the overhanging bank of dirt and roots scraped along the window. The right wheels spun; she had got into a drainage ditch. In panic, she jerked the car back toward the road. The bus, now just ahead, veered away, honking, and she passed it with a swish of dirt torn loose from the bank.

"Oh God," she said finally. Trembling, she drove on.

Gregg said, "Boy, that was a close call!"

Now the ground flattened; they had left the mountains and had reached the Valley. The road became straight. Far off, at the opposite end, she saw the town of Ojai. Thank heaven, she said to herself. Glancing at her wristwatch she realized that she had been driving only an hour and a half; the time was eleven-thirty. In time for lunch, possibly.

Anything, she thought, for a cup of coffee.

*   *   *

At the entrance to the school they both noticed more of the short, plump orange trees. The air was warm and dust blew ahead of them, among the trees and along the path. She enjoyed walking; a relief, certainly, from being in the car. But behind the school buildings were the mountains, the dreadful mountains.

"Are you at all carsick?" she asked Gregg. Beside her he had slowed and now he examined something in his coat pocket. "Put your spray away," she said, stopping his arm. "You aren't wheezing; you haven't since we left L.A. Evidently it is the smog. How do you feel?"

"Okay," he said, but he held on to his Adrenalin spray. Before he got out of the car he had used the spray, and on his pants was a spot that had dripped. His fright had increased, and as soon as she stopped walking he did so, too.

"I imagine they keep the horses over in that barn," she said, to cheer him. "Why, isn't that somebody riding?" She made him look toward the slope of grass and trees beyond the school grounds. A trail, a fire break, separated the shrubbery of the hill from the school's playing field. "I see they have football," she said.

A lemon bush, its leaves dark and shiny, grew by the steps ahead of them at the end of the path. Gregg tore loose one of the clumps of lemons; fruit and blossoms and leaves came apart between his hands as he and Virginia climbed the steps. On his face was an expression of forlorn savagery. Her own mood became dreary and she wondered if the school, the whole idea of sending him away from home, was going to work out after all.

"It's up to you, dear," she said. "If it turns out that you don't like it, you can come home. You understand that. But we want to give it a try."

Not answering, he gazed up at the main building, his eyes almost shut, his lips clamped together. And on his forehead the furrows and folds had gathered again, the wrinkles of worry, as if he were oppressed even by the size of the building. The school grounds, at this time, were deserted; one semester had ended and the children had gone home for a week. For that matter, she did not even see any teachers. But in a day or so, she thought. Then it would be more active.

"There's a trail up into the mountains," she said. "You can go on hikes. You can camp and build a fire and sleep in a tent, like your friend Bob Rooley did at summer camp." Remembering the pictures in the booklet accompanying one of Mrs. Alt's letters, she said, "And think of the rabbits and the goat and the horses—dogs and cats, all sorts of animals. Even a possum. In a cage."

The boy's face stayed hating.

Ahead of them the glass front doors of the building had been propped open, and Gregg shuffled inside. The lobby—dark and still—reminded Virginia of an old-fashioned hotel. Here was the desk, too. And all so silent. For dignity, she decided; to impress the parents. Stairs to a second floor. And, at the far end, the dining room.

"I'm going to try to get a cup of coffee," she said to her son.

No school official had appeared as yet to greet them. What, she wondered, should she do?

To her right, in an alcove serving as a library, two wide windows gave a view of the Valley. The school had been built on high ground; purposely, she decided, as she turned to the windows. The town of Ojai could be seen first, the Spanish-style buildings among which she had driven. Even the automobile garage had ivy growing up its walls. The single main street of the town had, along most of its west side, a park. On the other side, the shops, a single row of them, connecting one with the next, made her think of a mission. Or stalls, she thought. Each with its adobe arch. And the post office at the corner was in the shape of a tower; it occupied the ground floor, under what appeared to her to be a belfry.

The park, visible to her, had in it a series of tennis courts. Yes, this was where they held the tennis matches. And the music festivals, too. Beyond the town, the Valley extended to the mountains, surfaces perpendicular to each other, meeting at right angles. As if, she thought, she were down at the bottom, standing where she could see up the sides. But the Valley was large; she did not feel cramped. Yet the mountains existed in every direction. No other route back, except over them. Only two roads—according to her map—and each as hazardous and steep as the other.

"Isn't it lovely?" she said to Gregg, who had wandered over beside her.

"Yes," he said.

"We were in those mountains," she said. "We drove through them. Wasn't that exciting?"

"Yes," he said.

Feeling restless, she began to roam around, out of the library and into the hall, past the desk and then back again. An office door was open, and books in stacks covered the floor, a single book repeated over and over again, a textbook. It reminded her of her own childhood, this peeping into unfamiliar schoolrooms for the first time, the smells of varnish and paper, the storerooms such as this.

From a side doorway a woman appeared, noticed her, and said, "Can I help you?" This woman, middle-aged, with a strong beaked nose, wore slacks and a sailcloth shirt, her rimless glasses gave her a forceful look and she walked with that straight, practical authority that Virginia remembered so well: this woman had the unadorned vitality of the professional schoolmistress, a type that had kept order among the young since the days of the Roman country villas. Surely this was Mrs. Alt.

"I'm Virginia Lindahl," Virginia said.

"Oh yes!" The woman put out her hand. "I'm Edna Alt." Her hair was brushed back and tied with—heavens—a rubber band. And her cheeks, although firm, had a grayish cast, probably from hiking and from supervising leathercraft out under the sun. "I'll take a chance and address you as Virginia," Mrs. Alt said, smiling a smile that made Virginia think, This is how they smile at you when you join their active revolutionary party. "Is this Gregg?"

"Yes," she said. "You know, Mrs. Alt, I wish somebody had told me about the drive; those turns down the mountain . . ."

"If the school bus can make it, a twenty-year-old bus, you can, too," Mrs. Alt said, still smiling the underlying message which had to do with confidence and knowing to rely on your own ability. But it was a genial message, even optimistic; Virginia did not resent it. To Mrs. Alt, everyone had great potentialities, and it was a doctrine that Virginia applauded. The same tone had got into Mrs. Alt's letters, and that was one of the reasons why Virginia had chosen the Los Padres School over the others.

"I think I met your bus," Virginia said.

But Mrs. Alt had already transferred her attention to Gregg. "My," Mrs. Alt said, without making it sound fatuous or quaint; it was more of her enthusiasm, a spontaneous expression. "This is the little boy who has trouble with his breathing. Is that your Adrenalin spray?" She held out her hand. "You know what I bet, Gregg? I bet you won't need that up here."

Virginia thought, It's fine to talk like that if you can pull it off. And, she thought, I hope to God you can, Mrs. Alt, because it's going to cost me two-hundred-and-fifty dollars a month.

"Would you like to see your room?" Mrs. Alt asked Gregg, who stared up at her mutely. "You may, if you want." Taking his spray from him she held onto his hand and began to guide—lead, really—him toward the stairs. Gregg hung back. "Or you can go outside. I believe James is shoeing one of the horses. Have you ever watched a horse being shod?" In her voice appeared a hushed, mysterious tone, as if she were letting the boy in on some secret of worth. Virginia was reminded of the children's programs on the radio; those ladies talked that way, too. Perhaps it had become an occupational dialect. But Gregg, by degrees, began to respond.

Remaining where she was she watched Mrs. Alt pilot Gregg outdoors, onto the stone terrace, and then down a flight of steps. And now, Virginia thought, into the pot with you, young man. This is where we boil the new children.

But, she thought, the woman's good at it. She is no fool. My mother and Mrs. Alt; they would get along. What a pair.

Mrs. Alt returned at a great rate, striding as if she had been hiking for miles. "We stopped for a minute to watch them put up tents," she said to Virginia. "When it's warm enough we sleep outdoors. The air is excellent up here."

"His asthma's better," Virginia said. She felt a little afraid of Mrs. Alt.

"Yes, I thought he was breathing normally. How far back does his history of respiratory difficulty go? I'm thinking that it may be the result of an emotional situation in the home environment, rather than the smog. Could that be? Come into the office so I can get your letter from the file." Mrs. Alt had already started along the hall.

The office smelled of soap. As she arranged her coat over her lap, Virginia saw that the smell came from a washroom. A picture entered her mind: the faculty, all of them ladies with eyeglasses and encouraging smiles, washing their hands regularly, perhaps every hour. Perhaps at the ring of a bell. But the aura of the school seemed to be one of warmth, not harshness; the rule here was enthusiasm.

Lighting a cigarette, Virginia said, "The two-fifty is going to cut deep, but we feel it's worth it."

"Eh," Mrs. Alt said, pausing and glancing at her sideways. "I see."

Silence, then. Mrs. Alt found the letter and read it over; she finished, pushed it aside, leaned back, and scrutinized Virginia.

"Why do you want to put him in the school?"

Taken aback, Virginia said, "Because—it would be good for him."

"Why?" With a gesture of dismissal, Mrs. Alt spun Virginia's letter all the way around.

"Well," Virginia said, "the home situation is bad; tensions and—"

"I ask that," Mrs. Alt interrupted, "because I want to be sure you're not simply trying to get out from under the responsibility of raising a child."

"Now look," Virginia said.

"Is Gregg happy at home?"

"Well," she said, drawling with mortification.

"What does he think about living up here? He's never lived away from home before, has he? He's always been with you."

"I feel he's breaking down under the tensions that he has to cope with in the home, which aren't his fault." She stared at a place on the floor. What had she got herself into here?

"I see," Mrs. Alt said.

"Good Lord," Virginia said, "I'm not completely ignorant of my own motivations."

Folding her hands together on her desk, Mrs. Alt said, "How does your husband feel?"

"He's—not overly sold on the idea. I'll admit that."

"What's his relationship with Gregg?"

"Good. As far as it goes. That is, Roger is involved with his work." She added, "As I mentioned in my letter, he owns a retail television store. It takes a good deal of time. Usually he doesn't get home until after Gregg is in bed. The only time he sees him—you understand of course that the store is open all day Saturday—is on Sunday. And even then, Roger sometimes goes down to the store to get caught up."

Mrs. Alt said, "How are you and you husband getting along?"

"Oh," she said, "fine." How humiliating it was.

"What about these—tensions?"

Virginia groaned.

"Would you rather not discuss it with me?" Mrs. Alt asked.

"No. I don't care. It just seems a little gratuitous." After an interval she resumed. "Anyhow, I think I explained in my letter that I have done and am doing now, to some degree, a dance therapy that gives me some opportunity to gain an insight into psychological workings, including my own, and my husband's. And the home situation."

"You did mention that," Mrs. Alt said noncommittally. She did not appear to be impressed.

"It's important to realize," Virginia said, "that Roger and I have radically different histories."

"What on earth," Mrs. Alt broke in, "can you possibly mean by that? I get so impatient—" Arising, she paced around the room, slapping her arms together around herself, and then sat down again. "How old are you, Virginia? You're still in your twenties, aren't you?

Well, say thirty. And you talk like some decrepit psychiatrist from back in the—what would you call it?—let's say back in the Popular Front Days. I mean these—terms. Can't you come out and *say* what you mean, do you have to play these word games?"

Virginia said, "I guess a schoolmistress is used to treating everyone as a child to be corrected." She was angry, but she also was amused, in a sour ironic fashion; after all, she had sized up Mrs. Alt in much the same terms.

"Am I doing that?" Mrs. Alt considered. "No," she said, rejecting Virginia's account. "I'm just trying to get you to come down to earth. Look, let's get out of here; let's get outdoors in the sun and out of this stuffy office."

Starting off, she glanced back over her shoulder. Virginia put out her cigarette, collected her coat and purse, and followed her outdoors, into the hot, bright sunlight. Mrs. Alt led her from the building and down a long dirt roadway; the clumps of dried mud broke under their shoes, and once Virginia stumbled. Mrs. Alt, of course, had on low-heeled workshoes. The air burned Virginia's throat and again she thought of coffee. But she was being taken away from the dining room and kitchens, toward a series of wooden shed-like outbuildings.

"You can help us air out the canvas," Mrs. Alt said.

"Not in these clothes," Virginia said.

"Well," Mrs. Alt said, smiling, "then you can supervise." She slowed so that Virginia could catch up with her. "It won't hurt you, Virginia. What would you say if I told you I thought rolling out canvas, outdoors in the sun, is a lot better for a person than dance therapy or any of the so-called creative psychological therapies?"

"I don't know what I'd say," Virginia said, feeling low.

"I won't try you, then."

A gang of children, wearing nothing but khaki shorts, sat on a flat grassy plot, spreading out canvas tents. Most of them seemed older than Gregg. Gregg was not among them.

"Fine," Mrs. Alt said, supervising.

"Mrs. Alt," one of the boys said, "I found a toad in one of the tents; can I keep it?"

"Is it alive?"

"Well, it moves some. I think if I give it some grass to eat it'll be okay."

Watching the activity, Virginia could not ignore the fact that the girls—three of them, eight or nine years old—had no tops on; like the boys, they wore only shorts. Of course, eight years old was young . . . she debated in her mind. Not that it mattered. But there were certainly two schools of thought on the topic. The skin of the children shone dark brown. They did look healthy. It would be hard to imagine asthma here, she thought. Colds and asthma, turn elsewhere. The children seemed happy, but subdued.

"Take a careful look at your toad," Mrs. Alt was saying, "and see if it has a precious jewel set in its head."

Virginia laughed with outrage.

After no jewel had been discovered by any of the children, Mrs. Alt returned to Virginia, drew her to one side, and said to her, "Would you like a short little snap judgment of you, Virginia? An on-the-spot word picture? I'd say you're intelligent, very well educated, basically kindly, but rather nasty out of what I'd call ignorance. Arrogant nastiness, at that. You know, the more I talk to you the more I agree that Gregg should be here with us. You're convincing me." She put her arm around Virginia and squeezed her, an action that horrified Virginia.

As evenly as possible, Virginia said, "Well Mrs. Alt, I'll think it over and let you know."

"Let me know?"

"Yes," she said. "We have a couple of days, don't we, until the beginning of the semester . . . I'll phone you or write." As far as she was concerned it was all off. She had endured enough.

Mrs. Alt said, "You're capable of real anger, aren't you? I thought you were. Virginia, you drove up here with the intention of putting Gregg in the school. Now, you're old enough and bright enough not to change your mind because your feelings are a little bit hurt."

"Damn you if you do, damn you if you don't," she said in a state of despair. "What am I supposed to do?"

Leading her by the arm, Mrs. Alt started back along the dirt road. "Just calm yourself. Tell me about your radically different histories."

Virginia said, "Is it possible that I can get a cup of coffee?"

"We'll have lunch. It's at least twelve, isn't it? The children have already had their lunch . . . there're only a few of them here, so we don't open the dining room; we let them eat in the kitchen. Will it bother you to eat with some of the teachers? I think they're in there about now."

"I don't care," Virginia said.

In the kitchen two women and a man sat at a yellow wooden table, eating and talking. The cook, an immense Mexican woman in her sixties, prepared lunch at the oil-burning range and a younger woman, sweet-faced, also Mexican, set out dishes. The kitchen was larger than Virginia had expected; it was like an auditorium. The range took up one whole side. The glasses and plates were stacked on shelves, as clean as could be. Mrs. Alt introduced her to the teachers, but the names passed over her; she had fallen into a dulled, somber mood, and all she could think of was sitting down and getting the coffee.

"How long have you lived out here in California?" Mrs. Alt asked her, seated across from her beside the male teacher.

"Since 1944," she answered. The coffee steamed; she found it hot and fairly good. "Before that we lived in Washington, D.C. We met there."

Mrs. Alt said, "Gregg is a little undersize, isn't he? Is he eight?"

"Seven and a half."

"You know that we have a physical examination for each of the children during the first month they're here. We expect to have the usual ailments—we keep a trained nurse always on the grounds—but after all, this is a school and not a hospital. If Gregg's attacks become too acute we won't be able to keep him. However, I don't think they will be."

"The spray takes care of it," Virginia said. "He knows how to use the spray. If it gets worse he has an inhaler. But you'd have to help him with that; it means setting it up over heat and mixing the herbs or whatever they are." She was listless now. "He's never needed that. I don't even remember where I put it." She finished, "And anyhow that's the whole point. If he's not better off up here we don't want to leave him here. We really don't like the idea of sending him away from home. But as I started to explain, we don't agree on a lot of basic points—Roger and myself, I mean. He has his ideas and they're not the same as mine." She sipped her coffee.

"Were you both born in Washington?"

"I was born in Boston," she, said. "Roger was born in the Middle West."

"Why don't you want to tell me where?"

She shrugged. "Arkansas, I think." Whenever she said it she felt her flesh crawl. "He had a very poverty-stricken childhood. During the Depression they lived on relief and charity. I guess it was common enough. Potato peels from the family next door." The topic filled her with torpor; she recited the information mechanically. "My family was better off, but of course we all felt it. Anyhow—" She drew herself up and rested her elbows on the table, holding her cup at chin-level. "Because of his own childhood—he really doesn't talk much about it so I get it piecemeal—Roger worries about a lot of things that don't bother me, financial matters for instance. Food, for another. They never got all they wanted to eat, although I don't think they really went hungry. He's always afraid something will go wrong . . . if you understand. He's tense all the time. He spends most of his time down at the store, not doing anything; sort of—" She gestured. "More or less just keeping his eye on it. To be sure it's there."

"Won't the two-fifty a month increase his anxiety?"

"Well yes," she admitted. "But then Gregg won't be there. So presumably it won't affect him."

The three teachers had their own conversation going, but they were also listening.

Mrs. Alt said, "I can't see any improvement in your situation if this bankrupts you."

"It won't," she said shortly.

"We have an arrangement by which you could apply for a grant. Some of the children come in that way; the parents pay part of the tuition, interested groups pay the rest."

"We can manage it," Virginia said. "If we decide to go ahead." She drank more of her coffee. "And we don't agree on basic matters such as religion. Roger doesn't have any religious convictions; in fact he's against religious training. I don't want Gregg raised in that atmosphere. I don't want him raised, either, where there's a contempt for education and learning in general."

Mrs. Alt said, "What does your husband think of your dance-therapy?"

"Oh," she said, "he's indifferent."

"Do you have any interests in common?"

"Of course we have," Virginia said, not caring at the moment.

For several minutes Mrs. Alt discussed some trivial items with the teachers. Virginia ate the sandwich they had placed before her, finished her coffee, lit a cigarette. Nobody offered her a match; the male teacher—in sweater and slacks, with tie—was involved in conversation. She glanced at her wristwatch. The road, she thought. The god-awful trip back. Her great dread now was that for one reason or another she would be delayed and have to drive back after dark.

To Mrs. Alt she said, "I'd better go round up Gregg. We should start home soon."

"Bring him inside," Mrs. Alt said, "so he can have his lunch, too. He hasn't eaten, has he?"

"No," she admitted.

"You don't want to take him off without giving him his lunch. I left him with James; you can't miss the barn—you probably saw it as you came up from parking your car. It's down at the end of the playing field. Do you want me to go with you?" Already she had resumed her conversation with the teacher; it had to do with schedules for classes.

Virginia said, "We really should go." On her feet, she said, "Thank you for the meal."

"Why do you have to leave this minute?"

"The drive," she said.

"That does worry you, doesn't it?"

The male teacher—he was young, amiable-looking—said, "I wouldn't care to drive that very often. But some of the parents do. Every weekend; twice each way." To Virginia he said, "If you put your boy into the school would you want to pick him up on weekends?"

"Yes," she said. "That's what I told him, anyhow. I feel I should. It's part of the agreement between us."

"The children aren't dismissed on Friday until after three o'clock," Mrs. Alt said. "So you couldn't pick him up before then. And he should be back by six p.m. Sunday night. You'd have to drive it after dark, during the winter. From what you've said I don't think that would be a good idea; you'd be apprehensive about it, and that would be transmitted to Gregg and he'd feel that you didn't want to pick him up."

"This is all assuming—" Virginia began.

"Why couldn't her son go in with one of the other parents?" one of the lady teachers suggested. "Maybe they could arrange to share the driving."

"Liz Bonner picked her two boys up almost every Friday," the male teacher said. "Maybe you could arrange it with her."

"That's a good idea," Mrs. Alt said. "She'll be bringing her boys up sometime tomorrow." To Virginia she said, "Why don't you be here so I can introduce you to her? Unless you don't want somebody else to drive him."

"Mrs. Bonner is a good driver," the male teacher said.

"But real Los Angeles," one of the lady teachers said, and they all laughed.

The idea cheered Virginia. "Would she mind?" she said. "Maybe I could pay her or something. It would be worth it."

"Liz has to make the trip anyhow," Mrs. Alt said. "Let's do it this way; I'll talk to her when she brings her boys up, and then I'll phone you. If she's agreeable you can drive up and settle the details. You're living in Sepulveda and I think they live near there, toward San Fernando, near enough so it wouldn't be much out of her way. If necessary she could take Gregg to her place and you could pick him up there."

"Why couldn't she talk to Mrs. Bonner down there?" the young male teacher said. "Instead of having to make the drive back up here."

"I'd rather she talked to Liz up here," Mrs. Alt said. "So I can be sure it's settled. You know how Liz is."

Excusing herself, Virginia left the kitchen and set off for the barn. My God, she thought. It was settled. Decided. The burden of decision had faded away.

You'll love the Los Padres Valley School, she said to herself. Do as I tell you, young man. Love the Los Padres School. Because starting next week it's your home. And Edna Alt is your friend.

2

Poking his head into the store's office, Pete Bacciagalupi said to him, "Hey, you're still here, aren't you? I thought maybe you went home." The front door of Modern TV Sales & Service was locked and the shade was down; business had come to an end for the day. The overhead lights flickered as Olsen, the repairman, bent and shut them off at the switch. "You wife's looking for you," Pete said. "She parked in the yellow zone; she just now went back to get something."

"Okay," Roger Lindahl said. He closed the store books and stood up. Probably she was home from her jaunt up to Ojai. With Pete he walked through the store, checking the various switches to make certain everything was off. "The intercom," he said. "Get that."

"I got it," Pete said. "It's all checked; you can go home. I'll put on the night-light." At the cash register he punched the key and began winding a new tape. "You put the money away, didn't you? That's the main thing."

Olsen, at the front door, said, "Some dame wants in. Who gets to tell her we're closed?"

"That's Virginia," Roger said. "I'll let her in." With his key he unlocked the door for her.

"Hi," she said. "I'll drive you home." She kissed him and he smelled all the various road smells, cigarettes and heat and dust and the fatigue of fighting the traffic. Wilted, and yet unusually keyed-up, she clung to him and then stepped away, holding the door open. "Ready to go?" she asked.

"Wait," he said. "I have to get some junk from the office." He started back through the darkened store, and Virginia followed. When he reached the office she came after him, swirling her long coat, darting her head in a tic new to him; she seemed to be trying to view him from some covert angle, and he said, "Have I got a tail pinned to me or what is it?"

Virginia said, "Let's sit down for a second." She hopped onto the desk, crossed her legs, and slid off her shoe. "I drove with heels," she said. "It feels good to rest. Three hours on the road, and then God—the tramping around in the dirt." Her shoes had dust on them, reddish dry dirt, which she blew off.

"Oh yes," he said, not hiding his aversion. "The C.C.C. camps."

Pausing at the office door, Pete said, "Good night, Mrs. Lindahl. Good night, Roger. I'll see you tomorrow."

"Good night," Roger said. Virginia did not notice; she had opened her purse and was rooting in it.

"Good night!" Olsen bellowed, from the far end of the store. The door slammed as he departed.

After Pete had also gone, Roger said to his wife, "Where's Gregg?"

"Home. With Marion." That was her mother, Mrs. Watson.

"Did you find any schools you liked?" He let the words carry his attitude.

"I only visited one school," she said, her face thin with caution. "The Los Padres School. We had lunch there. And we watched a horse having his shoes put on."

"Now what?" he said. "Are you going back tomorrow?"

"No," she said. "Tomorrow is the day I'm over with Helen." Helen was the local ward boss of the Democratic Party; Virginia had got in deep on local issues, zoning and the like.

"And the next day," he said, "is dance day."

Virginia said, "How'm I going to tell you?"

In him, at that, settled the very thing she had rid herself of; the weight, the burden. "Did you give them a check?" he said.

"Yes."

"How much?"

"The whole first month's worth. Two hundred and fifty dollars."

"I can stop it," he said.

"Don't."

"Sure. Tomorrow morning." Absolutely, he thought. He had no doubts.

"She's wonderful. Mrs. Alt."

Roger said, "Is this so you can—have more free time? Is it going to be nothing but therapy classes and P.T.A.? Hell," he said, "that's the end of the P.T.A. sessions. You're taking him out of the public schools; you lose that. So what do you gain?" Across from him Virginia held herself in a fixed posture, her head tilted, smiling. "You have to have my permission," he said. "I'll go to a lawyer and see."

With a bright chirp, she said, "Do that."

The stared at each other.

At last she shuddered. "I know I'm right. You haven't even seen the school."

"Let's have the receipt." He stuck out his hand, waiting.

"You will go see it? Will you do that much at least?"

"I'll see it as I go up and get the check back."

"This is why I want him away," Virginia said. "You and I don't—" She broke off and swallowed, her eyes wide. Wetness rose, reached her lashes, glowed and quivered. But that was all.

"I'll call them tonight," he said, picking up the phone. "So they won't bank it." When he had got the operator he asked for the phone number of the Los Padres School, in Ojai.

Virginia said, "I'll leave you."

Hanging up, he wrote the number on the pad. "Why?"

"I'll—be ridiculous. Obviously. Or isn't that important?" Her voice sharpened, but always the reserve was there, the training; something was held back. "I go up, make arrangements to put Gregg in the school; I go over lists with Mrs. Alt to be sure I'm going to have everything he needs ready—things like labels on his clothes, all of them, medicines that he has to have—I stopped at the drugstore and got four different prescriptions filled; I've had the job all to myself of explaining to Gregg and getting him to understand; I drove that awful god damn drive twice in one day, a drive that would kill anyone, even you. Wait'll you drive it; you'll see what I'm up against." Plucking her handkerchief from her suit pocket she blew her nose and rubbed at her eyes.

Roger picked up the phone and dialed. He asked for the Ojai number. While he waited, Virginia pushed her handkerchief away, stepped from the desk and into her shoes, seized her purse, and ran from the office. He heard her heels on the floor, then the noise of the door opening, then the slam.

In his ear the phone buzzed. A voice, a woman's low voice, said, "Los Padres Valley School."

"I'd like to speak to Mrs. Alt."

"Speaking."

"This is Roger Lindahl." And at that point he was at a loss. "My wife," he said, "talked to you today."

"Oh yes. Virginia. Did she and Gregg get home all right?"

"Yes," he said.

"She told me how much the drive upset her." In his ear Mrs. Alt's voice was placid, but not unconcerned. "I imagine you've just now found out that Virginia's put Gregg in the school; is that so? She didn't tell me, but I had the idea that she was doing it on her own."

"Yes," he said.

"She's in a state of great tension," Mrs. Alt said, "but I think she knows what she's doing. Well, do you want to come up here and discuss it with me? I'll hold the check until I've talked to you about it. I can come by and visit you, if you'd prefer; I'll be down in L.A. tomorrow sometime late; I have a niece there."

"I'll come up," he said. "That way I can see the school."

"Good," Mrs. Alt said. "What time? Better make it in the morning."

"Ten," he said.

"Fine. Can you bring Gregg? The more he sees of it before you decide the better. I wish he could stay here a week, but the semester begins in a few days and we have to have the registration completed. I'll see you at ten, then. If you get lost and can't find the school, ask anywhere in town." The phone clicked.

Disconcerted, he hung up and then rose to switch off the office light. A real artist, he thought to himself, as he put on his coat. She could sell anything.

When he had locked the front door he realized that their Oldsmobile was still parked in the yellow zone. Virginia had not driven off; she sat at the wheel, waiting for him.

"I called her," he said, as he opened the door and got in. "I'm going up tomorrow morning, with Gregg."

Not speaking, Virginia started the car and pulled from the yellow zone, onto the street.

The next morning Virginia still had not begun talking, but neither had she left. He phoned Pete and told him to open the store, and then he shaved and bathed and put on a suit and tie and clean shirt. Virginia, moving silently about the house, disappeared into the kitchen when the time came for him and Gregg to leave; she said good-bye to neither of them.

"Is Mom sore?" Gregg asked, as they drove toward the highway.

"Just at me," Roger said.

The trip up the highway was a ball for him; he enjoyed each part of it. After the turn-off he stopped at a roadside drive-in and ordered beer and fried prawns for himself, scrambled eggs and bacon for Gregg.

"This is swell," Gregg said. "Boy, Dad, you sure fooled that truck." The boy had been fascinated by the great game of lane-switching. "Remember that truck?"

Later, they drove past short, round trees. Roger said to his son, "See those? I'll tell you what they are. They're pecan trees."

The drive raised his spirits. When they passed the stream and saw the men fishing, he stopped the car and got out.

"Come on," he said, leading Gregg down the trail from the road. For half an hour they helped the fishermen; once, Gregg was handed a pole and allowed to tug a fish from the water. It was a small, dingy fish, but all the fishermen exclaimed. One claimed that it was the only fish of its kind caught in that part of Ventura County. Gregg got the fish as a gift, wrapped in newspaper; it was tossed in the back of the car and then they drove on, speeding up the grades and around the curves to regain time.

"That's Ojai," Roger said, when they had left the mountains.

Gregg giggled. "Mom calls it O-hy."

Together, he and Gregg walked from the car, up the road from town to the school. He had left the car in a garage to have the thousand mile lubrication; there was no knowing how many miles Virginia had driven without a change of oil.

"That's the school," Gregg said presently. Ahead of them, on the right, began a low split-rail fence that enclosed an orchard. Beyond the orchard could be seen buildings, tall fir trees, and what looked like a flag.

"How do you feel about it?" Roger said.

"I don't know," Gregg said. He slowed. "There's a possum in a cage. I fed him a turnip."

Roger said, "Do you like this school? Do you want to live here?"

"I don't know," Gregg said.

"You could only see Mom and me on weekends."

Gregg nodded.

"Is it a nice school?" Occasionally he got an answer by asking the same question another way.

"Yes," Gregg said.

"Are the kids nice?"

"They aren't there yet."

"Are the teachers nice?"

"I guess so. James is. He's got real dark skin, like Louis Willis. He put a shoe on the horse." As they toiled up the road, Gregg expounded on the method of shoeing a horse.

A Negro, Roger thought to himself. You can't win.

They entered the school grounds. The land became flat. Gregg, running ahead of him, shouted back, "Hey, Dad, I'll show you the possum! Here's the possum!" Rolling, bounding, he disappeared from sight. His voice trailed off. "Possum . . ."

"Christ," Roger said. Without his son he felt nervous; he halted and reached for his cigarettes. The pack was back in his coat, in the car; he had tossed his coat over the seat when the day became warm. Looking around, he saw the steps leading up to the larger of the buildings. A woman had come out on a terrace and was gazing down at him, a lean, middle-aged woman wearing glasses, her hair tied back; she had on jeans and he saw at once that she was Mrs. Alt and that she was an I-take-no-shit-from-anyone woman.

His fear grew. Why? Like a child, he thought. Standing there he quaked. My God, he thought, perspiring. He felt as if he were going to faint.

"Hey Dad," Gregg shouted, scampering back, his face flushed, gasping for breath. "Can I ride a horse? Can I ride a horse? Can I ride one of the horses? Please, can I ride? James says is it okay if I can ride, please can I ride?" Dancing around Roger, he caught hold of his hand and tugged at him. "Please, Dad, please! Let me ride a horse, please! Dad, please! Come on, Dad! Let me ride one of the horses; can I? Can I?"

On the terrace the tough woman watched. Sunlight, hot on his face and body, made Roger sweat.

"Please, Dad!"

He saw trees. Off on a trail a horse clopped. Horses, Roger thought. Be damned. Nice-looking one. Nice rump. The air smelled of dried grass and it was hot, hot.

God, he thought. Not in years.

Wiping his neck he took a couple of steps forward. Sweat in his eyes. He wiped his eyes. Dizzying air. The farm-smell.

"Look at the horse!"

"Yes," he said. The farm-smell reeked: manure. Straw.

On the terrace the woman watched. She put her hands on her hips. Why do I feel so weak? Roger thought. Why?

"Roger!" the woman said sharply.

"Yes," he said. "I'm coming." The reek of horses.

He walked a step. Another. "Please," he said.

Please. He saw the barn. Dirt beneath his toes. Broken heap of wire. Line of hills, green and tree-caked.

At the back of the barn a slope of weeds; dirt descending toward rock. Quiet in the mid-day summer air. Buzzing, and it sprang by him, a black fly.

He ducked.

"Please," he begged, afraid of her. "Can we go?" Both he and Stephen trembled. Then she nodded.

He and Stephen ran over the weeds, the dirt, away from her and the house, past the rusted truck. In the wallow the pigs squirmed. Across the land by the wallow one hog, alarmed, got up to flee; his ears down he ran, bending and puffing, as far as the fence.

In the shed they slammed the door and fixed the wire so no one could open it. So their mother couldn't open it and get them.

"It's cold," Stephen said. "Hey, I can't see; can you see?"

Eventually they could see.

"This is where," he said to his brother. They had come here, to this safe locked place, to find who could pee the furthest.

"You go first," Stephen said.

"You."

"No." Stephen huddled nervously, listening. "It was your idea."

The shed floor had broken under the weight of dung and moldy straw. Jars, filled with preserves, were stacked in the corners, their lids corroded. In the centre of a web a dead spider twirled with the currents of warm air entering through the cracks in the shed, the spaces between the boards.

Standing at one end of the shed, he peed.

"Okay," he said to Stephen.

Stephen peed. When they measured, they found that he had peed almost a foot further than Stephen.

"But I peed more," Stephen said.

"That don't count."

"Why not? Let's see who can pee the most."

"I peed already," Roger said. "So did you."

"Then let's go drink something."

"It'd take hours."

"No," Stephen said. "It comes right out. If you drink milk you pee milk in around five minutes."

The coolness made him sleepy. He felt safe. This was their place; they could give up worrying, here. He threw himself down on gunny sacks, by the remains of a thrasher. Finally Stephen joined him.

"Let's go down to the squij," Stephen said. He meant the open sewer from the outhouse, the trench cut along the side of the beet fields. Yellowjackets hung around the trench and it was something to do to catch them. Or sometimes he and Stephen dammed up the trench and made side trenches. At least it was a place where something was happening.

While he and Stephen lay on the gunny sacks, a chicken crept through a space between two boards and into the shed.

"That's an old hen," Stephen said.

"What's she doing in here?"

The hen, noticing them, turned and crept back out again.

"She must have a nest in here," Roger said. He felt a stirring of interest. "Hey, she must be all the time sneaking in here to lay her eggs."

Stephen stood up. "Let's look for it."

Together they looked, without luck.

"Maybe she'll be back," Roger said. "We'll wait; don't make no noise."

For a long time he and his brother lay in the damp, cool, dark shed, on the gunny sacks. A mouse ran over Roger's foot, once; he shook the mouse off. Above their heads, in the rafters, many mice scuttled and rustled and squeaked.

Suddenly the hen appeared at the place between the boards, cutting off the sunlight. Stephen dug his fingers into his brother's arm.

The hen's head jerked, turned, lifted. Then the hen crawled through the hole and stepped into the shed once more.

Hurriedly, the hen settled herself in the corner of the shed, ruffled her feathers, sounded a triumphant rattle, and then hopped up and left the shed the way she had come.

"Why that no-good old hen," Stephen said. "Laying eggs in here so nobody'd find them." He and Roger ran to the corner. The support beam had broken away, leaving a hole in the dirt not much larger than a rat hole. The dirt and bits of wood formed a soft mass; Roger and his brother scooped away the mass—beneath it were eggs, many of them, some cracked, some dark with decay, some fresh-white. He and Stephen dug farther; below the layer of eggs was another layer of eggs, much older, so old that they looked like rock.

When all the eggs had been gotten out and laid in a row, he and Stephen counted twenty-six of them.

It was the biggest egg-find either of them could remember. They loaded the eggs into a bucket and carried them into the house.

By foot, along various sidewalks, Roger Lindahl slowly passed the liquor store and arrived at the house on Massachusetts Avenue in which he had lived from the start to the break-up of his marriage.

The front room was a mess of packed cartons and suitcases and crated books. His things had been separated from Teddy's but they had not yet been removed. In the dining room Teddy, under the overhead light, was feeding the baby. A sour smell filled the house; the dining room and kitchen smelled of unwashed dishes and food that had been spilled and left to dry. The bare floor was ankle-deep in trash and the knickknacks with which the baby played. On the couch, Teddy's two Siamese cats regarded him with hostility, their paws tucked under them.

"Hello little friend," Teddy said to him, as she spooned strained peas to the baby, who had already dribbled down her bib and onto her hands and stomach. "Go look at the lamp and the rugs in the other room; I want to know if you want them. Otherwise I have a friend who can use them."

The light blinded him and he shut his eyes. The two cats made no room for him on the couch. Their hair had got into everything; in the overhead light the sideboard showed grey streaks in the wood, scratches and hair. Both arms of the couch hung in tatters. Their smell, the stale pungency of the cooped-up animal, underlay the other smells of the house.

His wife—they had not yet arranged the divorce—put out her hand and shut off the radio plugged into the overhead light fixture. "My Devotion" sank away. She moved wearily and he felt sorry for her; she had her job with the Department of Agriculture and after that she had to pick up the baby from the child care center, drive to the stores and do the shopping, fix dinner for herself and the baby, and of course make some attempt to clean up after the cats. The cats, he thought; now she clung to them even more. On the couch the cats glared declaring: Come near us and we'll massacre you. We know your attitude. The cats, their feet under them, watched and managed their defense. Tirelessly, they guarded their lives.

"Would you do me a favor?" Teddy said. "Turn on the heater."

With a match from the stove he lit the gas heater and opened the door to the hall.

"Did you change your mind?" Teddy said. "You want to stay here tonight?"

"I just stopped by about something."

"How are Irv and Dora?"

"Fine."

"It's very nice of them to let you stay with them for a while. Where are you sleeping? Is there really room there?—they only have the one bedroom, don't they?"

He thought, at that, of a notice which he had written as a child to a children's radio show: "Dear Uncle Hank, this is a drawing of my little brother Stephen, he sleeps in the piano."

"Can't you answer me?" Teddy said, with venom. Her beaked face swung in his direction; under the bare light it glared. And then he saw hunger, and then fright.

"I wish I could stay," he said.

"What would you think," she said in a strained voice, "if I quit my job and came along with you out to California?" Her eyes, with the intensity that had always made him uneasy, flickered and refocussed. But the old hex had lost power over him. Nothing in the world was permanent. Even the stones became dust, finally. Even the earth itself.

In the beginning she had been the fiancée of his friend Joe Field. Joe and he and Irv Rattenfanger, for years, lived quietly within the W.P.A. At that time none of them had any money. They fashioned a mah-jongg set out of plywood and bathroom tile. Once a month they ate out in an Italian restaurant.

Teddy said, "I talked to an attorney and you can be arrested for desertion and child support. Any time I say the word."

"I don't have any money."

"How are you going to get to California?"

"I have some money," he said. "I'm taking Irv's car." With pride he said, "I got hold of a C sticker." He had already pasted it on the windshield beside Irv's old B sticker. It entitled him to all the gasoline he needed.

"Why don't you go by bus?" she said. "Wouldn't it be cheaper for just one person? If that old wreck of Irv's breaks down you won't be able to get parts or tires—you'll get stranded somewhere, out in the desert. And you'll be alone; it won't be safe. That's an awful car. I drove it once. It's ready to fall apart."

"I want to take my stuff," he said.

"And you can't ship it?"

He wanted it with him so that if he found a good deal along the way he could stop and settle.

"If you write for money," she said, "I won't answer." Wiping the baby's mouth with a damp cloth she said, "What about after you get there? Are you going to get in touch with me? Maybe after you get a job in one of those aircraft plants around Los Angeles—what about that? You'll be making plenty of money out there. By then you'll be lonely; I know you, you'll be glad to have somebody you can lean on." She spoke in a quick monotone, her attention still on the baby. "I know you, you slimy little snake. You can't get along by yourself, you're like a baby. You never grew up. Look at you, you're only two feet tall."

"Tall where it counts," he said.

"That thing?" she said. "Go find yourself a knot hole; that's all it's good for." She jabbed the spoon at the baby. Rose's hands lifted in reflexive self-defense; she jerked them away.

"Don't take it out on her," he said. The sight oppressed him and he turned to the rugs and lamp. He was allowing her to keep whatever she wanted. The marriage had lasted five years and in that time they had gathered together almost every variety of thing, a whole house full to its basement and its closets and shelves. Most important to him were his clothes, his sets of wrenches and bits, his oboe which he had played since grammar school days, certain copper ashtrays which his family had given them as a wedding present. And many small items, such as his hairbrush, his pearl cuff links, pictures and mementos. And blankets and cooking utensils, so that he could sleep and eat in the car during the trip.

"When are you leaving?" Teddy said.

"As soon as my check comes through." The Government was slow to make good on its final payment; for months it had been giving him compensation for a back injury suffered in a fall at his job at the Richmond Navy Yard. Now the Government doctors maintained that he was well. He had the choice of going back to work at an essential war job or being drafted.

"Let's go out," Teddy said. "Let's have some fun tonight; maybe your check'll come tomorrow." She put the baby's food away in the refrigerator and washed her hands at the sink. "I'll change and we can go dancing or to a show. Or we can have a good time here; we can make something of the last time we have together, before you go." Already she had started to unfasten her blouse; she kicked off her low-heeled shoes, coming towards him. Her hair flapped in its usual manner, the long, inert, lusterless hair. She had an elongated, narrow nose and as she approached him she gazed continually down both sides of it, a bird-like habit. Her legs had no grace to them, no lines but those of muscle and bone, and her feet smacked noisily. Her eyes glittered; her breath whistled in her throat.

"I don't feel like a party," he said. "I just came from a party." He remembered why he had come here and he said, "I want to get them a bottle of wine, something special."

"Can I come?" she said, panting. "Let me go back with you."

"No," he said.

"Then the hell with you," she said. "I won't give you any money; you want a couple of bucks so you can show up big with the wine, don't you?"

He said, "I told them I'd get it."

"That's just too bad."

For a moment or two neither of them spoke. Pushed close to him she swelled and ebbed, swelled and ebbed, like a pulse. How much she would have liked to stick him, to spear him with her nails. At her blouse her hands broke loose and snatched at air; they convulsed. And all the time she kept her eyes fixed on him.

Leaving her, he passed on back into the dining room where the baby sat in the high chair under the light. At sight of him the wan limpness left her and she began to smile. Suddenly he made up his mind to take Rose along with him. Why not? He seated himself beside her at the table, where Teddy had sat feeding her. On the table was a clean spoon and he waved it before her, slowly, until her mouth fell open in wonder. Light flashed from the spoon and the baby shouted. He laughed, too.

On the couch, the two Siamese cats also watched the spoon; they coveted it with hate. He felt their desire to destroy, and he turned his chair so that his back was to them.

3

On the terrace the woman said, "Hello, Gregg. I see you decided to come back and visit us again."

"Hello, Mrs. Ant," Gregg said, still tugging at his father's arm.

Descending the steps, Mrs. Alt approached Roger with her hand out. "How do you do. I'm very glad to meet you, Mr. Lindahl."

He unfastened his son's grip. "Later," he murmured to him. His confusion cleared enough for him to get a good look at Mrs. Alt. "I'm sorry," he said. "He wants to go ride the horse."

As they shook hands Mrs. Alt said, "You have a very striking wife, Mr. Lindahl. Everybody was quite impressed by her." She leaned down to speak to Gregg. "What would you like to do? Do you want to play down on the football field with the other boys? I believe they all went down there. Shall I take you down there?"

"I know where it is," Gregg said. "I was there yesterday." He ran off a few yards, halted, turned, and yelled back, "Good-bye! I'm going down to the football field!" And then he continued on past the trees and was gone.

"Will he be okay?" Roger said. "Can he get there okay?"

"He's there now," Mrs. Alt said. "It's just over the rise."

Roger said, "I didn't realize you had all the grounds. It's more like a farm."

"Oh yes. We keep the children outdoors as much as possible. We have animals—actually this was a farm, once. They raised prize cattle. Some retired people together. They owned the property and then one of them died."

"Where I come from," Roger said, "is where the prize hogs are raised."

"Yes," Mrs. Alt said. "I lived in Western Arkansas for a year or so. At Fayetteville."

"There's hogs all through there," Roger said.

"Did you grow up on a farm?"

"Yes," he said.

"Then this must seem like—" Mrs. Alt laughed. "I mean, it must seem familiar to you. The buildings and the smell. Some of the parents sniff the air and think What on earth can it be? Some unsanitary thing . . . I can tell by the way they prowl around."

"It smells fine to me," Roger said.

Folding her arms, Mrs. Alt said, "I have your wife's check inside. You can have it back whenever you want."

"Thanks," he said.

"Did your wife tell you that she and I got into a quarrel and kept at it all the time she was here? We started right out. On every conceivable subject."

Roger said, "I'm sorry to take off again, but I have a store. If you want to give me the check I'll round up Gregg and start back." He did not want to hang around; the school, the smell of hay and animals and manure, the sight of the barn, the dirt and dried grass, had too much effect on him.

"Suit yourself," Mrs. Alt said, immediately starting up the stairs towards the building.

His hands in his pockets, he followed after her. The woman moved rapidly, and he lost her; he found himself in a deserted hall, facing a desk and lobby. In a chair a small girl was reading a book; she did not look up or notice him.

"Here's your check," Mrs. Alt said, appearing. She handed him the check, and he accepted it and stuck it in his shirt pocket. Her tone was brisk.

"Does this happen very often?" he asked.

"Once in a while. I think we can take it in our stride." She did not seem angry, only impatient. He got the impression that she had learned to suspend judgement; she did not wish to approve or condemn. Probably she had a great many things to worry about; her head was full of details and items to be attended to. She was willing to stand here talking to him, but now that the business between them had been concluded she was anxious to get on to other work.

"I won't keep you," he said. "Thanks a lot for not—" His thought was unclear. "For letting me off the hook."

"Next time," Mrs. Alt said, "you and your wife perhaps should talk it over in advance." She smiled at him, the friendly but controlled smile. "It's been nice meeting you," she said. "Your little boy is a very sweet child. I hope his asthma goes away. I'm sure it will. He seems quite alert and curious about things; he enjoyed watching them shoe the horse. He asked an unusual number of questions."

They shook hands, and then he walked out of the dark lobby, onto the front steps of the building. The sunlight hurt his eyes and he shut them. When he was able to see he headed in the direction Gregg had gone.

The shock. Smells, so identified with his brother; terrible false shocking sense of his brother's nearness, end of loneliness. The rotting hay, the sight of the barn, the dry, crumbling soil . . . right by him, at his hand.

"Stephen," he said.

Broken eggs, calcified. The black cracks, leaking smells and slime; he carried the bucket.

"Oh good heavens," his mother said in her clear, firm voice. "What in the world is that? Get that out of the kitchen; don't you bring that in here."

We kept the eggs. Twenty-six eggs.

Two smashed.

In the yard the old hen running: searching in and out of the shed. Popping in and out, between the boards.

Ha-ha.

An adult, a man, got to his feet, said something to the woman beside him, walked out onto the field to take the football. He elaborately arranged the children in formation.

"Jerry, you stand over there. Walt, there. What's your name? Gregg? You stand there, Gregg. Mike, you stand there. Okay, now. Get ready." The man prepared to fire the football between his wide-apart legs. "Here!" he shouted. The football sailed a few yards and fell into the grass; screaming, the children sprinted towards it, arms extended, fingers grasping.

The man, grinning, sauntered from the field and sat down again with his companions.

A trail traveled down the slope, to the football field. After a time Roger started along it. He came out not far from the adults, and they noticed him; one of the women craned her neck to see him and the row of faces turned his way.

Ignoring them, he watched the children. Teachers, he decided. His position was not good, here. He was trespassing. Gregg had no right to be scampering around on their football field, playing with their football. The situation made him uncomfortable. He wanted to get Gregg and get right out.

But it's a swell place for a kid, he thought. Nobody could deny that.

He continued watching the children, standing restlessly by himself, until at last one of the adults arose, exchanged a few words with the others, and then approached him. "You're Mr. Lindahl, aren't you? Gregg's father?"

"Yes," he said.

"I'm Van Ecke. The arithmetic teacher." The man shook hands with him; he had an inoffensive manner, an informality that was probably professional. Both he and the other man wore short-sleeved Aloha sports shirts and lightweight trousers; they, and the women, seemed relaxed and in an affable mood and they smiled at him. With them was a portable radio, tuned to popular music, and a pitcher and glasses on a tray. "Why don't you join us?" Van Ecke said. "Is your wife with you? I met her yesterday when she came up with Gregg. In fact, we had lunch together."

"Not just the two of them," one of the women put in. Everyone laughed. "Mrs. Alt was along."

Seeing no choice, Roger walked back with Van Ecke. The arithmetic teacher introduced him around.

"This is Mrs. McGivern, the science teacher. Miss Tie, our English and physical ed teacher. And this is Mr. and Mrs. Bonner. Parents. Like yourself. Their kids are out there with yours."

Mrs. Bonner said, "One grade below. First teachers, then parents."

"Then children," her husband said.

"They're at the bottom of the scale," Van Ecke said.

"What about the possum?"

"He's at the bottom. Correction."

Van Ecke asked. "Is Mrs. Lindahl along?"

"No," Roger said. He seated himself awkwardly. "Just Gregg and I."

"How old is your little boy?" Mrs. Bonner asked.

"Seven and a half." He added, "He's undersize."

"After he's been up here awhile," Mrs. McGivern said, "he'll be six feet four." Again they all laughed, all except Mr. Bonner, who eyed him intently. They seemed easy-going, except perhaps Bonner. But his sense of discomfort grew. He was going to have to tell them the situation, and it was going to make him look pretty lousy.

The teachers chatted away, keeping their eyes on the children. Mr. and Mrs. Bonner were about his age, older than the teachers who looked, to him, like college students. Certainly Van Ecke was in his twenties. Miss Tie had a colorless, bland face; he guessed that she had got her credentials right after the war. Of the teachers, Mrs. McGivern seemed the most able, the most mature. Bonner had plump, furry arms, a pink face, receding but curly hair; next to him his wife sat with her arms on her drawn-up knees, her chin forward, a spear of grass switching back and forth between her fingers. Unlike the women teachers, who had on jeans, she was dressed in a skirt and blouse. A ribbon in her hair made her look younger than her husband and the teachers, but when she glanced up he realized that she was in her thirties. She had a pretty, round face and nice eyes; he liked her eyes.

She said, "Are you the one I'm supposed to talk to about the ride?"

"I don't think so," he said.

"Mrs. Alt said something about my driving your little boy in with me on weekends."

"No," Roger said, "not that I know of."

"Maybe it was somebody else," Mrs. Bonner said, tossing the spear of grass up and catching it. "I thought it was you; I'll ask her again." To her husband she said, "Didn't she say Lindahl? I'm sure she did."

Van Ecke said, "As I recall, it was Mrs. Lindahl who was talking about the drive. We were having lunch. She said something about how much it bothered her."

"Yes," Mrs. McGivern said. "That was Mrs. Lindahl."

They all waited expectantly. "I'm sorry," Roger said. "She didn't mention it to me."

Bonner tilted his wrist; underneath, on the inside, he had a watch. The dark leather strap passed along the strands of fur. "Maybe you better go ask her, Liz. We've got to leave pretty soon."

"She's probably up in the office," Mrs. McGivern said.

"I'll go see who it was," Liz Bonner said. "She said she wanted to get it settled today." Taking her purse she slipped to her feet and started up the trail to the top of the rise. Half-way up she said over her shoulder, "I know it was somebody." Then she was gone.

I had better get out of here, Roger thought. To those around him he said, "It was nice meeting you people. Maybe I'll see you again sometime." He stood up. "Time to head back to L.A."

"Are you leaving Gregg today?" Mr. Van Ecke asked.

"No," he said. "No, later in the week." He walked out onto the field, not looking back. "Gregg!" he called. "Time to start home."

"Not yet," Gregg yelled. "Please, just a little longer; okay?" Turning his back he dived into the group of children and vanished from sight.

Filled with anger, Roger said, "You get right over here." Following his son he seized him by the wrist and dragged him away from the other children. Gregg blinked in surprise and hurt, and then his face folded up in grief. Opening his mouth he began to wail. The other children became hushed; they all watched as Roger led his son from the field.

"Wait'll I get you off somewhere," Roger said. "You never had such a whipping; I'm not kidding you, I'm not kidding." Gregg stumbled and half-fell; he lifted him back on his feet and went on up the trail. The ground slithered and crumbled under their feet; clods of dirt spilled in a torrent behind them, carrying weeds and small rocks to the bottom. The group of adults watched without comment.

Wailing and whimpering, Gregg managed to say, "Please don't whip me." He had only been whipped once in his life. "I'm sorry; I won't do it again." Probably he had only a vague idea of what he had done. "Please, Daddy."

They passed the school buildings and reached the road that led back down to the town. "Okay," Roger said. "I won't whip you." His temper and anxiety began to abate. "But next time I want you to mind me. You heard me, didn't you?"

"Y-yes," Gregg said.

"You knew I wanted you to come."

Gregg said, "When are we coming back?"

"Oh Christ," he said, filled with despair.

"Can we come back tomorrow?"

"It's too far."

"I want to go back," Gregg said.

They plodded on down the road; Roger held onto his son's arm.

Both of them perspired, both of them became silent. What a foul-up, Roger thought. What a bass-ackward mess.

"Mommy said I could," Gregg said, once.

"It's too far."

"No it isn't."

"It is," he said. "And it costs too damn much. So stop talking about it."

On and on they toiled, feeling worse, losing all sense of where they were and what they were doing. Neither of them saw anything; when the road turned they turned with it. when they reached level ground they stopped while Gregg tied his shoe.

"I'll buy you a soda," Roger said.

His son, sniffling regularly, did not bother to look in his direction. He straightened up and started on.

"Okay," Roger said. "The hell with it."

They entered the town, the blocks of houses and then the business section.

"Look at the park," Roger said. "You want to go into the park?"

"No," Gregg said.

At the garage Roger picked up the car, paid the bill for the lubrication, and then started to back out onto the street. Beside him his son squirmed on the seat.

"I have to go to the toilet," Gregg said.

Pulling on the handbrake, Roger opened the car door and helped his son out and back into the garage. He left the car where it was and took Gregg into the bathroom. When they returned they found the car gone.

"Somebody stole the car," Gregg said.

"No," Roger said, searching around for one of the garage attendants. "Where's my car?" he said. "I left it here with the motor running."

"One of the men parked it across the street," the garage attendant said. "It was blocking the entrance. See it over there?" He pointed, and they made out the car, parked by a mailbox across the street.

"Thanks," Roger said. He and Gregg walked to the crosswalk and stood, as cars passed.

While they were crossing the street, a Ford station wagon halted beside them, and a voice, a woman's voice, called, "Mr. Lindahl; wait a minute, will you?" The station wagon then picked up speed, turned right, and came swiftly to a stop at the curb. Roger could not figure out who the woman was; he could not see her, and he did not recognize the voice. The car was totally strange.

The car door opened and Liz Bonner slid out, locked the door, and approached him and Gregg.

"Listen," she said breathlessly, "do you have to go back to L.A. right now? Can't you stay here a few more minutes? Mrs. Alt told me you changed your mind; you're not putting Gregg in the school. Why? What's wrong? You were going to. Did somebody do something?" Coming up close beside him she gazed up earnestly at him. She smelled of sun and fabric and perspiration. "Is it because of the way my boys jumped on him when they were playing ball? Chic—my husband—says it's because you saw us yelling at him and it made you sore. Is that it?"

He saw himself as the greatest rat that ever walked the earth. "No," he said, "I was already fixed up. Nothing to do with you."

"Oh," she said, unconvinced. "Really? But you brought him up here; you drove all the way up from L.A. And your wife arranged for me to pick him up on weekends. And she and Edna made out the lists of what he's supposed to bring; didn't your wife even pay her for the first month? I don't understand it; Edna seems upset about it and I can't get a clear story from her." The tumble of words ceased, at that point. Mrs. Bonner plucked at her shoulder strap and then seemed to become aware of her peculiar position. "How ridiculous can you get?" she murmured. "I guess I went off the deep end. Well, anyhow—we had good intentions."

Neither of them knew what to do next.

"Hi," Liz Bonner said to Gregg; she smoothed his hair back from his forehead.

"Hello," Gregg said.

"How are you going back to L.A.?" Liz Bonner asked. "Oh, you have your car. You don't want a ride."

"Thanks," he said.

"Well, it's too bad. It's a nice school. Maybe some other time." She smiled hesitantly. "I'm glad to have met you." She remained for a moment and then she said, "What we thought was—we thought you were a new parent, and you had this idealistic notion about the school, and you had just brought your boy up, and then you ran into us. And we fouled it up somehow." She shrugged. "Some way or other. And we thought Edna was sore because of that. Our doing that. I'll see you, then, maybe. Some time."

She dashed back to her car, unlocked the door, got inside, and, scrutinizing the traffic, drove off in the direction of the school. The station wagon needed a bath; dust and road grime covered it. He saw it again as it reached the first grade at the edge of town; he and Gregg watched the dull shape shoot up the hill down which the two of them had trudged.

"We could have come down with her," Gregg said.

They got into their own car, their Oldsmobile. The motor was running; the attendant hadn't shut it off.

"Back to L.A.," Roger said. Pulling away from the curb he headed in the opposite direction from the red Ford station wagon. "What a mess," he said to Gregg. "Did you ever see a mess like that?" He drove slowly, with both hands on the wheel. How did I get into it? he said to himself. How does anybody get into a situation like that?

The glare dazzled him. Straight into the sun, the whole trip back. God, he thought. Things were bad enough at home. Not more, he thought; please not more.

4

Saturday afternoon, as Virginia walked home from the bus stop to her apartment in the North East part of Washington, a dingy old car pulled up by the curb; the window rolled down and a voice hailed her.

At first she thought it was Irv Rattenfanger; it was his '34 Buick, but loaded with boxes and crates. A rack had been welded to the top and it was full, too. She halted, catching her breath, and then she recognized Roger Lindahl, the man who had drunk up her bottle of wine at the Rattenfangers' party. He was crammed into the front seat with the boxes. Waving merrily, he parked the car and got out to run around and leap up on the curb. Today his mood was buoyant, but she shrank away. One of those sub-rational forebodings, bound up in childhood experience and bad luck, began to plague her as soon as she recognized him.

"Hello," she said. "You seem happy today."

"I just got my Government check," he said. "I've been driving around; your roommate said you ought to be home any time. You just getting off work?" He was drawing her toward the parked car. "Hop in and I'll ride you home."

"There's no room in there," she said, with wariness.

"Sure there is." Opening the door he showed her the space he had made beside the driver's seat. "Look," he said, "I'm leaving for California!"

She could not help feeling excitement at the idea. "In that?"

"I'm leaving late tonight; I'm all loaded and I have my C sticker. Hey—" He paused, and a seriousness set in. "Look, I can't leave until after the traffic. How about going out with me?"

For just a second she thought he meant literally driving a distance with him in his loaded-down car, a sort of trial run to see if all the gears and engine worked.

"I mean, let's drive down into Rock Creek Park or something. For a couple of hours." His hand shot up and he examined his wristwatch. "It's only three o'clock."

She said, "Are you really just about to leave?"

"Sure." His face lit up; the frowns and wrinkles eased away.

"You didn't come back last night," she said. "To the party."

"I came back later," he said vaguely. "It was after you went home." His feet shuffled. "How about it? There's a bunch of animals or something down there, in buildings. I drove through there once." He did not bring up the subject of the wine, which he had sworn to replace. For some reason she knew that he never would.

"Okay," she said. The Park was not far from her apartment and she loved to roam around in it, especially near the river. Since it was so familiar she was less apprehensive. And anyhow, he was a friend of the Rattenfangers. He even had their old harmless car.

With the two of them in the car the doors would barely shut. She had to hold a cardboard box of clothes on her lap. At first his driving unnerved her; at the lights he shot forward and at corners he turned without slowing. But he was skillful.

"What check?" she asked, unable to think of anything else to say.

"Compensation," he said. "From Uncle Sam."

"Oh," she said, thinking of her own job at the Washington military hospitals. "Were you in the Service?"

"Yes." He nodded. "I was wounded in the Philippines." He glanced at her and said, "We fought it out with the Japs—I was taken off with a bunch of guerillas by means of a submarine."

"Where were you hurt?"

"My leg," he said. "A Jap machine gunner shot away most of the bone. But I got him. With a Filipino throwing knife." Again he glanced at her and she realized that he was making it up.

"That's a lie," she said.

"No," he said, "it's true. I have a silver plate there."

"Show it to me."

"It's inside." His voice sank. "It's all healed over."

She said, "I work with wounded servicemen; you couldn't walk as well as you do."

Protest started from him. And then it disappeared. A brief, sly elfish manner took its place and in spite of herself she was charmed. But he did not admit it was a lie; for a time he continued to nod his head.

"I have to stop at a gas station," he said, as the car entered a business district. Without any further word he swung the car from the street and up by the pumps of a Texaco station. Then he backed it to the grease rack and shut the motor off. But he did not get out; sitting there, he launched into a long story, without explanation, a rapid and nervous account:

"We had this milkman and we used to put a note out on the porch, you know, stuck on the door with a thumbtack, telling him not to leave any milk that day. One day I looked out the window and I saw he didn't come up on the porch; when he saw the note pinned up he just gunned his motor and drove off, to save time. So I got to writing different things; I wrote things like, Leave four gallons of cream and six pounds of butter and six pints of milk. I put notes like that up, and he just glanced out the window of his truck and gunned off. Then one day there was a new driver and he came up on the porch and read the note, and he left all that stuff. Twenty dollars

worth of butter and cream and milk. Even a quart of orange juice."
Roger became silent then.

"When was that?" she said. "When you were a child?"

"Yes," he said, but again she sensed the evasion. And even in her
childhood—and she was younger—the milk trucks had been horse-
drawn. She remembered the clop-clop of the hoofs at dawn, while
everyone was still in bed. But, she thought, perhaps it was in another city.

She said, "Didn't Dora tell me you're married?"

"Hell no," he said, horrified.

The station attendant in his brown uniform, wiping his hands
on a rag, walked over, "What can I do for you?"

"What's the chances of maybe my using your hydraulic jack for
a couple of seconds?" Roger said.

"Why?"

"Because my bumper jack won't lift this load I got in here and on
top." A servile, wheedling quality entered his voice which she had
never heard in anyone before. "Come on," Roger said, "be a good
guy."

Shrugging, the attendant walked away. At once Roger jumped
from the car and hurried to the hydraulic jack, which he had already
located. Soon he was back, dragging it behind him.

"I want to get the spare on the rear left," he explained to Virginia. "It'll only take a couple of seconds; okay?" The jack disappeared under the car. At that she opened the door and stepped out
onto the pavement.

Down on his hands and knees he was guiding the jack beneath
the rear axle. And she had the strange conviction that, silly as it might
seem, he was doing all this deliberately, because of her, not because
he really wanted to change the tire. In some oblique manner he
wanted to convey something to her.

Perhaps, she thought, he was showing his prowess. But she herself,
even with her limited experience, could tell that he was not doing

well; first he could not locate the proper spot for the jack and then he could not tell how the jack itself worked, and finally, when the back end of the car had begun to rise he could not figure out how to get off the hubcap. Searching around, he found a screwdriver that belonged to the Texaco station; he used that to pry the hubcap loose and it fell with a clatter. Meanwhile, the station attendant had approached to watch. She and the attendant watched together, neither of them speaking, both of them skeptical. To have the station attendant beside her, sharing her opinion, was pleasant.

Still, Roger remained happy; he twirled the wrench and dropped the bolts or nuts or whatever they were one after another beside him. The wheel wobbled off; he set it against the fender and then lifted the spare to take its place. Crouched with his bony knees stuck out before him, sweating and grunting, he struggled until the attendant stepped over to steady things for him. When the first bolt was in place the attendant departed and Roger finished alone. Cheerfully turning to her he said, "You think I'll make it to California?"

"I guess you will," she said.

He thanked the attendant—too elaborately, she thought—and soon they were on their way again. Beside her Roger told a long tale about himself and Irv back in the 'thirties, but she did not listen; she pondered until all at once she realized that by the tire-changing business he had wanted to show her that he could not get to California, that he was incompetent. It was not something he could say. Perhaps he did not understand it.

With that thought about him she felt a wave of emotion, a kind of gentleness. Now she saw that he was astonishingly malleable. Behind the wheel of his car he waited for her to direct him; he was not really taking her to Rock Creek Park. He had no idea at all, no plan, only the sense that he wanted to be with her. So he drove around corners and through lights, talking unceasingly, but without actually saying anything. And, she thought, he was hiding almost everything of importance about himself. There was no use asking him direct questions because the answers would be myths, tales, like his fighting in the Pacific. But he did not intend to impress her; he was not boasting, he was filling in.

But she found him likeable. She did not mind being kidded. She saw no harm in it.

"Do you know anybody in California?" she asked.

"Yes," he said. "I've got a lot of connections out there on the Coast around L.A. They sure are expanding out there; you can make plenty of money."

"Have you ever been out there?"

"Sure," he said,

"I never have," she said.

"I'll drive you," he said.

She did not answer. And he didn't say it again. But now, without warning, she felt as she had when she first met him, when she discovered him drinking up the wine for her party.

"You should see some of these veterans," she said, trembling with a sort of dim moral outrage, almost a sort of quaking. "The awful burns and injuries, and they have to be taught to move their legs and arms again as if they were children; they have to start again all over. People on the outside just don't understand how terrible it is. And they come in every day, they pour in from the different islands in the Pacific. People see the newsreels and that's nothing but the guns going off and the troops landing; they don't see how awful it is, what it's really like. They think it's exciting, like adventure stories. Like the stuff in the magazines. It's screened."

"It sure is," he said, but his tone lacked emphasis. "People here in the States have a funny idea what it's all about."

"I see them every day," she said, and after that there was no more to be said. But she let him drive her around; for one thing she was curious to know if he were really going to leave that night or if the California business had sprung into his mind to explain the loaded car. Perhaps, she thought, he was only moving from one apartment to another. Or these boxes and parcels were going to be stored at the Rattenfangers'. He so clearly was in transit . . . padding about the Rattenfangers' apartment in his stocking feet, rooting in their cupboards, buying their car and hauling his possessions. Maybe here she had met a tramp, a hobo. As a child, growing up in Maryland, she had peered out as her mother intercepted tramps at the front gate; the tramps had got into the yard, they ate their sandwich and drank their cup of coffee on the back steps, out of sight, and then they moved on. Once a tramp had left a sandwich uneaten and her mother had told her to throw it in the garbage can instantly and wash her hands. But she had given the sandwich to a dog.

Yes, she thought, he was a hobo. But in her mind the image of the hobo had become confused with the bright face of Tom Sawyer as he set out with his bindle over his back, his property tied up in a—what was it?—red pocket handkerchief, the huge old kind for the men who took snuff. Dancing down the road . . . blue eyes and guileless smile. Singing, talking, dreaming as he hopped along.

And the dog, she thought; it had not died. Although she had kept her eye on it, afraid that the hobo might have left poison in the sandwich. Or was it germs? Too long ago, she thought; now she could not be certain.

Propped up among his boxes Roger Lindahl carried on a conversation about something. She listened; it had to do with television. In the Post War world, television was going to be a giant industry and Roger had involved himself in television electronic engineering and design; a buddy of his, unnamed, had designed a scanner with more lines or with fewer—she could not follow the discourse because it poured out so fast, the words trying to appear at once. The tail of the discourse came first; he sputtered in his eagerness and became breathless, as if he had run to tell her, as if he had just now witnessed a surprise. She saw him hopping across the snow; she saw his spindly legs pumping over the fields of Maryland. In her mind the frail, hectic man beside her had become mixed with her view of the land through which they now drove; looking out the car window she realized, with a start, that he had brought them downtown almost to the Tidal Basin. Delighted, she exclaimed. And he stopped talking instantly, as if sliced off. To her the Tidal Basin and the trees had a mysterious quality; they kept the countryside here in the center of the city, as if it could not be completely suppressed. Actually she was afraid of the Tidal Basin; it was part of the lines and pools of water that had cut into the ground by the coast, the canals and rivers and streams; Rock Creek itself, and of course the Potomac. When she came near the Potomac she believed she had been removed completely away from the present; she did not accept the fact that the Potomac existed in the modern world.

Along the Potomac grew thickets, scrub brush, tangled bushes that had heaped up in mounds, and the ground, the land, was close to the water; there was no bank, no rise. The water had spread out, to the roots of the trees; even the birds skimmed at eye level when they coasted past, going out toward the Atlantic or west into the further woods. Once she had run along the banks of a canal, deserted, its locks shut for a century; weeds had split the wooden beams and in the trapped water thousands of tiny fish moved in and out, born there, she decided, peering down from the great height. How remote it was, even then. Desolation. Only the smallest living creatures remained; jay birds, a rat swimming with its tail after it like a rudder. And none of them made any noise, except perhaps the jay, and even the jay waited until he was safe, off in the brambles, before he squawked. And she walked, with her mother, along the cracked plank of the canal. When they arrived at a train track—grass obscured it until their shoes stubbed against the ties—her mother said she could walk on the rails; no trains, or few trains, came by. And if one did, she would hear it an hour in advance. The track passed beneath misshapen trees, and later across a stream. The water, beneath the trestle, was muddy brown, thick, inert. If a train came, her mother said, leading her across the trestle, they could drop off into the water. Striding, her mother took her to the far side. And there the trees began again as before.

"They fought here," her mother said. That was so indistinct to her, then (she was eight or nine). Only the idea of fighting; not people, just the idea of fighting among the brambles. Then her mother explained about the Army of the Potomac. A grandfather had been with the Army, McClellan's Army, in the Shenandoah Valley. They saw that, too, the Blue Ridge Mountains and the valley itself; by car they drove down along the floor of the valley; the mountains poked up like cones, each one separate from the others. And she could see cars up on the sides, traveling around and around, winding up to the top. She was afraid she would be driven up there, too, and later on she was. Her mother's family had come from Massachusetts and she saw on her mother's face a cold look as they drove through the valley; her mother's eyes got a withered, terrible meanness and she refused to talk. Everyone else enjoyed the trip, the fields and the maps spread out on laps and the soft drinks, but her mother sat with her face screwed into silence. Her father pretended he didn't notice.

And yet her mother had settled in Maryland, had bought a two-story stone house with a fireplace and considered herself part of the community. The town was peaceful. At sunset a band from the Guard Armory marched up the streets, the kids—including Virginia—whooping after it. Her mother remained indoors reading, with her cigarettes and glasses; she was a rather sparse, muscular New England woman, living in a town of Southern ladies all of whom were shorter, more voluble, much more strident. Virginia remembered the low voice of her mother among the strident Maryland voices, and in the almost twenty years that they had lived in Maryland, up to this moment in the fall of 1943, her mother's manners and habits had not changed a bit.

"Let's stop," she said to Roger Lindahl.

"This is the Reflection Pool," he told her.

She laughed, because he was wrong. "No it isn't."

"Sure it is. Those are the cherry trees over there." His eyes danced, a milk innocent fire of slyness. "It really is." He coaxed her; he begged her in a friendly way to take his word for it. And what did it matter?

She said, "Are you my guide?"

"Sure." He puffed up, but still joking. "I'll show you around."

This, the Tidal Basin, belonged to her. Part of her early years. Both she and her mother loved Washington. After her father's death she and her mother rode into Washington on the weekends, by bus usually, and walked along Pennsylvania Avenue and to the Smithsonian Institute or the Lincoln Memorial or around the Reflection Pool or here; especially here. They came into the Capital for the blossoming of the cherry trees and once for egg-rolling on the lawn of the White House.

"The egg-rolling," she said aloud, as Roger parked the car. "They called it off, didn't they?"

"For the war," he said.

And, as a child, while her father was alive, she had been brought in to watch a parade in which the Civil War veterans had marched, and she had seen them, the brittle dried-up little old men in brand-new uniforms, going by on foot or being pushed in wheelchairs. When she saw them she thought of the hills and brambles along the Potomac, the deserted train trestle, the jay who flew by her without a sound. How mysterious it was.

The air chilled both of them as they walked; the surface of the Tidal Basin rippled and a mist had come in from the Atlantic, so that everything looked gray. The blossoms of the trees, of course, had disappeared earlier in the year. The ground beneath their shoes sank and in some places water covered the path. But the air smelled good; she liked the mist, the nearness of water and earth.

"Kind of cold," Roger said, his hands in his pockets, his head lowered. He walked slowly, kicking at bits of gravel.

"I'm used to it," she said. "I like it."

"Are your folks here?"

"My mother," she said. "My dad passed away in 1939."

"Oh." He nodded.

"She has a house in Maryland, across the line. I only see her on weekends. Mostly she spends her time gardening."

Roger said, "You don't talk like you're from Maryland."

"No," she agreed, "I was born in Boston."

Twisting his head he peered at her sideways. "You know where I come from? Can you guess?"

"No," she said.

"Arkansas," he said.

"Is it nice there?" She had never been in Arkansas, but once when she and her mother flew to the West Coast she had looked down at hills and woods and her mother had, after examining the map, decided it was Arkansas.

"In the summer," he said. "It isn't damp heat, like here. This is the worst summer of anywhere, here in Washington. I'd almost rather be anywhere else in the summer than here."

Out of politeness she agreed.

"Of course there're a lot of floods and cyclones around where I come from," Roger said. "And the worst is after the water goes down there're rats. You know, in the junk. When I was a kid I remember there was a rat one night trying to get into the house up through the floor by the fireplace."

"What happened?"

He said, "My brother shot it with his .22."

"Where's your brother now?" she asked.

"He's dead," Roger said. "He fell and broke his spine. In Waco, Texas. He got in some kind of beef with a guy . . ." His voice receded and he frowned. On his face was an expression of disapproval; he drew himself up and shook his head, a feeble motion, as if the head of an old man had moved, from side to side, a palsy without meaning. His lips stirred.

"What?" she said, not hearing.

The lines of worry had spread out across his face and he hunched over, slowing, staring at the path. Then he summoned his strength; he grinned at her and some of his gaiety returned. "I'm just kidding," he said.

"Oh," she said. "You mean about your brother?"

"He's living in Houston. He's got a family and a job with an insurance company." Behind his glasses his eyes shifted and glowed. "You believed me, didn't you?"

She said, "It's hard to tell when you're telling the truth."

Ahead of them two women had got up from a bench, leaving it unclaimed. Roger made for it and she accompanied him. At the final step or so he ran like a boy; he whirled and dropped onto the bench, his legs out, his elbows back of him. As she seated herself beside him he fished a pack of cigarettes from his shirt pocket and lit up, blowing clouds of smoke in all directions, a sighing and snorting of contentment, as if he considered the finding of the unclaimed bench some significant event for which he was grateful. He crossed his legs, tipped his head on one side, smiled at her with affection. His smile was like a little confident breaking open of him, a coming apart of the rigid outside rind; as if, she thought, he swelled up just enough to break through, and, for a moment, emerge to look around at what she saw, the trees and water and earth.

"I don't have to go to California," he told her.

"No," she said, "I guess not."

"I could stay here. Any big city there's going to be a lot of television . . . like New York for instance. But these guys out on the Coast expect me. They're counting on it."

"Then you better go," she said.

He studied her for a long time.

"I mean," she said, "if that's what you told them. That you were coming."

At that, he put on such a circumspect expression that she knew he was really very smart; he had been shy, a little uncertain of himself, and he had frisked about while he searched for what he wanted, whatever it was, something to do with her, but as time wore on he lost that, he got over the awkwardness; the kidding and the half-boasting, the nonsense, rushed by. He got rid of them. Now he was more like she remembered from the night of the party: quiet, moody, even somewhat despondent. But how clever he was. He could do almost anything. In the beginning she had felt helpless because he sat drinking up her wine, and now a tinge of that helplessness returned; on the bench beside her he seemed so resourceful, so experienced, and of course he was older than she. And she had no knowledge of him really; she could not really trust what she heard from him, or even what she saw. It was, she thought, as if he had complete control of himself. He could become anything he wanted.

Especially, she thought, he had an enduring quality. Something to do with time; she did not understand it at all.

A long view, perhaps.

"I got to get going," he announced suddenly. Snapping his cigarette from him, into the wet grass, he stood up.

"Yes," she said, "but not right this minute."

"I have a lot on my mind," he said. But he remained where he was.

Virginia said, "Maybe you better go and get it done."

"What about you?"

"Oh, go to hell," she said.

"What!" he said, astonished.

Still seated, she said, "Go on. Go do what you have to do." They had surprised each other and made each other angry. But for her part she knew she was right. She looked past him at an object out across the water, in the center of the Basin; she pretended to herself that it had moved and she followed its course as it bobbed up and down.

"You don't have to get sore," Roger said.

His composure came steadily back, and again she thought that he needed only time. In spite of his size—when they were both standing he was an inch or so shorter than she—he managed to keep her respect; in the past she had regarded small men as ridiculous to some extent, their strutting and posing, their rituals of pride, but that was not so here, that was not the case with him. His resilience impressed her. And, while she still gazed out at the buoy on the water, Roger began to grin again.

5

A figure far off down the street reminded her of her daughter. A lank tall girl, wearing a coat, who marched so swiftly that her hair streamed behind her. And her hair had the ragged uncombedness of Virginia's. At the curb the girl stepped without looking, the same plunging forward with her head up, with no thought of where she put her feet. It gave her an ungainly quality, as it gave Virginia; the girl did not have a feminine walk, nor grace, nor even good coordination. She did not seem to know what to do with her arms. But her legs were long and smooth—the short war-time skirts showed them up to the knees—and her back was quite straight. When she came trotting up onto the last block Mrs. Watson realized that it was Virginia. For heaven's sake, had she come on the bus? Always in the past she had come with somebody in a car.

"I didn't recognize you," Mrs. Marion Watson said.

Virginia halted at the fence, flushed and breathing through her mouth, an asthmatic wheeze that seemed to rise out of good spirits rather than exertion. She made no move to open the gate and enter the yard; she seemed happy to remain on the sidewalk. After a pause Mrs. Watson resumed her work; she snapped off another growth from the tea-rose bush over which she crouched.

Virginia said cheerfully, "What are you doing? You're cutting them down until they're stumps; they look like sticks."

"I didn't expect to see you come walking up the street," Mrs. Watson said. "I was looking for Carl's car." Carl was the boy who usually brought her daughter; they had been going together, off and on, for a year.

Opening the gate, Virginia ducked under the arbor of cabbage roses, brushing at the branches without paying attention to them. Something to get past, as it had been with her all her life. The swipe of her hand, the impatience . . . she came up beside her mother, stopped a moment, and then started onto the back stairs.

"I have to finish this," Mrs. Watson said. "This is the time to prune them." She continued snapping the branches; here and there is the yard she had left piles of them, and along the side of the house. "I'm almost done."

On the steps Virginia surveyed the yard, swinging herself from side to side, her hands in the deep pockets of her coat. In the midday direct sunlight her face gleamed, lacking makeup, somewhat dry, but, her mother thought, pretty enough. A girl's bright thin mouth, a few freckles on her cheeks, the sandy, shapeless hair. Skirt and blouse of a college girl, the same low-heeled shoes—a pair of saddle shoes they had picked out together, on a shopping trip several years before.

Getting to her feet—her muscles ached from the gardening—Mrs. Watson said, "Now I want to rake them into the back so Paul can burn them."

"Who's Paul?"

"The colored man who comes around and does gardening and hauling." From the garage she brought the rake and began to strike with it at the cut rose branches. "Don't I sound like a Southern lady?" she said.

"I know you aren't."

She paused in her work. "I am. I wouldn't be out here in this—" Gesturing at the yard she said, "Of course now it's patriotic."

Most of the ground had become a victory garden; beets and carrots and radishes waved their tops in rows. "But let's face it."

"I can't stay too long today," Virginia said. "I want to be back at the apartment by dinner time. Somebody might call."

"The hospital?"

"No," she said. "A friend who's going to California."

"How can she call if she's going to California?"

"Well, if he doesn't go then he'll probably call."

"Is it somebody I know?"

"No," Virginia said. She opened the screen door and started on into the house. "He's a friend of the Rattenfangers'. They had a party for me—"

"How did it turn out?" She had been told about the party; it celebrated Virginia's first year at her job.

"Not bad. Mostly just sitting around talking. Everybody had to go to bed early to get up Saturday for work."

"What sort of man is this person?" Once, in town, she had met the Rattenfangers at Virginia's apartment. The two of them did not impress her as much as they impressed Virginia, but she did not mind them; at least they seemed genial, without claim to being anything other than they were.

Loitering on the steps Virginia said, "That's hard to say. I don't know. What kind of person is anybody? It depends on the circumstances a lot. Sometimes you're in a different mood."

"Well," she said, "what's he doing?" When her daughter did not answer she said, "Is he in the Service?"

"He's discharged. He got wounded in the Philippines or something. Anyhow he's on Federal disability. He seemed sort of nice. He's probably in California by now. Or on the way." She sounded glum. Next thing she had disappeared into the house, and the screen door closed behind her.

At the kitchen table the two of them sat rolling cigarettes on the odd little machine that Mrs. Watson had bought at People's Drugstore. It turned paper and pipe tobacco—almost the only tobacco still available—into half-way decent cigarettes, preferable at least to the peculiar ten-cent brands that had shown up on store shelves, which tasted as if they had been swept from the floors of barns.

"That reminds me," Virginia said. "In my purse I have some red stamps for you. Don't let me forget them."

"Can you spare them?" Her delight rang in her voice.

"Sure. I'm eating lunch at work. If the butcher asks why they're not attached to the book, say you got them for fat."

"I hate to take yours," Mrs. Watson said. "But I can certainly use them. Look, dear, I'll buy a leg of lamb for next Sunday; you can come out and eat it."

"Maybe so," Virginia said, as if she were not really listening. Her attention had turned elsewhere and she sat mutely, stiff and in an awkward position, with her chair too far back from the table. It gave her a skinniness; her cheeks had become sunken and she stared down hollow-eyed, her bare arms resting on the table before her. As she worked the machine she drummed on the table; her fingers, so lean and unusually strong, beat on the wood until she noticed what she was doing and stopped.

"You look like hunger," Mrs. Watson said, not pleased.

"Hungry? No—"

"Hunger. Somebody personifying the Axis concentration camps."

Her daughter's brow pulled together. "Don't be silly."

"I was merely teasing you."

"No," Virginia said, "it's your way of making a suggestion."

"You could use makeup," Mrs. Watson said. "Or do something else with your hair. You've stopped putting it up, haven't you?"

Virginia said, "I don't have time for that. There's a war on, you know."

"Your hair is really a sight," Mrs. Watson said. "If you go look in the mirror you'll agree."

"I know what I look like," Virginia said.

A moment of silence.

"Well," Mrs. Watson said, "I just don't want to see you detract from your pretty appearance."

Virginia said nothing. She resumed the making of cigarettes.

"Don't take things so seriously," Mrs. Watson said. "That's one of your tendencies, and I know you know it."

Virginia raised her head and gave her a hard glance.

"How is Carl?" Mrs. Watson said presently.

"Fine."

"Why didn't he drive you out?"

"Let's talk about something else." Her work slowed and she began to pick at bits of tobacco, catching them between her nails. For all its fierceness her energy had an early limit.

"He hasn't been sent back overseas, has he?" Mrs. Watson said. Of the different boys she preferred Carl; he seemed always to be on his feet opening doors, shaking hands, half-bowing from his great height. "There's so little stability during a war," she said. "How long do you think it'll last? I'll be glad when it's over."

"They should be opening up the Second Front pretty soon," Virginia said.

"Do you think so? Do you think the Russians can hold out? Of course, we're getting so much Lend-Lease to them . . . but I'm surprised they lasted this long." From the beginning she had been sure the Russians would give up; she still expected to turn on the radio and hear that they and the Germans had signed an agreement.

Virginia said, "You won't agree with me, but I think the war is a good thing because of the changes it's made. After it's over the world will be so much better that it'll make up for the war."

Her mother groaned.

"Change is good," Virginia said.

"I've seen enough change." In 1932 she had voted for Hoover. The first months of the Roosevelt Administration had horrified her. Her husband had passed on at about the same time, and in her mind the two events mingled, death and loss with the overturning of the order, N.R.A. stickers and, in the streets, the W.P.A. signs. "Wait until you get as old as I am," she said.

"Does it bother you not to know where we'll be a year from now? Why does it bother you? It's wonderful . . . that's the way it should be."

A deep distrust, an awareness of the most powerful kind came to Mrs. Watson and she said, "What's this boy like?"

"What boy?"

"The one who's going to call you. The one who isn't going to California."

Virginia smiled. "Oh." But she did not answer.

"How disabled is he?" She had a horror of maimed persons; she never let Virginia tell her about patients at the hospital. "He's not blind, is he?" That struck her as the worst, more awful than death.

"I think he just pulled something in his back. A slipped disc."

"How old is he?"

"Around thirty."

"Thirty!" It was something like being maimed; an image sprang up: Virginia with a balding middle-aged man who wore suspenders. "Oh my God," she said. She thought, then, of the time her daughter had frightened her the most; it had happened when they were staying near Plumpoint, at a cabin on the Chesapeake Bay. The children had run about collecting Coca-Cola bottles left behind by the bathers; they sold the bottles for two cents apiece and with the money they hurried off—gangs of them—to the amusement park at Beverley Beach. One afternoon, with money from bottles, Virginia had hired a man to row her out onto the bay in a rowboat, a leaky hulk of a rowboat covered with barnacles and stinking of seaweed. For almost an hour the boat had bobbed around, out among the waves; on the beach she and her husband watched with despair and fury until finally the fifty cents worth of time had been used up and the man rowed back.

"Maybe not quite thirty," Virginia said. "But older than I am."

She continued making cigarettes with the machine. "He's had a lot of trouble. But he doesn't seem to understand it; he just goes roaming around."

"What—does he want?" she asked. "In a woman, I mean."

Virginia said, "He doesn't seem to want anything." After a pause she said, "Maybe just to talk. He wants to be an electronic engineer after the war."

"When do I get to meet him?"

Again smiling, Virginia said, "Never."

"I want to meet him." She heard her voice squawk out.

"I think he went to California."

"No, you don't think so. Bring him out so I can meet him. Or don't you want me to meet him?"

"There's no point in it."

"Yes," she said. "I'd like to very much. Does he have a car? he can drive you out next time. What about next weekend?" Her desire was to get him here before anything happened. To get him to this place first. "Of course it's your life," she said. "You understand that and so do I."

Virginia began to laugh.

"Isn't it?" Mrs. Watson demanded. "Isn't it your own life?"

Nodding, Virginia said, "Yes."

"Don't try to put the responsibility on me. You have to make your own decisions; you have a job and you're an adult, out on your own."

"Yes," Virginia said, in a sober voice.

At two o'clock in the afternoon Virginia left and her mother walked with her as far as the bus stop. When she returned to the house the telephone was ringing.

The voice on the wire said, "Is Virginia there?"

"No," Mrs. Watson said, out of breath. She recognized Penny, Virginia's roommate. "She's already left; she just now left." At the end of the hall the front door stood open. A paper boy walked past along the sidewalk, folding his papers; he glanced in, hesitated, and then tossed the paper onto the porch.

"There's somebody here who wants her," Penny said. "I guess she'll be home soon if she's already left."

"Who is it?" Mrs. Watson demanded. "Is it that one who was going to California? Ask him if he's the one."

"Yes," Penny said. "He didn't go."

"Tell him I want to talk to him. Put him on the phone. Do you know his name?"

"His name's Roger something," Penny said. "Just a minute, Mrs. Watson." A long silence followed and she listened; she pressed the receiver against her ear. Off in the distance people stirred and murmured, a man and his voice, Penny's voice, then steps and jarrings of the phone.

"Hello," Mrs. Watson said.

"Hello," a man said, a muffled voice.

"This is Virginia's mother," she said. "Are you the man who was going to California? You didn't go, did you? Then you're going to be around for a while, is that right?" She waited, breathing as little as she could, but he said nothing. "I told Virginia to bring you out here for dinner," she said. "So I'm expecting you; I told her next weekend. Can you come then? Can you drive her out? You have a car, don't you?"

A stirring. And then he said in his muffled voice, "Yeah, I guess so."

"I'm looking forward to meeting you," she said. "Your name is Roger? What's the rest of your name?"

"Lindahl."

"All right, Mr. Lindahl," she said. "I'll telephone Virginia during the week and tell her when dinner will be. I'm very glad to have met you, Mr. Lindahl." She hung up the phone and walked away, along the hall to the front door, where she snatched up the newspaper the boy had thrown.

She found her glasses case, put on her glasses, and carried the newspaper to the kitchen table. After fixing herself a cup of Nescafé instant coffee she lit one of the cigarettes that she and Virginia had manufactured and began to read the news.

Do I really think she's that stupid? she thought, laying down the newspaper.

Through the kitchen window she noticed the piles of rose prunings; she had not finished raking them to the back. So she took her cigarette with her, outdoors to the backyard, where she had hung the rake. Soon she had dragged the piles together in one heap; she whacked at them with the rake, her cigarette between her lips. Now, she thought, I'm scandalizing the neighborhood. Shocking the Southern ladies by smoking in my own yard.

In less than ten minutes she finished her work. She took up her shears and gazed around for something more to do.

I don't care if she's that stupid, she thought. I just want to see him; I want to see what he looks like.

The desire to have an exact visual impression of him dominated her mind. The details; the color of his hair, his height, the kind of clothes he wore, his choice of words. Otherwise, she thought, anything was possible. Any act between them.

Her eyes fell on the wisteria, and she started toward it with the shears; clacking the blades of the shears open and shut she hurried across the garden.

6

When he got home from the trip to Ojai, Virginia said to him, "Did you bring back the check?"

"Yes." He handed it to her. "That damn school," he said. "You know what the hell it did? It reminded me of Arkansas. You didn't tell me it was a farm; it used to be a stud farm for some rich people."

Entering the house, Gregg said to Virginia, "Daddy wouldn't let me play football; he made me come back because I didn't mind him. And he got all mad at me." Dry-eyed, he advanced to his mother and put his arms around her hips.

"They even have a barn," Roger said. "The whole works—a cow, rabbits, a bunch of cats. That woman is a farm woman; look at her arms. My God, she's a farm woman. Couldn't you tell that?"

Virginia said, "Did you have lunch on the way?"

"No." Irritably, he started back out again, toward the parked car. "I have to get down to the store; I can't stick around here. What time is it? One-thirty? Jesus Christ. Will you call Pete and tell him I'm coming right away? He probably hasn't been able to get downstairs to the can yet today."

While she phoned, Roger roamed through the house. She found him in the bathroom, changing his shirt and tie.

"I stink like a Mexican," he said. "From the driving and the goddamn heat."

"You could take a shower," she said. She had never seen him so worked-up, in such excitement. "Are you all right?" she asked.

"It was just as if he was there," Roger said. "I expected to see him any minute. Everything was there but him." He washed his face in the bowl. "The day he and I found the twenty-six eggs in the shed. It was just that—he got it the next week. That was the last time we had any fun; she bawled us out because we brought the eggs into the kitchen. Hell!" Dropping the towel, he appealed to Virginia. "Naturally we brought them into the kitchen. That's where they taught us to bring eggs when we finished picking them up in the henhouse. You know what's in those damn nests in the henhouse? China doorknobs and junk like that, one in each nest. To fool the chicken. Christ, I used to grope down into the straw and by God, it'd fool me; I'd think—hey, I got an egg. And it was just a doorknob!" He stared at his wife.

She did not know what to make of him.

Following her into the kitchen, he continued, "Did you ever get to look into a chicken's guts and see the eggs? Before they're hatched? All sizes—it's weird. I never saw anything like it. It used to scare the hell out of me. And then we'd eat the chicken. Can you figure that out?"

She said, "I thought you told me your brother was still alive." She had never been able to get the actual picture of his family, his brother or his father or his mother.

"He jumped from the back of the truck—this old junk-heap in the yard—and landed on a bent piece of metal. It practically cut off his big toe. We thought it was funny. I remembered kind of sneaking around with my hand over my mouth, laughing. Anyhow, he got lockjaw and died." Roger threw himself down at the kitchen table and put his head on his arm.

"Then he is dead," Virginia said.

Taking off his glasses, Roger looked up at her vacantly.

"Years ago you told me he was living down in Texas," she said, feeling indignation.

He went on staring at her in his sightless fashion, holding his glasses in his hands. "Oh." He nodded. And then he put on an expression of such weariness that she at once seated herself next to him and rested her head against his.

"I'm glad you're back," she said.

Roger said, "What did you do? Tell them you wanted this woman to pick Gregg up on weekends?"

"Mrs. Alt said something about it."

"I met her," Roger said. "She and her husband were both up there, and their kids. Gregg played football with them. Liz and Chic Bonner. I guess they live down here."

"I think they live in San Fernando."

Rousing himself he said, "I have to get down to the store." He kissed her on the mouth—his body smelled of the Arrid that he had just used—and left the house. Still in the kitchen, at the table, she heard the Oldsmobile start up and then fade away down the street.

That evening, after dinner, while she was showing Gregg the use of different crayons, Roger said to her, "Come on into the bedroom. I want to talk to you."

"Just a minute." She finished setting up Gregg's coloring book and then followed her husband from the room.

In the bedroom he leaned against the wall, hands behind his head. He seemed in a good mood, and so, she also felt cheered. "You want to do it?" he asked.

Puzzled, she said, "Do what?" For a moment she imagined that he meant an action for which they used no direct name; it usually happened in the bedroom. She became embarrassed. But he did not mean that.

"Up there," he said.

"You mean the school?" So he had finally come around. "Isn't it too late?" she said, but already she calculated their best bet; both of them, she and Roger, should appear at the school with Gregg, his assortment of articles, and the check. No telephoning. No preliminaries. "We'd have to drive up tomorrow," she said. "And we'd have to get all this stuff packed tonight."

"You have a list." He grinned at her.

"Would you help?"

"Sure."

Together, they packed feverishly. At midnight they were still at it. Gregg was not told; they did not want to excite him and keep him from sleeping.

"Mrs. Alt is going to think we're crazy," Virginia said. "I wonder what she'll say. She probably won't be able to think of anything to say. You want to pretend—I mean just for a joke—that everything seems ordinary to us, completely ordinary? We'll just say, Here we are. Here's Gregg. Oh, yes. Here's the check."

"We'll tell her it's all in her mind," Roger said.

"Yes, let's say she's just imagining it—we'll look her straight in the eye." Sleepy and tired as they both were, they enjoyed the packing; it had the exhilarating breath of change, of some new level of existence. It marked the end of one period and the beginning of another, and neither of them was quarrelsome or anxious about it, now.

At one a.m. they finished and stacked the suitcases and boxes by the front door. Then, in the kitchen, they both had a drink.

"He can always come home," Virginia said.

"I don't think he wants to. He liked it up there."

"But he could."

"He won't," Roger said. "Except on the weekends."

Early the next morning they fixed Gregg up in his best suit, loaded all the baggage into the Oldsmobile, locked the front door of the house, and set off for Ojai.

Roger did the driving. They reached the Valley at eight-thirty; the sunlight was cold and white and all the trees dripped moisture from the night. The air smelled good, and they drove with the windows down.

From the moment he understood where they were going, Gregg kept up a ceaseless account of what he intended to do; he intended to ride the horse, shoe the horse, hike up to the top of the mountains and plant the U.S. flag and the California Bear flag there, feed the possum, win at football, help put up the tents, find out why James had dark skin, give up his room in favor of an underground cave equipped with atomic devices run by clock motor, bring Mrs. Alt (he still called her Mrs. Ant) home to dinner, take all his old friends up to see the school and him in it, bring all his new friends down to L.A. to see his old school, and so on. In addition, he cataloged and commented on each place and object that the car passed; he gave long spurious accounts of the trees, houses, condition of the road, make of cars, purpose of individuals seen in fields or by the road.

"All right," Roger said at last. "Take it easy."

Hugging the boy, Virginia said, "We're almost there." She had begun to feel sentimental and tearful; from her purse she got a comb and worked with Gregg's hair. He did not pause in his monologue.

"And then," to hold them, "I ran and ran and nobody could catch up with me; I ran so fast nobody even knew where I was; they all said, Where did he go? Where did he go? And I was up at the place where the water comes from. Maybe I swam part of the way. I think I swam part of the way. That was where all the branches were. And nobody knew where I was."

"Okay," Roger said. "Knock it off."

This time he parked inside the school grounds. Nothing had changed, except that today cars were everywhere. Other parents, with their children, could be seen wandering about, along the paths and trails between the buildings. The air smelled of breakfast.

"I guess we're not the only ones," Virginia said. How well-dressed the parents were. The mothers had on furs; all the men were in business suits. "It's an important day," she said.

Roger said, "Looks like a wedding or something, everybody dressed up." They got out of the car, leaving the luggage behind. At the sight of the other parents with their children, Gregg fell silent. He seemed awed.

"Wouldn't it be funny," Roger murmured, as the three of them walked up the steps to the main building, "if she says the register is full? We never thought of that."

The lobby of the building was crowded with parents and children, all formal and on their best behavior. Small groups had collected; conversation went on in low tones. Now the smell of cigarettes and perfume and pipes and leather filled the rooms and halls.

"We better start looking for her," Virginia said. "She must be around somewhere."

"Keep your fingers crossed." Roger said to his son.

"Okay," Gregg said, crossing his fingers.

They found Mrs. Alt talking with several couples. As soon as she spied them she broke away and came toward them. She did not seem surprised, only rushed and business-like. "Did you bring Gregg back after all?" She shook hands with Virginia. "I'm glad to see you again. You just got in under the wire. Did you bring his things? If not you still have a day or so. Actually, we have children coming in all during the first month."

"Hello, Mrs. Ant," Gregg said.

Mrs. Alt smiled. "Hello, Gregg. Welcome back." She propelled the Lindahls into the office and shut the door; the murmur of voices cut off behind them. "This is always a hectic day—the day the children arrive. It'll be like this from now on." At her desk she unscrewed her fountain pen and began writing. "I'll have James carry Gregg's things up to his room. They'll be six in a room. Some of his roommates are already here; he can meet them right away. What turmoil." She tore off a receipt and passed it to Roger; he gave her back the check which Virginia had made out.

"Fine," Mrs. Alt said. "What about some coffee? You can go in the dining room if you wish: the doors are open. When I have a chance I'll introduce you to some of the parents, especially of his roommates." Arising, she showed them to the office door. "I'll try to get hold of one of the teachers to show you around while you're here. Or did you see the grounds? Anyhow, you're free to go anywhere you want; this is open-house day."

A teacher approached her; she said good-bye to the Lindahls and hurried off.

"Well," Virginia said, "that's that." She was a little dazed. "It's settled."

From a phone in the hall, Roger called the store and told Pete that he wouldn't be in until later. When he had hung up he found his wife and son standing with a group of parents.

". . . Oh, it's a wonderful school. We've had Louis and Barbara here three years, now. When all the children are here, it's about evenly divided. You see more boys, now; for some reason they're the first to arrive. Some of the boys stay over between terms. I guess a few of the girls do, too. They keep them very well supervised. You don't have to worry. They'll write you at the end of each week and tell you how he's making out. Remember to tell them how much allowance he's to get. Don't forget about the laundry; that's extra. They send it out." The talk went on.

Leaving them, Roger wandered about, overhearing the various conversations, noticing the different parents. Most of them were young. All of them were well-dressed. The women, like Virginia, were for the most part thin and tall, pretty, with sharp faces; their voices were louder than the men's, and they seemed to be doing most of the talking. The men smoked, listened, nodded; exchanged a few remarks with one another. They had been pushed into the background.

The young arithmetic teacher Van Ecke passed by in his sweater and unpressed slacks, and Roger greeted him.

"Oh hello," Van Ecke said, obviously not recognizing him. "How are you making out?"

"Fine," Roger said.

Pausing, Van Ecke said, "This is the day the parents get to look us over and see if it's worth the money. Most of them don't show up again until the end of the term. Of course, a few drive up now and then, but not very many." He eyed Roger. "Let's see."

"Lindahl is my name," Roger said.

"Oh. Of course. How's your child? Say, did you get that all cleared up? Something about his room or his clothes."

"It's fine now," Roger said.

"I see your wife over there," Van Ecke said. "What an attractive woman. Mrs. Alt says she dances. What sort of dancing? Ballet?"

He explained.

"Oh, like Cyd Charisse," Van Ecke said. "Yes, they have a lot of that down in the town. Experimental art stuff—I'm afraid it's too deep for me. What line are you in, Mr. Lindahl?"

"I have a TV store in L.A.," Roger said.

"I'll be darned. I guess TV's the coming thing for everything. Plays and sports and comedy, everything."

Roger said, "Have you seen the Bonners around?"

Van Ecke shook his head. "No, they left early this morning. They stayed overnight. Their boys are here. I guess they're older than your boy; they're eleven or twelve." He edged away. "I hope to see you again, Lindahl."

The time was nine-thirty. He entered the dining room, attracted by the coffee smell. Most of the tables were bare, not in use, but in one corner of the room cups and cream pitchers and sugar shakers and silverware and napkins had been put out. One of those two-level metal carts had just now come pushing through the kitchen doors, carrying on it glass pots of coffee; the woman behind the cart, vast, dark, probably Mexican, began filling cups at the tables. Men and women clustered around. It all seemed pleasant. He walked over and took a cup for himself.

He had been sitting for a few minutes, stirring his coffee, when a man in a blue business suit took the chair next to his, glanced at him, found a cup for himself, asked someone for the sugar, and at last said, "You're not one of the teachers, are you?"

"No," Roger said. "A parent."

The man nodded. "Nice school they have here." He stirred his coffee, ill at ease. "Sure a drive up, though. Those turns."

"Just don't brake on the turns," Roger said. "Keep your foot on the gas."

"Then don't you get going too fast?"

"You never brake on a curve," he repeated. "You always have the engine pulling. Brake before you hit the curve. Otherwise your rear end will break away on you."

"I see," the man said. He continued stirring his coffee and then mumbled, "Pardon me," and got up and wandered off elsewhere.

I'm not doing very well, Roger thought to himself. He felt lonely. But he did not have any desire to rejoin his wife. At his table other people seated themselves, nodded to him or said hello, sat for a while, and then moved on.

Finally he put down his cup and left the dining room. He walked out of the building, through a side door, onto the terrace. For a few minutes he stood smoking and looking at the view. Eventually he continued down a flight of steps to the road, and from there into a grove of fir trees and out onto the dirt ridge overlooking the football field.

No children in sight.

His hands in his pockets, he stood meditating about nothing in particular, feeling no special feeling. The time was about ten o'clock and the first real warmth was beginning to get into the day. Far off, along a valley road, a truck moved. Its diesel smoke followed it like a tail.

From behind him he heard footsteps. He turned around. A Negro came toward him, carrying some folded papers. "Are you Mr. Rank?" the Negro said.

"No," Roger said.

"I beg your pardon." The Negro wheeled around and set off in the direction from which he had come.

That's James, Roger decided. Hello, James. Good-bye. And in him the fear, the always-present memory of them, the pain at his mouth.

After an interval he meandered on, in no particular direction.

Ahead of him was a small square concrete building from which stuck a funnel. Part of the school's heating system, he decided. He passed the building and climbed a steep trail to a bluff. Not far away was another building, tumble-down; from it came an odor of feed and manure and animals, but not a familiar smell. Not horses, he thought, walking toward it.

The building had no door. He entered into the gloom. A row of cages—nothing more. In the cages shapes shuffled and sniffed. Rabbits. He stopped by the first cage. The dark ochre rabbit peeped up at him, twitching. The smell was overpowering, but he did not object. He looked into each of the cages. Some of the rabbits noticed him; some had their broad backs to the wire, poking their fur through in patches. He chucked one rabbit; the rabbit shifted slightly and squatted down, away from the wire. And all the time the noses of the rabbits were in motion. Their great tepid eyes watched him.

He left the shed and walked at random. Once he saw a group of parents and their children. He stepped over a heap of boulders— a dry creek bed—and jogged up the far side. No sound. No stirring.

Forcing a path through bushes he stepped out. Onto the football field, the far side.

Walking with his head down he crossed the field, step by step, over the weeds. At the spot where they had been he stopped. Here, he thought. In the shadow, under the rise. Away from the sun. He fooled aimlessly, kicking at clumps of soil.

On the ground was a long straw of grass, several cigarette butts pushed into the loose soil. Right here. The straw of grass had been tossed down when Mrs. Bonner left to go find Mrs. Alt.

Bending down he picked up the straw of grass and put it in his pocket.

I must be nuts, he said to himself.

Then he walked on, up the same trail as before, to the top of the rise. No, he thought. What a mistake that would be.

I really am nuts.

He walked until he came to his parked car. Unlocking the door he got in and sat, with the windows down. He put on the radio and listened to music and news and commercials; then he shut it off, got out of the car, and locked the door again. The goddam windows. He hadn't rolled them up. Opening the door he stretched across the seat and rolled up the window on the far side.

After that he started back in the direction of the main school building.

In the lobby he found a chair and settled down. Some of the parents had drifted off upstairs to the children's quarters, or to the classrooms, or outdoors; the lobby was less crowded.

Mrs. Alt, noticing him, came over and dropped into the cane-bottom chair beside him. "I'm worn out," she said.

"It's a mess," he agreed.

"You know, I'm so glad you changed your mind."

He nodded.

"Can I say something about your wife?"

"Sure," he said.

Mrs. Alt said, "I think she's very cold with children. Withdrawn. I don't really think she's very good with children. That's my snap-judgment for the day. I told her that, or I wouldn't be saying it to you. I told her that was why I was willing to take Gregg."

"It's true," he said. "I guess."

"Did she want to have a child?"

"I don't remember."

"What's her mother like?"

"Worse." He grinned.

"She said something about her mother living near you."

"Too near," he said. "She followed us out from the East."

"I think you're doing the right thing," Mrs. Alt said. "Your wife passes on too much of a sense of menace to Gregg."

"So do I."

"Yes. You do, too."

"But," he said, "it's Virginia you don't like."

Mrs. Alt said, "That's true. I don't really care much for that kind of person."

"I'm surprised you'd come right out and say it."

"Why?" She turned toward him. "Virginia senses it."

"Virginia thinks you're wonderful."

"Of course she does."

He did not grasp that kind of utterance.

"I suppose the thing that set me off," Mrs. Alt said, "is her snobbery, her feeling about her own stock. I come from Iowa; I take that very personally." She laughed, a deep noisy laugh.

"Yes," he said, "I thought you were from the Middle West."

"Have you ever been through there?"

"Once," he said. "When I was a kid. My father took us on a trip. Buying some kind of farm machinery. We had a truck."

Mrs. Alt said, "You certainly upset Liz Bonner. She flew out of here . . . but she gets like that. She has an infinite capacity for misunderstanding what people say to her; she gets everything wrong and nobody can ever straighten it out. She's one of those sweet, earnest people who hang onto every word and then—God knows what goes on in their brains. If any. For example, we have to keep special toothpaste here for her two boys because she read somewhere that the regular toothpaste—the big brands—has diatomaceous earth in it and that wears away the teeth. I don't think they've used diatomaceous earth in toothpaste since the 'twenties. Maybe they do, though. Maybe she's right. That's the trouble; there's no way you can prove she's wrong. She's sort of a—" Mrs. Alt searched for the word. "I don't want to say lunatic. That isn't it. She's sort of an idiot with a touch of mysticism. In the Middle Ages she'd probably have been burned at the stake and sometime long afterwards canonized. Yes, she's the way I think Joan of Arc must have been. I can see Joan overhearing discussions about the war with England, and the Dauphin, and completely reconstructing the whole situation in her own mind . . . and then running out the door about the way Liz ran out of here when I told her you weren't putting Gregg in the school after all."

"She drove down to Ojai looking for us," Roger said.

"Really?" Mrs. Alt grimaced.

"What line is he in?" Roger asked.

"Oh, he's part of the bread company. A vice-president. You know. Bonner's Bonny Bread."

"Sure," he said, making the connection.

"Originally his grandfather operated a small bakery. Then his father merged it with some other independent bakeries in L.A. They kept the name." Mrs. Alt was quiet for a time. "You know, there's only one thing I can't forgive Liz Bonner for. No matter what you tell her, she swears you didn't. It just rolls off her back. As if she's in another world. Tell her something and the next day she stares at you with those big brown eyes—No, I didn't know that. What do you mean? She's amazed all over again. At first it's sort of—what should I say? Let's say, at first it doesn't drive you crazy. But wait until you see it month after month, her discovering the same thing over and over again."

"How does he stand it?"

"Oh, Chic's easygoing. He's off in his dream world, too. I don't think he hears her, to tell you the truth. They go their own ways."

Across the lobby two women came toward them. One of them was Virginia and the other was Mrs. McGivern, the science teacher. "What's the discussion?" Mrs. McGivern asked, drawing a chair over.

"Liz Bonner," Mrs. Alt said.

"There's nothing to discuss," Mrs. McGivern said. "She's just dumb."

To Roger, Virginia said, "I let Gregg go off with some other boys and Mr. Van Ecke. A hike down into town."

"Okay," he said.

"I don't think so," Mrs. Alt said. "Scatterbrained, maybe."

"That's the same," Mrs. McGivern said.

"No," Mrs. Alt said. "She isn't plodding. She's not slow; I always associate a sort of pedestrian, dulled personality with dumbness. Liz is alert—too alert. She picks up everything she sees and hears; that's part of the trouble. She isn't selective. She just grabs it all in, without sorting through it."

"She has no perspective," Mrs. McGivern said. To Virginia she said, "Aren't we clever? Sitting around here tearing down someone who's seventy miles away?"

"If we're going to talk about somebody behind their back we really better be sure it is behind their back," Mrs. Alt said.

"Oh, Liz wouldn't care," Mrs. McGivern said. She had her own slow, pedantic way; she was a rather masculine woman, with short hair and a rough, square face. "She'd think it was funny."

"I guess I don't know her," Virginia said.

"She's the woman I mentioned to you," Mrs. Alt said. "The one who comes up every weekend for her kids."

"Oh," Virginia said. "Well, I hope she's intelligent enough to be able to make the drive."

"She is," Mrs. McGivern said. "That has nothing to do with intelligence anyhow. Just lack of imagination."

Roger said, "Or an eye for traffic situations."

"What's that?" Mrs. McGivern said.

"The ability to size up the road," he said.

Mrs. McGivern made a gesture of dismissal. "With all these new automatic shifts and power steering and power brakes, all they have to do is turn the key."

"And go right off the road," Roger said, angered. "Driving is a skill. Either you have it or you don't. How much driving have you done? What do you do when you feel your rear end break away on you? Slam down on the brake?"

Mrs. McGivern did not answer. She drew her chair so that she faced Mrs. Alt. A conversation began, having to do with science lab tables. He felt Virginia's hand on his arm; she put her finger to her lips warningly.

"Okay," he said.

"I'm surprised at you," Virginia said.

"Okay." He lapsed into silence.

* * *

On the trip back to Los Angeles both he and Virginia were downcast. It was going to be hard on them; they felt it already. Roger drove. Beside him, she stared out at the scenery. The useless land, she thought. Miles and miles of it. Worth nothing to nobody.

"God damn woman," Roger said.

"Who?"

"That science teacher."

"Yes, she did seem sort of horrible." She remembered the occurrence, then, and she said, "But you didn't have to start yelling. What ever got into you?"

"The reason women are such lousy drivers is because they have that attitude," he said. "They figure all they have to do is turn the key; that's why they drive right into you."

"Mrs. Alt seemed tired."

"Yeah," he said.

"I'd hate to have all that responsibility." After a time she said, "I've been thinking of things we overlooked. We didn't pack his heavy wool socks, those long ones he puts on over his regular socks. I'd better make a list. We can take them up to him, or we can give them to him when those people, the Bonners, bring him down."

"You better call them," Roger said.

"Yes," she said. "That's right. That all got mixed up. I better get in touch with her myself; Mrs. Alt probably won't think about it again. Anyhow, the Bonners aren't up there now. At least, that's my understanding. Did you see them?"

"Not today," he said.

"I'll call them this evening." In her purse she found a pencil and note paper. She made out a list of things for Gregg, and she also jotted down: *Find phone number, call Liz Bonner*. But then she got to pondering the gossip between Mrs. Alt and Mrs. McGivern. "I don't know," she said. "From what they said about her, she sounds unreliable. Did you get that impression when you met her?"

"No," he said.

"What impression did you get?"

"She seemed all right."

"Maybe she'd leave him off somewhere along the way."

Scowling, Roger said, "Get a bunch of old women together and look what you have."

Virginia said, "Is she pretty?"

"No. Not particularly."

"What does she look like? Maybe I met her and didn't know her."

"She wasn't there." He chewed his lower lip. "They're both around thirty. He's getting bald. When I saw him he had on a sports shirt; he looked like anybody else. She has brown hair."

"I met Jerry and Walt," Virginia said.

"Who the hell is that?"

"Their children."

"Oh." He glanced at her.

"The boys have red hair. And freckles. They're—"

"I saw them," Roger said. "They're big."

"Well," she said, "they're twelve." She calculated. "Then she's older than thirty. Unless she was married at seventeen."

"Thirty-five, then," he said.

"I don't think Mrs. Alt likes me," Virginia said.

"She likes you okay."

"I always run into women like her head-on," Virginia said.

When they got back to Los Angeles, Roger parked the car in the yellow zone in front of Modern TV Sales & Service. "I'll see you later," he said. "If you start feeling lonely, go to a movie or something."

"He'd be in child-care anyway," she said. "During the afternoon." It was the evenings she was thinking about.

She drove home and parked the car in the garage. For an hour or so she did things around the house, and then, oppressed by the quiet, she opened the phone book and looked for a Charles Bonner who lived in San Fernando. Two were listed. She called the first, and got no answer. So she called the other.

"Hello," a girl's voice said, a breathy teen-aged voice close to her ear.

With great uncertainty she said, "Is—this Mrs. Bonner?"

"Yes."

"Are you Mrs. Elizabeth Bonner?"

"Yes."

Virginia said, "I'm Mrs. Lindahl."

"Who?"

"You have two boys up at the—" And then, at that point, she forgot the name of the school. "Up in Ojai," she said. "Jerry and Walter."

"Oh!" the voice said. "Yes, certainly. Who did you say you were?"

"Virginia Lindahl," she said. "Mrs. Alt was going to talk to you about me."

"Who? You mean Edna?" There was no recognition in the voice. "What about? Just a moment." The phone, at the other end, was put down; Virginia heard the noise of a radio and then the noise ceased. She heard footsteps and the phone being picked up again. "Say it again," Mrs. Bonner said.

Very distinctly, Virginia said, "Mrs. Alt said she was going to talk to you and your husband about driving my son Gregg home on weekends from the school up in Ojai." The name came back to her. "The Los Padres Valley School."

"Yes?"

Exasperated, Virginia said. "I'd like to discuss it with you. Maybe we can work out some sort of arrangement. Either I could pay you or we could alternate or something. Mrs. Alt thought we could work something out."

"Are you down here in L.A.?" Mrs. Bonner said.

"Yes I am," Virginia said.

"I thought you weren't going to put your little boy in the school." The voice rushed on in bewilderment. "Didn't your husband come and get him?"

"We changed our mind," Virginia said.

"Oh. That's fine. It's a wonderful school. Is he up there now? We already took our boys up; we left them there this morning. It was yesterday when we met your husband. I forget his name, his first name. What was your little boy's name? George?"

"Gregg," Virginia said.

"He's real cute. They were all out playing football. Sure, I'd love to bring him down when I come. I'm going up Friday night; I can get him then, if you want. Or maybe you should get him the first time; what do you think? It's up to you. I'm going anyhow. Or we could both go together; why don't we do that? Just take one car. I could drive up and you could drive back or something. What do you think?"

"That sounds all right," Virginia said. "I guess it doesn't matter which car we use."

"We better go in the station wagon," Mrs. Bonner said. "If the boys get tired they can crawl in the back and go to sleep and that way they won't be climbing over us all the time. I leave around one in the afternoon, on Friday. I'll drive by and pick you up. Or maybe you better come by here in your car, so when we get back you can take Gregg right home. Okay? I'll give you my address."

"I have it," Virginia said. "From the phone book."

"Oh," Mrs. Bonner said. "Okay. Well, then I'll see you Friday afternoon around one." A long hesitation, and then she said, "Well, I'm glad to have met you, Mrs. Lindahl. I'm looking forward to— seeing you."

"Thank you very much, Mrs. Bonner," Virginia said. "I appreciate your help a lot. I'll see you, then." She hung up and closed the phone book.

Real scatterbrain, she thought. They're certainly right. But she sounded nice.

7

During the winter of 1944, when his divorce became final, Virginia married Roger Lindahl. She quit her job with the Washington military hospitals, Roger quit his job as stand-by electrician at the Richmond Navy Yard, and by train the two of them left for Los Angeles, California.

The weather in California was warm; there was no snow, no icy streets, cars with chains, children wearing knickers and wool socks, or old men puffing along in overcoats and ear muffs. The sight of palm trees entranced her; it seemed to her like another country entirely, even another continent. The aircraft plants had become the center of all activity; nothing else mattered. Workers' cars were parked in lots as far as the eye could see. The plants never closed; as soon as one shift ended another began, day after day, the swing shift, the graveyard shift, the regular day shift. Men and women flowed into and out of the plants, carrying their lunchpails, the men wearing jeans, the women wearing slacks and bandanas. To Virginia they looked tired and quarrelsome and she saw fights break out on street corners and in cafés and bars and even on the public buses. The workers put in long hours, made more money than they could count or keep or even remember; they were tired, growing rich, most of them had come from the Middle West, lived in cramped rooms with children yelling under their windows as they tried to sleep. On their free time they drank beer in the bars, carried their dirty clothes to the launderettes, ate their meals, bathed and returned to work. It was a fast-paced, frantic life; they did not seem to enjoy it, but they realized that they would never earn so much again. Every day more of them arrived, searched for places to live, joined the lines at the plant gates. The jukeboxes in the cafés played the "Strip Polka" and at night, on the streets, soldiers and sailors from the nearby bases roamed energetically, stared at by rows of elegantly-dressed Mexican boys who lined the lit-up shop doorways looking, to Virginia, like wooden Indians in brand-new varnish.

After a day or so they found an apartment in a six-unit war-time housing building in a village of identical buildings. Special streets, blocked during part of the day to through traffic, connected the buildings, and at the entrance to the village a large sign read:

> 2,400 adults and 900 children
> live here! So drive carefully!
> Go slow! Don't exceed 15 mph!

Only white people lived in the village, but a mile away, on the far side of a steam laundry and supermarket, was a second village for Negroes, set up just like theirs.

Both she and Roger got jobs at once, she as an inventory clerk, Roger as an electrician; their shifts came at the same time so they were able to eat their meals together and shop together. Across the hall from them the young married couple had opposed shifts; the man arose from bed at noon, started to work at two, arrived back home after midnight, while his wife slept from ten o'clock at night to six in the morning and left for work at seven-thirty a.m. Several people in the building tried, from time to time, the business of holding down two shifts in a row, collecting time-and a-half overtime for the second eight hours. If the second shift took place on a weekend during the night their income from the two shifts was enormous. She and

Roger both worked a seven-day week. A sign on their door read: WAR WORKER ASLEEP. DO NOT DISTURB. Later on he nailed a sheet of galvanized iron over the door, to deaden the voices and noise from the hall. By the fall of 1945 they had a good-sized savings account and a locked box full of War Bonds.

It seemed to her that the long hours of work at the aircraft plant made both of them excessively tired. They became quarrelsome, like the people in the bars. Both of them became thin—they had arrived thin enough as it was—and somber. Most of their free time was spent lined up at the supermarket, buying groceries, or at the launderette waiting for their clothes. In the evenings they listened to the radio or walked down to the corner for a beer; some nights she read a magazine and Roger slept. On the radio the Bob Hope program held forth, and Red Skelton and Fibber McGee. That made up everyone's exhausted pleasure: lying fully dressed on the bed listening to the Hit Parade on Saturday night or the Jello program—Jack Benny and Dennis Day and Rochester—on Sunday night. The war came to an end by stages; the aircraft plants began to discharge groups of employees and cut down the number of shifts, the overtime, the seven-day week. But they did not move on like migratory workers; they had earned enough money to stay. By now they considered themselves Californians, as good as the Native Sons. Los Angeles had become the largest populated area in the world; everyone poured in and no one left.

Near their wartime housing village a colony of stores had come into existence, clustered around the supermarket. First, after the launderette, appeared a shoe repair shop, then a beauty parlor, a bakery, two bar-and-grills, a real estate office. Later, the real estate office moved elsewhere and the store became vacant. One day a new sign was hung up, announcing: ONE DAY RADIO REPAIR. Presently the first post-war table model radios appeared in the window beside displays of tubes, batteries, flashlight bulbs, phonograph needles. Within the store a man in a cloth smock could be seen puttering at the counter.

Their Emerson radio had stopped working, so one morning Virginia carried it to the One Day Radio Repair to be fixed.

"I think it's just a tube," she said to the man. "I don't think it's anything serious. It just stopped playing."

"Well we'll see," he said, plugging the radio in and clicking the knob on and off. Bending over it he tapped the tubes with his knuckle, peered inside, listened with his ear against the speaker. He was large, round-faced, and he reminded her of Irv Rattenfanger; he seemed pleasant in a preoccupied fashion. The little shop, new and barely open for business, had already become littered with discarded tubes and ads. "I'll make out a tag," the man said, reaching under the counter. "I can't work on it now."

She gave him her name and address, and he gave her a claim check torn from the bottom of the tag. Several days later when she stopped by, the radio had been fixed; the bill ran seven dollars and fifty cents.

"Just for a tube?" she protested.

"Filters," the man said, showing her the tag. "Dollar-fifty for the parts, the rest labor." He turned on the radio and it ran satisfactorily.

"Just to put in a part?" she said. But she paid him the money and left with the radio. That evening she told Roger how much it had cost. He listened solemnly. At one time, back in Washington, he would have run about in anger, but now he only picked up the receipt and read it, put it down, and shrugged.

"They're probably crooked," she said, thinking of a magazine article she had read.

Stretched out on the couch with his feet up on the arm, Roger said, "Maybe not. They charge around that." He had taken off his glasses; his arm lay over his eyes.

"I wish you had been along." She could not shake off her sense of aggravation. Prices for everything were going up; it was terrible. "You could have talked to him; I don't know anything about radios. And they know when you don't know anything; they always size you up and take advantage of you."

But he remained unbothered, apparently asleep; for half an hour he lay on his back, his eyes shut, sometimes sighing, shifting, smoothing his hair with the flat of his hand. Meanwhile she washed underclothes in the bowl. From the downstairs apartment a radio could be heard, and once a dog barked in the yard. A car motor started up. Children ran along the cement path beneath the window; a woman yelled for them to come indoors to dinner.

To Virginia the apartment was peaceful enough; the pressure on all of them had let up and they were glad of it. They had finished the war in a sprint, an ordeal lasting night and day, without humor and certainly without idealism. Now it had come to an end; they lay on the couch or washed a few things, or sat around discussing what to do with their money, which opportunity to take advantage of. They had earned their money. The servicemen had begun to return; they had little or no money and many of them wanted to go to school on the G.I. Bill, or they wanted to get their old jobs back— saved for them by law—or they spent their time with their wives and children, glad to be able to do that and nothing else. For the warplant workers something more was required, something tangible. They had got used to having something in their hands, some real object.

"I guess we can afford it," Virginia said.

On the couch he grunted.

"We have the money," she said. She got the real estate ad section of the newspaper and read it, as she had been reading it now and then, watching the prices, the new areas opening up. How high property prices had gone in the last year. A house that had sold for five thousand dollars now sold for ten. New tracts, subdivisions they were called, had started to advertise; each had a picturesque name. The smallest of the new houses, the tract houses, sold for seven or eight thousand dollars. It seemed to her to be too much. The tracts advertised low down payment to G.I.s, and she thought that it would be harder without the G.I. provision; in their case they would need one or two thousand dollars.

"They're not built as well," she said. "The new houses. Isn't the lumber green? Isn't that what we read?"

After a moment he sat up, rubbed his eyes, lowered his legs and reached about for his glasses.

"I'm sorry," she said. "I didn't mean to wake you up."

"Look," he said. "Let's go down to the market and get something for dessert. Some ice cream or a pie." Stepping into his shoes he looked around for his coat. "I'm still hungry."

She put on her coat, too, over her cotton shirt, and they strolled along the evening street to the supermarket, where all the lights had gathered into one colorful smear. The sidewalk was untidy with candy wrappers and trash, but nobody noticed; they had got accustomed to it. Inside the market blue white fluorescent lights flooded down on the stacks of cans and bottles. She and Roger lined up at the checker's counter with a cart of small items, beer and a jar of pickles, margarine, lettuce, and a berry pie. On the trip back to the apartment Roger stopped at a curb and peered around.

"Is that the radio shop?" he asked.

"Yes," she said. It was shut up for the night; the neon sign had been turned off. In the window the table model radios could be seen, illuminated by a row of small bulbs set behind them. Hoisting the bag of groceries Roger stepped from the curb and crossed the street to the window. She followed him.

"I wonder how much he's got invested in it," he said.

"I don't think he has much, just a few little radios and some tubes."

Roger put his hand to the glass and gazed in, past the window display, at the fixtures and shelves to the rear of the store. "You think he does the repair work himself?"

"Yes," she said. "He's the only one there."

"A couple hundred bucks worth of radios," he said. "Used fixtures. A tube checker. Repair parts. What else? A cash register, I guess. That's about all."

"There's rent," she said.

"He probably lives in the back." Turning away from the window he walked on. "I'll bet he opened that place for less than three thousand dollars."

"I don't think he's making very much," she said. She did not like the store; it was too barren. Too small and dismal. She could not imagine herself in a place like that and she said, "Do you think a place like that can last very long? Nobody goes in there; that's why he has to charge so much. In a month or so he'll give up. And he'll probably lose what he's got invested."

"There's nothing to sell now," Roger said.

"No," she agreed, "he just has those little radios."

"Later on," he said, "in a couple of years, he'll have television sets to sell."

"If he can stay in business that long," she said. He did not respond to that; she waited and then she said, "Is that the kind of place you mean? I thought you meant a larger place, like the shops downtown." She was thinking of the department stores with their carpets and warmth and salesmen and indirect lighting. The escalators and the whirr of the air-conditioning. All her life she had loved to wander through the big downtown department stores; she loved the smell of the fabrics, leather, the jewelry, the perfumed salesgirls in black, wearing flowers.

"My Christ," he said, "it takes a million dollars to open a department store."

"I just meant—" She did not know what she meant.

"I'm talking about something that's possible," he said. "We could buy a place like that. I can handle the repair work; no salaries to pay, like he works it."

"We only have twelve hundred dollars."

"That's pretty good," he said.

"It's awful in there," she said. "You've never been inside; I have. Ratty little hole in the wall—it's like a shoe-shine parlor or something. Just a place."

Nodding, he conceded that she was right.

"What would you do, then?" she said. "Why wouldn't it be like that?" That man probably thought his place would be nice-looking, she thought. And he didn't have enough capital to fix it up. "He probably wishes he never opened it," she said. But as a matter of fact the man had seemed content in his bleak little store. But, she thought, he was a pale, soft, clerkish man; a sort of neuter, humming to himself, smiling at the customers. Surely it was a miserable way to exist.

She said, "You don't want that; you want more than that. I know you wouldn't be happy. If you're going to get a little store of your own it ought to be something nice. Pretty—" She thought of a modern shop, a dress shop she had visited in downtown Pasadena; an attractive, stylish front and plants set into a moat the length of the window. "You want to be proud of your store, don't you? It wouldn't be to make money anyhow; it would be for something more."

Beside her Roger said nothing.

"If it were me," she said, "I'd rather work in a nice store than own a place like that."

After that neither of them said anything. They walked the rest of the way back to the apartment in silence.

Later, as she heated the pie in the oven, she said, "I can see if my family could help." Of course she meant her mother. The securities and annuities had been owned originally by her father. So they did not seem as much her mother's as the family's. In a sense, then, they were hers, too. She did not know exactly how much they amounted to, but as she remembered they were worth at least twenty thousand dollars. Enough so that her mother could begin thinking of a trip to Europe, now that the war had ended. In letters her mother had described various travel plans, including a visit to the West Coast. She had even considered going to Africa.

"What are you giggling about?" Roger said, at the doorway of the kitchen.

"I'm sorry." She hadn't realized that she had laughed at the idea, the vision of Marion in hip-boots, tramping across the veldt, a sun hat on her head, clutching a shotgun. Her calm, practical, New England mother . . . Good Lord, she thought. She remembered how Marion had looked when she came back from her vacation in Mexico: giant lacquered sandals on her feet, crimson trousers with gold braid, far too tight for her, a lace shawl, and a hand-carved cigarette holder as long as a ruler. At that she had told her that she looked like President Roosevelt, and the cigarette holder, at least, had vanished. But for months her mother had gardened in her Mexican outfit, until the crimson trousers split. The high sandals, she said, kept her feet out of the mud.

Beneath the kitchen window the woman from the next apartment gathered her washing in from the lines that crossed the lawn. A dog ran back and forth nearby. The woman—plump, in her thirties—wore her hair up in a net and Virginia thought, She looks like a waitress. In a highway café. Somewhere between—she had thought, between Arizona and Arkansas. Suddenly the woman screeched at the dog to go away from the clothes basket: her voice blared like a trumpet.

Lord, Virginia thought. Is that how I sound? Do I look that way? Automatically she dried her hands and lifted them to her hair; she patted her hair into shape. Now she kept it short, clipped close because of the machines with which she worked. For safety. And tied up in a red cotton bandana.

In the living room Roger had again sprawled out on the couch, his feet up on the arm. She thought, He can't have a hole-in-the-wall store like that. Even if he wants it.

It has to be better.

After they had eaten up the pie, Roger said, "I'll see you a little later." He had his watch out. "Go to bed if you get sleepy. I'm just going down to the corner for a while."

"Why don't you stay here?" she said.

"I'll be back pretty soon," he said. From his eyes shone the leisurely, confident look; it was the sly quality that always annoyed her.

"I thought maybe we could talk," she said.

He stood at the door, his hands in his pockets, his head tilted on one side. And he waited, showing his endurance, not arguing with her, simply standing. Like an animal, she thought. An inert, unspeaking, determined thing, remembering that it can get what it wants if it just waits.

"I'll see you," he said, opening the door to the hall.

"All right," she said. After all, it didn't come as a surprise.

"I've got some things cooking," he said. "I'll tell you about them later when they're more sort of settled." Mystical and cunning, he left. The door shut after him and she wondered what it was this time. She returned to the kitchen—which she liked to keep scrubbed and in order—and began to wash the dinner dishes.

8

In a particular bar-and-grill not far from his apartment, Roger found the men he wanted: they had taken a booth in the rear and he pushed past the bar toward them.

His friend, Dick Makro, waved a greeting and pointed at the man beside him. "Hi," he said. "Say, this is John Beth, only don't call him Mac, he doesn't go for that; and this is Davis. I didn't catch your first name; I'm sorry."

Davis shook hands with Roger and reseated himself, not speaking. His first name remained his secret. John Beth, never called Mac, stuck up his hand. He had smart, clear eyes, like glaziers' points, and his hard-woven sharkskin suit kept him looking in top health. His hair bunched in mounds, puffed from the use of pomade. To Roger he gave a firm handclasp, leaning upward and moving his mouth. He had an immense overbite, but his teeth were an even color, probably because he did not smoke. At a guess he was in his middle fifties.

"I'm glad to meet you," Roger said, taking a seat across from John Beth and Makro. Davis, a sunken-chested dour person, fiddled with his drink and did not appear to care what the others discussed.

"Is that right?" Beth said.

"I can't help being conscious of the fact that you're the owner of the Beth Appliance Center," Roger said.

Beth agreed.

"Say look," Roger said. His friend Makro scratched at the wall and looked vague, leaving Roger and Beth alone. "I want to talk to you about a matter," he said, jumping in. "Now I've been by your place and I know what a fine store you have; you have all the different appliances, stoves and refrigerators and washers, the major appliances, and when they're in supply again you're going to do a tremendous business there in that location you have. But this thing I want to mention is something I think you've overlooked. Now I know you've got what radios are available, and you're probably taking orders; you have table models and consoles and phonograph combinations—"

"I carry Zenith," Beth said, "and Hoffman, and Crosley, and R.C.A. I don't carry Philco or any junk brands like Sentinel."

"I see," Roger said. "Well, here's the thing; I was in your store and I noticed the extensive line of radios and combinations you have or will have, but I noticed you don't have a service department."

Beth said, "No, we have the work done outside."

"Well here's the thing," Roger said. "One of your salesmen showed me downstairs in the basement and I saw where you have stuff warehoused there, in the cartons, and it occurred to me you could put in a service department there."

"I need that space," Beth said.

"Well what are you using it for? You're using it to stack up boxes; you could rent a garage for that for five dollars a month on some side street and bring the stuff around on a dolly; uncrate it there in the garage and not have the packing waste where customers have to trip over it getting downstairs to see the phonographs demonstrated."

Beth swirled his drink.

"What I'm thinking about is the future," Roger said. "When you clear out minor lines like vacuum cleaners and steam irons—I noticed your display racks along one whole wall on those and you get in television. Then you'll have to have a service department."

"That's years," Beth said.

Davis, in an ordinary voice, said, "There won't be any television for another ten years."

"Oh no," Roger said. "That's where you're wrong; there's going to be television inside one year—I read all the trade journals and I know; it's the truth. This time next year you're going to have as big a television inventory as everything else put together; that's a fact. I'm not making that up."

"That's just talk," Beth said.

"It's the truth, I give you my word I'm not making it up."

Beth said, "What do you want me to do? Hire you to repair television sets they haven't even invented yet?"

Both Makro and Davis snickered, and that put an end to the business. John Beth raised a glance across to Davis, and then he lifted himself up to search out the waitress. Roger pretended not to notice the glance.

Later on, after a couple of drinks, when Makro had excused himself to go on home and Davis was off at the men's room, Roger said to Beth,

"I'm not asking you to hire me."

Beth merely moved his lips. "What, then?"

"I want you to let me open a service concession. I'll buy the equipment and pay my share of the overhead; you'll get a slice of the gross and if there's not enough business then I don't see what you lose, except some warehouse space you won't need for six months anyhow."

Beth closed his eyes.

"I'll do my own advertising," Roger said.

"Under what name?"

"Beth Appliance Center."

Beth let his head sink.

"You're not risking anything," Roger said. "And when you get in television you'll really be glad you have a service department. I know what television service is going to be like; do you realize those television chassis will carry fifteen thousand volts on them? I'm reading the manuals now, as fast as they come along."

"Are you?"

"There's ten times the parts in a television chassis than a radio chassis. There's the high voltage power supply alone."

Beth eyed him.

"Every set you sell will have to be serviced. The difference between making a dime on television and losing your shirt is going to be in service."

Beth studied him as if he had managed to fart through his nose.

"If you have to farm it out, they'll eat up your profit. I'll bet you pay out too much now. What happens if you have to do a lot of service work under your guarantee? You have to take that off the books; you write it off. It's a big item, isn't it?"

Beth studied him, smiling.

"Somebody else is making a profit out of you," Roger said. "Who's making the real profit, you or the outfit that does your service?"

At that point Davis returned.

"I'll tell you what," Beth said. "If I decide to put in a service department I'll give you a call and you can drop around and we'll talk about it. I want to see how good you are at a bench."

He shook hands with Roger, and then he and Davis arose and departed, leaving Roger alone in the booth with the empty glasses and ashtray full of cigarette butts and twisted-up paper. The three of them had been drinking mixed drinks, but before him were bottles of Golden Glow beer. And, he realized, he alone did not have on a tie and business suit. He had left the apartment in his workclothes, his trousers and canvas shirt and coat.

Finishing his beer he left the bar-and-grill and miserably took a bus home.

Virginia had already been laid off from her job, and a month or so later he received his dismissal notice. They drew California State

Unemployment checks, reported each week to tell about their efforts to find work, and began to spend some of the money they had saved. In early December of 1945 John Beth called him on the phone.

"Hey I want you to drop down to the Appliance Center," he said. "There's something I want to show you."

Putting on a suit and tie Roger went downtown on the bus. A gang of workmen had begun remodeling the basement of Beth's Appliance Center. Long service benches were going in.

"My repair department," Beth said. "Look, you want to go to work for me? Makro says you know your stuff."

Makro had worked with him at the warplant. Now Makro had got a job as parts buyer for a big supply house.

"I want to buy in," Roger said.

"You can't. It's my store." They sat upstairs in Beth's office, above the display floor.

Roger said, "It was my idea to put in the repair department."

"I don't know. We were all chewing the fat about it, as I recall. Well what do you say? Take it or leave it."

The situation dazed him. All he could think to say was, "I have around a thousand dollars to put in; I can buy the fixtures and stuff." He could not look at Beth; he felt as if his eyes and mouth had been stuffed full of cloth. He sat rubbing his upper lip.

"Well I got work to do," Beth said, when he did not say anything.

Getting up, he left the office and walked downstairs and outside onto the sidewalk.

He spent the afternoon wandering around downtown, inspecting store windows, wondering what to do. Finally he entered a radio repair shop and asked the owner if he needed a repairman. The owner said no, and he left. When he saw another shop he asked there, too. The answer was again no. He asked at two more places and then gave up. By bus he started home. The bus was crowded with women shoppers and their parcels.

What an awful deal, he thought. How could it have happened?

Perhaps, all in all, he had gone in the wrong direction. He thought of Teddy, his first wife, and their child, who had been put in a school somewhere in the East two years ago, and he had not seen either of them since. She had remarried. Well, he had got to California; he had got his wish. But things did not have the shape he wanted. The ordeal of the war work, sleepless at night, long bus rides every day, the cramped apartment. Shit, and what was it for?

Several blocks from the apartment he got off the bus and walked inside a barbershop. All the chairs were busy, and men sat everywhere, reading magazines and smoking. So he gave up and left; he crossed the street to a bar, where he ordered a bottle of beer.

But as he drank his beer he longed for the feel of the barber chair, the hair lotions and the hot wet towel, the comfort. From where he sat he could see the barbershop; he watched until fewer men were waiting, and then he recrossed the street.

"Give me a shave," he ordered the barber, when his turn came. "And a haircut both: I want both of them." Only once in a year did he get a shave from a professional barber; to him it was a luxury like nothing else. He lay back and shut his eyes.

Later on the barber had to rouse him. "What do you want on your hair? Just water?"

"No," he said. "Some of that oil that smells so good."

The barber let him sniff several of the bottles until he found the one he liked.

"You going out to a party or something?" the barber asked, rubbing the oil into his hair with the palms of his hands. "You sure are going to smell good: I guess that's what attracts the ladies."

He paid the barber and left the shop in a much better mood. His cheeks and chin had not been so smooth in years. That was the best shave I ever had, he thought as he walked along the sidewalk. The buses had let off workmen everywhere and he had to thread a path among them. They hurried to get home, saying nothing. Their faces, grained and stubbled, passed and passed until he stepped into a bar where he had gone a number of times before. For almost an hour he sat hunched over on his stool, drinking beer and meditating.

The bartender lounged by him, once, and said, "Did you ever see a horse that could run backwards?"

"No," he said.

"I'll bet there isn't no such thing. But a person can run backwards."

Another man, a worker in a black leather jacket and steel helmet, said, "He could run backwards if he tried."

"Hell he could," the bartender said. "He couldn't see where he was going."

When he had finished his beer Roger stepped from the stool, said goodnight, and walked slowly outside.

The street had darkened. The lights bothered him and he shut his eyes; putting his glasses in his coat pocket, he stood for a moment rubbing his eyes. Where else? he wondered. He had done that at another time. He thought about Teddy again, and Irv Rattenfanger, and the tune "Bei Mir Bist Du Schön" which had been popular when he and Teddy were going together. They had danced the "Dipsy Doodle" at a roadside tavern in Maryland, one night . . . in those days he had been a darn good dancer. Strange that Virginia, who used to be a dancer, didn't like to dance. They had gone dancing only once. Her coordination, he thought, as he walked out onto the sidewalk; no good. No sense of rhythm. Why? It did not make sense.

Ahead of him a big Negro stopped to talk to another Negro. Roger, walking with his head down, stumbled against the big Negro, who did not budge.

"Watch where you're going," the Negro said.

Roger said, "Look out for me."

"Watch yourself," the Negro said, as big as a barge.

"You watch it," Roger said. "You coal-black jig." But it was not soft enough; the Negro heard him and as Roger started past, the Negro raised his fist and hit him a blow in the ear. Roger spun and fell; bounding to his feet he jumped forward and hit the Negro with all his might. As he did the Negro hit him again, this time in the mouth, and teeth flew in all directions. He slid to his hands and knees. Then the Negro and his companion started quickly off. Other men appeared, white men, and two of them helped Roger up.

"What'd that jig do?" they yelled, attracting more white men. "Did he slash you, buddy?" They felt from head to foot, searching for blood as he swayed between them, his fingers covering his broken front teeth.

"A nigger jumped this guy," one of the men told the crowd forming around them. "Beat him up and got out."

One of the men offered to drive him home. They put him into the car, cursed all Negroes, wished him luck, and gave him his glasses, which had fallen from his pocket.

"There's more of them moving into L.A. every day," the man who was driving him said.

He rested his head on his arm, suffering the pain.

"Of course they're most of them up from the South," the man said. "They're mostly farm hands; they don't know how to conduct themselves in a city. I mean, they've got money for the first time in their lives, and it goes to their heads. They're having themselves a hell of a good time. I'd rather have them than the Pachucs, though, I'll tell you. If those Pachucs get you they'll hold you down and stomp on you; they got those cleated boots."

Speaking as best he could Roger said, "The god damn niggers."

"Well, it could have been anybody," the man said, as he drew the car up to the curb in front of the apartment building. "Is this the right place?"

"Yes," he said. He held his handkerchief to his mouth. His ear rang and he could not hear well; sounds hummed and then shrank away. "Thanks," he said, as he got from the car.

"It could happen to anybody," the man said. He stayed parked at the curb until Roger had reached the steps of the building, and then he drove off.

When Virginia saw him she leaped up, horrified. "What happened?" She ran to him and pulled his hands away from his mouth. "Oh my God," she said. "What was it? What happened?"

"A guy beat me up," he said. "I never saw him before in my life."

"I'm going to call the police," she said. "I'm going down to the phone." She started out into the hall.

"The hell with that!" he said desperately. Sinking down on the couch he said, "Get some ice cubes."

She brought him the ice cubes and he made a compress out of them. Lying on his back he held them against his upper jaw. Virginia wiped away the trickle of ice water.

"I got to go to the dentist," he said.

"Do you want me to call around now?"

"No," he said. "Tomorrow."

That night he did not go to bed; he spent the night on the couch, lying on his back. Several Anacin tablets helped the pain but he did not seem to be able to fall asleep.

What'll I do? he asked himself.

He thought of other places that he had liked better. Actually, he realized, he had not got any happiness out of being here, not even in the beginning. Washington D.C. had been much better, he decided. In spite of the weather. He liked the buildings there. And he did not mind the snow.

In Arkansas as a child he had slogged through the snow, and he remembered the spindly trees without leaves that stuck up along the hillsides, thickets of them, and all of them weak, frail, and yet they covered the uncleared ground everywhere. Probably they were still there. He thought of the time he had put an old earthenware vase up on a stump and pitched rocks at it until it shattered, and in the potsherds was a coin, stuck there when the clay was wet. When he cleaned the coin off he found that it was a twenty-cent piece. In all his life—he was eleven—he had never seen or heard of a twenty-cent piece before, and he carried it around with him for almost two years, believing that he had the only one in the world. And then, one day, he tried to spend it, and the salesclerk refused to accept it; she said it was a fake, that there was no such coin. So he threw it away.

Now, lying on his back with the compress against his mouth, he tried to remember what he had wanted to buy with the twenty-cent piece. Candy, he decided. Well, it would be gone now, in any case. The coin or the candy.

The next morning his mouth had become too swollen for him to eat. He tried sipping some coffee, but the pain stopped that. Yet he remained at the kitchen table, staring down at his cup and plate.

"You have to go to the dentist," Virginia said. "You can't eat, and you can hardly talk—let me go call."

"No," he said.

"But what are you going to do?"

He sat wretchedly in the living room most of the morning, doing nothing in particular, not speaking to Virginia or even thinking about anything. The pain from the broken front teeth became worse, and finally in the early afternoon he let her go downstairs to the public phone. She did not come back for a long time. At last she appeared and said,

"I finally got one who can see you today. His name's Doctor Corning." She had the address and he read it; the office was on the other side of town.

Taking the slip of paper he put on his coat.

"I'm going with you," she said.

"No." He shook his head.

"I am."

"No!" Pushing past her he walked outside into the hall and to the stairs. But she followed.

"You might faint," she said. "I want to go with you; why don't you want me with you?"

"Go to hell," he said furiously. "Go on back inside." He descended, and when he reached the sidewalk he saw that she had given up. So he walked on to the bus stop by himself.

The trip took over an hour. In the dentist's waiting room he tried to smoke, but he could not hold the cigarette between his lips, so he had to put it out. The dentist made him wait fifteen minutes. Three small children sat opposite him with their feet sticking out straight; all three stared at him, giggling, until their mother told them to hush.

The dentist admitted him at last and gave him a shot of Novocain. "I can save one," he said. "I can give you a cap for it. But the other two are right down at the gum." He began to remove the broken pieces of the teeth. "Your wife said on the phone somebody hit you."

He nodded.

"It'll take a couple of days to have the cap made. Anyhow, you should stop feeling the pain now that I've got the remains of the others out. I think you'll be able to eat soft foods, as long as you don't try to bite." With his mirror he inspected the other teeth. "How long has it been since you've seen a dentist?"

"A long time," Roger said. He had not been to a dentist since before the war.

"You have major work to be done. Most of your molars are decayed. You should have x-rays taken. You really shouldn't let your teeth go. Aren't they sensitive to sweets?"

He grunted.

"The cap and the other work I have to do will run you sixty dollars," Doctor Corning said. "Can you pay me that now? With patients I don't know I like to have it in advance."

He paid him with a check.

"On the restoration," Doctor Corning said, "I'd say you have between two and three hundred dollars worth of work needed. And the longer you wait the more it'll cost."

He made an appointment for the cap, and then he went downstairs to the street. The Novocain had made his face hard and misshapen and he continually raised his hand to touch himself. The amount of money that he had paid out put him into a frenzy. He realized—he knew—that he had been robbed, taken advantage of. But he was helpless.

God damn, he said to himself.

He had a vision of crooks, swindles of every kind; he saw up into the office buildings and the crooked activity going on, the wheels, the machinery. Loan offices, banks, doctors and dentists, quack healers preying on old women, Pachucs smashing store windows, defective equipment, food with filth and impurities in it, shoes made of cardboard, hats that melted in the rain, clothes that shrank and ripped, cars with broken motor blocks, toilet seats running with disease germs, dogs carrying mange and rabies throughout the city, restaurants serving rotted food, real estate under water, phony stock in nonexistent mining companies, magazines with obscene pictures, animals slaughtered in cold blood, milk contaminated with dead flies, bugs and vermin and excretion, rubbish and garbage, a rain of filth on the streets, on the buildings and houses and stores. The electric machines of the chiropractors crackled, the old ladies screamed, the patent medicine bottles boiled and exploded . . . he saw the war itself as a stupendous snow-job, men killed for fat bankers to float loans, ships built that went right to the bottom, bonds that could not be redeemed, Communism taking over, Red Cross blood that had syphilis germs in it. Negro and white troops living together, nurses that were whores, generals who screwed their orderlies, profits and black-market butter, training camps in which recruits died by the thousands of bubonic plague, illness and suffering and money mixed together, sugar and rubber, meat and blood, ration stamps, V-D posters, short-arm inspections, M-1 rifles, USO entertainers with corks up their asses, motherfuckers and fairies and niggers raping white girls . . . he saw the sky flash and drip; private parts shot across the heavens, words croaked in his ears telling him about his mother's monthlies; he saw the whole world writhe with hair, a monstrous hairy ball that burst and drenched him with blood . . .

"Shit," he said, walking along the sidewalk, his hands shoved down into his pockets.

Gradually he got control of himself.

"Jesus Christ," he said in a weak voice. His hands shook and he felt cold. Perspiration gathered in his armpits and as he walked his legs wobbled beneath him. At a drinking fountain he stooped and took a mouthful of water; he spat it into the gutter and then wiped his chin with his handkerchief.

Things weren't as bad as that, he thought. They still had seven or eight hundred dollars in the bank, more than he had ever had in his life.

But he was still frightened. He did not know what to do. So he continued walking, among the grocery stores and used car lots and drugstores and bakeries and shoe repair shops and dry cleaners and movie theaters, gazing into the windows and trying to think what was the best thing for himself and his wife.

In front of a used car lot a salesman stood picking his teeth and watching people go by. As Roger passed him he said, "What kind of car did you want, buddy?"

Stopping, he said, "How did you know I wanted a car?"

The salesman shrugged.

"What do you have?" he asked him.

"Lots of clean cars, buddy," the salesman said. "Come on in and look around. I'll give you a good deal, the best deal in town."

His hands in his pockets, he wandered onto the lot.

When Virginia heard him coming up the stairs she ran to open the door. He no longer seemed miserable and discouraged; he smiled at her in his old manner, the secret, meaningful smile, as if there was something he knew that she did not.

"What did he do?" she asked. The swelling had gone down; he seemed able to move his mouth. "Why were you gone so long?"

Roger said, "Come on downstairs."

"Why?" She hesitated, not trusting him.

"I want to show you something." Turning, he started back. "I bought a car."

At the curb a blue pre-war sedan was parked.

"A '39 Chevy," Roger said.

"Why?" she said.

On his face the cunning, the sense of having done an act of importance and daring, flooded out. He rocked back and forth, glancing at her and then at the car; finally he said, "Guess why. Go on. I'll bet you can't guess."

"Tell me," she said.

"We're going to take a trip East," he said.

"Back to Washington?"

Grinning, he said, "No, not that far. To Arkansas."

She saw that he meant it.

9

On Friday, at the store, Pete Bacciagalupi said to him, "Boy, you're all up in the air. What is it? Some hot deal cooking?"

Roger said, "My kid's coming home from school today."

The afternoon dragged on, hour by hour. He spent some time next door at the drugstore lunch counter, and some time in the basement with Olsen, going over service questions.

When he went back upstairs he found Pete clearing off the counter. "I finally moved the twenty-one-inch bleached-oak Philco," Pete said. His hand closed over Roger's shoulder and he turned him to face the back of the store. Without speaking, he nodded to point out the small side demonstration room. In the semi-darkness a man sat waiting, making no sound. "He showed up while I was busy," Pete said. "It's you he wants, naturally."

Going to the door of the room, Roger put his head in. The chair creaked as Jules Neame arose to greet him. The old man was in his shirtsleeves, smelling of perspiration and tobacco; he wheezed apologetically and in the darkness his gold tooth glinted as he smiled, excusing himself by raising his empty, helpless hands.

"Mr. Lindahl," Neame said.

"Hi, Jules," he said. "How's it going?" The old man owned Neame Lawn Furniture & Garden Supplies, the store next door on the right.

"You're so busy," Neame said. "I don't want to bother you. I thought maybe you or your young fellow could give me a hand." At the crucial words he fell into a defensive, ornate diction, an almost courtly manner of speech. "If another time would be better—" His hands sawed the air.

"I'll give you a hand," Roger said. "What is it?"

They walked together the length of the store, to the doorway. Mr. Neame's stomach wagged from side to side with each step; the top button of his trousers was undone and circles of wetness had spread out from his armpits, across his silk shirt. "A swing," he said to Roger. "We can't get it to the window." His face still quivered with exertion and the deep flush had not left; in the display room he had sat recuperating.

"Call me next time," Roger said.

"Well." Mr. Neame put his hand to his cheek, hiding his face. "I hate to bother you, Mr. Lindahl."

In the lawn furniture store, Mrs. Neame stood by one end of the swing, panting and shaking. The old woman had been trying to drag the swing alone, while her husband went to get help. Seeing Roger, she smiled gratefully, straightened up, glanced at her husband. Jules took her place and Roger got hold of the other end; together they dragged the swing to the front window and got it in place. Mrs. Neame followed, wanting it exactly right but saying nothing; her husband waved her off as she started to point.

"They're heavy," Roger said, when they had let go.

"It certainly is wonderful of you, Mr. Lindahl," Mrs. Neame said, "to let yourself be taken away from your own work to do something for us that we ought to be able to do on our own." Both she and Jules were embarrassed; the two of them drew together, not knowing what to say to him.

"Any time," he said, but his heart had yet to get back to normal. His voice choked off and he remained silent a moment, getting out a cigarette and matches. As always, after he had carried some heavy object, a TV set or a stove or a refrigerator, his hands were white and his fingers stiff and streaked. He felt as if his hands were about to break loose from his wrists; he put them in his pockets, out of sight. At that, Jules Neame started with agitation; he disappeared into the back of the store, through the curtains, and then reappeared with a box which he held out to Roger.

"Would you try a piece of Turkish Delight?" he said, urging the candy on him. "It's the real thing; it comes from my sister. Take a couple of pieces."

Roger accepted two pieces, for Pete, who liked them. He returned to his own store and placed the Turkish Delight on the counter.

"Thanks," Pete said, biting into a piece. "What was it this time?"

"Another lawn swing."

"Your wife called," Pete said. "While you were over there helping them move their swing." He showed Roger a note he had made on the phone-pad. "She says she's back from Ojai. She'll call you again in a little while." Munching, he said, "That's nice up there. A lot of wealthy retired people." He watched Roger stick the note in his pocket. "Old man Neame sure thinks a lot of you. You know, one of these days he's going to have another heart attack right there in the store and fall dead into one of those swings."

At five-thirty, Virginia called again. "I'm home," she said. "We just got back. Here's Gregg."

Much noise in his ear, and then his son's voice.

"Daddy! You know what I did? I fell out of the window where I was at; I fell all the way down to the ground. And then—"

Virginia replaced him at the phone. "He wasn't hurt. It was the window of the tent they use."

"How does he seem to be?" Roger asked.

"Fine. He certainly was glad to see me. He was waiting down by the parking lot. I'm glad I went along; I mean, I'm glad I didn't just tell her to pick him up."

"How was the ride?"

Virginia said, "Horrible. Worse than I remembered. But she zips right along. She goes almost as fast as you."

"Which way did you drive?"

"I drove back. So she could handle the kids."

Roger said, "What do you think of her?"

"They certainly were right."

"What do you mean?" he said.

"She certainly is dumb."

"Oh," he said. "I guess so."

"But she's real sweet. I'll talk to you later; Gregg's running around the house pulling down the lamps. You'll be home around six-thirty?"

"That's right," he said. He hung up.

"What's the matter?" Pete said to him. "Didn't they get home okay?"

"Sure," he said. He felt discouraged. "I'm going next door," he said. "For a cup of coffee." Leaving Pete in charge of the store, he set off for the drugstore.

That evening, after they had put Gregg to bed, he said to his wife, "What do you mean? Why do you say she's dumb? She didn't strike me that way."

Virginia, seated on the couch in her robe, said, "She doesn't hear anything you say, and when she does she doesn't understand it; she gets it balled up until it makes no sense at all. Isn't that what you'd call dumb?"

"I think you're all picking on her," he said.

"I just spent four and a half hours with her," Virginia said. "Take my word for it."

He said, "Then you don't think it's going to work out?"

"What do you mean? That has nothing to do with it."

"What's the arrangement?"

"She'll drive the three boys back to the school this Sunday. Then we'll go again together, next Friday."

Roger said, with bitterness, "If she's so dumb, maybe you better not get involved."

"I don't see the connection."

"You're asking her to do something for you, make a drive you're afraid to make, and then you come home and sit around talking about how dumb she is. I call that hypocrisy. Don't you?" He became more and more outraged. "Don't you feel ashamed?"

Virginia said, "You asked me what I thought of her."

That was true. "Let it go," he said. "Forget it."

But he, himself, could not let it drop.

"Did anything happen during the trip?" he asked, after an interval.

"No," Virginia said. She had picked up a magazine to read.

"You're sure?"

Dropping her magazine, she said, "What's the matter with you? What's this all about?"

He put on his coat, the older one with the missing button. "I'm going down to the store awhile." Hanging around the house made him too restless; he could not remain. "I have to open up some table-model TV sets and get them tuned up for Saturday."

"Really?" She trailed after him sadly, to the front door. "What if Gregg wants you?"

"For God's sake," he said irritably, "he's only been away three days. I'll see you later." He shut the door after him. The porch light came on; she had switched it on for him.

He got into the Oldsmobile, warmed up the engine, and drove back down to his closed-up store.

Downstairs, in the service department, the fluorescent overhead lights were on. Olsen sat at the repair bench, still involved in his work. Beside him was a cardboard container of coffee and the leavings of a sandwich. His back was to Roger, a great streaked, grimy back, his bulging head, irregular, fringed with choppy gray hair, swung slightly, but he continued working. "Hi," Olsen said.

"Hi," Roger said. "How come you're still working?"

"I don't know. You're paying me." The basement roared with noise from the radio Olsen had before him; he lowered the volume a trifle. The room smelled of his perspiration. He was a long-armed artisan, surly and individualistic, one of the last of his species. In his own crabbed, taciturn manner, he was an excellent radio repairman. He took responsibility for his work. Nobody knew how old he was; he looked at least fifty. He came, he had told them, from Utah. His clothes were always sloppy and ragged; between the buttons of his shirt the dark hair of his stomach could be seen. The only trait about him that Roger could not stand was his habit of spitting into the wastebasket.

"How long have you been here?" Roger said.

"I'm marking it down." Olsen pointed at the sweaty, bent imitation-leather notebook in which he recorded his hours. "Look in there if you want."

"You goddamn repairmen," Roger said. Anyhow, he was glad of Olsen's company.

Olsen grinned his broken, misshapen grin.

"How about a beer?" Roger said.

"You're standing?"

"Sure."

"Okay," Reaching up, Olsen shut off the bench. The hum and sputter and racket died, the meters and dials switched to no-reading. Unhooking his legs from the stool, Olsen clambered down, stretched, fastened his trousers, spat into the waste-box at the end of the bench, and then lifted his coat from the nail he had driven into the support beam of the wall. "Let's go," he said.

Together, the two of them sat at the bar down at the corner, drinking Budweiser beer from bottles. The jukebox played a Johnny Ray record. A few workmen and businessmen and one middle-aged blonde in a furpiece sat talking or meditating. At the rear of the bar two men played shuffleboard. The counters knocked now and then. A gas heater sizzled; the bar was pleasant.

"You got troubles?" Olsen asked.

"No."

"Then why aren't you home?"

He did not feel like answering. "I'm down at the store setting up TV sets," he said.

"Like hell you are," Olsen said.

Raising his head, Roger said, "What kind of troubles am I supposed to have? I've got a paying business; I've got a wife and a kid. My health is reasonably good. I've got no particular problems." He drank his beer, resting his arms on the surface of the bar.

"I'm married too," Olsen said, after a long period of time. "I got no kids but I got a fair-to-middlin job. Even though the guy I work for is a horse's ass. But I'm not home. I'm down in the service department at nine o'clock in the evening." He turned his head sideways and scrutinized Roger.

"What's the matter with you?" Roger said.

"Nothing." The bloodshot eyes shifted about. "I was just wondering something."

"Say it."

Olsen said in his grating voice, "How long's it been since you've had a piece of tail?"

"It depends on what kind you mean,"

"You know what I mean." Olsen put his thumb into his beer and then lifted it up to examine it. "I don't mean your front parlor."

"Two years," Roger said. In 1950, on New Year's Eve, he had gone to bed with a girl that he met at a falling-about, drunken party. Virginia had got offended at something and had gone home early, leaving him alone.

"Maybe that's what's wrong with you."

"Go to hell," he said.

Olsen shrugged. "That's what's wrong with a lot of guys. They fall sick without it. What you get at home don't count."

"I don't agree," Roger said. "You ought to be at home where you belong."

The broken smile returned. "You're saying that because you don't know where you can lay your hands on any."

"No," he disagreed. "I mean it."

"Aren't you glad for what you got two years ago?"

"I wish I hadn't," he said. Afterwards, he had felt remorse, and he had never done it again, or even tried to. "What's the point of getting married? How about your wife? You approve of her cheating if she wants to?"

"That's different," Olsen said.

"Sure," Roger said. "The double standard."

"Why not?" Olsen said, "It's natural for a man to play the field. It's just as natural for a woman to not. If my wife cheated on me I'd kill her. She knows that."

"Do you cheat?" Roger asked.

Olsen said, "Every chance I get. Every chance." He put on a righteous expression, a grim, elevated thing.

What a lousy business, Roger thought to himself. He drank his beer. I know it isn't right. But that has nothing to do with it. "Love is more important than marriage," he said to Olsen. "A man gets married because of love; isn't that so?"

"In some cases," Olsen said, going along with him.

"Then love is first." He pointed his finger at Olsen, who gazed down remotely. "You have to think about love as the primary thing. Marriage just grows out of it; love leads the way. In China they marry without love; they never even see each other before they're married. That's just like breeding cattle; isn't it? That's the difference between man and an animal; man falls in love, and if you don't go in the direction that love points then you're acting like an animal, and what the hell are you alive for? You tell me that. Are you alive just to work and eat and reproduce?"

"I see that," Olsen said, "but how can you be positive when you're in love? Maybe all you want is a piece of tail. That isn't the same; you can be in love and not want to go to bed with her, in fact maybe that's how you know you're really in love; you don't want to go to bed with her, you don't want to sully her. If a man really loves a woman he honors and respects her."

"There's nothing disrespectful about sex," Roger said.

"Sex is unfair to the woman. It robs her of her virginity. That's the most precious possession a woman has. Would you want to do that to a woman you loved? I'll bet you'd kill some guy that violated a woman you were in love with; you'd castrate him for doing that. I think if you really love a woman you're supposed to protect her. A woman don't get nothing out of sex. Most women hate it. They submit to it to please the man."

"That's a lot of bull," Roger said. "A woman enjoys it as much as a man."

"Only a certain type of cheap woman," Olsen said violently. "A real lady you could love and be proud of and would want to marry wouldn't enjoy it, and she wouldn't let you do it to her; I'll tell you that. You find a woman that'll go to bed with you and I'll show you a bum."

"Even after marriage?"

Olsen picked at a blister on his thumb. "That's different. There has to be kids. But it's a sin to have sex ouside of marriage. We weren't meant to have marital relations except for the production of children."

"I thought you said you got it every chance you had."

Olsen glowered at him. "That's none of your business."

"There's nothing degrading about sex," Roger said. "If you didn't think there was there wouldn't be."

"Do you have a sister?" Olsen said. "Answer me that; do you have a sister?"

"You talk about it being a sin," Roger said, "and then you sneak off and cheat on your wife. You sure are mixed up."

Setting down his beer, Olsen said, "You better not talk disrespectfully to me. Even if you are my boss. You're a swell guy and all that, but you better not talk disrespectfully to me, especially where my wife is concerned. I don't allow you to talk about my wife, even though you are a good friend of mine and I think a lot of you."

"I'm sorry," Roger said. He stuck out his hand, and after a prolonged moment, Olsen shook it.

"You're just riding for a fall," Olsen said, "when you talk like that." He picked up his beer and in a mood of deep sternness gulped it down. Roger returned to his own beer. After that neither of them said much. When they left the bar and returned to the store, Olsen descended to the service department, leaving Roger alone.

Going into the office he sat in the darkness, watching cars and people beyond the locked front door of the store.

What a mess, he thought to himself.

The time was nine-thirty. Not so late, he decided. He put on his coat, left the store without saying good night to Olsen, and got into his car. Very soon he was driving out to San Fernando.

At a Standard Station he parked and looked in the phone book for the address. Two Charles Bonners were listed, but he remembered the street name; Virginia had mentioned it. Getting back into the car he drove up to the Bonner house and parked in front of it, with his engine and headlights shut off.

The house looked like those around it, a small, recently-built one-story California ranch-style house, with a wide garage, a single pepper tree in the front yard, a picture window which showed drapes and faint light. In front of the house the red Ford station wagon was parked. Under the dull streetlight the car looked gray.

Now or never, he said to himself.

Stepping from his car he crossed the street, walked up the path and onto the porch, and rang the bell.

Sounds. The porch light flashed on. They're up, he said to himself. Not yet ten o'clock. And it's Friday. He doesn't have to go to work tomorrow. Or maybe he does. Panic—panic.

A latch rattled, and then the door swung open. Chic Bonner, in his shirtsleeves and stocking feet, peered out at him. "Oh," he said. "Lindahl. Come on in."

"It's pretty late," Roger said. "I just dropped by for a second."

"Hell," Chic said, "it's early." He shut the door after Roger, "Nice to see you. Take off your coat." Holding out his hand he said, "Let me have it; I'll hang it up."

"I can't stay," Roger said. "I just wanted to talk to you for a second."

"Let me pour you something to drink." The living room had a cluttered look; magazines lay everywhere, on the couch and on the floor. The television set was on, and Chic started towards it to shut it off. "I was looking at some damn TV drama, one of those half-hour things. You're in the television business, aren't you? You must see plenty of it all day long." He shut off the set. "Sit down."

Roger saw no signs of Liz Bonner. Maybe it was just as well. But now, in addition to panic, he felt an eerie cold feeling, a hollowness. Disappointment. "I wanted to thank you for the driving business," he said.

"Oh yeah," Chic said. "They both drove up together, didn't they?"

Lowering himself onto the couch, Roger clasped his hands together and said, "I've been thinking. If this business is going to work out, it's got to be split fifty-fifty."

"No, that's okay," Chic said. He seemed uncomfortable. "Let it go as it is."

"No," he said. "Here's the way I feel. It isn't fair for your wife to take on a job we're supposed to do. Here's how I think it should work, if it's going to work. Virginia's afraid to make that drive, so I'll do our share of the driving. If you and your wife can pick the kids up on Friday, I'll take them back to the school Sunday evening. For me it would have to be Sunday; I work on Friday."

"So do I," Chic said. "That's why I can't go up Friday." His hand traveled over his hair, halting at the bald place and then beginning again. "I've got an admission to make; it's hard to make to people. I don't drive. I don't have a license. Liz does all the driving."

Roger shrugged. "That's nothing to feel bad about." He had lost his own license, a couple of times.

"I know. Anyhow, as far as I'm concerned, this would be swell." Chic sat down facing Roger. "She's been making that drive four times a week. Now you can cut it down to two. I appreciate that. She says she likes it, but that's too much for one person."

"True," Roger said.

"Well, then do you want to take them back this Sunday?"

"Yes," he said. "I'll come by around four o'clock and pick up your two kids."

"Fine," Chic said, smiling with satisfaction. "I mean, it was swell anyhow, but—you understand. The less times she has to make the trip the better I feel."

Arising, Roger moved towards the door. "I'll see you Sunday."

"Better make it around two," Chic said.

"Okay," he said. "Good night. Say good night to your wife for me."

Chic, accompanying him, said, "Too bad Liz isn't here. She's down the street visiting some woman she knows. They have kids; we're going somewhere tomorrow. Don't ask me where—I wasn't consulted."

A moment later, Roger found himself out on the front porch. Chic said good night and shut the door.

His legs wobbled under him as he crossed the street to his car. Anyhow now he had put himself in the middle of it. Four and a half hours a week on the highway, with the boys romping around the car. His mind groaned under the weight of plans: he could leave early, spend most of the afternoon up at the school. And he would be out of the house; he would have a legitimate excuse for taking off on Sunday afternoon. And—Christ—he was not left sitting by himself, on the rim of the pot. Whatever that meant. His thoughts were cloudy. He let them stay cloudy.

As he got into his car he noticed that Chic had left the porch light on. Probably for his wife. She would be coming back, soon.

Roger closed the car door and then moved over until he was less visible from the outside. But it was still too risky. Instead, he stuck the ignition key in the lock and started up the engine. Switching on the headlights he drove off, around the corner, and then back to the next street. Shortly, he had parked several houses away from the Bonner house, behind a parked milk truck.

Fifteen minutes passed. A dog trotted along the sidewalk, sniffed at a bush, then went on. Several cars came by. Once, a man stepped out of a house, waved good night, and set off rapidly on foot.

I'm crazy, Roger thought. Suppose Virginia calls the store? I'll say I was downstairs. I couldn't reach the phone. But suppose Olsen comes up and answers it. He won't; he never does.

But suppose Olsen happened to be upstairs near it.

While he was meditating, a door far off down the street slammed. A woman hurried down the path of the house, onto the sidewalk. His eyes had got used to the dim light; he could see her quite well. The woman skipped along, her head down, half-running, then walking, then half-running again. Her hair, tied back in a pony tail, bounced up and down. She wore a short coat, and as she ran she hugged it against her with her hands. Her skirt flared out behind her.

Liz, he thought.

He watched her until she raced up the steps of her own house and vanished inside. The door slammed. The porch light died away into darkness.

After a few minutes he started up the engine of his car and drove away, back towards his own house.

The living room light had been turned off. As he reached about uncertainly, Virginia called from the bedroom,

"Is that you?"

"Yes," he said. He found a floor lamp and put it on.

"I went ahead to bed. I'm sorry."

He said, "Can I bring you anything? Have you really gone to bed? Or are you sitting up reading?" Looking in, he saw that she had really gone to bed; the room was dark.

"I called the store," she said.

"When?"

"About half an hour ago. I didn't get any answer."

"I must have been down in the basement. Olsen and I worked on some new sets."

"Are you going to fix anything to eat?" Stirring about, she raised herself up and switched on the lamp by the bed. "If you are, I might want something."

"I don't know," he said. He did not feel hungry, but he went into the kitchen and opened the refrigerator. "I might have a sandwich." He rummaged aimlessly around until he had found the Swiss cheese. "Olsen and I were out for awhile," he said. "We had a couple of beers."

"I thought you went down there to work."

"We talked."

Virginia appeared, fastening her robe. Her hair, long and tousled, hung in her eyes; she brushed it back. "Don't make a lot of noise and wake up Gregg. He's still restless; I had to go in there a couple of times."

"I've come to a decision," Roger said. "I don't want you driving that drive. I'll split it with the Bonners. They can drive on Friday, and I'll drive on Sunday. That's the best. It'll be even."

"Fine," Virginia said, with a huge gasp of relief. "I know I'm selfish, but I really love you; can you really do it? On your one day off?" Her delight flowed from her. "Maybe I could go along and hold onto the boys. So they wouldn't climb all over you."

He had not thought of that, both of them going together. "It'd be too crowded," he said.

"Maybe so. Maybe once in awhile, though." She looked at him with such fondness that he felt leaden with guilt. "I love you," she said. "You know that? What did you do, sit down there at the store figuring out how you could do the driving?"

"I can't do it all," he said, evading. "Not the going up on Friday. So we'll have to split it with the Bonners."

"You know what Liz told me? Her husband lost his license. I guess he drove erratically. She wouldn't tell me why . . . but she has to do all the driving for them. Should I phone Liz tomorrow and tell her? I guess you can tell them when you go over with Gregg." As he fixed his cheese sandwich she considered the matter. "If I have a chance I'll call her."

He said, "I already told them."

"Oh," she said. "Good. What'd they say?"

"I just talked to him. He liked the idea."

"I've never met him. He was at work, when I was over there. They have one of those little tract houses; ordinary furniture inside, the usual TV set and drapes, coffee table, couch and rug. The furniture you see in those carload-sales places, those complete living room outfits for thirty dollars down and the rest at a dollar a week."

"Where the Okies go," he said.

She rushed on, "Yes, where they have those loudspeakers and Okie music." Then she put on her subdued, mannered smile. When she was not sure of his meaning she passed through a formal stage, a moment of becoming a hostess, hearing and not hearing. "Oh come on," she said. "I know you don't like other people to say that."

"No," he said, with venom.

"She says they're buying the place. Most of their money must be in the bread factory. Of course, I shouldn't judge everything by her housekeeping; I wouldn't want my house to be judged by some woman coming in and snooping around. But that's what they do; I've had it happen to me. The P.T.A. wives. I don't think Liz cares. If she did she wouldn't leave everything lying around. It doesn't seem fair to him, but maybe all he cares about is his work. He's a vice-president; it's that Bonny Bonner Bread—we've used it."

"Maybe this bread I'm using," he said, in a shaky voice.

"What's wrong?" Virginia said.

"They have a little house, ordinary furniture; she's dumb; she's a lousy housekeeper; when you meet him you'll say, He's bald."

"Is he bald? Really?" That visibly nettled her. "How old is he?"

He didn't answer. He busied himself at the refrigerator, feeling moral outrage, the stricture in his throat. I'm not going to squeak, he thought. Through the blockage his voice would be high-pitched. Better not say anything at all. His pulse pounded as he bent; his wrists swelled.

"It worries you to have me drive," Virginia said. "You get like this."

He raised his head.

"Now don't look at me that way," she said. "I know you don't approve of my driving."

"I don't give a damn about your driving!" His whole body shook. The studious desire to misunderstand. But maybe it was better. Let her go off into her own worries. Because she feared the drive she assumed that he must doubt her ability, too.

"Is that why you want to make the trip?" she asked.

"No," he said. "That's not why."

But her expression said, That is why. I can tell. But I agree anyhow. It's the truth. We both know it.

10

At the Los Angeles airport Mrs. Watson scouted for a blue '39 Chevrolet sedan, and when she found it she found her daughter.

"I wouldn't have recognized you," she said, as Virginia caught up her suitcase and shoved it into the back seat. "Stand up so I can get a good look at you."

Virginia shut the car door and stood up, facing her mother. "I had to cut my hair," she said. She still wore her long coat, the one she had taken with her from Washington. But her hair was short, like a boy's, and ragged, as if cut at home. "Because of my job. It's growing out again." Leaning forward she kissed her mother. "Thanks a lot for not stopping in Denver."

"I'll stop on the way back," Mrs. Watson said.

"Are you disappointed in me?"

"What do you mean?"

Virginia said, "I don't look very ladylike."

"No," Mrs. Watson said. But she had never put much of a premium on that. "But you're thinner," she said. "And," she said, "I think you look a little mean." Around her daughter's eyes were lines, not wrinkles but grooves of intensity. Her daughter had a cool, detached, competent look; she wore no makeup, or nail polish, and in her gray suit she reminded her of some of the young career business women. "I'd be afraid to get into an argument with you now," Mrs. Watson said. "You'd probably throw me with some jujitsu hold."

As she drove, Virginia said, "Roger didn't come along because I told him I wanted to talk to you without him around."

"How are his teeth?" On the long distance phone Virginia had told her that he needed dental work done and that he had started having it. The idea repelled her. Naturally it would be his teeth. His eyes were bad, his teeth had holes in them, and two years ago, as soon as she laid eyes on him, she knew, by the way he walked, that he had some sort of back injury.

"He got one of them capped," Virginia said.

"He better get them all capped," Mrs. Watson said.

Virginia said. "I paid one week's rent for you on a nice room with cooking privileges."

"I'll have to see how it looks."

"It's nice. They just painted it. Anyhow, it'll give you a place to stay; I wish you could stay with us, but we only have one bedroom and then just the living room."

"Is this the car he wants to drive to Arkansas in?" She did not know much about cars. "It looks like a good one."

"Except for getting a new car it's about the best."

Mrs. Watson said, "If you don't want to go to Arkansas, tell him you don't want to go."

"He'd go alone."

"Oh," she said. "Is that how he feels?"

"He'd just disappear," Virginia said, with a quick little flick of her head. "He'd fool around with the car, make sure it worked okay and had plenty of gas and oil and whatever else it needs, he'd stick stuff in the back, in the trunk place, and he wouldn't say anything; he'd just go. While I was shopping or asleep. I'd get up and he'd be gone." After a moment she said, "Every day he thinks about it. He goes out and hoses off the car and starts it up; he drives around town, talking to people. He's getting ready to go, but he hopes I'll come along. So far he's come back. He hasn't actually left."

"But that's against the law." Hearing about it, she was not surprised. Now that the war had ended and the easy money had stopped. Now that the aircraft plants had started shutting down. He had come out to California to get in on it; now he intended to leave. The money for the train trip had been hers. With Virginia's money he had financed himself out to the West Coast. There was nothing complex about the situation.

Virginia said, "He feels he can't get anywhere out here."

"He could get a job."

"He wants to open a television shop."

"Maybe he can do that in Arkansas," she said. "By himself."

Virginia glanced swiftly at her and then back at the traffic. She said nothing.

"Why don't you let him go?" Mrs. Watson said.

"That isn't worth answering."

"Let him go and then divorce him."

"What if I told you I'm pregnant?"

She flinched. That was the thing she had most dreaded; she knew it would happen sooner or later.

"I am," Virginia said. "Four months."

"Leave him anyhow."

"No," Virginia said, smiling. "I'm not going to leave him. I want him to stay here; I think this is the best place for him. If he had some money he could open a shop. I think he could run it if he once got it started. He's resourceful. He's energetic. You'd be surprised. For two years he's been working a seven-day week, and all that money has gone in the bank; the only money we've spent is on rent and food and for his teeth and then this car. We can sell the car. He's been working since we got married."

"So have you."

"I was working before I met him."

"Not in a warplant."

"What do you say?" Virginia said.

"Oh heavens above," her mother said. "Don't ask me. I can't give you money for that, so he can run off to Arkansas with it."

Virginia said, "Give me the money and I'll fix up everything in my name. He can't run off to Arkansas with it then. How can he? He can't take the store with him."

"You certainly are a prize sucker," Mrs. Watson said.

"A sucker! You never saw her, did you? I wouldn't be that for anything—"

"Who?" Mrs. Watson said.

"His first wife."

"No," she said. "I never met her."

"I did," Virginia said. "What an awful spectacle. She came around once, before Roger and I were married. She had their little girl with her."

"Did she want you to take the girl?" Mrs. Watson said, abhorring the idea.

"No, of course not. She just wanted to see him and see me, see what I was like. What an awful situation to be in; don't you understand how that would be? Imagine seeing her husband with me." Virginia raised her head. "I thought—Suppose some time it's my turn. He gets tired of me and decides to go off by himself or with some other woman. I made up my mind—" On the steering wheel her fingers clamped and strained. "I'm never going to be in that woman's position; I'm not going to let him go off with somebody else and then come around begging for scraps, like she did."

"Scraps," Mrs. Watson said. "You mean he just left her to starve?"

"No, I mean she had nothing. What was she left with?"

"The child."

Virginia said, "That's the awful part. The child, too. That won't happen to me. I promised myself then, and now I have to face it; now's the time I have to do what I said. This would work out; I talked to the loan people at the bank   "

"They wouldn't loan anything on something like that."

Virginia agreed. "But they told me a lot. How much it would cost, how much net profit we'd have to make, the sort of location we should look for. One of the men even drove me around in his car."

"They like to have something they can foreclose on," Mrs. Watson said.

"They can't foreclose if they don't make any loan."

Beside Mrs. Watson her daughter sat bolt-upright behind the wheel, steering with great vigor. "I didn't know you drove," she said. "When did you learn to drive?"

"Roger taught me."

"You have a license, don't you?" She felt a pang of nervousness. "I mean, it's all legal, isn't it?"

The car had entered a shopping district. Virginia slowed and then pointed to a row of stores. "Look. See that second one?" The store passed before Mrs. Watson got any kind of look at it. "I'll drive around the block," Virginia said. "I want you to see it. Mr. Browminor showed it to me. He's the bank man. He says the lease will expire in another couple of months; the woman is retiring. He says it's an excellent location."

Again they drove by the stores. Virginia turned into an empty parking slot and shut off the engine. From where they had parked they could see the front of the store, the window displays and sign. It was a hat shop.

"The bank owns the building," Virginia said. "The Bank of America. They're the largest bank in California. They're up to their neck in real estate. They used to be the Banco d'Italia in the old days; they held the mortgages on all the farms in the Imperial Valley after World War One, and in the Depression they got all the land."

"Did Mr. Browminor tell you that?"

"I read up on it," Virginia said. "I have nothing to do all day; I'm not working. I don't feel like sitting around a war-time housing unit listening to other people's radios and kids." She spoke so fiercely that her mother felt uncomfortable.

"It's a nice-looking store," Mrs. Watson said.

"The building was put up in 1940. So the wiring and plumbing are modern. And the front is modern. It won't have to be remodeled for at least ten years."

"Is this the one you want?"

"He showed me a couple more. And he gave me the name of a Realtor who specializes in small businesses. Do you realize how many people are moving out here to Los Angeles? In ten years there'll be more people here than in New York."

"I doubt that," Mrs. Watson said.

Virginia blushed.

"You always go at it so," Mrs. Watson said, "once you start. Try taking it a little more slowly."

Virginia eyed her. "I want to get it arranged."

"There's no rush. How much do the bank people say you ought to have?"

"They suggest at least ten thousand dollars. Preferably fifteen or twenty. No less than ten, anyhow."

"How much do you have?"

Smiling just a little, Virginia said, "About seven hundred dollars, including the market value of this car."

"So," Mrs. Watson said, "I'd have to put it all up, when you get down to it."

"It's a good investment. You can't make a mistake putting money into real estate in California."

"But you're not buying real estate. You'd just be leasing. You'd own nothing but the stock and fixtures."

"And the location."

"Why don't you buy lots? Land for subdivision."

"Because," Virginia said, in her old inflexible way, "that's not what we're interested in. We want a store we can run."

Voices, his wife's and another woman's, drifted down to him as he started onto the hall stairs. At once he realized that Mrs. Watson, his mother-in-law, had arrived from the East. The two of them, he thought. Sitting together in the living room, waiting for him.

However, he continued on up and opened the door.

His mother-in-law lifted her head, and both she and Virginia stopped talking. The room smelled of cigarettes and women's clothing. Over a chair their two coats hung, with their purses, and beside the chair was Mrs. Watson's suitcase. All the windows had been shut; the room was stuffy, overly-warm. On the bookcase the radio—fixed by the One Day Radio Repair—played light music. He did not find the sight, or the smells and sound, unpleasant; in a sense he was glad to see Mrs. Watson.

Back in 1943, when he had met her, she had treated him with courtesy. The meal at her home in Maryland reminded him of the best restaurant meals, pot roast and baked potatoes and rolls, linen napkins. He wore his good suit and a tie borrowed from Irv Rattenfanger. The conversation revolved around his plans, and that was all right; he expected that. He explained to her about his trip to California. At least she listened to him. Later on, when Virginia told him that her mother had not cared much for him, he accepted it as natural. His first wife's mother had not liked him either.

"Hello," he said, laying down his package. "I'm glad you got here okay."

Mrs. Watson put out her hand, so he shook hands with her. Her hand was small, rough, muscular. Her skin, he noticed, had darkened and become spotted, especially around her throat. On the back of her hand were liver spots, and her veins stood out. She was even thinner than Virginia, and somewhat shorter. For a middle-aged woman she looked good. At least she lacked the soft, flowery clumsiness of Teddy's mother.

Mrs. Watson said, "It's nice seeing you again."

"What did you get?" Virginia said, picking up the package.

"Just some stuff." At a hardware store he had bought one of the new soldering guns just now appearing on the market; it had two elements, one extremely hot, both of which heated instantly. At a radio wholesale supply house he had got schematics on a new type of phonograph cartridge invented by General Electric; it operated on a radical principle called variable reluctance. He spent much of his time visiting such supply houses, and the new cartridge had them all interested.

"Virginia says you had trouble with your teeth," Mrs. Watson said.

"Yes," he said. He wished the two women would sit down, and he started uncertainly towards the couch.

"When they bring out that needle," Mrs. Watson said, "I always wish I could die quietly of a heart attack and save them the trouble." Her tone was the flat, calm, measured declaration that he remembered.

"Sit down," he said, seating himself.

Both Virginia and her mother sat down, then. For a moment nobody spoke. He began to feel oppressed.

"They laid us off," he said. "From the plant. They're laying everybody off."

Here, in the living room of the apartment, his apartment, he became suddenly conscious of size. He and the room were both small, unimpressive; even, he thought, flimsy. What did he have? What did he show? As always he wore his work trousers, his coat and canvas shirt, his flappy, bent, dirty shoes. Then he thought how he had sent out his suit to be pressed for tomorrow; she was not supposed to arrive until tomorrow. The sense of pressure, the mashing down of him . . . he struggled to breathe.

In his mind, inside him, he longed to leave. The tugging at him, the need; outside the building his car was parked, pointed towards the highway, Route 66. Barstow, first, then the Mojave Desert, then Needles, and the Arizona border. Seated in the cramped living room, with the window shut, facing his wife and mother-in-law, he heard the car about him, the nearness of the road.

God, he thought. Could he stand it?

On his lap his fingers plucked at his coat; he smoothed the fabric, examined it. He could not sit still. Getting up he went to the window.

"Can I open a window?" he said. "It's sure stuffy."

Neither of the women answered.

"I guess I will," he said, perspiring. The window opened and he remained by it, savoring the air.

Offering her package of cigarettes to her mother, Virginia said, "What do you think about your room?"

"Oh I think it'll do for a while," Mrs. Watson said. "I may look around if I'm going to stay very long."

"I picked that place out," Roger said. "I found it."

Mrs. Watson said, "That's a good car you have. Virginia says you just bought it recently."

"I'm tuning it up," he said. For several days he had had it down the street at a Shell Station, cleaning the plugs and tinkering with the carburetor settings. He had got to know two of the boys at the station; one of them was married and earlier in the month he had brought his wife over for dinner.

"If you can't work on your own car," Mrs. Watson said, "you really are at their mercy."

"That's a fact," Roger said.

Again no one spoke.

On the table was the FM unit which he had started wiring from the diagram. Virginia lifted it up and said, "Marion asked me about this."

Mrs. Watson said, "Yes, I was wondering what it was."

"I didn't know what to call it," Virginia said. "It's a radio, isn't it?" She set it down. "All I could tell her was that you were making it."

"I'm wiring it," he said, wanting for a reason too vague to pin down to clarify that it was not a kit, a model. "This is going to be the band," he said. "This is the new band." He could not explain it. The whole new world, the opening up of regions and levels . . . the hell with it, he thought, feeling futile. Yes, he thought, I call it a telescope. Something to make the time go by. After that, I'm inventing the microscope and then the printing press. If I have time I'll invent the steam engine. Toys to hang from the ceiling of my room . . .

"Look," he said, "this is what Colonel Armstrong developed. It's as important as the superheterodyne circuit. He developed that, too."

They listened attentively.

"The problem with these is drift," he said. "The plates expand when it heats, and it drifts off the station. So you have to retune it." He picked up the incompleted FM tuner. "Somebody'll figure that out, though."

He felt like a boy.

Mrs. Watson said, "Virginia says you bought the car to go back to Arkansas."

"Yes," he said.

"Have you asked her if she'd like that?"

He could think of no answer.

"I think you ought to ask her," Mrs. Watson said. "Maybe she doesn't want to go to Arkansas."

"It's a nice state," he said, not looking at either of them.

"What are you going to do back there?"

"Look around," he said.

"Why can't you do that out here?"

"This isn't like I thought it was," he said. "It didn't turn out to be what I want. My luck isn't any good out here."

"You think your luck will change back in Arkansas?"

He said, "That's where I grew up."

"Do you want your children to grow up there?"

"I don't know," he said.

"Is that any kind of place for children? What are the schools like?"

"I don't know," he said.

"You know what I think?" Mrs. Watson said. "I think you're blaming everyone else for something that's your fault."

He nodded, staring down.

"Yes, it's your fault," Mrs. Watson said. "Why don't you look at me when I'm talking to you?"

He looked.

"That's just an excuse, that luck. It has nothing to do with luck. You know that, don't you? I know you know that. You know that as well as I. Now let's stop talking about that and face up to the situation. You wanted to come out here and now you're going to have to stick with it. You have a wife to support and pretty soon you'll have a child, and by then I want to see you with a job. Anybody can get a job out here. All you have to do is look. You've just decided it's time to move on, haven't you?"

He tried to think of something to say. Across from him Virginia showed no expression.

"I have a lot of things to do," he said. "I have to finish getting the car tuned up." Arising, he said, "I think I better go down to the station for a while."

Mrs. Watson said, "You sit down and listen to me."

"I have to get going," he said.

"That car isn't yours," Mrs. Watson said. "According to law it doesn't belong to you; it belongs to both of you, you and Virginia. If you run off with that car it's stealing."

"It's my car," he said, feeling panic.

"Don't you listen? I told you that you don't own it and you just stand there repeating that it's yours. It's half yours, but you can't run off with it. Anyhow you can't leave the State without your wife. You know that. You can be arrested and brought back. You can't run out on your family."

He said, "We're both going to Arkansas."

"Virginia's not going to Arkansas. She's staying here. So you can't go. That's desertion, and taking the car out of the state is grand theft."

"I have to go get the points cleaned," he said. "There's no law that I can't drive my own car down to the gas station and have it worked on." Moving toward the door he waited for Mrs. Watson to say something or to stop him; he expected her to leap up and fly at him and catch hold of him. But she remained seated, smoking her cigarette, and beside her, Virginia still showed no emotion of any kind; her face remained blank, as if she were deep in thought.

"I'll be back in around an hour," he said, speaking to his wife, hoping for some word, some remark that would release him.

The two women glanced at each other.

"If you're going to take the car," Virginia said, "you could drive Marion over to her room."

"I have to take some things from here," Mrs. Watson said.

"Sheets," Virginia said. "What else can you think of? Pots and pans, dishes."

"If you're sure you can spare them," Mrs. Watson said.

"I have two wool blankets. That should be enough. Where's the list we made?" Virginia searched among the papers on the table. "Let's see, you'll need some face towels and bath towels."

The two women collected everything, wandering here and there in the apartment checking for items they had missed. He did not stir; he stood by the door, not leaving, not helping or speaking, not knowing what to do.

"I think that's enough to get me started," Mrs. Watson said practically. "I can shop at the store for food; don't pack any food." Virginia had filled a cardboard box with silverware and dishes, a skillet and double boiler, a salt and pepper set.

"You want to carry this down?" Virginia said to her husband.

Picking up the box he carried it downstairs and set it in the car. Virginia followed him with the bedding.

"Hurry back," she said. After the bedding she put a wastepaper basket full of china packed in newspaper into the back of the car.

"Aren't you coming?"

"No," she said, "I still have to go to the launderette and pick up your shirts."

Mrs. Watson appeared, carrying her suitcase. "There's probably a waiting list for phones," she said to Virginia.

"We can try anyhow," Virginia said. "I'll call them and talk to them."

Opening the front door of the car, Mrs. Watson said to her daughter, "I'll drop by in the morning."

"Fine," Virginia said. She stayed on the sidewalk, her arms folded, as he drove his mother-in-law off in his car.

After they had gone a few blocks he said, "I wasn't going to leave Virginia."

Mrs. Watson said, "You just better forget about this Arkansas business."

"I'm telling you the truth!" he said.

"You were married once before," Mrs. Watson said. "Isn't that right?"

"Yes," he said.

"Where is she now?"

"I don't know. Back East."

"Did you have any children?"

"One."

"Do you ever hear from them?"

"No."

"Do you contribute any money toward their support?"

"No. She remarried."

"I knew it would work out like this," Mrs. Watson said. "As soon as I laid eyes on you. But Virginia wants to stay with you. It's up to her. I told her originally how I felt about you."

He said bitterly, "I don't think much of you either."

"I'll tell you one thing," Mrs. Watson said, "and that's this: you're not going to walk off and leave my daughter, especially now that she's going to have a baby. You better make up your mind to that. You're staying right here and support them. What is this business you want? Some sort of radio fixit shop? Are you competent to do that?"

He concentrated on driving.

"As far as I'm concerned," Mrs. Watson said, "you'd be better off at some kind of laboring job. But Virginia thinks you could manage a little store."

Horrified, he said, "It's none of your business. You mind your own business. That's my affair, between me and my wife; you have nothing to do with it."

"Don't you dare talk to me like that."

His voice stuck in his throat. "Don't you meddle in my family," he told her, at last.

Mrs. Watson said, "She's my daughter and I've known her a lot longer than you have. I'm much more concerned about her welfare than you'll ever be. All you care about is loafing at some easy job where you won't have to do any work. You're what the people back home call trash. Isn't that the truth? Now you know that down inside you; you know you're just a no-good man with a lot of trash talk. I told my daughter not to have anything to do with you, but she was working there in the Washington hospitals and she had a noble thing about the war and helping crippled people. If she wants to waste her own life, give up her life and devote herself to trying to patch you together into something worthwhile and useful, I know she can't be stopped by me from doing it. Of course I think some day she'll wake up and realize. Anyhow, I came out here with the determination to aid my daughter as much as I can, because I've always been behind her, even after she married you; I'm not like some who'd turn against their child because they disapproved of what their child did to them. There's no mean or wicked streak in Virginia, just ignorance like everybody else when a war's going on and people have lost their good sense." Her speech took on the sharp, sing-song Southern whine, the accusation and sense of suffering of the Southern lady. But all at once she ceased; opening her large leather purse she began searching for her cigarette lighter.

"Don't you go too far with me," he said.

Having lit a cigarette she resumed. But now she had gone back to her dry, controlled manner; she had calmed down and become more business-like. "While I'm staying out here," she said, "I want to do something for Virginia to help her along the lines she wishes. I think she's got her mind set on fixing it up so you can have your fixit shop, and if that's what she wants I'll naturally do everything in my power to bring it about. I always intended to do the best I could by her. It has nothing to do with you; it's between me and my daughter, Virginia."

Then he saw the drift of it. He saw her getting ready to talk about giving them money for opening the store. Up to that moment the idea had never occurred to him; he was taken completely by surprise. A wave of excitement flashed into his bones, his hands and feet; he began to dance up and down behind the wheel of the car, trying not to let go of it, trying to see the cars and street ahead, the signals and pedestrians and signs. Then he began to yell at Mrs. Watson, "I don't want your fucking money, you hear? I wouldn't touch any of your fucking money!" He yelled at the top of his lungs. "You keep your trashy hands off of my store, you hear? I don't want nothing to do with you, I want you to go back home to your place and live there and have nothing to do with us. You hear me? You understand? If you keep coming around I'm going to do something to you. I mean that, Mrs. Watson. I don't care who you are or how much you've got; I mean what I say. You keep your fucking money. I mean that too. I don't want it. I mean to open my store and I don't want no help from you."

Her face wavered and faded, as lifeless as rock.

"Get out of my car!" he yelled, driving steadily along the street. "Open that door and get out, you hear? Or I'm maybe going to do something to you right now; maybe I'm not going to wait any longer." Stepping down on the gas pedal he speeded up the car; he shot forward, around a corner and along a side street. Faster and faster the car flew; he paid no attention to speed. "You take all your stuff and get out! I'm telling you what you better do. Get that trash out of the back of my car; I don't want all that trash cluttering up my car. I need my car. When you get out, take it with you."

The house in which her room was located appeared ahead of them, to the right, among other buildings. Driving along the curb he brought the car to a bucking stop; Mrs. Watson, bouncing up, raised her arms to protect herself, twisting her body as she fell forward against the dashboard and door. He yanked on the brake, leaped out of the car and ran to open the door on her side. With both hands he dug out the suitcase, and then from the back the boxes and bedding and wastebasket, throwing them onto the sidewalk. Mrs. Watson remained in the front seat, following his actions wide-eyed, motionless.

"Get out of my car," he said.

She gazed at him, utterly disconcerted.

"Get out." He stood yelling at her, not touching her. "Go on, get out of my car."

Sliding her legs, she stepped shakily to the pavement, holding onto her purse, sunglasses, and cigarettes.

"Now when you come back tomorrow," he said, "you talk to me with respect. You hear? You understand what I'm telling you?"

Without waiting for her answer he ran back around the car and leaped in. Slamming the door he drove off in low gear, not shifting, pushing the gas pedal flat. He did not look back.

He thought of himself, years ago, a child in school, in the second grade. Nobody paid any attention to him; nobody listened to him or cared what he had to say. Sitting at their desks they were served at lunch time a meal of bread sandwiches, tomato soup, and milk. He took the crusts of his sandwich and stuck them on top of his head. It was the funniest thing that had ever been seen, and all the children laughed. The next day at lunch time he did it again, and again they all laughed. Every day for a month he stuck bread crusts on his head, and everybody looked at him and applauded; he got to his feet and jumped up and down and waggled his arms and made faces, and they all laughed and laughed. It was the happiest moment of his life.

Now, as he drove, he thought to himself that he was finally going to have his store. He began to cry great tears of humiliation that dripped down his face and splashed onto his shirt and arms. The wetness slithered among the hairs of his wrists and stained his trousers. At a red light he got out his handkerchief and wiped his cheeks and neck. Hating himself and his wife and Mrs. Watson and the Negro who had hit him and the dentist who had charged him sixty dollars and the salesman who had sold him the car which he had no use for and John Beth who had not let him open the repair department at Beth Appliance Center, he continued crying and wiping his face as he drove back to his wife and the wartime housing unit in which he lived.

11

On Saturday morning, after Roger had gone to work, Virginia got a telephone call from Liz Bonner about their shopping date. She drove over to the Bonner house and parked.

"Hi," Liz said, opening the front door and letting her in. "I'm giving the dog a bath. Come on inside; I'm almost finished." She looked quite plump and fetching and brown-eyed in her cotton shirt and cord pants; her feet were bare, and her sleeves were rolled up past her elbows, and splotches of foam and water clung to her. She had tied her hair back with a ribbon. Under her shirt her breasts bounced as she ran ahead of Virginia, through the house. "You want a cookie? I baked them last night, but they taste like soap. Anyhow, that's what the paper boy said when I gave him one. It's supposed to be coconut."

The glass dish of cookies was in the center of the dining room table, a platter of white squares like small red bricks.

"When did you want to leave?" Virginia said. They had talked about going down into Pasadena before noon.

"Anytime," Liz said. "Excuse me." She hurried off somewhere, and Virginia heard the sloshing of water and Liz's voice addressing the dog. She heard, too, the noise of a lawnmower. Beyond the dining room window a red-faced man wearing a blazing sport shirt passed with the lawnmower. His big furry arms attracted her attention. The man, to her, looked like a gym instructor or a scout leader. He had that sober, responsible, out-of-door manner. It did not seem to her that he was especially bald. In the morning sunlight his face shone and perspired, and he stopped to wipe his forehead with his arm. Then he plowed on. He did not appear to mind the task.

Following the sloshing noises, she came upon Liz kneeling in the garage by a tin tub in which a collie dog stood dripping water. "That's Chic," Virginia said, "isn't it? Out in the yard mowing the lawn."

"Yes," Liz said. "Oh, you didn't meet him." She scrambled up. "I'm sorry; I forgot. Do you want to meet him now? Come on," she said, snapping her fingers at the dog. "You're finished with your bath." The dog hopped from the tub and shook himself; water flew, and Virginia retreated. Liz picked up a towel from the doorknob and began to rub the dog dry. "Go outside in the sun," she ordered the dog. "Go on out. Go on." The dog started toward the door of the garage. "Go sit out on the front sidewalk," Liz said. "Keep out of the shade so you don't catch cold."

The dog obeyed more or less. He left the garage, and she and Liz watched him stop to shake himself once again. Then he set off along the sidewalk.

"You're all dressed up," Liz said. "I better go change. I didn't know what you were going to wear so I waited. That's a nice suit. Don't you think people back East dress better than they do out here? Do you know—" She started from the garage up the steps that led to the kitchen. "I wear these pants six days a week; I wear them to the store and around the house, and nobody cares. I guess part of it's the weather; it's so mild out here." At the bedroom door she stopped, turned, and said, "Where's Gregg today? Can't he come? The boys are coming."

"He's with his grandmother," Virginia said.

"Bring her along, too." Within the dark bedroom—the shades were down—she began to throw off her clothes. "Chic's coming. He thought maybe he could get a look at Roger's store. It's along the way, isn't it?"

More confusion, Virginia thought. Kids and dogs, a flock of them trailing along into the crowded downtown department stores. "I'll go out in the yard," she said. She had not seen it, yet, and she was curious. "While you're dressing." Without waiting for an answer she left the house, opening the back door of the garage to find herself suddenly in sunlight.

His lawnmower halted. "Hello," Chic Bonner said. "Are you Mrs. Lindahl?"

"Don't stop working," she said. "You look like you're having fun."

Chic said, "It's a chance to get outdoors. I'm cooped up in the office five days a week. The only chance I have to get out is on Saturday and Sunday, unless I take some time off."

By the side of the house, beds of flowers grew; she turned her attention to them. The beds were well-kept, weedless. The blooms on the flowers—she did not recognize them—were immense. The entire yard had a professional tone, as if a Japanese gardener had been let loose. But, she thought, he probably does it himself. How tan he is. She pictured him with sacks of fertilizer and heavy spray-tanks and imported English pruning shears. A proper schedule of plant-care. And the interior of the house . . . so messy. The contrast: order, here. Chaos within. The two domains.

"How nice it is out here," she said.

He accepted her compliment. "Are you a gardener?" he asked. "By that I mean, do you get the itch once in a while?"

"I'm not," she said. "My mother's more the gardener in our family. She kept a wonderful garden back in Maryland. Out here she hasn't done much. She's not used to the dryness."

"You have to water," Chic said. He started up his lawnmower again; it was manual, not gas-operated, but it had fat balloon tires. The paint on it was shiny, new. To Virginia it had the aura of the garden-supply shop window; she imagined a price tag dangling from it, a wheelbarrow display directly beside it.

"I never had much luck with flowers," Virginia said. "I planted a few glads, but neighborhood kids knocked them down."

"I see," Chic said, mowing.

"That's something that really offends me. I had tulips along the front path, but the kids in the block picked them as fast as they bloomed."

"Tulips are limited to one bloom per plant a year," Chic said. "From a gardener's standpoint they're more trouble than they're worth. You have to really love them to make it worth it."

One bloom, she thought, or a hundred; it didn't matter since the kids were going to steal them anyhow. The kids had even uprooted the plants in their eagerness to snatch the blossoms. She had come outdoors in the morning and found the hairy white bulbs littering the walk.

Don't they run through your garden? she thought. Apparently not. You have it all like a model, a world. And if I could get the darn things to come up in the first place I was never able to protect them. After the kids had yanked up the tulips (what did they do with them? Sell them? Give them to their mothers? Teachers?) I stood at the window, ready to deal out justice, but I never caught them; they didn't come back, at least not that week. And I couldn't stand there forever, just for a few flower bulbs.

I admire you, she thought. I admire anybody who can keep a garden operating with kids around.

The two Bonner boys shoved open the side gate and came toward her and Chic, carrying armloads of comic books. "When are we going downtown?" Jerry asked. "Hello, Mrs. Lindahl," he said to her.

"May I see those?" Chic said, resting the handle of the lawnmower against his stomach and reaching out his hand toward the comic books.

The two boys held the comic books so that he could go through them, one by one, examining the covers. He withdrew several. The boys accepted his judgement as a natural event; neither of them protested.

"Does your boy ever get his hands on these things?" Chic said to Virginia. He held up one of the bad comic books; it had a banner reading *Tales of the Crypt* and the picture was of a young girl's head being baked, on the end of a rod, by a loathsome fiend. "It makes you wonder sometimes." Rolling up the bad comic books he stuck them into his back pocket and resumed his lawnmowing. "I think if that was the only way I could figure out to make a living, I'd forget it," he said.

The two boys departed with their comic books.

"Better get into the car," Chic said. "You can read in there."

"Okay, Dad," Walter said, at the gate. The two boys disappeared past the side of the house.

"Who do you suppose puts out those things?" Chic said to Virginia.

"Somebody in New York," Virginia said.

"A lot of that stuff is printed here in L.A.," Chic said. "There's a regular industry here. What they have on TV is bad enough. I don't remember that there used to be horror comic books. When I was a boy there weren't any kind of comic books, and we didn't miss them. What do you suppose it'll be like when they get to be our age?" He squatted on the lawn and began cleaning the blades of the mower. "They pick it up outside the home. There's nothing you can do."

"Even up at the school?" she said, thinking of Gregg.

"This stuff—" He tapped the bad comic books in his back pocket. "They go everywhere. All over the world. It's a big business, like oil or shoes."

The back door of the house banged open and Liz appeared, all powdered and perfumed, with her hair in soft ringlets, wearing an orchid-colored dirndl and a puff-sleeved blouse. "Ready to go?" she said to Virginia. "Chic, you better go change; shouldn't you change? You can't go downtown on Saturday like that. Go in and put on a suit." She smiled at Virginia.

"Wait until I put the lawnmower away," Chic said, spinning the blades with his thumb. Bits of wet grass fluttered.

"What do you have in your pocket?" Liz bent down and caught hold of the rolled-up comic books. Flattening them, she studied the first cover. "What's all this?" She seemed unable to imagine where the comic books could have come from; carrying them over to the back step she seated herself, spread them out on her lap, and began to read them. "This is awful," she said, in a bewildered voice. She did not seem offended, only confused.

Chic winked at Virginia as he straigntened up.

While he wheeled the lawnmower to the garage, Liz remained seated on the back step, poring over the comic books. The wind blew her hair and ruffled her skirt; she reflexively smoothed her skirt. In the sunlight she looked flushed, charming; the color of her clothes stood out, and Virginia could not help admiring her hair and the smoothness of her skin. And there you sit, Virginia thought. Struggling with a comic book, holding it with both hands, frowning and moving your lips.

Glancing up, Liz said, "Where'd he get these?"

"From the boys," Virginia said.

"Did you look at them?"

"No," she said.

Liz said, "Is it true that a corpse can come back to life and point out its murderer? That's what it shows here. That's absurd." Leaning on her elbow, Liz drew up her legs, crossed them, and resumed her reading of the comic books. Then she closed the comic book and tossed the stack indoors, behind her, into the house; her legs stretched out to balance her and Virginia saw that she had on high heels but no stockings. I have not seen that since the War, Virginia thought. Liz patted her waist, tucked her blouse into her belt, brushed her hair back from her eyes. Sprawled on the step, she said, "I guess we better go. It's almost ten." With reluctance, she got to her feet.

Appearing from the garage, Chic stepped by his wife and gave her a spank. "Let's go," he said.

"How do I look?" Liz asked Virginia. "Okay?"

"Fine," Virginia said. But the comic books, she thought. Then she felt guilt. I am mean, she said to herself. Mean and unfair. But, she thought, with delight, wait until I tell Roger. I wish I had a snapshot of her sitting there. It would be something to keep.

In the back seat of the station wagon the two boys read their comic books with great seriousness, uninterested in the drive.

"Don't read in the car, boys," Chic instructed them. "It's bad for your eyes." At his voice, the collie started up. "Come on now, boys."

Gradually they ceased to read. They put away the comic books. How obedient, Virginia thought. They had the same gravity that their father had, his making something important out of every act. She herself felt lazy and lulled, as she always did on Saturday; the idea of shopping carried with it the atmosphere of prosperity, as if money was left over, beyond the demand of necessities. She could go as slowly as she wanted, pick over the skirts and dresses, try on what she wished; she did not have to buy or not buy, and if the girls behind the counters did not approve, then it was too bad; she did not need their approval. She could leave. She was mobile; she could go somewhere else or even back home. And she liked the buzz and pressure of the crowd, the hectic pushing and shoving of the downtown shops on Saturday. The air of drama . . . the gathering of many.

While she meditated about that, she became aware that Chic and Liz had begun to argue in low, snappish voices.

"No stockings," Chic was saying, seated so that he faced his wife, his back to Virginia, "and what do you have on under that blouse? Nothing at all, do you?"

"I have a slip on," Liz said, driving with her eyes on the traffic.

"You don't even have a slip on."

"I do. Look." Letting go of the steering wheel with her left hand, she showed him the strap of her slip.

"What else?" He waited and got no answer. "Nothing else. Why don't you put on a bra when you're going out? Why do you always leave some part of your clothes missing? Do you like to go out in such a way that you attract attention? Is it some infantile drive toward exhibition or noncomformity, or are you just so habitually careless that you don't know when you're dressed or not? Tell me, why didn't you put on the rest of your clothes? And if you just forget, why does it happen so many times?"

Liz said, "I couldn't find a pair of stockings that didn't have a run; all my bras are on the line or in the wash or something, and I didn't have time to put on pants."

"You better turn the car around and drive back and put them on."

"We don't have time. And what do you care? Why are you always so concerned about things that aren't any of your business? Can anybody see I don't have on stockings unless they happen to get up right next to me?"

"You ought to wear a bra. You shouldn't go out of the house without a bra. I can see right through your blouse. That's how I knew you didn't have a bra on. Look when the sun strikes you; look down. I'll hold the wheel." He took hold of the wheel but she did not let go.

"You told me to hurry up," Liz said. "I didn't have time to iron a bra."

Turning in his seat, Chic faced Virginia. He had got really angry. "You notice she blames me, but she also defends what she's done as being perfectly natural. Actually she doesn't know why she does things. It's whatever enters her mind."

In the back seat the two boys appeared unbothered by the argument. They had begun reading their comic books again, with the same sobriety as before. But to Virginia the argument was offensive; she felt they should settle it and forget it. "It seems simple enough to me," she said, to both Chic and Liz. "We're going shopping; she can pick up what she needs." Otherwise the day was falling into a decline.

"That's right," Chic said. "That's a good practical suggestion." His face lost some of its weight of anger; it cleared until he was smiling.

"I'll look around," Liz said. "I'll see if there's anything I want." As she stopped for a red light she said, "What I need more than anything else is shoes. And both the boys need shirts. I have a list in my purse."

Chic had abandoned the argument. To Virginia he said, "Should we pick up your mother and Gregg first, or go by the store first? You know better than we."

"We should pick them up first," Virginia said. "I think. They may have gone somewhere. She said something about going over to see some woman she knows who's a real estate broker; she's debating about getting a license. The woman is urging her to."

"That's a good field," Chic said. "You have no investment to lose, except your office fixtures. But it's overcrowded. And it takes time to get the state license." He was at ease, again. "How about yourself?" he said. "Did you ever consider something like that? A lot of active young women are giving that a try. They can do it during the day."

"I know, she said. "But I have plenty to do. I have my dancing."

He pondered. "Of course," he said, "my own interest runs toward business sites. I could never ferry old ladies around, buttering them up. A lot of being a real estate broker involves being able to tell one whopper after another. Do you agree with me there?"

"Yes," she said.

"They're marginal," Chic said. He frowned earnestly at that. "Some of those operators—they collect their commission and get out."

She nodded, wondering to herself what he would think of the store. Evidently he had a strong moral idea of how business should be done; she was conscious of his judgment.

"Are you not interested in the store?" Chic said.

"I'm interested," she said. "But I don't have to be there; it isn't necessary. He's doing fine without me."

"What's the kind of dancing that you do?" He asked in such a fashion that she realized what was in his mind; he thought of night clubs or at best such dance teams as the Castles, or possibly Ginger Rogers and Fred Astaire.

"Have you ever heard of Martha Graham?"

"I believe so," he said.

She described for him the kind of modern interpretive dancing that she taught. She told him about group therapy and participation drama, and the like; he appeared to listen, but she did not feel much real emotional response.

"Can that be a living?" he said. "By that I mean, can you make it pay?"

"No," she said. "Not really."

He did not comment on that. But again she was conscious of his judgment. So it can't be your main purpose in life, he was saying to himself. It's a sort of hobby, to fill vacant time.

"I don't do as much dance therapy as I used to," she said. It's so hard to arrange, she thought to herself. So difficult to interest people in.

12

On Saturday the store usually had its busiest day. At the counter Roger fell into a somnambulism; he let this Saturday join those in the past and those to come. The phone rang and customers came and left. We are not sick today, he thought. Nobody is sick on Saturday. Nobody is down the street or across the street or sealed up in the bathroom. This is the hub, whether we want to be here or not. He wrote out a tag for a customer. This is where our minds have to be.

Early in the morning Olsen had left in the service truck and had not been seen again. People on his route had phoned in to ask where he was.

Where are you? Roger thought. The people were waiting in their houses. Why hasn't he shown up? the people said.

"He musta got stuck somewhere," Pete said, looking cross. "He had that set he was taking all the way over to San Bernardino."

"Today?" Roger said. "On Saturday?" He felt dull rage.

"It's the only day the guy's home. Olsen figured on beating it over there before the traffic. He musta got behind a truck coming back. It's that guy Flannigan we've had all the complaints from."

"Okay," Roger said. "Tell me if he phones in." He returned to the customers at the counter. "Yes ma'am," he said. "What can I do for you?"

"I bought this needle here the other day," the middle-aged woman in the tan dress said. "And it doesn't fit my phonograph. The man—I think it was the other man there you were talking to—told me it was the one I needed."

While he was inspecting the needle, he heard voices at the doorway. Looking up, he saw an astonishing sight. His wife Virginia and his mother-in-law Marion Watson had come into the store, and with them was Gregg, and two freckle-faced red-haired boys, and a dog, and then Chic and Liz Bonner. The four adults conversed amiably; the children immediately spread out into all parts of the store, clutching at the television sets and squeezing in front of customers. The dog, a collie, settled down in the doorway, obviously trained to stop at that point.

Roger exchanged the needle for the woman, and then he left the counter and went over to his wife. The four of them moved in a gradual course toward the back of the store; Virginia seemed to be showing the Bonners something. For a time none of them noticed him and then Virginia said cheerfully,

"Why didn't you tell me you went over there last night?"

"I did," he said.

"Oh. Well, if I'd known you were going I would have gone along."

Chic and Liz Bonner greeted him, and he nodded back.

"What's up?" he said to Virginia.

"Liz and I had a date to go shopping down in Pasadena today. I thought we all might as well go along. And then I was talking to them about the store, and Chic suggested we drop by so they could see it."

"You've got quite a nice little place here, Lindahl," Chic said. "You own it? By that I mean, you're the sole owner?"

"That's right," Roger said. When Chic had gone off a few steps, he drew Virginia aside and said to her, "You didn't tell me about any shopping date."

"It was tentative. We just talked about it, on the trip back from the school. Then this morning she telephoned me."

"Oh," Roger said. "She called you."

"I think she wanted to have the boys meet you before Sunday," Virginia said. "So you wouldn't be a stranger. She's always driven them up herself."

The two Bonner boys had started downstairs to the basement; Chic Bonner called for them to wait. He and Liz followed after the boys. Chic had on his short-sleeved sportshirt, either the same one or another like it, and slacks; Liz looked lovely in a skirt and blouse. They did not seem to be in a hurry.

"Can you get off for coffee?" Virginia said.

"No," he said.

"Even for a couple of minutes? We could all go next door."

"You can see how busy it is," he said. "You know how Saturday is." Mrs. Watson had come over beside Virginia. "How could I possibly leave the store on Saturday?" Roger said. "You know darn well I'm stuck here."

Virginia and her mother rejoined the Bonners, leaving him alone. He felt a rebirth of the frantic sense of being off somewhere on the edge. Here, in his own store, he felt it. Even here.

"Phone for you," Pete said.

"Who is it?"

"I don't know. Somebody about a set." Pete put the phone down and went back to showing TV combinations to a young couple.

"Hello," Roger said into the phone.

"I've been sitting here waiting for your repairman to bring back my set," a man's ponderous voice said. "And he isn't here yet. How long am I going to have to wait? He was supposed to be here this morning. I have to get downtown; I can't stay around here."

After he had finished hassling with the man on the phone he waited on an elderly lady at the counter who had a paper bag full of tubes to be checked. One by one she brought the tubes out and laid them on the counter; each was wrapped in newspaper.

Carrying the tubes downstairs he gave them a slipshod check and then brought them back upstairs. "They're okay," he said to the elderly lady. "Must be something else. Bring the set in."

"Oh it's too big," the elderly lady said. "I'd have to get someone to carry it for me."

It took a long time to get rid of her. When next he had a breathing space he discovered that Mrs. Watson, Chic and Liz Bonner, Virginia, his son Gregg, the two Bonner boys, and the collie, were all leaving; they had got almost to the doorway. The dog was on its feet, ready to start off. He felt utterly futile.

"Good-bye," Virginia said to him. All of them, more or less, said good-bye. Chic Bonner seemed to be expounding on some topic; he peered up at the ceiling of the store, paced off the width of the doorway, and then went out to examine the windows.

What the hell is he up to? Roger wondered. What now? What else is there?

After the group had gone, Pete came over to him. "Friends of yours?"

He said, "Their kids are in the school Gregg's going to."

"The dame isn't bad-looking. Real sort of—what do you call it?—fresh-looking. You know?"

He nodded, feeling despondent now.

"Olsen didn't phone in, did he?" Pete said.

"No."

"He better show up. He'll be delivering sets until midnight tonight." Moving off, Pete reached to take hold of the phone.

At the counter Roger began sorting the tags. His hands worked reflexively. So she had called, he thought. After she had heard that he had come by. Did it mean anything? If so, what did it mean? What did anything mean? he wondered. And how did a person tell?

We can never be certain. Not until our dying day. And maybe not even then. All of us, he thought, are down here fumbling around, guessing and calculating. Doing the best we can.

A noise caused him to glance up.

Liz Bonner came rushing back through the doorway, into the store. She glided up to the counter and placed herself before him; in an instant there she was, directly in front of him, not a foot away, a dark vivid merry-eyed little shape in a long skirt. His hands continued sorting the tags. He was too startled to put the tags down. He felt as if he were a tin mechanism, under a dome of glass; his arms lifted and fell, his fingers selected the next tag in order and brought the wire up to the hole. But at least he did not watch what he was doing; he kept his eyes on Liz. He felt so lacking in control, so helpless, that he thought, I'm lucky to be able to do that.

"I forgot my purse," Liz said. All the colors of her had deepened, become more intense. She's blushing, he realized. But even her skirt, and her hair, were dark: her eyes had dilated and he saw that they were coffee-colored. They had in them an alert, active expectancy, as if she were prepared for something, for him to do or say something.

"Oh yeah?" he said, in a faint voice. "In here?"

She regarded him coolly, still with that color and delight, as if she had wanted to come back, as if it meant a great deal. "I think I left it down in the basement," she said. "Where all those big TV sets are."

"Okay," he said. He could think of nothing else to say; he had lost his ability to talk.

Across the counter from him her warm, shiny face reflected equal confusion; the darkness of her eyes shrank and she started to say something, hesitated, and then, without a word, she skipped off in the direction of the stairs, her long skirt trailing out after her.

What? He thought, what should I do? Before him, on the counter, his hands sorted tags, wired and selected. Just stand here, he said. Let your life run out of your fingertips, until you go blind and your legs curl up and you die.

In a moment she returned, with her purse. The purse was leather, new, with a strap that she now fixed over her shoulder. She seemed happy, relieved to find it.

"I'd hate to lose it," she said. "I've got all sorts of junk in it." At the doorway she paused breathlessly, turning back toward him.

"Are you leaving?" he said. She nodded. "Good-bye," he said, then. "I'll see you," he said.

Without answering, she ducked her head and hurried on, out of the store and along the sidewalk.

After a time he said to himself, I don't know. How can I know? Am I supposed to read something into that? Make something out of it? Or, he thought, maybe I have got to the point when I see something in everything, because I want to see something.

The next thing, he thought, is voices. I'll start hearing voices.

What can I count on? What can I believe?

Behind him the intercom to the basement hissed. One of its tubes had a partial short, and the hissing kept up day after day. I am almost hearing things in that, he thought. Why not? What would the difference be, between hearing something in the hiss of the intercom and in what I just now witnessed . . . that act put on here in the store, in my own store where I know everything and own everything, in front of me.

Look what I am lost into, he said to himself. I'm hanging on the merest hiss of noise, so low that it's barely audible. On the threshold of audibility. A hum.

Hummmmmmmmmmmmmmmmmmmmmm.

How precarious it is. I have to strain. Reach.

Christ, he thought. I'll probably pull my gut doing it. Wear myself to death, listening.

Hummmmmmmmmmmmmmmmmmmmmm.

The fatigue. It can be tough. It's not easy. It's not something that happens to you while you stand idly by; it's something you do at great labor and over a great deal of time. You have to blow on it, cull it, fan it, breathe your life out onto it to keep it there.

You invent it, he thought to himself. And then you maintain it until it's true.

Going to the intercom he pressed the key and said, "Is anybody down there?"

He waited. Nobody.

Hummmmmmmmmmmmmmmmmm.

"Get to work," he said into the intercom. Downstairs, in the empty service department, his voice would be booming out. He imagined it, the echo in the darkness. "Get off it and work," he said. "Get off your ass, down there."

I'm talking to myself, he said.

"What are you doing?" he said into the intercom. "Are you just sitting there? Asleep?"

You're sound asleep, he said to himself.

"Answer me," he said. "I know you're down there." I'm not alone, he said to himself. I know it. "Come on," he said, pressing the key. He rotated the control on the intercom to the maximum volume. "Answer me!" he said. The floor beneath him vibrated. My voice, he thought. Under me. From under the ground.

Hanging up the telephone, Pete approached the counter. "Hey," he said to Roger, "what are you doing?"

"Talking to the service department," he said. He let up on the key of the intercom.

The intercom hissed.

That night, after dinner, Virginia showed him the sweaters that she had bought on her shopping trip with the Bonners.

"See?" she said, holding them up. "Aren't they nice?"

"Fine," he said. "Did you have a good time?"

"You know I enjoy shopping over in Pasadena."

"Why the hell was Chic measuring the front of my store?"

"Was he? I guess he was measuring the frontage."

"Why?"

"You'll have to ask him," Virginia said.

After some thought, he said, "I sure was surprised to see the eight of you come wandering into the store."

"Eight!"

"Sure, counting the collie. Whose is that?"

"It belongs to Walter and Jerry. It's very gentle and mannerly."

From where he sat he could not see her face. He wondered if he should raise the question about his having gone over to the Bonners. Which was worse, raising it or not raising it?

No way to know that, either. No way to know anything for certain. Unclear glimpses. Possibilities. Leads, hints . . . he gave up.

Maybe I'm lucky, he thought. That there's no real knowing. Just suspecting. What a difference between the two.

Confirmation—that was the thing that was lacking. They could wander forever without getting it. Or it might drop in their laps. Confirmation for him, for what he suspected; or for Virginia, if she suspected anything.

I suspect, he thought, that you suspect. And, he thought, what do you suspect, for Christ's sake? Because right now it's just too vague.

Virginia said, "Oh, I meant to tell you. You'll probably get mad, but anyhow—" She smiled. "Liz left her purse in one of the downtown department stores. We had to drive all the way back to Pasadena for it; we just barely got back by closing time."

"Was it there?"

"Yes, one of the clerks put it behind the counter. Chic says she does that all the time."

So there vanishes that, he thought.

See? he thought. Look what can be done with the hiss. Look at the voices you can hear in the hum for no reason.

Hummmmmmmmmmmmmmmm, the world said to him. On all sides. Everywhere. Hiss and hum. Trying to reach him, speak out to him.

"What are you thinking?" Virginia said. "You look so gloomy."

"I'm thinking about color TV."

"Don't think about it."

"I can't help it," he said. "I'm thinking about a warehouse full of black-and-white TV sets that I'll have to practically give away."

"Try to think of something pleasant," Virginia said.

"I'll try," he said. "I'll try the best I can."

*　*　*

On Sunday afternoon he put Gregg into the Oldsmobile and drove over to the Bonners'. In broad daylight their small tract house looked shabby; it needed paint around the windows, but at least the lawn had been cut. The red station wagon, parked out front, still had its coat of dust. On one fender somebody, probably the two boys, had traced letters in the dust, indistinct initials.

As he closed the door of the Olds, he thought, I might even be able to read something in those initials traced on the car fender.

"Are we going back now?" Gregg asked, as they crossed the street.

"Pretty soon." The time was one-thirty. They had some latitude.

"Mommy isn't coming, is she? I thought Mommy was coming." The boy blinked morosely.

"Mommy asked me to drive you," he said. "I'm driving Walt and Jerry, too." In his tone of joking he said, "Of course, if my driving isn't good enough for you, maybe you'd like to hire a cab with the forty cents you've got saved up."

Gregg said, "Couldn't we go a little later?"

"We'll see," he said, leading his son up onto the porch of the Bonner house and ringing the bell.

No one answered the bell. He rang again. The house had an air of emptiness.

"Maybe they're not home," he said to Gregg. And then he discovered that he was standing on the porch alone; Gregg had slipped off. Son-of-a-bitch, Roger said to himself. He left the porch and walked across the lawn. "Gregg!" he said.

His son appeared from around the side of the house. "They're in the backyard," he said. "They're out back."

"Okay," Roger said. He accompanied his son along the path between the side of the house and the fence, through a gate, past a bush, and into the backyard.

The collie dog sat in the center of a terraced lawn, its feet before it. The yard looked better than the front. At the rear were several fruit trees and an incinerator and a heap of dried branches and leaves. Flower beds had been planted along the side fences. The two Bonner boys were in the process of building a hut out of scrap lumber, up against the back fence; they had it almost finished. Both boys worked in their jeans, bare from the waist up, and barefoot. Chic Bonner had taken up a position nearby, on a brick border; he sat with his head down and his eyes almost shut. In the sunlight his head sparkled damply; the remains of his hair had a transparent quality, as if its final day was almost upon him. His scalp had turned pink and spotted, and when he glanced up, Roger saw that his eyebrows, too, were pink. Shading his eyes, Chic squinted at him and then brought out a pair of sunglasses.

"I can't see a damn thing in this glare," he said.

"It's me," Roger said.

Liz Bonner stirred and sat up. She had been lying stretched out in the grass, in a swimsuit. "Is it that time already?" she murmured. She turned over and rested her weight on her elbows, putting her hands to her cheeks. "Hello, Greggy," she said. "Come over here for a minute." When he did so she reached up and took hold of his shirt. "Do you make him wear his shirt? Can't he take it off?" Sliding to her knees she unbuttoned Gregg's shirt and tossed it over the brick border at the end of the lawn. "Take off your shoes," she said to Gregg. "Ask your Daddy if it's all right."

"Can I take off my shoes?" Gregg said, returning to him.

"Sure," he said. "Go ahead." To Liz and Chic he said, "You people look comfortable."

Liz sat now with her legs out before her, learning backward on her flattened palms. Bits of grass had stuck to her swimsuit and to her legs and midriff. Her skin was lighter than he remembered. She was stockier than Virginia, and shorter, and her hips seemed to him much more feminine. She really had a good figure, he thought. Like the two boys laboring on their hut, she had taken off as many of her clothes as possible. She looked perfectly natural stretched out on her bath towel; she fit in with the sun and the collie dog and the yard itself.

"Join us," Liz said.

"What do you mean?" he said.

"Stretch out. Take a nap. Take off your shirt and your shoes."

"It sounds wonderful," he said.

Gregg, now wearing just his pants, began to explore the yard. His gyrations carried him closer and closer to the hut in the rear, until at last he began to circle it, not looking in its direction, but nonetheless involving himself with it. The two Bonner boys viewed him with disgust. They continued their building.

"Lindahl," Chic said, his legs apart, his arms resting on his thighs, "that isn't a bad-looking store you've got. But you don't have much frontage on the street, do you? It seemed to me your windows, your displays, are awfully small. Maybe I'm wrong. I've never known anybody in retail selling. It's something that's always intrigued me but I never got into it. That place next to yours has more frontage, doesn't it?"

"Yeah," he said. "I guess so."

"You just lease, don't you?"

"That's right."

"What's your rent run a month?

"About three hundred."

"I'll be darned," Chic said. "As much as that? Well, you're in a good location. The store's deep, isn't it? I used to be interested in architecture, back when I was going to school; I took a couple of courses—I horsed around with designing. I guess everybody goes through a period like that." Lifting his head he scrutinized Roger through his dark glasses. "Is there much satisfaction in retail selling? Now, I'd guess dressing the window provides you personally with some satisfaction; I don't know why, it just seems that way to me. On the other hand, while I was in there I noticed all those old ladies. I'd imagine retail selling involves a certain amount of loss of dignity; anyhow, I'd guess that you feel you're lowering yourself when you got involved with those old people and their complaints. That's a guess, too, but I bet I'm right."

It gave Roger an odd feeling to hear such an accurate report on his situation. The man had a real knack.

"The windows are a lot of fun," he said guardedly.

"How about the buying? It seems to me there's the matching of wits, sort of pitting yourself against your jobber. That would appeal to me."

"That, too," Roger said.

At that point, Chic appeared to lose interest. He returned to his interior world.

"Gregg," Roger said. "We're going to have to get started." His son had begun tugging at a piece of lumber, wanting to set it up as part of the hut's roof. Walking in that direction, Roger said to the two Bonner boys, "It's about time."

Both boys ignored him; they continued with their labor.

Liz scrambled up from her bath towel and came over beside them. Her bare arms and shoulders sparkled, and he saw how far down the top of her swimsuit had slipped. Her left breast, full and smooth, was all but exposed. "They're mad at me," she said. "Because I'm not going." She tugged up the strap of her swimsuit.

"Oh," he said. Obviously the boys were sore at him, too. They pretended neither he nor Gregg was anywhere about. "That's too bad," he said, glancing at her, uncertain of himself.

Chic said, "Snap out of it, fellows. Go get dressed and hop into the car."

"Yes sir," Walt said in a grumbling voice. He threw down his lumber and shuffled off. Jerry accompanied him.

To her husband, Liz said, "What'll we do? Is it serious?"

"They'll get over it," Chic said.

"Look at it from their point of view," Liz said. "I don't blame them."

Chic said nothing.

"I'm going along," Liz said.

"They're old enough to go up without you," Chic said stolidly. "You manufacture a dependence that doesn't exist. That's one reason why this business of splitting up the driving appeals to me. When I was twelve I'd rather have walked the whole distance than show up with my mother. Let them go up a couple of times without you and they'll get along fine after that." He turned to Roger. "Isn't that so?"

"Leave me out of it," he said.

"Don't you think a twelve-year-old boy is old enough to go places without his mother?"

The back door slammed; Jerry and Walt reappeared, fully dressed.

"Why do you want your mother along?" Chic asked them.

They muttered and hung their heads.

"Go get in the car," Chic ordered them. "Sit there until it's time to go."

The boys slow-poked off in the direction of the car.

"Let me go this time," Liz said. "I'll drive up and Roger can drive going back."

"You just can't let those kids out of your sight," Chic said. "I'm surprised you sent them up there at all."

"I'll go change," Liz said. Snatching up the bath towel she disappeared into the house.

"It gets me down," Chic said to Roger. "What about Virginia? She impressed me as a sensible woman. She doesn't coddle your boy, does she?"

"It varies," he said, not wanting to get into it.

"Just between you and I," Chic said, "don't repeat this, but you know, Liz plays it by ear. She has no rules; she treats them according to mood."

"Come on, Gregg," Roger said to his son. "Put on your clothes and go get into the car with Jerry and Walter." Taking his boy by the arm he guided him over to his shirt and shoes and socks. Standing by him he prodded him along, keeping him from stringing it out, and then sent him off along the path by the side of the house.

Chic Bonner said, "You don't let your tongue wag, do you Lindahl?" He looked at Roger with resigned respect. "I guess if you're going to operate a business you have to be able to do that."

Time passed. Neither of them spoke. Finally, from within the house, Liz called, "I'm ready. I guess we can go."

"Don't put me on the spot like that," Roger said to Chic.

"You're right," Chic said. He sounded chastened. "I don't have a sense about things like that. Have a good trip. If the boys give you any trouble, smack them down. You have my permission; otherwise you won't be able to handle them."

Going around the side of the house, Roger came out onto the front lawn. Gregg and the two Bonner boys had got into the Oldsmobile; they glared at one another and then all three of them looked out and glared at him. But he did not bother to worry about that. I have other things on my mind, he thought.

The door of the house opened and Liz Bonner came down the path, her coat over her arm, her purse swinging by its strap. She had changed to a starched, striped shirt and flowered skirt. "Are you going to make remarks about my driving?" she said. "Oh, it's your car," she said in dismay. "Are we going in your car?"

"Makes it even," he said.

"Can I drive your car?" Hesitantly, she peeped inside. The three boys stirred somewhat; both Jerry and Walt began to perk up as they realized she would be coming along. "What kind of a shift does it have?"

"Automatic shift," he said. "You won't have any trouble."

"You drive up," she begged.

"Okay," he said, holding the car door open for her.

She got in; he slammed the door and walked around to the driver's side.

Here she is, the voices said in his ear. They no longer hummed; they spoke. But what did it mean? Anything? Nothing? He did not know; he could not tell.

13

Fixing dinner, her hands buried in the egg and mustard and bread and onion and ground beef that would become the meat loaf, Virginia heard a man's steps on the front porch. He's home, she said to herself. But then the doorbell rang and she underwent a tremor of fright; a vision of highway patrolmen formed before her, notification of the catastrophe in the mountains between Ojai and Los Angeles.

She wiped her hands with a paper towel and ran through the house to open the front door.

On the porch stood Chic Bonner, with a flat packet under his arm. "Hello, Virginia," he said docilely.

"He's not back," she said. "Did something happen?"

"Not that I know of," Chic said, with his sturdy calm.

"Shouldn't he be back?"

Raising his arm he held his wristwatch up to the light. "No, not necessarily. Liz usually never got the thing tied up until six or seven." Lowering his arm he proceeded into the house, a steady moving-forward that brought him deep into the living room. At the coffee table he put down his packet; he removed his coat, and Virginia found herself closing the door and coming after him to accept the coat.

"You startled me," she said, taken aback by his entry into her house. He seemed to consider himself welcome; he did not go into an explanation or apology, or make any attempt to find out what she was doing, if she had company or if she was busy, or even if she was willing to have him come in and lay down his packet on the table.

"Ahhh," he said, sinking down on the chair that faced the fireplace. "Say listen," he said. "Go on with what you're doing. I can talk while you work."

"I was fixing dinner," she said, uncertain as to what she should do.

He accepted her statement. "Go ahead. You know, I think your husband's smarter than I am. I brought over some stuff I want him to see." His tone was melancholy.

"Excuse me," Virginia said. "I'll go on with what I was doing." She went into the kitchen and resumed her kneading of the meat loaf ingredients; she poured the milk in and began stirring with a wooden ladle. In the living room Chic Bonner occupied himself with his packet. She could hear him opening it: once she glanced behind her and saw that he had put out a row of manila sheets the length of the table. His approach had a thoroughness and silence to it that reminded her of the activity of provident mammals, those that set about collecting materials for winter. Chic surveyed things and saw where they would be ten years from now. He was unimpressed by the present.

"You have a second?" Chic said.

"Not right now," she said, adding salt to the meat loaf; she had almost forgotten it.

He entered the kitchen. Immediately his size became evident; just by standing there he made it impossible for her to get from one side of the kitchen to the other. He had planted himself, and now he watched her go about her work.

"Let me ask you," he said, "if you don't mind me talking to you while you're working. What does that store of his gross in a year?"

She did not know. "You'll have to ask him."

"I imagine his mark-up runs between twenty-five and forty percent. How many salaries does he pay? Can I assume he draws a regular salary out of the gross—it shows on the books like any other salary, is that right?"

"You better ask him," she said, pushing the meat loaf pan into the oven.

Chic said, "Let's see. He's got a repairman. And that salesman. Anybody else?"

"No," she said.

"He has his bookkeeping done outside?"

"That's right."

"Do you ever help out? Say, at Christmas time?"

"I go down at Christmas," she said. "I answer the phone and wait on people. And he hires a boy to drive the truck and make deliveries."

He noted that. "It's actually a small operation. Do you have any idea—just a general idea—what he's got tied up in it?"

"No," she said.

After that he merely stood.

"Would you like anything to drink?" she asked.

"All right," he said.

"What, then? Coffee? Wine? Beer? There's some Bourbon in the pantry."

"Beer is fine," Chic said.

She opened a can of beer and poured him a glass, which he accepted and drank and then put down on the table.

"I wanted to discuss this with you first," he said. "I want to be certain of his reaction before I broach it with him. He's the kind of person that could turn it down flat. He makes up his mind and does what he feels is right. And then nobody can change his mind. That's probably why he's been able to build up a successful retail business."

"What do you want to broach with him?"

Chic said, "How do you feel he'd respond to the notion of expanding his place? Come on into the other room, so I can show you my designs. Come on." He moved off, back into the living room, and she went along, curious and feeling as she did when some powerful insurance salesman began to unlimber his charts and graphs and predictions, his representations of the future.

Here, on the table, Chic had spread out his respectable calculations. She bent down, drying her hands on her apron, and at the sight of the sketches she was dumfounded. The sketches had a professional touch, like illustrations she had noticed in the newspaper from time to time of proposed public buildings. One sketch showed a long, low storefront, a horizontal broken by a perpendicular sign. Another showed a counter arrangement. The big, slow man had a tangible genius.

"His counters are bad," Chic said.

"Why?" She was fascinated. To her it was like receiving some exclusive service, an analysis, a test; in college she had taken aptitude tests, intelligence tests—the results had always made her shiver with interest.

"Too close to the door. They intimidate the customer. Customers want to be able to get in freely. Serve themselves, have access to the racks and displays without having to account for themselves." He tapped the sketch. "With the counters by the door, the customer is accosted—or thinks he'll be accosted—as soon as he crosses the threshold. I noticed it as soon as we entered the store. The only plea for a counter in the front is that it cuts down on shoplifting, and it makes it possible sometimes to reduce the staff and have one man double in two jobs—salesman and clerk. Now, if he were operating a grocery store, where there's no real selling, just clerking, and plenty of small merchandise . . . he'd have to have his counters by the door."

"I see." She studied a sketch of lighting. She saw a great deal in what he had laid out before her. Yes, she thought, I see all right. "You must let him look at these," she said.

Without a trace of humor, Chic said, "What do you think he'll say? I thought I'd talk to you first because you know him better than I do. As long as he's tied up to a one-man operation he'll never—"

"What would you do?" she interrupted, catching the drift of it, the real idea under the surface. "Sell your bakery?"

Chic said, "It's not my bakery. I hold a percentage of the stock and I draw out a salary. What I'd do is resign my job there and sell a part of the stock, convert it, and put that in to match what Roger has in inventory and fixtures and so forth."

"Would you work?" she persisted. "You're not talking about a silent partnership, are you?"

"I'd like to try my hand at retail selling."

"You'd be in the store, then."

He nodded.

"These sketches," she said, sitting down on the arm of the couch. "They're for a new store, aren't they? Or are they for remodeling?"

"Either," he said. "A lot would depend on how he feels about his location. That's something he'd know more about. And to remodel, the leases of at least one adjoining store in the building would have to be bought up, preferably the lawn-swing place. That would give the frontage he needs."

Virginia said, "And you're really serious, aren't you?"

On Chic's face was such a sober look that she did not have to hear his answer.

"But you just saw it once," she said. "And you hardly know anything about us."

"It's all in the books," Chic said. "I'll know what I need to know when I can see the books. When I know the yield and the overhead and what he's had to write off and so forth."

To her the idea had begun to sound fabulous. Going to the phone, she said, "Can I call my mother and talk to her?"

"If you want," Chic said. He began to rearrange the sketches, preparing them for Roger.

The phone buzzed in her ear, and then she heard her mother's dry voice. "Hi," Virginia said. "Say, listen. How about coming over here awhile? There's something I think you'd get a kick out of."

"Well, you could come and get me," Marion said tartly. "That would give me time to do a few things I have to get done."

"Just a second." Turning to Chic, she said, "Can we go pick her up in your station wagon?"

"Certainly," Chic said, bending over his sketches.

"We'll come and get you, then," Virginia said. "In about ten minutes."

"What is it?" Marion said. "Why don't you tell me?"

"You'll see," she said. "Good-bye. We'll be over in ten minutes." She hung up.

"Yes," Chic said, "I'd like to get her view, too. She'd probably be able to help me get a line on his reaction."

As she got her coat, Virginia said, "Why didn't you bring Liz?"

Chic said, "At the last moment she got nervous and had to go along."

"Up to the school?" It surprised her. "Did they both go?"

"Yes, both of them. She was worried about the boys. They didn't cotton up to the idea of riding with a stranger. She's always been the one who's taken them in the past."

Oh no, Virginia thought to herself, wanting to laugh out loud. Four and a half hours of listening to Liz Bonner's conversation. Poor Roger.

"I see you smiling," Chic said.

"I was just thinking back," she said, making up a more politic explanation. "Roger had this big theory about making the driving efficient—you'd do it on Friday and we'd do it on Sunday, and now they're both going up together."

14

When they arrived at the school—at three-thirty in the afternoon—all three boys awoke from their lethargy and began talking in grandiose terms. As soon as Roger had shut off the engine the boys spilled from the car, onto the dusty ground. Walter and Jerry set off at a trot, in the direction of the main building; Gregg remained behind, looking to his father to tell him what to do.

"I should take him inside," Roger said to Liz Bonner. "Shouldn't I? Or what?"

Liz, still seated in the car, said, "Yes, let's go in." Neither she nor Roger had said much during the trip. They had both watched the countryside, commented on the scenes that passed; after the car had left the mountains, Liz had kicked off her shoes and curled up on the seat to nap.

"Are you coming?" Roger said. He stepped out, stiffly, and came around to her side of the car. Both his legs felt as if they had knots in them, and his head ached. After Liz had gone to sleep he had turned on the car radio and tuned to crime and humor programs for the boys. By the time they had reached the school, none of them even cared to listen. The trip was a real grind, he realized. No joke about that. He was relieved that he did not have to take the wheel going back. The traffic on Highway 99 would be terrific.

Lowering her feet to the ground, Liz straightened laboriously to a standing position. "Mind if I go in like this?" she said to him, stretching her arms. She had left her shoes on the floor of the car. "They won't care; they're used to me." She picked up her purse and started after the boys.

"It's good to get out," he said, keeping up with her.

"Did I snore?"

"No," he said, startled.

"Chic says sometimes when I go to sleep in the car I snore. Have you got a cigarette?"

He gave her his cigarettes and then lit a match for her; both of them halted and stood with their hands shielding the match. A late-afternoon wind had appeared; Liz's long skirt pressed against her legs, and as she stepped away with her cigarette a gust of wind untied her hair and spread it in a sheet across her face. Holding her cigarette away from her she turned aside, throwing her hair back.

"Will they be given dinner?" Roger asked her.

"Yes," she said, "at six. That's why Edna makes us all pop up before then with the poor little prisoners."

Gregg, slowing ahead of them, said, "Daddy, when will you and Mommy come back?"

"Next Friday," he said.

"Oh I see," Gregg said. Hanging back, he drooped and scuffed at the dirt beneath his feet.

"What do you see?" Liz said, catching the boy around the waist and propelling him up and forward; Gregg stumbled and she hugged him against her. Giggling, he struggled. Liz let him go and he raced off, circled her and Roger, and came rushing back with his arms out. "Take it easy," Liz said, fending him off. She gave Roger a breathless smile.

"Don't get burned on her cigarette," Roger said to his son.

"He won't get burned," Liz said, holding her cigarette high. "You worry too much. And suppose he does get burned. Look." She brought her bare wrist close to Roger's eyes. "See?"

He saw a white scar. Her skin was warm and smooth as he took hold to see better. Both of them stopped walking.

"Let me see!" Gregg yelled. Ahead of them, the two Bonner boys had disappeared onto the terrace of the building; they knew their way.

"The little boy down the street did that to me," Liz said. "With the head of a match. I bet him I wouldn't pull away. I was in love with him."

"Did you?"

She said, "You bet your life I did. I ran all the way home screaming. I told my father, and he went down the street and told Eddie Tarski's father, and he whipped Eddie half to death. I didn't tell them it was my idea."

"How old were you?"

"Eight. I had no stamina." She kicked a stone; it rolled to one side of the path. "That was in Soledad. Have you ever been to Soledad?"

"No," he said.

"It's up in the Salinas Valley. Right on the S.P. track. There's a minimum-security prison near there . . . we used to hang around and kid with the prisoners; they had them in the fields. We used to put pennies on the train track. They came out flat. I still have one . . . I carry it around for good luck."

Gregg said, "Didn't it make the train go off the track?"

Coming to the steps, they started up. "How soon do you want to head back?" Roger said to Liz. He hoped she wanted to stay awhile; he was counting on it.

"Any time," Liz said.

"I'd like to stick around awhile," he said. "I like it here. I was born on a farm."

"Oh you were?"

"In Arkansas."

"This isn't like a farm," she said, with certitude. "There's no crops, no beef herds or sheep; it doesn't do anything except keep the little prisoners chained up. Does it remind you of a farm? Why?"

"The animals."

"What animals?" She looked at him blankly.

"The horses," he said. "The rabbits."

"Oh." She seemed to remember. "That's right. I pay five dollars a month so Jerry and Walter can learn to ride. Or maybe it's five dollars for the laundry."

At that moment Mr. Van Ecke, the arithmetic teacher, in tie, sweater, and khaki shorts, came by and noticed them. "Hi, Liz," he said. "Hello there, Mr. Lindahl. You finally got it all straightened out, did you?"

"Pretty well," Roger said.

Van Ecke fell in beside them. "Where's the chief baker, Liz? Home with his loaves?"

She wrinkled her nose at him.

On the terrace, at the doorway of the building, the two Bonner boys had met a group of their compatriots. Gregg avoided them, conscious of his inferiority. Without appearing to do so, he edged away until he stood with Liz and his father and Mr. Van Ecke.

"Dad," he said, "you want to see my room where I live with the other boys?"

"Okay," Roger said. "Lead on."

"I'll meet you here," Liz said to him. "Or if something goes wrong, I'll meet you at the car. Don't leave without me." She called after him, "Even if you can't find me, I'm still here somewhere."

Led by his son, Roger ascended to the small boys' dorm, and was shown the clean, plain, large room in which the six small boys slept in three double bunk units. One of the dressers had Gregg's name pasted on it, and on top lay a heap of Gregg's comic books and Little Golden Books.

"Fine," Roger said, unable to be interested.

"Would you like to meet Billy, Dad?" Billy was his son's new friend. Over the weekend Gregg had rattled on about him and about their doings. "I think he's downstairs. Or maybe he's across the hall. I think he's across the hall, Dad."

Roger said. "I think he's downstairs." He prodded his son back down the stairs to the lobby of the building.

Outside, on the railing of the terrace, Liz perched by herself, smoking the cigarette that he had given her. When she recognized him and Gregg she hopped down, smiling.

"Where's Van Ecke?" Roger said.

"Off on his chores."

"Where're Jerry and Walter?"

"Off helping some kid build a shortwave receiver. You should go over there; that's your specialty. Can't you do that? Didn't you build shortwave receivers when you were a kid?"

"A few," he said.

"You could really impress them," Liz said. Ducking down pursing her lips, she said to Gregg, "Does your father impress you by being able to build shortwave receivers?" She arose, so close to Roger that he had to step back to avoid the sweep of her hair. "Boy," she sighed. "You really have Chic buffaloed. The way he has it figured is that you're the only one who isn't afraid of Edna Alt—" She lowered her voice. "And who has the guts to walk out of here not impressed. He's really afraid of her. I am, too."

"She's tough," Roger said.

"Down on the field," Liz said, "when we met you and you grabbed Gregg and hustled him off—Chic mulled over all that—first he thought you were mad at us; so did I. We both thought we said something, or the boys picked on Gregg. You know. I guess I told you." She eyed him pensively. "Then when he found out that you got your check back from Edna, he worried that around, and he came up with the announcement that you saw through her. All the way home he talked about that. 'That Lindahl knows his own mind.' 'Lindahl doesn't lick up any of that line she puts out.' "

"What did he think when he found out we'd put Gregg back in the school?"

"Oh, he pondered that, too. Finally—I was vacuuming the living room—he came in and said, 'Lindahl made his point. He had to show the old—whatever—that it was going to be on his terms. It was a matter of principle with him.' And so on. And he asked me if I knew what kind of work you did. I told him I thought Edna said you were in the shirt business."

"Great," Roger said.

Liz said, "He really went overboard about your store."

"I'm glad he liked it." He could see letting the topic of her husband drop. As far as he was concerned, Chic was a large blur, and he wanted to be the same to him, too.

Voices drifted along the terrace to them, Mrs. Alt's voice and those of a man and woman. Presently Mrs. Alt appeared, accompanied by a young well-dressed couple. Trailing behind them came a timid, rabbity-looking girl, perhaps six years old, in a starched dress with embroidered red and yellow roses. Her face had puffed from crying.

Liz, in a low voice, said in Roger's ear, "How would you like to be sent up here to this penal institution?"

"Depends," he said.

"You wouldn't like it."

Roger said, "You talked me into this thing, for Gregg."

"I did?" She stared at him.

"When you cornered me down in Ojai."

"O-*hy*," she corrected.

"You persuaded me to do it." He saw what Virginia meant, all right.

Her forehead wrinkled. "I thought you were mad at us; I was trying to apologize."

Mrs. Alt and the couple and the rabbity-looking child moved along the terrace in their direction. Seeing them, Mrs. Alt paused in her conversation and nodded. "Hello, Liz. Hello, Mr. Lindahl."

Gregg said, "Hello, Mrs. Ant."

The young couple smiled. They looked worn out by the ordeal of putting their child into a new school.

"Mr. and Mrs. Mines," Mrs. Alt said, "I'd like you to meet Mr.—" The slightest hestitation, a narrowing of her brows so that her eyes became brighter, and then she finished, "Mr. Lindahl and Mrs. Bonner. And this young man is Gregg Lindahl, Mr. Lindahl's son. I think Gregg and Joanne might very well be in several classes together."

They all said hello and shook hands. The two groups commingled for an interval.

Gregg said to the Mines, "One day I fell out of the window where I was; everybody ran to see if I hurt myself. I think that was just yesterday."

Cordially, Mrs. Mines said, "Were you hurt?"

"No," Gregg said. "But everybody thought I was hurt."

To Liz, Mrs. Mines said, "How long has your little boy been in school up here?"

"He's not my little boy," Liz said. "I never saw him before in my life."

For some obscure reason, that struck Mr. Mines as funny. Laughing, he said, "I know just how you feel."

"It's true," Liz protested, to everyone in general. "I'm no relation to him. I have two boys—where the hell did they go?" To Roger, she said, "Did you see where Jerry and Walter went?" She seemed absolutely unable to cope with the situation.

Mrs. Alt, in her energetic fashion, said to Liz, "Come on now, Liz. You know perfectly well you have seen Gregg before in your life. You drove up here with him." To the Mines, Mrs. Alt explained, "With Liz we sometimes wonder who's the parent and who's the child."

The Mines smiled, and then they and their child and Mrs. Alt continued on, along the terrace and into the building.

With gloom, Liz said to Roger, "Why did I say that? Do you know?"

"It's okay," he said. Like Mr. Mines, he, too, saw it as funny.

"I must be crazy," Liz said in a despairing voice. She put her arm around Gregg and patted him. "I mean—well, look at how awkward it was. Those people—what was their name?—naturally thought we were married and Gregg was my son. It got me upset as hell. Even Edna Alt started to introduce us as Mr. and Mrs. something."

"She salvaged the situation," Roger said.

"I guess now she's sore at me."

"Nobody's sore at you," Roger said

"I get so mad at myself," Liz said. "Gregg," she said, "I didn't mean that."

Obviously, Gregg had not followed the interchange. He knew Liz was not his mother; he had paid no attention.

"Gregg hates me," Liz said. Suddenly she leaned against Roger and rested her head against his shoulder. Her hair brushed his face; it scratched at him, and he smelled the warm, fragrant presence of the woman. "Can I rest on your shoulder?" she asked him.

"Sure," he said.

Then, just as suddenly, she whisked herself away and started off along the terrace. "We better get started back to town. It's worse going back; the traffic is enough to kill you. I forgot about that, or I wouldn't have asked you to drive going back. I can drive both ways, if you want; I don't feel tired."

"You didn't drive up," he said. "I did; remember?"

"No," she said, "I think I drove up." All at once she was indignant. "I know I did; you're supposed to drive back. Wasn't that the agreement?"

"I'm happy to do it," he said. At that she subsided and became doubtful. "It's okay," he said. He did not want to leave the school; that was what he was thinking of. But he realized that she was right about one thing; the longer they waited the worse the road conditions would be.

"I'll go inside to the powder room," Liz said, "while you're saying good-bye to Gregg." She turned back towards the doorway and then halted, saying, "Suppose I meet Mrs. Alt and those people again."

"Go on," he said. "Don't worry about that."

She looked at him uncertainly, depending on him.

"Honest," he said.

"Okay." She nodded and continued on into the lobby.

On the drive back through the Ojai Valley, Liz said, "Your wife is a wonderful woman. Really extraordinary. We talked and talked; I don't know when I've ever been so conscious of being in contact with a person who seemed so aware of what's going on in the world." She glanced at him.

"That's true," he said.

"She told me about her dancing. She's going to let me watch one of her lessons she gives. She explained about the therapy part . . . I don't understand that—I told her I didn't. She's very patient. I mean, it didn't seem to bother her that I didn't have the background to follow it. It seems to me she likes me. I had that feeling. When I called her Saturday morning she got all enthusiastic about going shopping; when Chic said something about wanting to see your store sometime, Virginia right away said we should go down and drop in for a couple of minutes. Mrs. Watson is her mother, isn't she? Not your mother. I like her, too. I really think you're very lucky to have a wife like that. She has the most beautiful muscular legs. Is that because of her dancing? She dresses a lot better than most of the women I know. When we were shopping I got her to pick out a couple of dresses for me."

"Good," he said.

"And Gregg is darling. You're really lucky, Roger. To have a wife and a child like that, and a store like you have. Even your mother-in-law is nice. You ought to be glad. Are you glad? Do you appreciate what sort of wonderful woman Virginia is? Even Edna Alt likes her. That's something."

Roger said, "I don't think Mrs. Alt likes Virginia. They tangled the minute they met."

"No," Liz said, with insistence. "I know Edna likes her. Where would you get an idea like that? What do you mean, they tangled?"

"That's what Virginia said."

"I can't imagine Virginia quarrelling with anybody. She's so bright and merry; she's always in a good mood, isn't she? Is that because she comes from Washington, D.C.? She told me about meeting you there during the war. She was working as a nurse and you had been discharged because of your wounds." Swiveling around beside him, she rested her arms on the back of the seat and stared exhaustively at him. "Where were you wounded? Did she take care of you? I can see Virginia as a nurse—she's just the type to care for the wounded soldiers. I remember during the war—you know what I did? You won't believe it. All I contributed to the war effort was that during the war I worked as a stenographer at the Bonny Bonner Bread plant, in Los Angeles, California. I met Chic before that—we were already married. What I mean is, when the men all got drafted I went to work to help out. Jerry was born in 1940 and Walter was born in 1941, in the middle of the summer. I met Chic in 1938. We had moved to L.A. My father was a doctor. He still is . . . only he's retired now. We've been married fourteen years. God, it doesn't seem possible."

To himself, Roger thought, This is another now-or-never moment.

"Doesn't it feel strange?" Liz said. "Without the boys? The car's so empty."

"Yes," he said. He could feel his hands sweating on the steering wheel; the surface beneath his fingers felt like glass. His nervous tension had increased, and as a result he found himself driving too fast. Liz noticed.

"You really drive this car," she said.

"I better slow down." He took his foot off the gas; the car lost momentum and began to glide.

"Now we're just coasting," Liz said.

He said in as clear a voice as possible, "How late is it? Do we really have to hurry?"

Liz did not appear to hear him. Leaning against the back of the seat, she had turned her attention on something behind him. "Look," she said. "Walter left his pocket telescope in the car; it must have fallen out of his pocket."

"Want me to stop?"

"Why?"

"So you can go around and get it."

"I'll get it later," she said. "Remind me. I sent away for that, for him. You know what it cost? Fifty cents and some Swan soap wrappers or something; I forget. It works pretty well."

"How late is it?" he said.

"I don't know. Don't you have a watch?"

"Do we have time to stop anywhere?"

"Why? What for?"

"Just stop," he said, feeling himself to be clumsy and foundering. Her absentness made him irritable.

"I don't want to stop."

He said, "I do."

"Suit yourself." She settled back, away from him, and seemed to be thinking. "You're driving," she said vaguely. "It's your car."

Ahead of them the road started up into the mountains. The land on each side was overgrown and poor. No houses or signs could be seen anywhere.

"There's a man hitchhiking," Liz said. At the side of the road a Mexican, a farm laborer with his coat draped over his back, a straw hat on his head, stuck his thumb toward them and smiled hopefully. "Give him a ride," Liz said. "I always give them a ride over the mountain range; otherwise they have to walk all the way back—they're going to Santa Paula."

He did not stop. The Mexican dwindled behind them; in the rearview mirror Roger saw the man's face sag and became hostile. Then the rocky slope and heaped bushes interfered with the image.

"Don't you give people who're hitchhiking rides?" Liz asked, not accusingly, but with concern.

"Too risky," he said.

"Is it? Maybe you're right. But I feel so sinful shooting by without picking them up—they don't have anything but what they're wearing, and here we are with money to send our kids to a private boarding school, and you own a store, and Chic has stock in the bread company, and we both have houses and everything we want. It doesn't seem fair. But maybe you're right." She made herself comfortable, her knees drawn up, her elbows stuck out so that her thumbs supported her chin.

At each turn in the road a shoulder had been cleared overlooking the Valley; he saw cars that had pulled off the road to take advantage of the rutted, bumpy parking areas.

"Not here," Liz said.

By that, she could have meant anything. "Why not?" he said, wanting to know, determined to pin her down.

She said, in a tight, agonized voice, "Listen, I'm not a teenager."

"What do you mean?" he demanded.

"I mean—I think you're thinking something dumb. Parking on the shoulder and smooching. Roger, I'm thirty-four years old, I've been married fourteen years. And you're married. Don't you think in fourteen years I've had enough—sex? I can't be tempted with that; I'm not going to sneak off with you to a motel or something." She gazed at him starkly.

At last he managed to say, "Of course not."

Neither of them said anything, then, until they had come out of the mountains on the Santa Paula side. Liz put on the car radio and tuned in a string orchestra.

"Do you like classical music?" she said. "Chic hates it."

He kept his eyes on the road. Trees grew on both sides. The car passed houses and narrow side roads. The countryside was fertile, flat, and well-tended.

"Don't be sore at me," Liz said.

"I'm not." But even to him, in his own ears, he sounded as sore and disappointed as a child. As a teenager.

Liz said, "I won't deny it would be nice to get off somewhere and make mad, passionate love. But I'm not going to do it. I find you very attractive. I have from the start, since I first saw you. You were up on the hill by the football field and we saw you and Mrs. Mc-Givern wondered who you were. But—for one thing I'm scared of Virginia and your mother."

"Mother-in-law," he said.

"And I'm scared of Chic."

"So am I," he agreed.

"I wanted to make this drive with you. I came along on purpose: I told Chic I was worried about the boys. All the way up I thought about the drive back, after we left off the boys, your boy and my boys."

He said nothing.

"What time is it?" Shivering, she took hold of his sleeve and drew it back to see his wristwatch. "Four-thirty. We could pull off the road for about an hour. No longer, though."

"And do what?"

Liz said, "I'll let you buy me a drink."

"Okay," he said.

"When we get to Santa Paula, turn right. There's a café and bar along the road. It's quiet. Nobody would know us, there. It's back from the road . . . not one of those highway places." Suddenly she scrambled around on the seat; her fingers dug behind him and she wrapped her arm around him. "Can you drive like this?" she said.

"Maybe I better not."

She drew away. "Roger," she said, "you don't tell everything to your wife, do you? You can keep some things secret if they're important . . . if they ought to be kept secret."

"Sure," he said.

On her face was concern, an ambivalent pall. "This could be a hell of a mistake I'm making. Isn't this what you've had on your mind? I want to be positive. Isn't this why you came over to the house the other night? You fixed this up on purpose, didn't you? Tell me; I want to hear you say it."

"Yes," he said. He put it as it was: a commitment.

"I feel nervous," she said. "And it seems hopeless when you start thinking about it. Maybe I can see you an hour or so, now and then . . . what good is that?"

"It's something."

"God," she said, with a sigh. "You know, my kids won't have anything to do with your little boy; he's too young for them. It's sort of strange. Here you and I are. We both have kids; they know one another. What were you doing fourteen years ago, in 1938?"

"I was on WPA." Roger said.

Liz laughed. "No kidding. That seems funny to me. So bizarre." Pulling back from him, she shaded her eyes to peer ahead down the road. "You know, I really want a drink. That's how I discovered this place. I stopped by myself a couple of times. I get lonely. All Chic does is sit around preparing his business charts. You're not like that, are you? You care about something besides your business. He reads those business trade journals—in college he had a business ad major. I majored in French."

He drove on, looking for the cut-off that led to the bar.

"Slow down," Liz said. "It's pretty soon."

He reached the intersection of the two highways and made a right turn, toward the Coast. Presently they drove by a gas station and stores.

A motel appeared ahead, modern and attractive. Both she and Roger watched the motel.

"I've changed my mind," Liz said suddenly. "Stop. Why can't we go in there? Who would know?"

"Nobody," he said, trying to see what was really there and not what crowded up into his mind from his own thoughts, hopes, imagination. But it all had gone in the direction of reality. It was not his imagination. Not any longer.

"It looks clean," Liz said, shading her eyes with her hand. "Doesn't it? Not run-down. Don't you think so?"

He brought the car up onto the gravel and stopped, with the motor running. "Whatever you want," he said. They both sat. He rubbed the perspiration from his hands. "Well?" he said.

"Let's go in," Liz decided. She opened the car door and hopped out, onto the gravel. The late-afternoon wind fluttered her long skirt about her; she held onto it and reached up to protect her hair. "Will you talk to them?" she said. "I'm scared to. I'll leave it up to you. I just want to get indoors where I can throw myself down and rest and be with you."

While he made the arrangements at the motel office, she drove the car through the ivy and lattice arch, into the court where the cabins were.

"You open the door," she said, when they had gone up onto the porch of their cabin. Without warning she put her arms around him and kissed him; she pressed her mouth against his with such force that he felt the impact of her teeth. "I'm really scared, Roger," she said, lifting her face up with her mouth at his ear. "But I want to do it. How long do we have? An hour? That's not very long."

An unromantic notion appeared in the uppermost part of his mind. "What about precautions?"

Liz said, "I put on my diaphragm back at the school." She passed on indoors, ahead of him, and tossed her purse down in a chair. "Remember, when I left you, just before we got into the car. It's good for a couple of hours yet."

Reaching behind her, she unhooked the snaps of her skirt. He saw, with surprise, that she had on nothing under it, and when she took off her striped shirt he saw that she had on nothing under that, either.

"I never wear underclothes," she explained. She glided toward him and put her cool, small hands to his shoulders. "I don't know why. I just don't like to. I want to be able to feel the sun."

In proof of that, she insisted on having the shades of the cabin up; she even had him move the bed so that the dimming sunlight streamed down on them. It warmed both of them as long as they were there.

15

They got back to San Fernando after sundown. The streetlights had been put on, and the neon signs; the streets were dark as Roger searched for the house.

"It's in the next block," Liz said. "What time is it?"

"Six-forty," he said.

"It's not very late. I usually get home this late. If he says anything I'll tell him about Mr. and Mrs. Mines and Mrs. Alt asking me to tell them about the school so they'd put their daughter in it." Beside him, she withdrew to study; she pressed her hands to her face, squinted, and then said to him, "I think you better come in with me. It would be natural, wouldn't it? Just for a second. Then say something about having to get right home for dinner. But don't stay."

From the time they had left the motel, Liz had churned the difficulties into every combination. She had insisted that they work out a complete account together, covering the interval from the moment they left the school to this moment, when they drove up before her house.

But she was animated and cheerful; she fidgeted about in the car, clung to him as he drove, commented on everything they saw along the road, asked him questions about himself, how many girls he had been in love with, how long he and Virginia had been married, was this the first time he had done a thing like this. . . .

"Roger," she said, "you know what this is? Adultery!" She clapped her hands to her cheeks in horror.

"Take it easy," he said, feeling deep affection for her, even for her confusion and fragmented recall.

"Isn't it?" she demanded, sitting up on her knees so that she was above him. "It's a crime; it's against the law. Oh my God, suppose people found out—like Edna Alt. Everybody up at the school." She really did look stricken; her face was pale and her eyes grew larger and darker.

"Don't worry about it," he said. "They won't know unless one of us tells them."

"I might blurt it out!"

He had to concede, to himself at least, that she might very well. "You won't," he said, however. But the idea did not increase his own sense of security. He could imagine her suddenly, on the spur of the moment, declaring to Chic, "I have to tell you—on the trip back from Ojai, Roger and I stopped at a motel and went to bed together."

"I feel so wicked," Liz said. "I feel as if I've betrayed my two boys and Chic and Edna and everybody. How do you feel?"

"I feel swell," he said, truthfully.

"You don't regret it?"

"No," he said.

"Neither do I." She subsided beside him, pressing against him, her arms around him. Then she leaped back. "We're almost there. It's past that telephone pole. Where's the station wagon?" At once she was alert. "It's gone. And I don't see any lights. Something's happened. Maybe he drove out looking for us. Do you suppose? My God, could he have followed us or something? It's possible; he might do that."

Roger parked the car across the street from the Bonner house. It did look dark and deserted.

"Come in with me," Liz said, clutching at him. "I'm scared. If anything happens I don't want to have to face it alone."

He opened the car door and assisted her out.

"Don't say anything to me," she said in a low voice. "Or look at me—you know. Don't make any signs or anything. You understand, don't you?"

Closing the car door he walked with Liz across the street to her house. Pinned on the front door was a typewritten note; she tore it down, then got her key from her purse, unlocked and opened the door, and switched on the porch light in order to see.

"Shit," she said.

"What is it?"

"He's over at your place." She handed him the note, groaning. "Now what? Oh God, let's not go there. See, he wants you to drive me over there. I'm not going over there; I'm not going to face your wife. All she'll have to do is take one look at me; she'll know."

"We better go over," he said. "You better come along."

"Can't you go and tell them I have a headache or something?"

He considered. "That might make them wonder."

Suddenly Liz bolted into the house. From the depths of the darkness she called back urgently, "I'm going to take a bath and change my clothes. No, I can't take a bath; it has to stay in at least six hours. Anyhow I'm going to change my clothes. Come on inside. Do you think we ought to telephone them? Oh Christ, suppose he comes back and finds you in here and me in the bedroom changing my clothes—" From the bedroom she burst forth; she had already taken off her shirt. "What'll he think? He'll kill both of us, me first." Buttoning her shirt around her as fast as possible, she said, "Let's go; let's get out of here. It'd be the end if he found us here together."

Roger put her into the car and drove to his own house.

"Roger," she said, as they made the last turn before his street, "are you in love with me, do you think? What a problem it is. Fourteen years . . . how long have you been married? You told me, but I forget what you said."

"A little under nine years," he answered.

"Chic and I were married five years before you and Virginia had even got married. We were married before you even met her, weren't we?"

"I guess so," he said.

"Jerry and Walter were in kindergarten when you got married. They were born before you met Virginia." She sighed. "What a mess. How'll we ever get it straightened out? No wonder people are against adultery; look at all the complications. Maybe we should just walk in there and tell them. You tell Virginia and I'll tell Chic." She began to laugh. "Or you can tell Chic and I'll take Virginia aside and say to her, 'Virginia, I have something to tell you. Your husband and I stopped off at a motel and went to bed together. What do you think of that?' How would you put it to Chic? What would you say?"

"I don't know," he said, wishing she would stop talking about it.

"It's sort of funny," Liz said. As he parked the car before his house—the living room lights were on and the red Ford station wagon was parked in front—she said, "Let's walk in there and hand them a note. Here, I'll write it out." She dug into her purse, but he stopped her hand. "No?" she said. "It would be sort of funny, in a way. Announce it like that . . . I guess not."

They got out of the car and walked up the path.

"Look," Liz said. "Your car parked right behind ours. It makes me feel funny." In the darkness she reached out, caught hold of his arm, and squeezed him. Then she let him go and skipped on, up the steps, onto the porch. Without knocking or ringing the bell, or waiting for him, she opened the door and flung herself into the house.

"Hi," she called merrily. "Hello, Mrs. Watson. How are you? What's going on?"

Virginia, hearing the front door open, looked up expecting to see Roger; instead, Liz Bonner burst into the house crying in a sharp, gay tone to each of them in the room, to her, to Chic Bonner, to her mother. Then, after Liz, came Roger, looking tired. Liz rushed about the room, her eyes shining; she seemed to be in a kind of trance.

"What's all this?" Liz demanded, seeing the sketches on the table. "Oh my God, did you bring them over? I thought you were kidding." She dropped her coat and purse into an empty chair and then ran over to Virginia, so close to her that her collarbone and breasts bumped against Virginia's arm. "Do you have an aspirin I can take? I have an awful headache. Thank God I didn't have to drive back." To everyone in the room, she said, "It sure was lucky Roger was along. Even so we had to pull off the road awhile. The traffic was terrible."

Virginia went into the kitchen for the Anacin. Liz came right along with her, staying close to her.

"I just love your kitchen," Liz said. "Don't go to any trouble; I don't even need water with it."

"What do you mean? You can't take it without water." She filled a tumbler with water and presented it to Liz, along with the Anacin tin.

"Thanks," Liz said, turning aside to gulp down the tablet. "Ugh," she said. "I can't swallow a pill sometimes when people are watching." Putting the tumbler of water and the tin on the drain-board she seized hold of Virginia. "You're always so good to me," she said, with an imploring expression that Virginia did not see the need for.

"It's just an Anacin," Virginia said, wondering what had got Liz so animated. Her face was strained and she had on no makeup; her hair was disarranged, probably by the wind, and she had about her a dark, musky scent, something like that of cigarettes and fabric and perspiration and deodorant. She looked very pretty and round, and Virginia could not help liking her in spite of her meaningless chatter.

"Are you sore at me?" Liz asked, her mouth hanging partly open. Without waiting for an answer she grabbed Virginia and buried her head in Virginia's neck. "I think so much of you and Roger," she said. "Listen, what is all that stuff Chic's got spread out there in the living room? Is that those drawings for the store? Tell him to go to hell." She broke away from Virginia. "Don't pay any attention to him."

Virginia said, "Liz, you really are a screwball." She did not know whether to laugh or be disgusted.

"Why?" Liz said. "What'd I say?" Then she shrugged and wandered back toward the living room. "I don't think I am. Is that your opinion?"

Virginia said, "Liz, I can't any more follow your thought-processes than I can—" She gestured. "Why don't you go sit down and I'll fix you some coffee? Have you and Roger had anything to eat?"

"No," Liz said, remaining in the hall. She drooped wearily.

"What about some food, then? Come on back in the kitchen."

"No thanks," Liz said. "You're very kind to me. I don't deserve it."

Coming toward them from the living room, Roger said to his wife, "Did you say something about food? We were going to stop and have something to eat, but we got involved in the heavy traffic."

"You look tired," she said. "You both look worn-out."

"What's there to eat?" he said. "What's going on? What's all the pictures?" He had a haggard, rumpled look; his eyes were red-rimmed, probably from the glare. "How come your mother's over?"

"We went and got her," Virginia said. She felt a little in the wrong at having done so; she knew how little her husband liked to come home and find Marion there. "You and Liz sit down here in the kitchen and I'll fix you some soup or something. Liz, look in the refrigerator and the pantry and see what you want; I don't know how hungry you are." To Roger, she said, "Suppose I heat up one of those frozen chicken pies for you?"

"Anything's okay," he said. "Anything hot."

Liz said, "Can I use your bathroom? It's just down here, isn't it?" She disappeared; the bathroom door closed.

Sitting down at the kitchen table, Roger said, "It's good to be home."

"Did she talk the whole way, both ways?"

He gave her an odd look.

"Never mind," Virginia said. She knew what it was like; she had made the trip with Liz, herself.

In the doorway, Chic Bonner materialized with some of his

notepads. "Excuse me," he said to Virginia. "Hi, there, Lindahl. Virginia, where did Liz go?"

"She went in the bathroom," Virginia said. "She'll be right out."

"Thanks," Chic said. He lingered in the kitchen, regarding Roger with his thorough gaze. "We got kind of worried about you."

"It's a grind," Roger said. "Be glad you don't have a license."

From the bathroom came sounds of moving around. Then the bathroom door was unlocked and opened. "Virginia," Liz called.

Virginia went to the bathroom door. "Are you okay?"

"Come on in." Liz sat on the closed toilet, gazing up at her wanly. "What's all that stuff he's doing?" Liz said. "Is he going to talk to Roger about buying into the store?" She rubbed her forehead with the heel of her hand. "You know, Virginia, I really do feel sick. Can I ask you a favor? Can I go lie down for a while?"

"Sure you can," Virginia said. "That's a good idea."

"Thanks," Liz said, coming along with her, from the bathroom and into the bedroom. "Oh," she said, "not on your bed."

"Where, then?" Virginia said.

"I don't know. Whatever you say." Liz sank down on the edge of the bed and folded her hands in her lap. "Gregg's bed? No, I guess that wouldn't do."

"I'll close the door," Virginia said. "If you need me or Chic, call." She started out of the bedroom.

Liz kicked off her shoes and then lay back with her head against the pillow. "Virginia," she said, "I hope you and I will always be good friends. Do you think we will?"

"Why not?" Virginia said, thinking to herself that it was a dismal prospect. And yet, there was that appealing quality in Liz; she showed it especially when she was with her children. It made her feel a little tender toward her. "You go to sleep," she said, and shut the door after her.

"What's the matter with Liz?" Roger said, when she reentered the kitchen.

"Just tired," Virginia said. "Car sick. She'll be okay."

Scowling, he said, "I'm probably responsible." He eyed Chic Bonner.

"No, I don't think so," Chic said. "She has moods like this. After we fight. She's trying to get sympathy from me for the long hard drive. Show me how she's suffered. She just wants somebody to hold her hand."

To Virginia that sounded likely. "How long does it last?" she asked Chic. It fitted Liz.

"Not long. She'll realize I'm not coming in, and she'll get up out of it."

Slumped over in his chair, Roger said nothing. She hadn't seen him so tired in months; he barely followed what was going on around him.

"Did Gregg act glad to get back to the school?" she asked him.

"He showed me his room," Roger said. His response came tardily and it was so vague that she repeated her question, knowing that he had not actually heard. "Yeah," he said. "He was glad. He likes it up there."

Chic said, "Say, Lindahl, come on in the living room for a minute."

Opening his eyes, Roger said, "Why?"

"I've got a few things here I've been showing your wife and mother-in-law Mrs. Watson. I wanted to get their opinion on them, too. They gave me some valuable pointers. I think your reaction was favorable, wasn't it, Virginia?"

"Yes," she said. "In the main it was."

After a pause, Roger said, "What have you got? Pictures?"

"It's about the store," Virginia said.

From the living room, Mrs. Watson said, "Roger, you come on in here, now. We have something to show you."

"What do you mean," Roger said, "it's about the store?"

"I have a few ideas," Chic said, smiling at Virginia, "that I want to discuss with you." Catching the excitement, she smiled back. "Let's all go in there," Chic said.

Roger said, "Look, Chic, Sunday's the only day I have off."

From the living room, Mrs. Watson said, "Roger! Mr. Bonner wants to show you his plans for the store."

"I'm too tired to care," Roger said. "Use your common sense. I have to think about the store six days a week and that's plenty." Removing his glasses, he stuck them in his shirt pocket. He rubbed his eyes, grimaced, and then got up and walked over to the sink.

"I'm sorry," Chic said, looking at Virginia with injury. "I guess I should have realized. I didn't mean to offend him."

Virginia said, "Roger, I'm surprised at you."

"What do you want to do," Roger said, his back to them, "buy into my store?"

"Something like that," Chic said. "But we can talk about it some other time."

"You don't know anything about my store."

"Does he always get mad like this?" Chic asked Virginia. "Lindahl, I really beg your pardon." With dignity, he returned to the living room, and when she looked in she saw him gathering up his designs.

"Don't put them away," her mother said. "Leave them out. If I have to I'll show them to him myself."

"No, mother," Virginia said. "You stay out of this." To her husband she said, "Sit down at the table again and I'll fix the soup for you. Both you and Liz—you're like a couple of children home from an all-day hike."

"I'm tired," he murmured, at the sink.

"I know you are." She kissed him on the cheek; his skin was dry, rough with beard.

At the doorway, Chic said, "We'll be going, Virginia." He had his packet of designs with him, and his coat over his arm.

She made him go back into the living room where she could talk to him. "You can see he's tired. Tomorrow he'll be wondering why he was so cross. Don't think he isn't interested."

"I guess I got carried away," Chic said. He had a diminished manner, now; his voice had ebbed and his enthusiasm was gone. "Should I telephone him or what?" He allowed her to put a sketch into the packet that he had overlooked. "Thanks," he said. "I appreciate your help, Virginia." He gave her that humble look, his look of deflation. Almost whispering, he said, "He carries a lot of weight on his shoulders, doesn't he? You know, sometimes I have to go around to supermarkets and chainstores and talk to them about handling our bread . . . I've had my share of dealings with the public. He isn't the only one who gets tired. Of course he's had more of it than I."

Virginia said, "Chic, I have a favor to ask."

"What is it?" he said, large and tame, but conscious that he had been ill-treated.

"Before you and Liz go, I wish you'd drive my mother home—so Roger won't have to. I don't want him to do any more driving tonight."

"Certainly," Chic said, recovering some of his sense of worth. He set his packet down again. "Is she ready to go, though?"

Virginia turned to her mother. "Do you want Chic to drive you home before he leaves? I'm going to fix Roger something to eat and then we'll probably go to bed early."

"I'd just as soon stay awhile," Mrs. Watson said. "I don't think I'd get in the way—"

"Please," Virginia said.

"All right," Mrs. Watson said, arising. "What did you do with my coat?"

Finding her mother's coat, Virginia sent her and Chic out of the house. Then she returned to the kitchen. Roger again had seated himself at the table.

"Chic's driving Marion home," she said, opening the pantry door. "How about cream of chicken soup?"

"Fine," he said dully.

She put on the soup, and then she poked one of the frozen chicken pies into the oven.

"I feel responsible," she said.

"Let it go."

"We all got excited. He really has some good ideas—you know, he's serious; he means it. He's not just fooling around."

"Means what?"

She said, "He wants to go in with you, dear."

At the table, Roger said nothing.

"He likes you," she said.

"I like him."

"He looks up to you. Think what it would mean if he bought in. A new front—maybe even a new store from the ground up." She plugged in the electric coffee pot.

"I guess he's got money to throw around."

"It wouldn't be throwing it around. He knows a good investment. He reads the business reports on television. Do you know what interests him the most? Color TV. He says color TV is going to mean that a retail TV store will have to put three times the amount of money in for the same inventory."

"At least," Roger said.

"He's an investor," Virginia said.

"I guess he is."

She said, "Poor thing, you sound so far away."

"I'll be all right." He fitted his glasses back in place. "How's Liz?"

"Asleep, I suppose. I forgot about her."

"Are you going to take her anything to eat?"

"No, not unless she wakes up and asks for it."

"Go see if she wants anything to eat."

"The heck I will," she said. "If she's hungry she can ask for it. I'm not going to wait on her."

"What a day," Roger said.

After she had served him his soup he devoted himself to eating; he spooned the soup up noisily, and she thought, watching, that he had not eaten this way in years. When she had first met him, he had crouched over his food, lowering his head and swallowing in huge gulps.

Their dinner at her mother's. The first meal, out in Maryland. When he and Marion had met. He had eaten in this relentless fashion, ignoring her, saying nothing.

The doorbell chimed. Drying her hands she hurried to let Chic back in.

"Thanks," he said. As he took off his coat he said. "How does he feel now?"

"Better. He's eating."

They both entered the kitchen. Roger glanced up at Chic. "I apologize," Chic said. "For disturbing you."

"I'm just tired," Roger said. "I'll get over it. Have a cup of coffee."

"You can stay long enough for that," Virginia agreed.

"Thanks," Chic said. He seated himself across from Roger. She poured coffee for both men; Chic drank his as he had drunk the beer. He seemed to appreciate anything, and she liked him; she wondered how he had got mixed up with Liz.

"Liz is asleep," she said. "I didn't want to wake her, so I didn't fix her anything."

"She shouldn't be messing up your bed," Chic said. His reddish face had got on it an expression of contentment. She saw that he enjoyed it here in the kitchen, drinking coffee with her and Roger. In Chic's mind the decision had been made to shelve discussion of business; he accepted Roger's position as final, and now he meant to take things easy until Roger changed his mind. The lack of pressure affected her, too. They did not have to solve it immediately. Roger was right. Sunday evening was not the time to undertake to deal with business problems. Bringing a third cup and saucer down from the shelf, she poured herself a cup of coffee, too, and joined the men at the table.

"What an attractive kitchen you have," Chic said.

"It's small," she said. "But it's warm in here."

Roger said, "Why would you want to go into retail selling? You've got a good set-up."

"I'm interested," Chic said.

"You won't make much money. There's too many guarantee repairs on TV sets. Service eats up the profit."

"It isn't the money," Chic said. "It's the idea that I'd be in a line where I could experiment. I want the experience. I feel it would give me room to turn around in." He told them, then, about his own work. On and on he droned. Virginia ceased to listen, but her husband seemed to care, at least enough to keep his eyes open and on Bonner. But his look of scorn remained. His lack of real attention. The subject did not seem to rouse anything deep in him, the exciting notion of the business merger and expansion.

What a little view, she thought to herself. Puttering about in a small land. Happy, she thought, at polishing one TV set in the morning, another in the afternoon. The ring of the phone . . . he dwelt in such a piddling kingdom.

"In TV," Roger was saying, interrupting Chic, "it's the big tube that has to be handled with kid gloves. If that cracks, stand back."

"I'd imagine," Chic said.

"Usually it cracks back at the neck. That's not too serious. Of course, you're out fifteen or twenty bucks, wholesale."

"Every business has its occupational hazards," Chic said. "In any foodstuffs it's the problem of spoilage and contamination."

"In the old days," Roger said, "we were more scared of the picture tube than anything else, even the high voltage. I remember hearing about a workman on the assembly line; one of the big tubes busted and the socket end, with the male prongs, went through the guy's stomach and out the other side."

Chic then told about the rat that was baked into the loaf of bread and sold to an old lady in Sacramento. "She collected something like forty thousand," he said. "Rats are a problem."

A sound caused Virginia to turn her head.

"Hi," Liz said. She had come out of the bedroom. Now she stood drowsily in the doorway, leaning with her arm against the wall. "The coffee smell woke me up," she said.

"How do you feel?" Virginia said.

"Better." Steadying herself, she walked over to Chic and he patted her, drawing her to him. "Can I have some coffee?" she asked Virginia. "I'll pour it; don't you get up."

"Don't you want anything to eat?" Chic said to her.

"No," Liz said, fumbling at the sink with the coffee pot and cups. "Is this a meat loaf, Virginia?" she said. "It doesn't look like anybody ate any of it."

"I forgot about it," Virginia said. "We got to talking."

To his wife, Chic said, "You look awful. You better go slap some cold water in your face."

Returning to the table with her cup of coffee, Liz said, "I never could make good coffee, Virginia."

"There's nothing to it," she said. "Just get the exact amount of water and coffee, and when you reheat it, make sure you don't let it boil."

"How do you know when it's ready?"

"You have to time it," she said.

To Chic, Liz said, "You're not going too fast with this partnership business, are you?"

Roger said, "What do you think about it?"

"What do you mean," Liz said, "what do I think? Do you mean, do I approve of it?"

He nodded.

Liz said, "I don't think anything. How can I? It's too soon to talk about it, either way. If Chic wants to look at your store, that's fine. But it's your store."

"Maybe so," Roger said.

"That's not the question," Virginia said.

Chic said, "You don't know anything about it; you have no idea of the situation."

"I know it's silly," Liz said.

After a moment Roger said, "Well, as Liz says, there's no hurry."

Chic said to his wife, "On what are you basing your statement? Have you any knowledge or experience of business relationships?"

"Common sense tells me that," Liz said. "Look at Gilbert and Sullivan; they wound up not even speaking to each other."

Chic said, in Roger's direction, "They made an awful lot of money."

"Did they?" Liz said.

"Personally," Chic said, "I'm not too concerned with whether I'm going to be speaking to my partner or having him to dinner or swapping trout flies with him. I'm primarily concerned with whether he's a competent and reliable business partner."

"But we couldn't help getting tangled up," Liz said to him.

"You'd both be working together in the store—both Virginia and I would be coming in."

"Yes," Virginia said. "But it's natural. Partners' wives always go in and out of the store. Employees' wives, too. Isn't that right, Roger?"

Roger said, "Somewhere I heard something to the effect of, don't do business with your friends or they won't stay your friends."

"This is all so pessimistic," Virginia said. "There's no reason why we should assume we're going to lose anybody's friendship."

To Liz, Chic said, "We were doing fine until you came in."

"Thanks," Liz said, sipping her coffee.

"Anyhow," Roger said, "we don't have to carry it any farther tonight."

"Shall I call you?" Chic said. "Sometime tomorrow or the next day?"

"No," Roger said. "It's hard to get me in the store. I'll call you, maybe some evening."

Clearly disappointed, Chic said, "I'll be expecting to hear from you. If I don't hear from you in a couple of days, maybe I'll take some time off and drop by the store."

"Suit yourself," Roger said, with no evident interest.

I could just kill you, Liz Bonner, Virginia said to herself. I'd like to get my hands around your throat for coming in here and spreading gloom and doom. What's the matter with you? Why, when everyone else is involved in something serious, do you have to appear with your idiotic remarks? What do you know about anything?

You are a stupid woman, she thought. A pretty, young-looking, big-chested, empty-headed woman. Go home and get into your own kitchen where you belong.

"Why are you so gloomy?" she said to Liz.

"I'm not gloomy," Liz said. "Maybe it would work fine. But it's easier to get into a thing like that than to get out."

"Are you afraid to take a chance?" Virginia said. "That's the only way anyone ever got anything in the world."

"Especially the business world," Chic said.

Both Liz and Roger stared down at their coffee cups.

"Well," Chic said, "I guess we better hit the road, Virginia. We'll give you people a call, maybe in the middle of the week."

"Fine," she said. "Did you have a coat?"

"Mine's in the living room," Chic said, standing up. "I think Liz had one."

"Yes," Virginia said. "I put it in the closet; I'll go get it." Leaving the table, she strode down the hall and into the bedroom to the closet. She took down Liz's coat. The bedroom was dark, but she made out the wrinkled bed, the indentation that Liz's body had left. What a lump, she thought to herself. She tossed Liz's coat over a chair and spent a few minutes remaking and smoothing the bed.

When she came out of the bedroom she saw Chic standing at the front door of the house with his coat over his arm, waiting for his wife. "I like the idea," she said to him.

"Thanks, Virginia," Chic said. "I wouldn't pay much attention to Liz. She just wants to be able to say something on the subject."

Virginia went along the hall and to the kitchen. In the kitchen, Roger and Liz stood facing each other by the kitchen table. A cigarette stuck from Roger's mouth, and he patted his pockets, searching for his lighter.

"I have it," Liz said. She opened her purse and brought out his lighter.

"Thanks," he said, accepting the lighter and lighting his cigarette.

"Here's your coat," Virginia said to Liz.

As Liz put on her coat, Virginia thought to herself, What was that? Why did she have my husband's lighter?

He must have given it to her on the trip, she decided. He was driving, she asked him if he had a match, he said no, here, take my lighter, and she never got around to returning it.

But how peculiar, she thought to herself. It was in the way they spoke to each other. The directness.

"Let's go," Chic said, from the open front door.

"Coming," Liz said. To Virginia, she said wearily, "Thanks for the aspirin."

"How's the headache?"

"It's better," Liz said. Roger moved along with the two women, until they had all three joined Chic. They moved down the path—Virginia switched on the porch light—to the sidewalk. Liz and Chic started towards the red Ford station wagon.

"Good night," Chic said. "We'll see you."

As Roger waved good night and started back toward the house, he thought to himself, There she goes. Off with her husband. Back to her own house.

When again? he wondered. Already, he longed for her. His hands and arms ached. He needed her now, as he started back into the house with his wife.

"Oh God," Liz said, from the station wagon. "I forgot something." Her heels clicked on the pavement. "Roger," she called, "I forgot the goddamn telescope."

"Oh yeah," he said, halting on the porch. In the back seat of the Oldsmobile; she had wanted to get it. "It must still be in the car."

"What's that?" Virginia said, beside him.

"Walter's toy telescope," he said. "He left it in the car."

At the Oldsmobile, Liz tugged at the door handle. "It's locked."

"I'll open it for you." He walked down the path and along the sidewalk, to the car. With his key he unlocked the door; Liz squeezed into the car and rummaged in the back. The engine of the Ford station wagon came on; Chic switched on its headlights. Back on the porch of the house, Virginia waited for him, shivering.

Softly, Liz said, "I'll call you."

"When?"

"Tomorrow. At the store." She found the telescope. "Here it is," she said. "Thanks."

Cheered up, Roger returned to the house and his waiting wife.

As she shut the front door and put off the porch light, Virginia said, "She always forgets something, doesn't she?"

"The boys forgot it," he said.

"I don't care much for her," Virginia said. "Why is she so set against things that would benefit somebody other than herself?"

"Like what?" he said.

"Let it go," Virginia said.

16

Monday, the entire day, passed without any call from Liz. That night he drove home in a mood of morbidity. He did not notice what he ate for dinner or what Virginia said to him; he placed himself before the television set in the living room and watched, without understanding, hour after hour of programs until it was time to go to bed.

I'll call her, he said to himself. But I can't. How can I call that number? Chic Bonner would answer.

Then, he said to himself, I'll say something about his damn designs.

While Virginia was occupied, he picked up the telephone and dialed part of Liz's number.

No, he decided. He hung up. If she wanted to call she would have called during the day. Something had gone wrong.

The next morning, she called him at the store.

"For God's sake," he said, when he recognized her voice. "I've been going nuts."

"I'm sorry," she said airily. "I intended to call you yesterday, but things kept happening. The man was here all afternoon working on the refrigerator. Do you know anything about refrigerators? It got so it didn't defrost."

"How are you?" he said. He had carried the phone off, away from the counter, to the limit of its cord. Squatting down on his haunches, he held the phone on his lap, keeping his eyes on Pete Bacciagalupi who had gone behind the counter to wait on customers.

"I'm fine," Liz said.

"Did Chic say anything?"

"About what?"

"About," he said, "anything at all."

"No," Liz said. "He was sore at me because I don't think his big schemes amount to anything. He'd like it if I raved about every idea of his." She sighed. "You know, Roger—can you talk, by the way? Is this a good time?"

"Yes," he said, ignoring the customers waiting at the counter.

"I'm lying here," Liz said. "In the bedroom. We have an extension in the bedroom, by the bed. I feel very lazy, today. I really feel good. Do you think Virginia suspects anything?"

"No," he said.

"She kept looking at me funny. I really had to get out of there— I couldn't think of any other way except to go lie down. I certainly felt strange lying down on her bed. Your bed, I mean. Do you see? It's certainly complex . . . how'd we ever get into it?"

He said, "Do you want to get out of it?"

"Oh no," she said. "Roger, that was really wonderful. What we did. It was never like that between me and Chic. That's the truth."

The store had filled up with customers. Olsen had appeared from the basement to talk to a man about repairs. The din of a TV set made it impossible for Roger to hear; he settled back against the wall, evading the racket.

"What's all that?" Liz asked.

"Nothing," he said. "Go on."

"What do you think Virginia would do if she found out? She's oo ovreet . . . she's one of the most adorable women I've ever known. I wish she liked me better."

He said, "When can I see you again?"

"I've been thinking."

Her tone made him apprehensive. "How about tonight?" he said.

"Roger," she said, "is this really right?"

"Christ," he said, "this is not time to start talking like that."

"No," she agreed. "You're right. I just wanted to make sure how you felt. You know Roger, you can get out of this any time you want. You understand that, don't you?"

He said, "When can I see you?"

"Well," she said, mulling. He could imagine her, her scratchy hair, the heat of her skin. The elaborate convolutions of her ear, the short, stiff fuzz growing at the back of her neck. She cut her hair herself, she had told him. "You know what I have on?" she said. "All I have on is the bottom part of my swimsuit. I've been lying out in the garden, getting some sun . . . I came in to change and then I decided to call you. I was afraid to call; it wasn't that I didn't want to. I'm not used to this. I don't know how to act. It was so strange—you and me sitting here in your kitchen, only a foot or so from each other, and I couldn't say anything to you or touch you. I wanted to touch you so bad . . . once I almost reached out and touched you. But God—if Chic saw that. Or Virginia. Wasn't that strange . . . the four of us gabbing away about nothing, and all the time I was just yearning to throw my arms around you and hug you."

"When?" he repeated.

"What about tomorrow night?"

"Okay," he said.

"Chic has to go to a business meeting. He goes every Wednesday. He takes the car."

"What time?"

"I'll call you when he leaves."

"Not at home," he said. "I'll come down here to the store. When? Seven or seven-thirty?"

"Yes," she said. "And then you can come over here. Or I can meet you somewhere. Only, he'll have the car."

"Is it safe for me to come there?" he said, thinking about neighbors and thinking about Chic coming home.

"I think so," she said. "Or you can pick me up and we can go somewhere." Suddenly her voice took on urgency. "Somebody's at the door; I have to go. I'll call you Wednesday at the store."

"Good-bye," he said.

"Good-bye," she said, and the phone clicked dead.

That evening, Tuesday evening, Virginia heard him say from the other room, "I better get down to the store. I gotta get some sets set up."

"Oh?" she said, feeling herself grow wary.

But he remained in the house, reading a magazine, going over some order sheets. At nine o'clock he said, "I guess I won't go down tonight. I'm too tired."

"Have you thought any more about what Chic said?"

"No," he said.

"Are you going to call him?"

"That horse's ass," he said.

"Don't use expressions like that," she said, her wariness becoming anger.

"I think he is," Roger said. "He's nothing but a fat soft jerk who's had things easy all his life. He was born with a silver spoon in his mouth."

"How absurd," she said.

"Him and his schemes. I know what kind of ideas he has; he'd put me out of business in a week. He'd have gardenias for the ladies and dishes and spotlights—he'd hire salesmen to stand around doing nothing. Potted palm salesmen, we call them. I see them down in those department stores. All a bunch of fairies."

Her indignation was so great that she gave up talking to him; she went off into the kitchen and sat at the kitchen table, smoking.

"I hate guys like that," his voice sounded, along the hallway. "They're like pants salesmen. Oily."

"Chic isn't oily," she said.

"No, but he'd hire them. I know Chic—he's the kind of fat well-dressed partner you see in stores; hanging around the back somewhere. They're always hanging around. They don't do anything; they're just there. He wouldn't get up off his ass all day long, except to go down front when the newspaper boy brings the paper in. Believe me, I know that type."

"And you're so industrious," she said.

"I do my share," he said.

"Pete does the work. You drink coffee next door and lie over at the steam bath talking with the other—" She started to say, other little merchants.

"Say it," he said.

"Say what?"

"I don't know." He came into the kitchen. "Whatever dirty remark you started to say and didn't."

"You can't tell a good man when you meet him," she said. "I read somewhere that that's the best use college has, to teach you to recognize a good man. It's too bad you didn't go to college, then."

"I can tell a good man. Pete's a good man, and you treat him like he was dirt. Olsen's a good man. Chic Bonner's nothing but a horse's ass." He started out.

She said, "You don't deserve to have a store. I wish I hadn't worked so hard so you could have it."

Pausing, he said, "Too late now."

"I know," she said.

"What do you want," he said, "gratitude?" He continued on back into the other room.

"Just some decent response from you," she said. "Something rational and intelligent."

"For Christ's sake!" he shouted. "I'm not going to take that guy into my store; it's my store and nobody's buying into it. Liz is right."

"It's interesting," she said, feeling bitter. "You find her opinion to be worth more than mine. I wonder why."

"Because she's right."

"Is that the reason? You know," she said, "I finally figured out what Liz reminds me of. In those big supermarkets on Saturday you go in and there's some little fat jolly woman at the back, with a tray of crackers and some new cheese they're selling; she has on a yellow uniform tied at the waist—you know. And when you go by wheeling your cart, she calls out in that bright cheerful voice, 'Say, honey, don't you want to try a free sample of Kraft's new bacon and cheddar cheese spread?' or whatever it is."

Roger said, "I think I'll go down to the store."

"Wait," she said, not wanting him to go. "I'm sorry. I shouldn't say that." But then she said, "Why do you think so much of her? What is it about her? Is it because she's sort of sexy, in an oozy way? I'd like to know. Really."

"Go to hell," he said.

"What I'd like to know," she said, unable not to say it, "is how a man like Chic Bonner could get himself mixed up with a woman like that."

The front door closed. Instantly, she leaped up and ran through the house. Now I've done it, she said. She opened the door. Roger stood on the porch, his hands shoved in his pockets, his body hunched.

"I'm sorry," she said, going out to him and putting her arms around him. "Don't go down to the store. I won't say anything more. Maybe we could do something; could we take a walk, or go to some club for a while? Maybe there's a band playing."

"No," he said. "I'm too tired." But he came back into the house with her. "I don't feel like talking about it," he said.

"Maybe it's because I miss Gregg," she said.

He said, "Doesn't that dance stuff take up enough of your time?"

Again she felt anger. But she kept her mouth shut. In her anger was a quantity of dread. I don't quite understand this, she said to herself. What is it? What's going on?

Maybe I don't know everything, she thought.

And then she thought, Could he be getting to where he's falling in love with her?

But she's such a fool, she thought to herself. That was the word for Liz. She was just a plain fool.

A comedienne, she thought. With a floppy cap and a trident, or whatever it was that fools carried. Little Liz Bonner, keeping them all in stitches.

But, she thought, remembering an unbreakable Decca record that Gregg owned and treasured, Danny Kaye's recording of "Tubby the Tuba" . . . in the end the funny little thing won out.

The next evening, Wednesday, when Roger got home he said to her, "I just have time to eat and then I've got to get back to the store."

"Okay," she said, expecting it.

At dinner he ate almost nothing.

"Worries?" she said, wishing he would say something to her, tell her about them. "Why don't you let me come along—maybe I can help you. Or keep you company."

"No," he said. "Thanks."

"Is it hard work you have to do down there?"

"Some. I have to shove a few crates around. Bring some table model TVs upstairs."

She said, "Be careful of your side."

Putting on his coat, he started out the door of the house, his car keys in his hand. As he passed her she noticed something odd. He smelled unusually good. Stopping him, she reached up.

"What is it?" he said, jerking away.

She thought, It's aftershave that smells like that. He must have shaved.

"I may go out on some prospects," he said. "A couple was in the store today; I got their name. I might drive a set out to their place and leave it."

"Oh," she said. In the past he had done that. Certainly it was possible. "Then if I called the store you might not be there," she said.

"That's right."

She said, "Can I call you Pee-wee the piccolo?"

With suspicion, he said. "What's that? Why?"

"That's Tubby's friend," she said. "In the recording."

For an interval he studied over what she had said, and then he understood and he got on his face an expression so strong and yet so hopelessly complicated that if she had not known what he felt she would not have had any idea of what it meant.

"God damn you," he said. "God damn you." Turning his back he went off down the path to the car.

I shouldn't have said that, she said to herself. Why did I say that? What's happening to me?

All during the drive to the store, his hands shook and he could scarcely see the traffic ahead of him. He drove by habit, parked in an empty slot, and walked across the sidewalk to the dark, closed-up store.

I'll leave her, he said to himself. I'm never going back.

Unlocking the door, he entered, and relocked the door behind him, leaving the key in it.

Christ, he said. He felt as if his head were going to burst; the pressure inside was terrific. Going downstairs to the bathroom he washed his face in cold water.

She must have smelled the fucking aftershave, he said to himself. In a fashion it was funny.

What'll I do? he thought. Pull out now, before she has anything to go on? Before she really has something?

Upstairs the phone rang. The sound of its ring reached him barely; had it not been for his practice at hearing it down here in the basement he would not have noticed.

His watch read seven. Too early. Anyhow, even if he sprinted up the steps, he would probably not make it in time. So he finished washing his face, drying himself, and then he walked leisurely up to the main floor. By that time the phone had become silent.

In the office he sat at the desk, smoking and thinking things over. What if Chic comes home? What if Virginia hops into a cab and drives over here? What if she drives over there?

And he thought to himself that in any case, even in the best of all possible cases, with neither Chic nor Virginia coming home or appearing at the door, or hiring private eyes or whatever, he still had the unsolvable, hopeless problem. He still did not know how really serious he was towards Liz, how far he wanted to go with her. Because, after all, there was only one serious place to take it, and that was straight to the courts for a divorce or two and then, after the year of the interlocutory decrees, a remarriage. He and Liz Bonner. Or rather Liz Lindahl. And how many children? he asked himself. She would probably keep the two boys. No, he thought, not if the divorce was by Chic. Not if she was divorced on the grounds of adultery. And Virginia, in any case, would keep Gregg. So at best he would wind up with Liz and her two boys; he would lose Gregg, and he might find that Jerry and Walter were no substitute, even Jerry and Walter and Liz together.

Of course, he and Liz would have children. Realizing that, he felt a little better.

God, he thought. How far ahead his thoughts had gone. It seemed a little premature. And yet, while they were in the motel, after they had gone to bed together and were just lying, doing nothing, Liz had said suddenly.

"You know what?"

"What?" he had said.

"I'd like to bear your child. I really would. That's what I want more than anything else."

And he had thought of her as being an instinct-driven female body, prowling about in search of a man to impregnate her, and then, after that, she would search for a place at which to give birth to that child. A secure, peaceful place. It would not end simply with the impregnation. It would not end here; she had to have the rest. How could she not have the rest? If he did make her pregnant, then he had only just begun to get himself mixed up with her. And even if she did not actually become pregnant, the notion was there, the idea. When they went to bed again—if they did—she would be thinking of that. Of course, she would not dare let herself become pregnant until he had shown that he could and would leave Virginia. In a sense he was lucky to be married to someone else; Liz could not possibly take such a risk—she could not, in her scatter-brained haste, leave the cap off the tube or the diaphragm in the box. So he did not have to worry about a surprise announcement from her. Unless it happened by mistake.

But he knew perfectly well, whether Virginia did or not, that Liz had all her wits about her. Especially, he thought, when she was do-ing such a thing as fitting on her diaphragm. There, she was beyond foolishness. She could not err. And, he thought, not because some instinct held her hands steady; it was because she could not afford to err. The situation was too serious.

Did he love her? he asked himself. Do I love her?

What kind of a question, he wondered, did that really amount to. No, he decided, I guess I do not. On the other hand, I never loved Virginia, nor Teddy, nor the girl in high school whose name was Peggy Gottgeschenk who was the first girl I ever took out and got. Nobody loves anybody in this century, nor does anybody pray, or open gulls to examine their gizzards for a harbinger of the future. But, he thought, I would stand up for her. That's as close as anyone can come. If it were a question of her or me, I would let myself get the ax between the shoulders rather than her. Isn't that enough? The rest, he thought to himself, is talk.

I used to feel like that, he thought to himself, about my brother. That was before he died. In a sense, I felt like that about all of them, my brother and then Peggy Gottgeschenk and then Virginia Watson and now Liz Bonner. But, he thought, does that prove anything? Does that prove I'm a liar? Or that I am kidding myself? No, he thought. It only proves that nothing is permanent. Even the Bank of America Building, where all the money and all the property deeds in California eventually wind up. Even that will pass away. We will all be gone in a little while. But my love is as great as theirs, and theirs is practically a legend.

The phone rang. He lifted the receiver off the hook.

"Hi," Liz's close, breathy voice came.

"Hi," he said.

"How are you?"

"Fine."

"He's gone," she said. "Come on over."

"Okay," he said.

"Hurry," she said. She hung up.

He locked the store after him, got into his car, and drove over to San Fernando as fast as he could manage it.

At eight-thirty that evening, Virginia called the store. She got no answer. Later on, at nine, she called again.

Depressed, she called her mother.

"Have you gone to bed?" she asked.

"At *nine?*" Marion said. "You must think I'm getting to be a regular old lady."

"I'm here alone," she said. "Roger went down to the store to work. He took the car."

"Poor Roger," Marion said. "Has he talked to Chic Bonner again about the store?"

"No," she said. "What do you think about it? You like the idea, don't you?"

"It seemed promising."

"You like Chic, don't you?"

"Yes," Marion said. "He impressed me as a forthright man, and of more than usual capability."

"You think he'd make a good partner for Roger?"

"I think he'd make an excellent partner. Provided that Roger can work with him and not feel—how should I put it? Not be conscious of certain disparities."

"What do you think of Liz Bonner?"

"Do I have to answer that?"

"Please," Virginia said. "You won't hurt my feelings."

"As far as I'm concerned," her mother said, "she's about what I'd expect to run into out here in Los Angeles. By that I mean she's not particularly anything. I don't really have an impression of her. Just a sort of blank space. She doesn't talk well, or stand well; she doesn't know anything; I'd say that the drive-ins and department stores and cafés out here are full of girls like her."

"That's my feeling," Virginia said. "She's the type you see in the supermarkets giving away free samples of some new cheese spread."

"Oh no," Mrs. Watson said. "I'll tell you what type she is. She's the type—you listen to me, Ginny—she's the type that when you want to get at the mayonnaise counter for the jar of mayonnaise that's on sale for forty-nine cents instead of seventy-nine, you find a cart parked in your way. And there's a plump, short woman who pushed that cart there, in your way, and that woman is at the mayonnaise counter herself, and while you're fuming and saying to yourself, 'Does this woman intend to block the aisle indefinitely?' that short, plump woman is smiling vacantly in your direction and she's taking the last jar of that forty-nine cent mayonnaise."

"Why do you say that?"

"I just know," Mrs. Watson said.

"You mean you think she's smarter than she acts? What do you mean?" She felt cross. "Be more specific."

"I just mean that cart of hers—interpret that whatever way you like—is going to be parked where you want to go, one of these days."

"I don't follow such imagery."

Mrs. Watson said, "Let's talk about something more pleasant."

They discussed various topics, and then Virginia excused herself and rang off.

What coyness, she thought to herself. Nevertheless, she herself had started it.

Again she telephoned the store. Again she got no answer. And then she did something that she knew was wrong. Looking through the front window, she made certain that the Olds was not anywhere nearby. She opened the front door so that she would hear its engine if it came up the street, and then she went into the bedroom, to the dresser, and opened the bottom drawer. It was the drawer in which Roger kept his personal articles; she had never looked into his secrets in all the time they had been together. But, she said to herself, this is different. This is the only thing I can think of, and I must do something. I can't just stand here.

But it disgusted her.

She felt as if she had got herself into a degrading position. Let it go, she said to herself. Forget it. This, surely, is worse. This is the worst of all, this rooting around. Peering and searching, and at the same time listening with one ear for the sound of the car.

What would I say, she wondered, if Roger walked in and saw me? It would be the end.

But she kept on; her fingers flew. She examined papers, photographs; they turned out to be business papers, and the photographs were mostly of herself and of him. How fitting, she said to herself. Pictures of them, their marriage license, his divorce papers from Teddy, tax statements, physical report from an insurance company, deed on the house, fire insurance on the house, countless papers that had to do with the store . . . her shame grew until she felt her skin simmering and red.

At the bottom of the papers she found a manila packet. Should she open it? She unwound the string and opened it.

Inside—to her disbelief—were pictures torn out of girlie magazines. One was Jane Russell standing with a bow and arrow. Another showed Marilyn Monroe wearing a slip, sideways at a window so that the light showed through her slip and showed her bra. Good grief, Virginia thought. She sat down on a chair to examine the picture. It looked as if the light shone through the bra, too. It looked as if, by a freak brilliance of illumination, the naked breast and nipple could be seen. What a large nipple, she thought. Like a bean.

Fascinated, she searched farther into the packet. Next she came upon a calendar for the year 1950. The girl, young, with a rather drab face, had been photographed undressing. She had on only a sort of wrapper at her waist, and it, too, was unfastened to show her bare thigh and most of her pelvis. The girl's breasts were somewhat soft, she decided. They hung down. And, curiously, instead of nipples they seemed to have on each a smear of red, and nothing more.

After the calendar she found a regular three-cent envelope. In it was a sheaf of paper, rolled up and tied. She unfastened the string. The sheaf fell apart on her lap; the paper was unbleached, coarse, the pictures were so dim that at first she could not make them out. The first showed something anatomical, and she traced it until she discovered that it was a woman's body, twisted into a shape she had never seen before. What was shown? she wondered. She looked at the next picture. It showed a woman and a man, and then she realized that for the first time in her life she was seeing a genuinely obscene picture. This was pornography, and it was not like what she had always imagined; it was vague, tortured, almost funny. It was revolting. She glanced at the rest. How could human bodies get into such postures? she asked herself. It was worse than an old medical book she had come across, once, in a doctor's office. But it was similar. She rolled up the sheaf and stuck it back in the envelope.

She closed up the packet and put it back in the drawer, with the business papers.

Any person, she thought, who would enjoy looking at a picture like that, had something wrong with him.

She thought to herself as she left the room, if he would own those pictures, he certainly had some unnatural quirk. Folding her arms, shivering, she walked into the kitchen and stood before the oven.

There's always been something the matter with him, she said to herself. She felt a presence; pressure of his thin, bony body. His breath in her face.

God, she thought. She shuddered.

Her own fault. Why did she look? It served her right. The pictures swam in her mind. I must get rid of them, she said. I have to. Why did I have to go rooting around? Will I ever be able to think of— sexuality as I used to think of it?

She lit a cigarette, smoked for a few minutes, and then put the cigarette out. Opening the refrigerator, she searched for something good to eat, some candy or dessert. She found the last of a pint of ice cream in the freezer; after she had finished the ice cream she felt better. Lighting another cigarette she began to wander about the house.

Her peace of mind gradually returned. She felt herself return to normal. What hysteria, she thought. Men, from the age of eight years and up, get and prize such pictures. Roger is normal. At the store such pictures probably pass from hand to hand; probably he had acquired them from another merchant along the street, or from Pete, or from Olsen.

Even boys, she thought. Writing on the walls of bathrooms. Writing on fences. Words, pictures. Natural and universal . . . from the time of the Egyptians to the present.

So it showed, after all, that she had got herself into an irrational frame of mind. She was ready to fly apart at any sign. Her perspective was gone; she had witnessed it leave her. My judgment, she decided, is faulty. At least this incident has one good outcome; it has made me aware of myself.

She turned on the radio and listened to music and then the news about Korea. On top of the bookcase was a collection of short stories by *New Yorker* and *Harper's* writers; she made herself comfortable on the couch and began to read, starting at the back story and skipping first paragraphs and then pages, until she had gone almost through the volume without really reading anything at all. Finally she found one story that interested her; it had to do with New England, and she noticed the author's name. A woman, she realized. She finished the story, enjoying the deft style of the writer.

I wish I could write like that, she thought. Perhaps her sense of rhythm would help her. Rhythm was important in everything.

Laying aside the book, she went into the bedroom and changed from her skirt and blouse into her leotards and cotton T-shirt. In the living room she put on a record of Ravel's *La Valse* and after a bit she began to dance.

While she danced, a thought matured in her mind. I could call the Bonners, she thought. I can make sure.

She sorted through all the possibilities. If nobody answered the phone, she could assume that either nobody was there, or that Liz and Roger were there. If Chic answered the phone, she could assume that Roger was not there, but that Liz might or might not be there. If she was there, then everything was fine. But if she was not there—

"Oh God," Virginia said aloud. She stopped dancing. The hell with it. It wasn't worth it.

Picking up the phone she called her mother.

"Were you asleep?" she asked. "No, I asked you that before."

"Maybe this time I was," Marion said. "Roger isn't here: I can tell you that."

"I know where Roger is," she said heatedly. "I'm not calling to find him. He's down at the store, down in the basement working. I just called to find out whether you would like to have lunch with me downtown tomorrow." It was the first notion that came to her mind.

"I suppose so. Is there something in particular you wanted to discuss with me?"

"No," she said. "I'll come by about twelve and pick you up. We can decide where we want to go after we get started."

"Should I dress up in my finest? Are you going to take me to some fancy place?"

"No," she said, "just wear your street clothes." She hung up the phone. Now she felt better. Thinking about lunch with Marion cheered her up. They could talk.

To pass the time she considered the various limitations of Liz Bonner; she told herself that only by the remotest stretch of the imagination could Liz be conceived of as dangerous or effective. She elaborated the image that she had constructed of Liz, the short plump woman in the supermarket giving out free samples of crackers and cheddar cheese. With her name on the back of her uniform, she decided. The word LIZ in red thread, so that if anybody wanted to call her they would know how. Ernie's Supermarket, the red thread declared. And I am called Liz, if you should happen to want me. Just call. I am here to serve you.

17

She held him in her arms; she held him in her, as close and far as he would go. She patted him and stroked his back and breathed through her mouth against his ear, so that she heard her own breath rushing back at her. The bedroom smelled of cinnamon.

"I've got you," she said. "I could kill you." I love you, she thought. What would your wife say?

Raising her hand she let up the window shade; she wanted to view him. Enough light entered the room, and she could see. In the next house the living room lights were on, and so were other lights in other living rooms, in the houses across the street. A porch light shone more brightly than the others; she saw, on that family's front walk, a tricycle and a toy wagon. Lying there, she listened to radios and voices.

"They're sitting around the living room," she said. "Watching TV and darning socks."

"Who?" he said.

"They all are. They're talking about—" She considered. "Mr. Daniels is saying that county taxes are going up this next June. Mr. Sharp is saying that he likes to watch accordion players better than dramas. Mrs. Felton is saying that Tide soap is on sale at fifty nine cents for the giant size. What time is it? Nine o'clock? What's on TV? You'd know that; you sell TV sets."

"I don't know," he said. His voice was muffled because his face was buried in the pillow and in her hair. She smoothed his hair back into place. The scratchy underside of his jaw pressed at her shoulder; she felt the bristles penetrate her skin as he spoke.

"You have a very nice back," she said.

"Why?"

"You're not fat. You don't have rolls of fat all over you." She shifted so that she could lift herself; she wanted to look through the window and see the entire street, each of the houses. "I like to think about them," she said. "The people living out there. What do you think they'd say if they could see us?" She thought about Virginia; she always thought about Virginia. I'm lying here with her husband, she thought. That's how I think of it. I have your husband, Virginia. Don't hate me.

"Aren't I hurting you?" Roger said.

"No. Don't move." She hugged him until she heard her own ribs crack. "You're not heavy." Much lighter, she thought, than he is. How different bodies are.

If they could see us, she thought, they would turn to stone. Yes, she thought; I can see them, marble statues, with weeds and brambles growing around them. The cracking apart of the walls. She saw the houses fall apart and decay. She saw the rosebushes grow over them, weigh them down, cause them to collapse. And the stone statues gaped. We have got old watching, the statues said. We could not look away.

"Why would it kill them?" she said. "Couldn't they stand it? It's not that bad . . . something else must do it to them."

"Jealous," he murmured.

She kissed him. You're wrong, she thought. I love you, but you don't understand. Why would they be jealous? Men are so odd. Walking along with a girl and telling other men by a certain code, Hey fellows, look what I get to lay. I know about you, she thought, holding him tighter. And maybe you do make a few of them jealous, a few who haven't had any for a while. But the others;

I'm thinking about them. Mr. Sharp and Mr. Daniels and Mrs. Felton.

She thought, they would stand gaping because they would feel themselves getting weak. Every second, the tiring out. The fumbling. When I am like this, she thought, I don't get old. As long as I am lying here, holding him inside me, I neither sink nor fall. I do not go in any direction. I am simply me. As long as I want. As long as I can keep him here.

Superstition, she thought.

"Do you believe that?" she asked.

He seemed almost asleep. "What . . ."

"That you don't get any older as long as you're having sexual intercourse?"

Stirring, he said, "I never heard that." He drew himself back onto his haunches, and then he slid to one side of her and lowered himself out; he put his face next to her throat and his arm on her stomach.

"You know why she hates me?" she said. Because I'm here, she thought. "Because she has to," she said. "I'd hate her. I don't blame her. You can only do this with one person . . . isn't that so? If you're here doing it with me, you're not with her; you've left her out. I've taken you completely. I want to. That's what I was after from the beginning." What does Virginia get back? she thought. What do I leave when I'm through? What comes trembling back to the house, putting its feeble hand on the doorknob . . . a worn-out thing. Colorless. I got everything out of it, she thought. He poured himself into me; I felt him. He came into me with everything he is and has. The wet life inside the skin. The actual life. There is that one tiny place where it can come out, that imperfection. And if you know how—and I do—you can gather up that and tuck it away, and pretty soon, if everything is right, the person you love spurts across. And the part that tells you is the moment that he knows what he has done; he knows that he is coming, and he can't stop; he has no control. He is leaving himself, leaving his body, and he tries to go back, and he can't. Then you know you have him. You have got him.

Why, she thought, does he think he has got something? What has he got? Show it to me. He has only been somewhere; he has been here (she took a Kleenex from the box beside the bed and began to wipe herself off) and now he has left again. But I took in something, and it is still there. Despite what I've read in the Brittanica, I believe that what I took in is absorbed into my system and becomes a permanent part of me. I can feel it all through me. She lifted her hands and pressed them over her eyes. Powerful lights flashed, color and shapes. All the way, she thought. Everywhere. And if somebody knows, they can tell. Virginia could tell that night, as soon as she saw me. She saw it like a color around me.

"Are you happy in bed?" she said. In some woman's bed, in the safest place. Stretched out peacefully. With her handkerchief she wiped herself. "It's sticky," she said. "Is that so it'll stick to me, inside me? So it won't slip out?" It stuck; it remained in her. Have you any more? "Is that all? You're worn out, aren't you?" You don't have much. Most of it's for her. But I want it all. It's mine; it belongs here, inside me. "I want to have your baby," she said. "Think how he would be. I'd be a good mother." I am his mother, not Virginia. I know how.

Even if I stay with Chic. I can have my baby, hold him with me, inside me. Raise him until he's big . . . it's mine. When I first saw you I knew that.

"Why are you small?" She knelt down on the bed and put her hands on him. "Do you want to be?"

"No," he murmured.

Go to sleep. Sleep here with me, in this woman's bed, not hers. I'll take you as you sleep. I will hold onto you. What have you brought me? "I love you," she said. She put her arms around him; she crushed herself onto him, and then she sat up, away from him. And then she stepped from the bed and stood. I will wrap you up, collect you in the tiniest bit. Smaller and smaller. But you will not be gone. A tiny bit, still.

"O God," she said. I want to go on and on with you. Can I? Can anybody? Why are we here at all? How did we even get this much?

Nobody offered it to us; nobody wants us to have it. I am not supposed to let you in here, tuck you in me—never. I'm supposed to get old and die.

She thought: One day he was fishing and he fell into the water and down to the bottom, away from land. He lived with the princess who was a turtle. The fisherman and the turtle.

Along the street the people were different; the houses were different; the dog that had greeted him was gone, dead and buried. The flowers were changed; the shape of all things had changed, so that he recognized nobody, nothing, not the grain in the towers, the stones, the ants on the ground. The lizards had gone away. The big trees, too. The marshes. The water itself had cooled. He thought, it's getting toward nightfall. The water, no longer warm, became cold and clear, and he saw back up to the land and started toward it, remembering it. But all changed. Nobody knew him.

"What do you say to her?" she asked.

He mumbled, half-asleep in the middle of the bed, on the sheet. They had tossed the blankets back, to the floor.

Do you know who she is? What about her name? Can you open your mouth and say what her name is? If I asked you now, what would happen? Would something disappear, fly from the room as if pulled out backwards? Would objects spin off and disappear, as you see when they run a film backward? The feathers, from the heap, fly in clouds and fix themselves onto the turkey. The spray forms on the water, a figure rises feet-first from the water and ascends at great speed; the water collects and descends to cover the spot. Fragments of the burst balloon collect into the balloon again. The ground stirs and beneath it things move about. Through a crack, things are seen to be moving far below. And then the old withered senile things get up out of the ground; they sit up. They stand, they step out, they begin to wave their arms and talk. And gradually they return to the town and take up where they left off.

If she shouts her name, then everyone must wake. If anyone says her name, or their name.

In the street, the houses lit up, radios and TV sets playing, kids on the carpets, women in the kitchens, appeared to him to be different, and he looked for his own house. He searched for the garage and the front walk and the rosebushes growing on the trellis by the front door, and the boy's toys left on the porch. The door was open but the porch did not look the same. The house was gone, too, and the garage and the rosebushes. Only the thorns and brambles remained. The weeds that had been cut, cut, every week. Over all the house.

While we're here she got old and died. If I point at her, she'll recede faster and faster, her mouth open, her hands up; her mouth moves, but she says nothing; I hear no sound, no name.

The door of the house opened and he entered, wearing the same suit and shoes and tie. Inside was only a dried-up crone. And when he asked her who she was, *she did not remember.*

But I did not do it to her. It was happening anyhow. I only lay here and held you down; I pinned you down here, to my bed.

"Hey," she said, throwing herself down beside him. "Let's go out back."

"Where?"

"Outdoors." She scrambled from the bed, caught hold of his hand, and tugged him after her. When he was on his feet she led him from the bedroom and to the doors that opened up on the garden.

Cold wind blew at them as they stepped out onto the grass. The grass was wet and all the yard was in darkness.

"I'm not going out here," he said. "Somebody'll see us."

"They can't see us." Tumbling down to the grass, she brought him with her, to her. "Here," she said. On the ground, in the dampness, where they could breathe. I can find you in the dark. She found him and put him into her, where he had been. Is it dark? Don't get lost. I'm here, she said. Beneath you. Around you. Feel me on all sides? Don't you know that's me? His weight came to rest on her, pressing her into the grass. An insect, probably a spider, traveled across her leg and onto her hip. The blades of grass made her itch. She wanted to squirm. Move every part of me. I feel each muscle stir. I'm everywhere, now. In the dark she touched him and she clasped her arms about him, flattening him to her.

Union with me, she said. What am I? The same as I always was. I don't change. But everything else changes. I feel her getting old and hating me; I feel that as much as I feel the big life in me. Virginia, she said, I am right here: can you find me in the dark? Yes, you can. You know me by the way I smell; you recognize me. The smell of grass.

"Is she like me?" she said.

"Who?"

"Virginia."

He grunted.

Virginia, you're thin. You have a narrow body. What would you be like? Hard, cold as a stone. Dry as a leaf. Would you yell? Move?

I married him when I was nineteen. I was still living with my family, in Los Angeles; he and my father played cards, and my father, being a doctor, went to the dresser drawer where he kept the samples of medicine from the pharmaceutical houses and loaded him down with pills and tablets, everything he might want. My father liked him. They talked about the Japs and Roosevelt and the Soviet Union and Freud and Joe Hill. In the summer he and I drove up north, to the Salinas Valley, and looked at farms. We found a fine truck farm, vegetables and grazing land for cattle or sheep. He hates sheep.

"You hate sheep," she said.

He grunted.

After a year or so I got pregnant. Jerry was born first, and then Walter. Gregg came last; he was always his favorite. We bought more land and had hogs, and we always had chickens and ducks. We raised alfalfa. He knows a lot about farming. He has made even a small farm pay. In fourteen years we've made it a going concern. Now Jerry is thirteen and Walter is twelve. Gregg is seven.

"Seven," she said. "Isn't Gregg seven?"

"About," he said.

I pick apricots and peaches and the green satsuma plums from our trees. I dry the apricots on the flat wood door of the basement. I make jam from the plums and I make jelly from the grapes. On the stump behind the barn I hack off the chicken's head; the chicken flaps about, scattering feathers. In the kitchen, Gregg stands by the table watching me as I open up the chicken to clean it; I explain to him what each of the inside parts is for. I show him the gravel in the gizzard. I let him handle the eggs that were going to come out some-day. In the front room the baby is asleep.

I love you, she said. I've got you. Out in the world the people grow old. She felt them age; she heard them creak; she heard their bones snap. In the different houses dust filled the bowls and covered the floors. The dog did not recognize him; he had been gone too long. Nobody knew him. He had left the world.

She felt his arms go about her waist, so that he had lifted her middle with his hands. She felt herself bend. Lifted up, higher and higher. She put her hand over her eyes to shield herself. And then she wanted him to kiss her. At the same time, she said. She waited, let-ting him find his way into her. You are going to cover me up, she said. With yourself. She caught hold of his face and turned it toward hers, so that she could look at him; she brought her face so close to his that perspiration fell from his cheeks onto hers. She made him open his mouth; she put her open mouth near his, her teeth to his, holding him there as he moved inside her, and then she pressed her mouth to his mouth as she felt it happen again inside her, for the third time. Did you ever do it so many times before? With her? She kept his mouth against hers. You are inside me and I am inside you, she said, putting her tongue into his mouth, as far as it would go. I am as far into you as I can be: we are exchanged. And which am I? Maybe I'm the one who must go back to her, all worn-out and empty. No, I'm the one who will never wear out. I am here forever, lying here on the ground, holding you down where I can reach you and get at you and inside you.

18

At ten o'clock a knock at the door startled Virginia. Putting down her book of short stories she went to the window and peeped out at the front porch. The porch light was on—she had switched it on for Roger—and on the porch stood two men; one was Chic Bonner in a business suit, and with him was an older man, tall, lean, with large ears. The older man wore a suit and overcoat and he smoked a cigar as they waited.

Opening the front door, Virginia said, "Hello Chic."

With an apologetic air, Chic said, "I'm sorry to barge in on you people, Virginia. Roger didn't call me, and I thought maybe I'd take a chance and drop by with Mr. Gillick here, so Roger could meet him. Earl, this is Mrs. Lindahl, the wife of the man I've been telling you about."

"I'm glad to meet you," she said. She shook hands with him. He unobtrusively pushed aside his overcoat, and she saw on his lapel a hearing aid. "Would you like to come in?" she said.

"Thanks," Gillick said. He and Chic entered. Gillick had a hearty largeness, something like that of Chic. Glancing around, he said, "Very attractive place you have here, Mrs Lindahl." He winked at her. "And I'm a builder, so I should know."

"Earl is a contractor," Chic said. "He's an old friend. He built the new building the bakery's in." Both he and Mr. Gillick had a dithering quality about them. She realized that they were expecting Roger to appear from the other room.

"Roger isn't here," she said.

Chic's face fell.

"He's at the home of a prospect," she said.

"I see," Chic said. "Well, it's my own fault for not calling. I sort of hoped maybe he'd be in the mood to look over my sketches tonight." He and Gillick exchanged disappointed glances. Neither of them seemed to know what to do. They shuffled their feet, glanced at each other again.

"Sit down," she said. "Let me take your coats."

"Can't stay long," Gillick said. But he let her take his big overcoat; it smelled of cigars.

After she had hung their coats up, she said, "This customer is only home in the evenings." She added a few details to her small story. "Roger took out a table-model R.C.A. last week for them to try. Tonight they're making up their mind."

So you're not home, Chic, she thought. You're out somewhere.

"Chic," she said, as she seated herself on the arm of the couch, "what are you doing running around at this late hour?"

Gillick answered, "Charles and I attended a meeting of—" His eyes twinkled. "The Los Angeles Hardwaremen's Ethical Practices Association. We wanted to see how they made out with the Justice Department."

"They're protesting an off-beat operation," Chic said. "One of the big chain department stores—Kerman's—is putting in a sideline, aluminum cookware. The hardware people have been trying to boycott their jobbers through their association, but it may get the ax for—what is it?—restraint of competition or some such."

"What's that got to do with bread?" she said, feeling edgy and uninterested.

"It's a business decision involving free outlets," Chic said, and he elaborated at length, as Gillick, beside him, nodded.

You are not home, Virginia thought, and you have not been home all evening. You have probably been away from the house since dinner time.

Gillick concluded, "That was one long session. They argued on and on. I was beginning to think it'd never break up."

"I'm sorry Roger isn't here," Virginia said.

"Well," Chic said, "maybe another time."

"I'm looking forward to meeting your husband," Gillick said. Both he and Chic seemed shy in her presence. Presently it occurred to her that she still had her leotards and T-shirt on. "I've heard so much about him," Gillick said, puffing clouds from his cigar.

"Are you interested in the store?" she asked Gillick.

"Well, to this degree," Gillick said. "Charles asked me if I'd give him my opinion on the building and the front. I told him I would."

"Have you seen the store?"

"No," Gillick said. "Not yet."

She said, "Chic, you have your station wagon, don't you? Why don't we drive down to the store so Mr. Gillick can look at it?"

"That would be great," Chic began, "although I hate to ask Gillick to get into this if your husband isn't—"

Thumping him on the knee, Gillick said, "I don't care. Let's take a look at it." He arose and moved toward the door.

"I'll get your coats," Virginia said. She went quickly into the bedroom and took their coats from the closet. Should I change? she asked herself. No. She put on a long coat that would cover her; grabbing up her purse she returned to the living room. "Here," she said, presenting the two men with their coats.

"We didn't stay long," Chic said, as she herded them out onto the porch. "You think if we waited a few minutes Roger might come back? I'm anxious for—"

"I doubt it," she said. "Sometimes he stays late on these home demonstrations. Where's your car?"

"Over there," Chic said. Gillick strode on ahead, and Chic fell in beside Virginia. "Say, Virginia," Chic said in a muted voice, "you know, I have a little problem. I hate to drive, if I can help it. Sometimes I have to drive. I drove down to the meeting, and I drove Earl over here . . . I lost my license last year, you know. It'll be awhile before I can get it back, probably not this—"

"I'll drive the station wagon," she said.

"Thanks," he said. He gave her the key and held the door open for her to get inside behind the wheel. "I appreciate it," he said. Both he and Gillick got in; she had started the engine by the time Chic slammed the door.

Here's where I find out, she said to herself. Maybe you are down in the basement unable to answer to the phone, and maybe you are not.

The store, when they reached it, was dark. The street in front of it was empty. She saw no cars parked nearby.

He's not there, she said. It's true.

"Good location," Gillick said.

"That's right," Chic said.

Parking the car in front of the store, she said, "Can you see well enough from here?"

"We better get out," Chic said. He and Gillick stepped out onto the pavement. "Store's old," he said. "Ought to have a facelifting."

"Too much wood," Gillick said.

"That's what I told him," Chic said. "That's why I went to so much trouble to draw up designs."

Gillick peered up. "Can't see much in the dark. Sign's old, too. Bad style. Jeez, the windows are narrow." He paced off the store's width. "Much too narrow." Placing his hand to the window he strained to see into the store. "Long, though. Basement?"

"Yes, with a toilet and washbowl."

"I can't make out the interior fixtures too good. What's the overheads?"

"Fluorescents," Chic said.

Seated in the car, Virginia listened to the two men as they

walked about on the pavement. You weren't here at all, she said to herself. Were you?

"Counter is obsolete," Gillick said. "Look at that old till. What a relic."

"I told him that," Chic said.

Gillick tried the knob. "Locked. Too bad we can't go in."

"Maybe during the day," Chic said. "If you happen to go by sometime—"

To Virginia, Gillick said, "Mrs Lindahl, do you have the key? Can we get in?"

"Yes," she said, opening the car door. "I'll let you in."

She entered the store ahead of the two men. In the rear, the ghostly blue night light lit up the television sets and displays. The air was cold and the stale left-over smell hung everywhere, coming up from the ashtrays and from the trash box under the counter.

If he were here, she thought, his key would be in the lock. He has that neurotic habit; he has always been afraid of being trapped in the store, so he makes sure the key never leaves the door if the door is locked.

"Downstairs," she said.

"Yes," Chic said. "Let's have a look at that. So Gillick can see the foundations."

"I can't see the foundations from inside," Gillick said, as they descended. Virginia led them down the steps; she put on the basement light.

The service department was empty.

You bastard, she said to herself.

"Okay?" she asked, her hand on the light switch.

Gillick glanced at her. "Any time you want to leave, Mrs. Lindahl," he said.

"Maybe we should," she said. "It's so late."

"Yes," Gillick said.

Virginia said, "Do you like my husband's store?"

"Why sure," Gillick said.

"I helped buy it for him," she said. "My mother and I."

"Is that so," Chic said. "I didn't realize that." Both he and Gillick eyed her. "Then it's in your name, is it?" Chic said.

"No," she said. "He holds the legal title. I let him have it made out that way."

Chic said, "That was certainly wonderful of you and Mrs. Watson."

"You know why I have on these leotards?" Virginia said. She pushed aside her coat and showed herself, how she was dressed, the way they had seen her in the beginning, when they had first come. "This is what I do my dance-work in," she said. "I gave up my dance-work so he could have his store. Isn't that a shame? Isn't it too bad? I really made a mistake."

Gillick and Chic were silent.

"You look very nice, Mrs Lindahl," Gillick said finally. He puffed on his cigar.

"Let's go," Virginia said, snapping off the light. "Come on. Come on." She started back upstairs; the two men followed. At the front door she stood waiting. "Let's go," she said again, as they passed by her, out onto the sidewalk. She locked the door and hurried to the station wagon. As soon as the two men were in, she backed out onto the street, shifted into a forward gear, and turned in the direction of her house.

"Take it easy," Chic said once, during the drive. Both men, failing to understand, were troubled and alarmed. "Slow down, Virginia." The car had gone close to a parked truck as Virginia made a sharp right-hand turn.

Not answering, she continued to drive as fast as possible. When she reached the house she stopped the car and hopped out.

"Good night," she said to Chic and Gillick; she tossed the car keys back, onto Chic's lap. Clutching her purse, she ran up the path and onto the porch. A moment later she had entered the house, switched on the living room light, and had seated herself at the phone.

She dialed Liz's number. Time passed, and then, at last, the receiver at her ear clicked, and Liz's voice said, "Hello?"

"Is Roger there?" she said.

"W-what?" Liz said.

"Is Roger there?"

"No," Liz said.

"Let me talk to him," she said.

"He's not here," Liz said. "Why should he be here? I haven't seen him in a week."

Virginia said, "Let me talk to Chic."

"He's taking a nap," Liz said.

"You're a goddamn liar," Virginia said. "And I know you are, because Chic is here; he's outside the house in the station wagon. He and Gillick. They haven't even left. Chic wasn't home all evening. He was at a business meeting."

The phone clicked dead.

She put the receiver back on the hook, then lifted it and dialed again. She let the phone ring on and on. Finally Liz answered.

"What do you want?' Liz said.

"Don't you ever come near my house again," Virginia said. "You stay away from here. You're nothing but a no-good little bit of a cracker; you hear me? You keep away from here. I don't ever want to see you switching your tail around my house again."

On the other end of the phone, Liz began to say something, but she did not listen; she hung up. Leaping to her feet she walked away from the phone, to the window, and looked out. The station wagon had gone. The street was empty.

Fifteen minutes passed. She remained at the window, with her coat still on. After a half hour had gone by, she saw the Oldsmobile turning onto the street. It parked in the driveway, the lights and motor were shut off, the door opened, and Roger stepped out. He locked up the car and then made his way up the front walk onto the porch. There he stopped. The front door was wide open; she had not shut it. For a moment he stood, and then he entered the house.

As soon as she saw the expression on his face she knew he had been there when she called. He had that closed-up look. His face was pulled together in the tight, unyielding scowl that she remembered from the years back; his body was hunched and his hands were jammed into his pockets. At first he did not speak. He merely stood, glancing up at her now and then. His mouth worked, he started to say something; then he wiped his lips with his thumb and fingers, grunted, and returned to silence.

Virginia said, "You were there."

"Where?" he muttered.

"When I called. You were there with Liz. You hadn't left."

"No I wasn't," he said. And then, gradually, he got on his face the sly, superior grin. You can't prove a thing, the look said. He shuffled his feet, glanced at her, and grinned. But he was afraid of her. The fear shone through the grin and lit it up.

"Where were you, then?" she said.

"At the store." He rocked back on his heels.

"I called the store."

He said, "I was downstairs. Working in the basement."

"All the time?"

"Yes," he said. "I had a lot to do."

"You're just as big a liar as she is," she said. "We drove down to the store."

"Who?" He stared at her.

"Chic and I and Gillick."

Now he had nothing to say. He stroked his chin and gazed down at his feet. And he still grinned; the grin remained on his face, empty and witless. It maddened her.

"You trash," she said.

He blinked.

"I know all about it," she said. "You better go down to the drugstore and get something to put on yourself, or you'll probably get a disease." As she said that, she believed it; but as soon as she had finished, she felt foolish. And, as he heard her, his look changed.

He seemed to draw some kind of energy from what she had said. It made him stand better; he stopped plucking at his chin. The grin expired, and, instead, a look of solemnity took its place. He unfastened his coat and passed by her with it, carrying it to the closet. When he returned, he said,

"What did you do, call her up?"

"Yes," she said. "As you know very well." She felt weak.

"Don't call her up," he said. "Leave her alone."

"Why?" she said.

"Just do what I say."

She found herself beginning to cry.

"That's a big help," he said, with irony.

Going into the hall she stayed by herself awhile, wiping her eyes on the sleeve of her coat.

My own fault, she said to herself. For saying that. Why did I say that? Never again, she said. I'll walk out before I say something like that again.

She returned to the living room. Roger was sitting down, in the middle of the couch, regarding her carefully.

"Have—you had dinner?" she said.

"I stopped at a drugstore and had a hamburger."

She said, "On your way home?"

"I stopped by a customer's house," he said. "I got the hamburger on the way here." He put his hands behind his head, extending his arms on either side. "Why are you going around the house with your coat on?"

Going to the closet, she hung up her coat.

"I didn't tell Chic," she said.

He said nothing.

"If she doesn't get panicky and tell him, there's no way he would know." She seated herself in the kitchen, in the dark. From where she was she could see down the hall and into the living room, the couch and her husband with his arms stuck out. "For a couple of minutes," she said, "I almost told him. I drove back here as fast as I could so I wouldn't tell him."

He did not stir.

"What do you plan to do?" she said.

"Like what? What do you mean?"

"I mean with her."

"I don't get you," he said.

She knew she would never get an answer. "You can't marry her," she said. "I'm not going to let you marry her."

Again he said nothing.

"I can't stop you from meeting her," she said, "If that's what you want to do. If you really want somebody like that. But it's not worth it, is it? Suppose Chic caught you? Wouldn't he kill you?"

"No," Roger said. "That doesn't happen."

"I thought that happened."

"He's just a bag of hot air."

"I think he'd kill you," she said.

Roger got up from the couch. "Let's forget it," he said.

"You better not see her," she said. "For your own safety. Can't you find some girl who isn't married? If he did anything to you, the law would be on his side. He'd know that. What would you do if he caught you with her? Suppose he had come home early tonight? You know she's too stupid to be able to cover up very long. Look what she said when I called. Of course, there wasn't much else she could say. If Chic had come home, what would you have done? Run out the back door?" The image of it made her sick with distress. "How awful," she said. "I don't think it would be worth it. I really don't."

Roger said, "He always drives Gillick home first. Gillick lives on the way. Then Gillick's wife calls Liz."

"Oh," she said. "I didn't understand. Does she have a system all worked out? Has she been doing it for years?"

He didn't answer.

"I guess," she said, "I shouldn't ask you any more about it."

"No," he said.

"Is that why you changed your mind and decided to put Gregg in the school? Because you met her?"

"No," he said.

"But that's part of it."

"No," he said.

She knew that he had reached the point where he would say nothing, answer nothing. "I want to tell you one thing," she said. "Since Chic stopped by here, he knows you weren't home this evening. So you better be extra careful. He knows she was alone this evening, too. So if he gets to thinking, that might be enough. You better not call her or talk to her for a while. When Chic gets home he'll undoubtedly tell her he was by here, and then she'll figure out—I guess she will—how I knew for certain that you were over there. I assume she has enough practice in this kind of thing to see she has to keep away from you for a while." She listened, but Roger said nothing. So she said, "I'll do this, I'll call her for you if you want. Not tonight, but sometime tomorrow."

"Christ no," he said, with such vehemence that she gave up the idea.

"It's up to you," she said. Sitting at the kitchen table, she listened; she waited for him to do something or say something. Off in the other room he was waiting, too, she realized.

The next morning, after breakfast, Roger said, "I'm going to take the Olds down to work today."

"Where'll you park it?" she said.

"In the lot around the corner."

"You almost never do that," she said.

He said, "I feel beat-out, today."

"I need the car," she said. "I have to pick up Marion at noon. We're going downtown shopping and to have lunch."

"The hell with that," he said. "I worked until ten o'clock last night; I'm beat-out. I need that car. My work comes first."

"I'll drive you to work," she said.

"What about after work?"

"I'll pick you up and drive you home."

He had no answer for that; his forehead wrinkled and twisted, but he could not answer her.

At eight-thirty she got in the car and started up the engine. Roger appeared on the front porch of the house, in his suit and tie, glaring at her.

"Come on," she said. "Or you'll be late."

With sleepy, embittered reluctance, he got into the car beside her. She drove him down to the store. Along the trip neither of them had much to say.

"Have you met Gillick?" she asked, once.

"No."

"He impressed me. He's a contractor, Chic says."

In front of the store she let Roger off.

"Thanks," he murmured, starting onto the sidewalk. A shaft of early-morning sunlight caught the side of his face, and she saw that he had shaved badly; a tuft of bristle discolored his cheek, near his ear. He always had trouble with that spot.

"I'll see you tonight," she said. At the sidewalk he lingered, waiting to be released, his back to her.

She drove away.

19

On his left, merchants rolled down their awnings with elaborate arm-motions. By the doorway of the West Coast Savings and Loan a group of secretaries clustered. Warm sunlight shone on his face, early-morning sunlight; the damp sidewalks had already begun to steam upward toward the sky. Debris from the night lay scattered in the entrance of his store and he kicked it out onto the sidewalk and then into the gutter. As he did so he took his key from his pocket. He unlocked the door and entered.

A Zenith sign clicked on and off above the row of television sets, but otherwise the store was dark; it smelled of cigarettes and furniture polish and fabric, a stale smell, the absence of life, cold and deserted, an uninhabited place. He put on the overhead fluorescent lights, opened the skylight, and illuminated the big R.C.A. display sign over the doorway. His hands in his pockets, he stood in the entrance, watching the street through the closed door.

At nine o'clock Pete Bacciagalupi appeared, jaunty in his blue single-breasted suit and pastel tie. "Hi," he said, opening the door wide, to let in the morning air. "You look like you've got a hang-over." He passed Roger, on his way to hang up his coat

Several minutes later the store truck slowed and entered a parking slot; the door flew open and Olsen jumped out. He spat on the pavement, grimaced, picked up a screwdriver that had fallen from the truck onto the street, and then sauntered toward the doorway of the store.

"Greetings," he said to Roger.

Roger said, "I want to take the outside calls, today. I want you on the bench." When Pete returned from hanging up his coat he said to him. "Don't let anybody take the truck out today. I want to use it. I told Olsen to stay down at the bench."

"Suit yourself," Pete said, "but a lot of those calls have to be taken care of today."

"I'll take them," Roger said.

"You're sure grumpy today," Pete said. He put his hand on Roger's shoulder. "Why don't you go over to the drugstore and have a Bromo?" He peered at him.

"Maybe so," Roger said. But he stayed by the front counter.

"Can I do anything?"

"No," Roger said. "Except wait on the customers."

On and on he stood, doing nothing, ignoring the people who came into the store and the phone and what Pete was doing. Just before ten o'clock he made out on the far side of the street a familiar flash of coat. At once he started from the store.

"I'll be back," he said to Pete, who was on the phone. Without pausing he started along the sidewalk in the direction that she was going. He reached the corner and crossed, against the light, and arrived as she did.

She had on little high heels and her checkered coat; her hair was up in a kerchief and her face was heavily made-up. Her lips were almost brown. When she recognized him her eyes filled up, strong and dark and wet, so that passers-by noticed her and some of them glanced back at her. She had stopped; when he reached her and took hold of her arm she did not budge. "No," she said. "I just wanted to go by and look in at you."

"Come on," he said, propelling her into motion.

"She might see us."

"Let's go down here," he said, leading her around the corner and onto a side street.

Liz said, "I came downtown to get a watch I left. I have to go by the jewelry store."

"I'll go with you," he said.

"I lay awake thinking about it all night," she said. "I kept thinking maybe she'd call again, or even come over. I kept listening for the phone or the doorbell." Two businessmen came out of an office doorway, and she had to step behind him for them to pass. Both men had fat, pink faces, chinless; they looked enough alike to be brothers. One picked his teeth, and both of them glanced at her in their fashion.

"Where's the jewelry store?" Roger said.

"In the next block, I think." From her coat pocket she brought out a small purse; as they walked she rummaged in it. "I have the claim check; the address is on it."

When she found the check she passed it to him to read.

"We should stop," she said. "Shouldn't we?" She took the claim check back from him. "Good-bye," she said. Pulling away, she hurried off, between two parked cars, onto the street; a taxi slowed for her and she crossed to the other side and disappeared among a group of people, women shoppers at the entrance of a clothing store. He followed after her. No you don't, he said. I know you. I knew you'd show up and then run off.

In the middle of the block he caught up with her. She had the claim check held up and she was reading the numbers of the storefronts.

"Give it to me," he said. "I'll find it." He walked along with her.

"I have to get right back home," she said. "I have a lot of cleaning-up to do around the house; I have to vacuum and wash the windows and this afternoon I have to go see about a chair. Chic wants me to get one of those big smoking chairs for the living room, those green leather ones. Not the old-fashioned ones; they make a new kind. It looks a lot better. It's like an office chair."

He said, "Are you going to deny me?"

"No," she said. "I love you. But I came to say good-bye. Maybe I'll see you again sometime later on, and even if I don't see you for a long time I'll be thinking about you; I won't forget you. Good-bye." Her fingers brushed his face, over his lips and chin. "I'm not sorry," she said. "It was fine. Wasn't it for you, too?"

Sayings, he thought. The commonplaces which she had picked up here and there, from books and movies and TV and magazines.

"I know I'll see you again," she said, still close to him, touching him. "You can't keep two people apart when they really belong to each other."

Her words. Everybody's words. Deliberate emptiness, prepared in advance. As if he were hearing an edict of some council, read aloud to him. A group of persons who continued on and on, with nothing else in mind, sorting the phrases. Reciting them back and forth among one another in their cold voices. At the end they had sent her out to deliver it to him; she was a clerk.

Now, he thought, he either accepted this nonsense or he tossed it up in the air, right now, with no delay. Nothing else was fair to her. If he strung along, listening to her, nodding and responding, trying to argue, he would find himself laughing. I can't take you seriously, he said to himself. Now I'm hearing what the rest of them hear, the scatterbrained talk, the ridiculous conversation you turn on them. You're turning it on me. Aren't you? I'm getting it, too. And I can see how it feels. In just a second—in the barest fraction of a second—I'll be able to view it the way they view it. I'll slip over. It isn't far. I can almost do it now, he thought. Damn near.

He said, "Liz, when I woke up this morning I lay in bed awhile and I said to myself, I'm in love with Liz Bonner."

She accepted that calmly. She seemed to take it for granted. "I know," she said. "But I wonder if that's what it really is. Last night after your wife called I got to thinking about it. Maybe it's just that we just stimulated each other physically. Couldn't that be?"

Only from a book, he thought. From a textbook or an article. From a popular magazine she had picked up in a bus.

"Sex is a complicated thing," she said. "Nobody really understands it. Even when you're asleep it works on you. When you have a dream, it has to do with sex; did you know that? The different things that happen in a dream are sexual symbolism. The other night, for instance, I dreamed about a long low building, like a courthouse. That represents a female sexual organ, according to this book I read on psychology. It was a book I had when I first got married, before Chic and I began to have intercourse. According to the doctor who wrote it, a woman should always be careful to take an active part during marital relations. He said that most women are frigid because they don't realize that they have to really participate in the act. So I always tried to participate. I mean, maybe because I was trying to live a healthy marital life I somehow over-stimulated you or something. I don't know."

"Did he say anything else?" Roger said.

"He explained about different muscles. Most of them lie dormant during the woman's entire life and she isn't even aware that they exist. I used to know the names."

She walked on a few steps, along the sidewalk. He followed her. People hurried past them in both directions.

"Chic has never been much good," she said. "Concerning marital relations. He always wanted to put it in immediately, if you understand what I mean. Does this bother you, my talking like this? I've been thinking . . . I wanted to talk about it openly with you. He never liked any of the foreplay. I guess that's what it's called. But to a woman that's terribly important. If a woman is going to reach climax she needs that. Actually the lining inside a woman isn't sensitive beyond a certain point. So once it actually enters her she may stop responding. There's a place that's very sensitive but I forget what it's called. Do you know?"

"No," he said.

"It's a sort of bone and if you go in right it's stimulated at the same time. You can reach that with your hand. If a woman, especially a young girl, one who isn't married, wants to stimulate herself she usually does it that way. And that's outside. A lot of men think that isn't the way it is, but it is. Sometimes afterward, after a climax, a woman can't bear having that touched. I wish I could remember the name of it. It starts with s or c. Anyhow, they actually scream if it's touched. But a woman can go on—most of them—and have climax after climax and a man can't. So if a man comes too fast then it isn't fair to the woman. He's all done and she's hardly started. So very seldom, maybe not ever, a woman gets anything out of the act."

"Meaning?" he said.

She said, "It's usually just for the man. For his enjoyment. The woman sort of submits to it, to please him. But that isn't right. A woman shouldn't do it if she doesn't get something out of it. Don't you agree? If she realizes that she's not, even if she wants to, very often she can't. It isn't her fault. In most cases it's the man's fault. It all depends on how he is, and if he doesn't care about her enough then naturally she can't get anything out of it."

At the corner she started down a side street. He held onto her arm; she allowed him to.

"It's bright," she said. "I should have brought my dark glasses."

In a yard, a plump Pomeranian dog yapped at them and Liz started away from him, toward it, with her hand out.

"I love dogs," she said, bending. "What's your name, little fellow?"

"Watch out," Roger said.

Kneeling, she patted the dog's sides. "He won't bite me. See?" The dog's tongue lolled, a small red tongue, like a cat's. The animal's ears were pointed. Liz flicked them.

"He's cute," she said, as Roger started on.

Across the street, in a fenced yard, a vast dahlia plant with shaggy cactus blossoms, yellow and thick, as large as dinner plates, caught Liz's attention. Before he could stop her, she had started across the street. When he caught up with her she had reached the fence and had broken one of the blossoms from its stalk. An elderly, heavyset woman in a print dress was sweeping the walk and when she saw that she hurried toward them.

"What do you mean?" she shouted. "I'm going to call the police and have you arrested; you have no right in the world to pick flowers from other persons' yards!"

Liz held onto the dahlia. "Give her a dollar or something," she said to Roger, as if she did not really see the woman. "I want to keep it." To the woman she said, "It was practically ready to fall off anyhow. And look, you have plenty of them; you have a whole bushful of them."

Feeling conspicuous, Roger paid the woman for the flower. Without a word she grabbed up the money and returned to her sweeping. Dust flew in clouds from her broom.

As they continued on, Liz fitted the stalk of the blossom into her belt. "How does it look?" she asked.

"That was a lousy thing to do," he said.

"She has more."

"Do you have to do dumb things like that?" he said.

Liz gave a snort, a suppressed noise, deep in her throat. Without warning she ran on ahead of him, breaking away from him and leaving him behind.

He thought, she's in no condition. He hurried after her and she jerked away. Shaking her head she ran; her arms flailed and then she had fallen. Crying, she rolled with her coat flapping; her fingers caught at the pavement and her purse bounced open and hurled out its mirror and lipstick and papers and pencils in all directions. He got down by her and pinned her to the pavement, halting her rolling motion. Ludicrous, he thought. Horrible and ludicrous; how could such a thing happen? He gathered her up in his arms, clutching her against him. Her face was scratched. A drop of blood shone on her cheek and she smeared it away. Her eyes were glazed.

"It's okay," he said

A few people halted to peer. Furiously, he waved them to go on. They went, but still glancing back.

Sitting on the sidewalk he held her tightly. She breathed irregularly and now she was staring at him; her face was flaked and without color.

"You're okay," he said. He began to collect the things that had spilled from her purse. Some had rolled a long distance.

Helping her to her feet he started to lead her back in the direction that they had come. She seemed to remain stunned, and he realized that she was limping. Maybe, he thought, she was physically hurt.

"I'd like to wash my face," she said. She put her hand down to her foot. "I think I broke off the heel of my shoe." From her foot she took her shoe, holding it up. The heel had been broken off, and he did not see it anywhere. Probably it had rolled into the gutter. "I'll take them off," she said. Leaning against him, grasping him with her fingers, she took off both shoes. "Is that it over there? Over by that wall."

He found the heel—she was right—and brought it to her. Now she had taken off her stockings and put them into her purse. Barefoot, she began to walk, slowly, and with great stiffness.

"I guess the dahlia got lost," she said.

He led her back to the business street, and together they found a shoe-repair shop. Inside at the machines, a boy in a blue uniform was stitching the sole of an Oxford; the shop screeched with racket.

"Be right with you folks," the boy said.

Liz seated herself in one of the cloth and chrome chairs, by the ashtray. "Do you have a cigarette?" she said to Roger, in an unsteady, weary voice.

He lit a cigarette for her, and put it into her hand.

"Isn't it strange?" she said presently.

"What," he said, rousing himself.

"How we found each other. You came up to the school to put your little boy in . . . there Chic and I were, watching them play football. We had never heard of each other . . . and now we're completely together. Nothing separating us, nothing holding us apart. And a month ago we had never heard of each other."

He said nothing. What could he answer to that? She is dumb, he thought. Yes, there is no doubt.

"What do you think it was that brought us together?" Liz said.

His voice answered, "Nothing brought us together. We brought ourselves together."

"Don't you think that Something watches over us?"

"No. Why should it?"

Considering that, she said, "Do you think in the world there's just one person?"

"No," he said.

The boy shut off his machine and hurried cheerfully over. "Sorry to keep you waiting. I see you got your shoes off, lady, all ready there." He took the broken shoe and heel from Liz and examined them. "Catch it in a grate? The other day a lady caught her heel in one of them sidewalk grates—you know? I can fix it back on right now; cost you seventy-five cents." Without waiting, he trotted back behind the counter and began working with a hammer and small nails.

"What do you want to do?" Liz said. "I'll leave it up to you."

"I want to go on," he said.

"So do I," she said. "It's worth it. I know how I feel and I know how you feel about me. I don't care about anything else. I don't even care if she knows. In a way I'm glad she knows. Does that sound silly?"

"No," he said, lying, wanting to keep going and knowing that he had to listen to her and believe her if he really meant to.

"Are you willing to run the risk?" she asked. "Maybe she'll tell Chic. He'd probably kill me. Or you. Maybe both of us. And the courts will uphold him."

"I don't think he will," he said.

"You're not afraid, are you? No, I know you're not. Or you wouldn't have gotten into this in the first place."

"I don't think she'll say anything to him," he said.

Liz got to her feet, swayed as she pressed out the cigarette against the ashtray. Then, very slowly and cautiously, she walked in her bare feet across to the boy working with his hammer. To the boy she said, "This man and I slept together last night."

The boy worked feverishly, not looking up. Probably he had been listening to the whole conversation.

"Come on," Roger said, standing up. "Leave him alone."

She came back. "I wanted him to know," she said. "He knows anyhow." Turning to the boy, she said, "Didn't you already know?"

The boy poured himself into his work, ignoring her; the hammer clacked in a frenzy.

"Why do we have to hide?" Liz said, seating herself. Her face still had the dry, set look, the shock. "I want to tell them. They know anyhow. I'm going back to your store with you."

"No," he said.

Finishing the job on the shoe the boy came around the counter, wiping his hands on his apron. "That'll be six bits," he said, staring past the two of them. He was flushed and a little hysterical; he shoved the shoe at Roger and started back again.

"Thank you," Liz said to the boy. "I appreciate it." She stepped into the shoe and then into its mate. "It's fine," she said to Roger. Now, in her shoes again, she picked up her purse and started toward the front of the store. Roger dug into his pockets, found a dollar, and gave it to the boy.

"Thanks," the boy said, glancing at him and swallowing.

Liz, at the doorway, said, "Why are you so embarrassed?"

The boy ducked his head and snapped on one of the machines. But she walked back toward him.

"Why shouldn't we sleep together?" she said to the boy. "We're in love. Isn't that what counts? I have two children and he has one little boy, a real cute little boy. What else can we do? We can't get married; we would if we could. It's not our fault."

Roger took hold of her arm but she resisted.

"Wait," she said. "I want to ask him. Why does he think it's so wrong?" To the boy she said, "Have you ever slept with a girl? You have, haven't you? You weren't married to her, were you? Why do you blame us and not blame yourself for doing it? You ought to be consistent." To Roger she said, "He isn't consistent. That's all I want him to be. He can think anything he wants, but he should be consistent; we're not any different from anybody else. Everybody does it. Then everybody must be guilty. Isn't that right? Maybe that's what they mean by original sin." The boy had left the counter; he had gone to the rear of the store. Liz followed after him. "I just want to ask you," she said. "I want to find out, that's all. Can't you answer me? Wouldn't you go to bed with me if you had the chance? Is there anything wrong with it?"

The boy did not answer. Roger led her from the shoe repair store, outside onto the sidewalk.

"This is our punishment," Liz said. "It's what we deserve. We've lost any contact with them, haven't we? We're in another world from them. They can't hear us and we can't hear them. That boy never heard a word I said; I could have said anything. He had his eyes completely shut."

"He heard, all right," Roger said, thinking that the shoe repair store was only a couple of blocks from his own store.

"No," she disagreed, as they walked along the sidewalk. "He didn't hear anything. I could stop anybody and they wouldn't hear what I was saying."

"Don't," he said.

"You haven't changed your mind, have you?" she said. "You still want to go on, don't you?"

He nodded.

"I just wanted to be sure," she said.

Seeing her like this, he did not know what to do with her. He had to get back to the store, but he was afraid to leave her. Yet they could not keep walking along the sidewalk; they had to go somewhere, make up their minds.

"I better go home," she said. "I shouldn't be down here, in this area. But I have to go to the jewelry store; otherwise Chic'll wonder what I was doing today. He might call the house while I'm not home, and I have to have something to tell him. You better not come in the jewelry store with me. They've seen me and Chic together; I'll get my watch and go on home and wait for you."

He said, "It's too risky."

"What?" she said. "Oh, you mean your coming by the house. It's too risky now."

"Later on," he said.

"Yes," she said. "That's so. Explain what you mean. You mean you want to call it off?"

"No," he said. "I don't mean that."

"Yes," she said. "You mean you want to call it off."

He was silent.

"What if I hadn't come by?" she said. "Would you have gotten in touch with me?"

"I would have," he said.

She peered at him, her eyebrows up. "Are you trying to get even with me for something? It isn't my fault that Chic came by your place and your wife found out where you were."

"I know," he said.

"Can't you tell me what's going on in your mind? I don't want to leave you; I don't want you to leave me. Let's try to make it work." She drew herself down into her coat, like a brown bird.

"Sure," he said. "But we have to be careful."

"Well, I don't understand," she said. "But it's up to you; I can't make you do what you said you were going to do." She started slowly off. "Maybe you can call me sometime."

"I think I'm right," he said.

"You probably won't call me," she said. "Anyhow I'll be thinking about you." Her voice wavered. "What a surprise. You didn't say anything at first."

"I'll give you a call," he said. Going after her he put his arm around her; she pressed against him and then she caught hold of him and kissed him. A group of kids, driving by in a Mercury sedan, loudly whistled and honked and waved. She let go of him and looked up seriously.

"Kids," he said.

"You're right," she said. "I know you are. I came down here to see you just one last time. I want to see you again, but I can't. Take care of yourself, you promise?"

"Yes," he said. Leaving her, he walked off, in the direction of the store.

Customers surrounded the counter, a flock of them hiding Pete from sight. He felt guilt. His own store, he thought.

"I'm sorry," he said as he stepped behind the counter.

Pete, ringing up the sale of a table model radio, said, "That woman wants her radio. Here's the number." He passed Roger the claim check.

After the customers had been taken care of, Roger picked over the tags by the register; he involved himself in the business of the day. "A good hour of business," he said to Pete. "Is Olsen downstairs?"

"He's next door," Pete said, writing down the sale of the radio in his book. "Having a cup of coffee."

An elderly lady appeared in the doorway, carrying a fat cloth shopping bag. "Are you the radio repairman?" she said to Pete. "I have a radio here I want to get fixed." She began to unfasten the shopping bag. "It just went dead. It's worked fine for thirteen years; I don't understand why it should go dead. Maybe it's a broken wire."

Or a worn-out sazifryer, Roger thought to himself. He helped her free the radio from its bag, and plugged it in. Pete brought the push broom from the closet at the rear and began sweeping.

"Afraid you'll have to leave it," Roger said. "I'll make out a tag." He unclipped his pen and wrote the date on the top tag.

"Oh dear," the old lady said. "I don't know what I'll do without it; I depend on it for the news."

After the old lady had left, he said to Pete, "There's a bunch of dead flies in the window. And the sign in front of the Emerson 21-inch is on its face. Maybe you can reach it without moving anything big."

"Okay," Pete said, sweeping. "Hey, you know, you look sort of hung over today. Why don't you go over to the Finnish steam bath place for a while? It'd do you some good." The telephone rang; he leaned his broom against the wall and walked over to answer it. "Modern TV," he said.

A young couple entered the store and stopped before the display of Westinghouse television sets. "Good morning," Roger said to them. "Something I can show you?"

He did his best, but nothing came of it. The young couple thanked him, said they would return and buy either the ivory or the plain plastic set, and left with a handful of literature.

"Time-wasters," Pete said, again sweeping.

At eleven o'clock Olsen returned from having his roll and coffee at the Rexall Drugstore. Passing Roger, he jerked his thumb and said, "There's an old fart over there who wants to see you. The old guy from next door."

"Jules Neame," Pete said. "I saw him ambling over there."

"Me?" Roger said. Christ, he thought. I know. I see.

"More lawn swings," Pete said. "Get your sleeves rolled up and pitch in."

Leaving his coat under the counter, Roger walked next door to the drugstore. At the soda fountain Jules Neame, big and untidy, sat eating a roast beef sandwich. The top button of his trousers was undone, and he had stuffed a paper napkin into his collar so that it hung, like a bib, down the front of his shirt. When he saw Roger he motioned him over to the vacant stool next to him.

"Hi, my friend," Neame said, smiling at him.

"Hello, Jules," he said.

"How's everything going?"

"Okay," Roger said. "As well as could be expected."

"It comes a lot of different ways, doesn't it? You never know. I guess we ought to be glad of what we have. We shouldn't look too far ahead: we should enjoy it now." Neame gnawed at his sandwich, speaking with his mouth full. "Here we are, Mr. Lindahl; we know that, but what else do we know? They talk about heaven and the afterlife. I think we'd be better off not worrying about that. Life is too short. We torment ourselves with worries about that, when we have enough to worry about already. We have enough travail in our lives. Guilt is useless. The world torments us, and we react by tormenting ourselves. I wonder how we can ever have such a low opinion of ourselves that we join in. I suppose we agree that they're right about us. We don't merit any happiness, and when we do get a trace of it we feel we've stolen something that doesn't belong to us."

Barely listening to old Neame, Roger toyed with the cream pitcher that the waitress had put on the counter.

"Good morning, Mr. Lindahl," the waitress said, pretty in her red blouse and tiny white hat. "How's business today?"

"Fine," he said.

"What will it be today?"

"Coffee," he said, reaching for a dime.

Neame stopped his hand. "Let me pay for it, Mr. Lindahl."

He shrugged. "Thanks."

"You seem so downcast today," Jules Neame said to him, as the waitress went off. "I hope whatever it is that's bothering you turns out to be nothing at all. You're a deserving man, Mr. Lindahl. Believe me when I say that. I know how you do business; I know how you treat your employees and your customers. Everybody in this block has a high regard for you. If there's anything I can do to help, I wish you'd tell me. I have a lot of respect and confidence in you. They say—you hear people say—there's a lot of good in everyone, but I don't go along with that; to me that's a terrible thing, taking on the role of judge that way, putting up a standard and passing judgment, as if they were in a position to tell what's good and what isn't good. A man has to determine for himself what's the best thing, and those who are fond of him, if they really respect him, leave it up to him to decide. I know the religious people don't feel along those lines, but that's too bad. Human beings are more important than their theories of morality. You know, when I was young I did a lot of speculating about philosophical matters. Did you ever by any chance run into a great thinker by the name of Spinoza? He had something he said, once; about a procession of musicians—a street band, you know, like they have down in the South—going past a funeral. And the music of the band—" He rambled on and on. The coffee came and Roger took up the cup automatically, paying no attention to the large old man beside him.

"Now my store," Neame was saying, drinking down a glass of buttermilk, "has all that space in the back, where we keep the merchandise. It's practically a world of its own, back there. Nobody ever goes back there except myself and my wife, and usually we're too busy to go back there ourselves. I rememember once I went back there and found a cat asleep on one of the sacks of grass seed. How it got into the store I don't know. We never notice who passes in and out. If they want to come in, let them come in." He leaned close to Roger and spoke in a lower murmur of sound. "Why don't you walk back to the store with me—I have to go back there." Wiping his mouth he pushed his empty plate away and stepped from his stool. "Just for a moment. I want you to see something. I told your repairman I wanted to talk to you; I saw you in there when I went by the front of your store, but you were busy talking to a young couple so I didn't go in. I don't want to stay away from my place too long. I'm not sure how long she'll stay there; she was so upset. But my wife calmed her down, so I think she's probably feeling a lot better by now. She didn't want to go in your store because she didn't want to cause you any trouble. So she came walking into our place and explained the situation to us; not the whole situation, but just that she wanted to see you for a moment and that she couldn't go into your store, or she felt that she couldn't. So I told her to stay there and I'd go over and get you and bring you back." His hand on Roger's shoulder, he steered him from the counter, toward the door; the smell of buttermilk blew down the back of Roger's neck and he felt the weight of the old man's hand on him, the heavy, boneless paw. "What's her name?" Neame asked him, as they reached the sidewalk and started toward the lawn furniture shop. "We didn't want to ask her. You don't have to say if you don't want. No, maybe you shouldn't."

Pausing before his own store, Roger signaled to Pete that he was going over to Neame's store. Pete winked at him and made a motion of lifting some heavy object.

"She's a very pretty woman," Neame said.

"Yes," he said.

"She has a very sweet face. Here." Neame held open the door of his shop, and Roger passed on inside.

In the back, beyond the partition, Liz sat in the middle of one of Neame's swings, her hands in her lap, her purse beside her. As soon as she saw him she started to her feet and dashed breathlessly toward him; her figure grew and she came with her arms out. Without a word she reached him and flew against him.

"Please," she said.

He said, "What did you do, come right here?"

"I couldn't go home," she said. Her face was strained, and all her features had slid sideways. The distortion amazed him. "I know it's a mistake," she said, "but I don't care. The hell with her. The hell with Chic and the boys and all of them. You feel like that, don't you?"

God damn, he thought.

"Is it wrong?" she demanded. "I love you. They all seem so vague. I knew I had to come back. They're out there, like those people." She meant the passers-by along the sidewalk, and the cars and buses. The office buildings. The stores. "Even my own kids," she said. "I don't even care about Jerry and Walter. Do you care about your store? It doesn't mean anything. I never felt like this before. It's strange." She stroked his arm, waiting, examining him, holding onto him.

He said, "Are you going to be home?"

"Yes," she said. "I'll be home the rest of the day."

"Suppose I come over after noon."

Liz said, "That would be fine." She drew away from him. "I'll see you, then. In a couple of hours."

He watched her as she hurried out of Jules Neame's lawn furniture store; he watched until she disappeard from sight.

The hell with them, he thought. The hell with my wife, Virginia, and her mother, Mrs. Watson; the hell with your husband, Chic, and your two boys, Walter and Jerry. I agree with you. The hell with all of them, even my son, Gregg. Family and friends, things, store, our lives, the plans we have had, everything we have had or thought about, except this.

But they will get us, he said. You are too dumb, too stupid to realize that. But I realize it. They will all come back.

20

When she got home Virginia fixed herself a dish of cottage cheese and canned pears; she sat at the kitchen table for a while, and then she put the breakfast dishes into the sink. She telephoned a friend, a woman named Rae Phelps who was one of the mothers from the nursery school to which Gregg had gone. Mrs. Phelps' name was on a ditto-graphed card stuck in the front of the phone book.

"I'd like to borrow your car today," Virginia said. "If I can."

In her ear, Mrs. Phelps' voice boomed, "What'll I use? I don't want to sound antisocial, but I have to take the darn kids to school and pick them up and shop. Otherwise I'd be more than glad to let you have it."

Virginia said, "I'll give you my Olds for the day."

"I don't understand," Rae Phelps said.

"It's just a thing I'm doing," she said. "I don't want to take the Olds." Her relationship with Rae Phelps was so remote that she did not even remember what color or make of car the woman owned. All she remembered was that the car was large and fairly new.

"It sounds crazy to me," Mrs. Phelps said, in her hearty way. "But if you want to swap cars, it's fine by me. You want to come by then?"

She thanked her and hung up.

Next she changed to a suit that Roger had never seen, a dark blue suit with a white collar. She put on gloves, and a small hat, stockings and heels, and transferred her things from her usual purse to a small shiny-black leather purse that Marion had given her for a present and which she had never used.

He'll call here once, she said to herself. To make sure I'm home.

A little past eleven o'clock, the phone rang.

"Hello," she said.

"Hi," Roger said glumly.

"You just caught me," she said. "I was just on my way to pick up Marion."

"I wondered," he said, "if I left a tag book there. I'm missing one."

She searched about the house, somewhat. "No," she said, back at the phone. "I don't see it."

"Okay," he said. "I must have it here somewhere. Thanks."

As soon as she was off the phone she locked up the house, got into the Olds, and drove over to Rae Phelps' house, a little over a mile away. There she traded Mrs. Phelps the Olds and received a well-waxed dark green Imperial.

"I'll be careful with it," she said, feeling anxious.

"Don't worry," Mrs. Phelps said. "It's insured." She was a tall, kindly, active woman, and she did not seem to mind giving up her car. "Whatever it is, I hope you make out all right," she said. "What is it, some sort of surprise party or something?"

"Yes," Virginia said.

In the Imperial—she found it marvelously easy to control—she drove by way of the freeway to the industrial part of town and the Bonny Bonner Bread Factory. She had never seen it before, and it impressed her; it was immense.

"I'd like to see Mr. Charles Bonner," she said to the girl at the reception desk. She told the girl her name.

"Yes, Mrs. Lindahl," the girl said. "Mr. Bonner is in and he says to show you in. It's just to your right, through that door."

She entered Chic's office. "Hello," she said.

"What a surprise," Chic said, standing up behind his metal desk on which were mimeographed reports and a typewriter.

"I can't stay more than a second," she said. "Do you have your designs here?" God, she said to herself. Let's hope not.

"No," he said. "They're home."

"I want to show them to our attorney," Virginia said. "I'd like him to see them."

A gratified expression appeared on Chic's face. "That's a top-notch idea, Virginia. You mean now?"

"Where's a phone?" she said. "I'll call and see if Liz is there. If so I'll drive over and pick them up. Mr. Charpentier is expecting me, and it's almost noon."

"Yes," he said, pushing his phone towards her. "She ought to be home, unless she's out shopping." He hovered nearby, as she dialed. She dialed her own number, and of course there was no answer. She let it ring; she let him hear it. "Damn," he said. "Wouldn't you know Liz would be out somewhere? Probably chewing the rag with some neighbor-lady."

"Well," Virginia said, hanging up the phone, "maybe I can make another appointment with Charpentier later on in the week."

Digging into his trouser pocket, Chic said, "Suppose I give you the key? You could get them; they're in the living room, on the coffee table."

"All right," she said, looking at her watch. She had only a little time left, as she calculated. Taking Chic's keys she left the Bonny Bonner Bread Company, got into the Imperial, and drove through the downtown business section until she saw a key store. There, she had a duplicate of Chic's door key made for her, at a cost of thirty-five cents.

She then drove back to the bread factory and returned Chic's keys to him. "I missed Mr. Charpentier," she said. "He had already gone to lunch."

"Oh," Chic said. "That's too bad."

"I'll make another appointment with him," she said.

"You people are getting pretty serious, aren't you?" Chic said. "I could tell by the way you got out of the store last night. You were afraid you might say something—" He smiled. "That would commit you. Am I right?"

"Yes," she said. She said good-bye and left the building.

At noon, she picked up Marion.

"What's this?" her mother said, peering about at the car as they drove. "Did you get rid of the Olds?"

"I borrowed this," Virginia said. "Now listen to me. We're not going downtown; I've changed my mind."

"Why are you all dressed up? You look very stately. I've never seen you dressed up like this before. Why don't you dress up this well all the time? You make me feel dowdy." Mrs. Watson noticed the purse. "That's the bag I gave you and you've never used. I wondered when you'd get around to carrying it. It goes wonderfully with your blue suit. Do I know that suit?"

Virginia said, "We're going by the store for a while. I don't want you to do anything; I just want you along with me."

"What kind of thing?" Her mother eyed her. "Look at me, Ginny," she said. "What is this?"

"I can't look," she said angrily. "I'm driving."

"Are you having trouble with that woman? That Liz Bonner?"

"I just want you along," Virginia said.

"I have a right to know what the situation is," Mrs. Watson said.

"The hell you do. You just sit there and watch. That's all. Now you do as I say; you hear?"

"My goodness, Virginia," her mother said.

Across the street from the store she parked in a parking slot and tilted the rearview mirror so that she could watch the entrance. The store truck had been parked in the loading zone.

"He'll use that," she said. Thank heaven, she thought, he hadn't been able to leave yet. As always, he had got tied up.

"Is he meeting her?" Mrs. Watson asked.

She said nothing.

At twelve-thirty, Roger appeared in the doorway of the store, carrying a TV chassis. He loaded the chassis in the truck, went back into the store, and emerged with another chassis.

"He's going out now," Virginia said.

"What are those mechanical things he's carrying?"

"For delivery," she said. "You know," she said to her mother, "you can get the key to anybody's house, just by asking them. All you have to do is tell them you want the key." She took the key to the Bonner house from her purse and laid it on the floorboards of the car, by her right foot, where she could immediately get hold of it.

"I'm surprised at you," her mother said, in an injured, disturbed tone.

Virginia lit a cigarette and continued to watch. She felt no sense of pressure, now; as soon as she had seen the store truck she had felt a kind of relief. Inside the store, Roger conferred with Pete; he inspected the big tablet on which the house-calls were listed, and then he made a phone call at the counter.

"Almost," she said to her mother.

I am not going to have it happen to me, she said to herself. I am not going to wind up like her.

In Washington, D.C., Teddy had come by; they had heard voices in the hall and Roger had leaped up to go to the apartment door. At first she did not understand who Teddy was; she had greeted her as a friend of his, and she had said how pretty the little girl was. Roger had fallen into such a melancholy state that, as she knelt down by the little girl, she had suddenly realized that this was his daughter and that Teddy was his former wife, from whom he was getting his divorce.

"I wanted to meet you," Teddy had said. Her legs were too thin; they were not much to look at, and when she walked, her feet turned outward, duck-footed, and they were flat. She had a penetrating voice; when she spoke to the child she took up a singsong pattern of accusation that made both Virginia and the child uncomfortable. So this is the woman he was married to, she had thought. This is she.

Afterward, she had said to Roger, "How could you ever have gotten interested in her?"

"I don't know," he had said morosely.

And she had thought, then, What a repulsive woman. Can he possibly see something like that in me? Is that what he wants?

"He likes that type," Virginia said to her mother. "It's a reversion. Liz is the kind he used to go around with, back when he was working in the shipyard and on the W.P.A. and probably before that, in Arkansas." And he would leave everything for that type, she thought. He would leave me.

"Did you just walk out on her?" she had asked him.

"No," Roger said. "It was falling apart. We agreed on it."

"But she wants you back."

"No," he said.

"Certainly she does. That's why she came by. She wanted to see if she could make you change your mind. She wishes she hadn't given you a divorce; she almost said it out loud, in front of me."

He repeated, "We agreed on it."

"And your child," she protested. "You just—abandoned them. I wonder if you'd ever do that to me."

She smelled the cold presence of snow, the ice, the Tidal Basin, the hills and woods around the Potomac. She saw around her the trees along Pennsylvania Avenue, the mansions. She saw the colored maids in their coats and red-cotton bandanas going to work in the morning on the bus, the town band in Maryland at night, marching along the street, leaving off its players at the different houses. The white-picket fences, the weight of summer.

"He just deserted her," she said to her mother. "They do; they always do. It's their nature."

"I warned you," her mother said.

"How dare he do that to me," she said. For someone like that. "I knew he would sooner or later, when he got the urge."

Coming out of the store, Roger halted, blinking in the sunlight. He removed his glasses from his nose, polished them with his handkerchief, glanced up and down the street, and then got into the truck.

"Here we go," Virginia said. She started the engine of the Imperial; it flooded and died. "God damn," she said, starting it again. "I'm not familiar with this car; it belongs to Rae Phelps. I hope I can manage it."

"You be careful, now," her mother said. "Maybe you ought to reconsider what you're doing, Ginny. I think perhaps you're acting a bit too hasty. What do you care if he's running around with the Liz Bonner woman? You can go to an attorney and get a divorce easier than pie; you know that. What do you need to mess around with all this kind of thing for?"

She backed from the parking slot and followed the truck.

"Can't he see you?" Mrs. Watson said.

"He doesn't know this car," she said. And she knew that the truck had bad rear-vision.

For almost an hour the truck moved about town, stopping at houses to deliver TV chassis and to pick up others. She began to wonder if she were making a mistake.

"He's doing his work," Mrs. Watson said. "He's doing what he's supposed to. And what are you doing?"

I'm waiting, she said to herself.

"How'd you get that key?" Mrs. Watson said. "Is that really a key to her house?"

I hope so, Virginia thought. I would feel darn strange if it turned out to be a key to their garage. But the clerk at the key store had assured her that of those on the ring it was certainly the front door key; it was the only Yale key of the bunch

"I think you've gone crazy as a loon," Mrs. Watson said. "It wouldn't surprise me to discover that you have a gun in your purse. You read about that in the newspapers; I don't see why you'd want to lower yourself in this manner."

Virginia said, "I have to catch him at it. Otherwise he'll always deny it. He'll never admit it."

"Why do you care?"

She didn't answer.

At two o'clock the truck turned in the direction of San Fernando. When it had gone most of the way it stopped at a Standard Station. Roger stepped out, stretched his legs, and walked into the men's room. When he came out again he entered the station office and made a phone call at the pay phone.

"He's phoning," Virginia said, from where she had parked.

"He's just calling the store to see if any changes have happened to his route," Mrs. Watson said. "He doesn't want to have to come all the way out here for nothing."

True, Virginia said to herself.

Returning to the truck, Roger started out again into traffic. She followed, keeping a large distance between them. Then, at an intersection, she lost the truck; she found herself the first car at the red light. The truck disappeared at a leisurely pace around a corner.

"See?" Mrs. Watson yelled in her ear. "You went and lost him! Now look what you've gone and done!"

When the light changed, Virginia made a right turn and drove directly to the Bonner house. She parked at the cross street, between two other cars.

"He'll be along," she said.

Five minutes later the store truck passed them and parked nearby, somewhere else. As she and her mother sat in the Imperial, they saw Roger walk along the sidewalk, glance here and there, and then continue, on foot, down the street to the Bonner house. He ascended to the porch, the door immediately opened, and he went inside. The door shut after him.

So that's that, Virginia said to herself.

"Let's go," she said. She started the car and pulled out onto the street.

"Are we leaving?" her mother said.

"Yes," she said.

"What about your key? Why'd you go and have the key made if you're not going to use it?"

"I don't want to," she said, driving away from the Bonner house.

"You've got a key; you know they're in there; you said yourself you have to catch him at it."

"Okay!" she said. At an intersection she made a U-turn; a dog, sleeping in the street, scrambled up and stood in confusion. She drove back in the direction they had come. "Will you come in with me?" she said. "I won't gone in alone."

"I'll come in," her mother said. "I'm against it, but I feel I should."

Virginia parked a few houses away. For a moment she sat.

"We better hurry," her mother said. "He might leave."

Virginia opened the car door. On the other side, her mother did the same.

"Don't let the door slam," her mother said, closing hers quietly. "You don't want to let them know you're coming."

Leaving the car door hanging open, she walked up the sidewalk toward the Bonner house.

"Did you have the key?" her mother asked.

"No." She returned to the car and picked it up from the floor boards.

"Now don't you be scared," her mother said.

She did not feel scared. She felt light-headed as if she were floating. As a child she felt like this as she walked up the steps to the stage of the school auditorium.

"I feel like I'm going to make a speech," she said. "A patriotic speech or something." She laughed.

"Never you mind about that," her mother said. "Just you get on in there."

Now it did seem funny to her. On the path she stopped. "I can't do it," she said, still laughing. "I'm sorry, but it's too absurd. You go in, if you want."

Snatching the key from her, Mrs. Watson said, "I will go in; I most assuredly will."

"Wait," Virginia said. "I don't want you to put your oar into this." She took the key back, climbed the steps, and unlocked the front door. Tugging along her mother, she entered the house. The living room was dark and cool; the drapes at the window were drawn. The room seemed messy to her, and it smelled of wood. Why wood? she wondered, and then she remembered the fireplace. Oak logs had been stacked near it, and the logs gave off the smell. In the fireplace itself was a heap of newspapers and magazines to be burnt.

From the hallway Liz appeared, her mouth open and her face elongated and stiff with fright. "I was out in the garden," she said. "What do you want?" She had on the bottom part of a woolen bathing suit, and over it she had thrown a shirt. She was barefoot. The tails of the shirt hung down almost to her knees, and between the buttons Virginia saw her tanned, bulging skin. She had nothing on underneath the shirt; she had not even finished buttoning it. Her legs sparkled with perspiration.

"I don't want to go in there," Virginia said to Liz. "In fact I'm not."

"In where?" Liz said in a faint voice. She shook her head and tiny particles of lint dropped from her hair, onto her shirt.

"Into your bedroom."

"How did you get into the house?" Liz said. "Wasn't the door locked?" Standing in the hallway, she finished buttoning her shirt; she stuffed the tails into the trunks of her bathing suit. "I was in the garden," she repeated. "What do you want? What's the idea of breaking into my house?"

Going past Liz, she went along the hall to the closed bedroom door. Opening the door she looked in.

On the chair, Roger's clothes were neatly piled, his coat and trousers and underpants, his tie and shirt and socks. His shoes had been placed at the foot of the bed. The bedcovers had been folded up and placed on the dresser. Roger lay on the bed, under the sheet. He had covered himself with it, so that only the top of his head and his eyes showed. He was watching her. Since he did not have his glasses—he had put them on the dresser—he could not make her out too clearly. Going closer, she saw that he was staring at her suit. He did not quite recognize her.

She seated herself on the edge of the bed. And still he held onto the sheet, keeping it over him, as if he was afraid she would drag it off and see him.

"Are you afraid I'm going to look at you?" she said. "I won't if you don't want me to."

"Who's with you?" Roger said.

"My mother." From the hall came the sound of her mother's voice and then Liz's voice. Virginia walked back to the door. "You want me to go outside while you dress?"

"No," he said.

"Shall I shut the door?"

Finally he said, "Yeah, shut it."

She shut the door. But still he remained in the bed, with the sheet held over him.

In the bed, he tugged the sheet up and kept it in place; he held it with both hands, watching to see if she came any closer. She had discovered him, and he waited to hear what it would be. A dreadful thing, he thought, trembling on the bed and feeling the doom, the closeness. It was here. The years of waiting to be discovered, the locking of the door, the preparing and listening. The door flew apart; she burst in; she stood by the bed, high above him. Her suspicions—she had previously suspected—had brought her in, and he faced her with what he had done, unable to hide; here he was, alone, and it had happened exactly as he had always known it would.

What a dirty thing, he thought. How could she stand to see him? Surely she would want to shut the door at once, go back out again. But the woman remained. Well, she seemed to say, I expected it. Now I have to decide what to do about it; I have to accept it and accept you as one doing it.

Yes, he thought. I have done it; I do it; I am caught here doing it. Everyone else does it, but that makes no difference; you are right. Have mercy on me, he thought, watching her. I'm sorry. I'm ashamed of it. I wish I had never been born. How could I begin to practice such a thing? It will drive you crazy, and it has done that; it has driven me out of my mind so that I imagine various other things. But you have shocked me awake and out of that. Can't you see that I am lying here dreamless, with nothing over me to protect me? So be kind to me. Don't make it too terrible, the judgment with which I agree. Yes, he thought, I agree; I must be punished for a sin like this. But not too much. Leave me something.

"I'll turn my back," she said. "While you dress." She carried his clothes from the chair and put them on the bed next to him, where he could reach them.

"Thanks," he said, laying his hand on them.

"You better get up," she said.

Trying to defend himself, he said, "Stephen does it too."

She shot him a look of impatience. I said the wrong thing, he thought, shrinking back.

"Was that you in the green Imperial?" he said.

"Yes," she said. "I didn't realize you saw me."

"Christ," he said, "you followed along after me. I just thought I was letting it get me. I saw a big car with a couple of dressed-up women in it, talking . . . I thought it was my imagination working on me."

Standing by the bed, she looked around the room; he saw her take it all in. So this is your place, her expression said. This is where you come, to this little room where you can lock the door and get at it in secret. But I interrupted you, and you had to break off.

"I won't do it again," he said. She did not seem to hear him; she had folded her arms and walked in the direction of the windows overlooking the yard.

Through the back windows of the bedroom, Virginia could see the garden. A glass door from the bedroom opened up onto it. Beyond the garden was another yard, and then a house, and telephone poles. He could have run out that way, she thought to herself. Why hadn't he? Maybe he was too frightened.

What an awful thing, she thought. To be trapped like this. To have people burst in . . . he lay in the bed naked and helpless, without even his glasses. But I had to do it, she said to herself. It was the right thing, for both of us.

"Now listen to me," she said. From the bed he gazed up at her, small and not in good health, not even able to make her out very clearly. "I guess I have to tell you what to do," she said. "Don't I? You don't know enough to take care of yourself."

His lips turned down, like a wrinkle; showing his lower teeth he said, "Why'd you bring your mother?"

"I wanted her to be a witness," she said.

"Are you going to divorce me?"

"No," she said, "I thought maybe Chic might want to have witnesses."

His eyes strained; his chin sank down and his lips moved. After an interval he said, "Does he know?"

"No," she said.

He considered that, pushing it about in his mind, frowning and trembling.

"I don't want to harm him," she said. "I don't have any desire to break up his marriage. If he found out about you, he'd divorce Liz and he never would have another thing to do with you. He wouldn't consider doing business with you."

"No," he said.

"I'm not going to tell him," she said.

Raising his head he peered up at her fearfully, but with a clumsy resentment.

"I don't want to ruin the plans for the partnership," she said. With Chic Bonner as your partner, she thought to herself, you might amount to something. You might turn out to be something after all. And the store, too.

Otherwise, she thought, you are a nervous little spindly man lying under a sheet without your glasses, and that is not enough for me. I must have more. I have given up my own life, my work, and I insist on getting something back that I can be proud of.

I am not going to come out of this with nothing, she said to herself.

"Listen to me," she said. "I want the store in my name."

He stared up at her, grinning with fear.

"And when we sign the papers with Chic," she said, "I want his side to be just in his name, not both of theirs. I don't want Liz's name to show up anywhere on the papers." I want, she thought, to have what I deserve. "How does that sound to you?" she said.

His grin lolled; his head fell first to one side and then the other.

"All right," she said. You have had what you wanted, she said to herself, and now you are getting what you deserve. You brought it on yourself. It is your own fault. "Put your clothes on," she said sharply. "Get up out of that bed and get dressed."

His thumb tugged at the clothes, pulling at his shirt. Concentrating on the clothes he fooled with them; he sat up and bent forward, gathering them onto his lap, over and onto the sheet.

"And as far as I'm concerned," Virginia said, turning her back to him, not intending to watch, "you and she can do any darn thing you please. As long as you keep it quiet."

Without answering, he sorted among his clothes. She heard the rustle.

Just don't bother me with it, she thought to herself. Just don't bring it into my life. I have my child, who is up at the school getting the kind of education he should have, and in a very short while I will have my work. And I do not want to be bothered; I do not have time.

While he dressed, she wandered about the room. The top drawer of the bureau was partly open, and she pulled it out to see what was inside. A heap of colored scarves covered small boxes in which were earrings; next to the boxes was a glazed pottery knickknack, a red-nosed Irish face with top hat and bulging cravat, to be hung on the wall. Somebody probably gave it to her, she thought. A present. Stuck away, hidden in the drawer. Maybe he gave it to her. She opened the second drawer of the bureau; it was filled with underwear. The corner of a box attracted her attention, a flat box; she drew it out and found that it was a diaphragm and tube of spermicide.

Stricken, she said. "Look—she's not wearing it; it's still in the drawer." She turned to show it to him.

"She has another," Roger said. He stood by the bed in his trousers, slumped over, unbuttoning the cuffs of his shirt. "Two sets."

"Oh," Virginia said. One to fool Chic; one to leave in the drawer. And the other, she thought. To be worn all the day. Day and night, wherever she went. Just in case. She put the box back in the drawer and shut it up again. "What an awful way to live," she said.

He pretended to be concerned with his shirt.

"Doesn't it bother you?" she said.

No answer.

"No, you're not fastidious," she said.

Again no answer.

"It would bother me," she said.

21

On May 1, 1953, the new store opened. From six to ten o'clock in the evening an open house was held; gardenias were given away to the ladies, pictures of all children were taken without charge to the parents, coffee and a cookie were served to everybody. Each person who entered the L & B Appliance Mart received a ticket for the grand drawing at which television combinations, Mixmasters, electric irons, and Sunbeam shavers, would be awarded to the winners. For a week, searchlights parked at the curb split up the sky with streams of light, and on Saturday night several members of the Los Angeles Angels baseball team showed up and were put on display on the lighted stage, along with the ten-piece Western band hired for the opening.

The new name, L & B Appliance Mart, had been chosen in order to give old John "Mac" Beth and his appliance center a run for his money. Both stores were in competition for the same market.

The L & B Appliance Mart had a long front, and all of the front was window. The building had been a grocery store; Chic Bonner had got wind of its availability for next to nothing through his contacts in the retail grocery-sales world. Earl Gillick had brought his crew and set to work completely remodeling the building. The glass was tilted to avoid reflecting glare in the eyes of passersby. The sign was not mounted onto the building, as it would have been in the old days; instead it was the letters of the name cemented directly onto the wall, each letter separate from the next. At a corner where Gillick had cut a wide entrance, an upright neon sign had been erected according to the designs which Chic Bonner had drawn and which Virgina Lindahl had approved. The doors were double, solid glass except for the plastic and copper handles, and the mail slot in the center of the right door. The entrance was at a slight incline. The exterior color was a pale green; the interior colors were also pastels. The interior lighting—Roger Lindahl had picked out the units—were recessed fluorescents. The building was newly air-conditioned and heated, in winter, by pipes under the nylon tile floor which carried a flow of hot water back and forth. At the rear of the building, unseen by patrons, a raised concrete loading dock had been built to receive merchandise and to load the several store trucks. Warehousing was done at the store itself.

By the summer of 1954, the gross intake had begun to pay off the cost of remodeling. The auditors could predict eventual amortization of the huge initial overhead.

On a Wednesday morning, in October of 1954, Herb Tomford, the floor manager of L & B Appliance Mart, unlocked the glass doors with his key and entered the store. The window washer, outside, was hard at work, and Tomford waved at him. The window washer waved back.

Good morning, Tomford said to himself.

He put on the air-conditioning system and the overhead lights. I'm the first, today, he thought. Bully for me. Going upstairs to the office floor, he hung his topcoat in the closet. Then he drew a chair up to one of the desks and began to sort through the final tags from Tuesday. Neither of the owners had arrived, so he could not get into the safe to fill the registers. It always made him uncomfortable to be in the store before the money had been brought out; what if a customer appeared and tried to buy something? I can give him pennies, Tomford said to himself. Thousands of them. Returning to the main floor, he opened the first register and wound the tape so that it read properly. While he was involved in doing that, Mrs. L's car came to a stop at the entrance of their parking lot, turned sharply, and entered the slot which she kept reserved for herself.

Number one, Tomford said to himself. The lady herself. He slammed the register and walked across the store to the small appliance counter. There, among the shavers and toasters and irons, he opened and set that register.

The lady who was his employer had left her parked car and was walking toward the front door of the store. Her coat flapped about her legs. How fast she goes, Tomford thought. She gets right across the parking lot; no time lost, there.

"Good morning, Mrs. L," he said, as the door swung open.

"Good morning, Herb," she said, pausing at the counter to lower part of her armload of papers.

"Will Mr. B be coming in today?"

She smiled at him with her absent, harried smile. "Why wouldn't he be in? Oh. His hayfever." Picking up the phone she dialed. "I'll find out."

"Looks like a nice day," Herb Tomford said.

"Hello," Mrs. L said. "Chic, are you coming into the store today?" A silence. "Dig them up," she said. "If you're sure that's it. I'd pull them up. I hate them anyhow; they're just weeds as far as I'm concerned." A silence. "Okay. Good-bye." Hanging up, she said, "He'll be in around noon. He says now they think it's the broom bushes he has down at the end of his lot."

"He said he thought that's what it was," Tomford said. "When the flowers came out originally."

Mrs. L put her coat away in the closet and then she opened the safe. "Here's your money," she said. "I'll be upstairs until you need me."

The salesmen were beginning to straggle into the store. They worked on a commission and draw arrangement, and as fast as they entered the door they darted quick glances to see if anything was stirring. One of them lit a cigarette and stationed himself behind the front counter; another seated himself at his table of pamphlets and began to fill out names in his prospect-book. A third, portly and dignified in his pin-stripe suit, folded his hands behind his back and placed himself near the doorway, in the vicinity of the display of television floor models. None of them exchanged more than a formal greeting with the others; each withdrew and prepared himself, according to his inclination. The last to enter made directly for the phone, laid out a pencil-written list, and began to make calls.

After the salesmen had come in, the two repairmen appeared. They had been having breakfast together across the street. Without speaking to the salesmen they went directly back to the service department. At nine o'clock, the boy who drove the delivery truck came hurrying in, and after him came the outside repairman, driving the service truck, which he parked near the loading dock behind the store. The last to arrive was the bookkeeper, who climbed the stairs to the office and said good morning to Mrs. Lindahl. He then uncovered the adding machine and began his day of work.

I guess I can go to the bathroom now, Herb Tomford said to himself. The fort is properly manned.

"I'm going to the head," he told one of the salesmen.

"Right," the salesman said.

Taking the morning newspaper with him, Herb Tomford made his way to the bathroom and locked the door so that nobody could disturb him. After he had made himself comfortable he opened the newspaper and read the sports page and then the letters to the editor.

While he was reading the newspaper, somebody came along and rattled the locked door of the bathroom.

"Is that you in there?" Mrs. L called. "Herb?"

"Yes," he said.

"I don't think you should be in there all the time. For what I need you for you ought to be out here."

Herb Tomford said, "For what I'm doing, Mrs. L, I got to be in here." He folded up his newspaper and tossed it over into the corner. "I'll be right out. What do you need me for?"

"We have to take out a Magnavox TV in the next ten minutes. Fred's setting it up right now."

"Who sold it?"

"Fred did. Somebody he knows."

"Does he get the commission?" Some dispute had arisen as to whether the repairmen deserved to get commissions on sets they sold.

"Yes," she said.

"That's okay by me," he said. He drew a flat one percent on all the major appliances sold, no matter who sold them. Washing his hands, he said, "That may make some of the potted palm brigade march out the door."

No answer. She has left, he decided. Drying his hands he picked up his newspaper and opened the door.

At noon, while he was considering where he wanted to have lunch, he looked up to see Chic Bonner parking his red Ford station wagon. Ah, Herb Tomford said. The mighty man himself.

Chic's face, swollen and red from his hayfever, showed no particular emotion as he entered the store. "Morning, Herb," he said. "Anything stirring?"

"Couple of things," Tomford said, showing him the tags.

"Yes," Chic said vaguely. "Say look, Herb. I want to see the floor-sanding man in here after we close up tonight. Can you get hold of him?"

"I think so," Tomford said. "I have his number around somewhere."

Kneeling down, Chic ran the palm of his hand over the floor past the edge of the carpet. "See those indentations? You know what does that? High school kids' cleated shoes. I'm going to put up a sign that any kids with cleated shoes have to take their shoes off before they come in here. What do they want anyhow?"

"What does anybody want?" Tomford said, thinking to himself that a floor had to be kept up whether kids came in or not. "I sold a kid a Zenith portable, the other day. If that's what you're alluding to."

"Did he make that rasping noise as he walked?"

"You mean, with his mouth?"

"I mean with his shoes."

Tomford said, "I'm sorry, Mr. B. I was so hungry for the sale I didn't stop to notice."

Gazing around the store, Chic said, "It seems to me the Philco display has been up since September."

"I'll take it down."

"Did they put in that window? Or did you?"

"I let them put it in," Tomford said, knowing that Chic did not approve of letting the wholesalers climb into the store's display windows. "That's their job," he said. "They have all the junk, the stapling guns and junk. I'm not going to tear my pants crawling around in the window. I wasn't hired to do that. If you want us to do the windows you better get some gal or some fairy from one of the department stores. The last time I was out in the window a bunch of children stood there making faces at me as if I was something to be laughed at."

"I see your point," Chic said. "Well, we'll see." He passed on, then, into the general activity of the store.

Later, when Herb Tomford went upstairs, Mrs. L called him into the office. "This is your tag, isn't it?" she said.

Something more, he thought to himself. "Yes," he said. "That's my tag. Tell me the part you can't read."

"Neither I nor the bookkeeper can read the street address." She handed him the tag and he seated himself at the desk to read it. "Why don't you use a ballpoint pen?" she asked. "Like everybody else. Those machines are made to work with ballpoint pens, not fountain pens. Fountain pens don't create a firm enough impression." She sat waiting. The tag, on blue paper, was the fourth carbon; the store operated a complex system to discourage employees from stealing.

"I can't read it either," Herb Tomford said. "I'll look it up in the telephone book." He returned the tag and picked up the phone book from the other desk.

"What was Chic talking to you about down at the front counter?" Mrs. L asked.

"The windows."

"Don't you consider it part of your job to do the windows? You have all the stuff supplied to you."

Herb Tomford said, "When I came here Mr. L was doing the windows. I didn't know it was going to become my job."

"You know Roger only comes in at night to use the bench."

"What's he working on?" Tomford said.

"Ask him. Don't you see him before you leave?"

Embarrassed, Tomford said, "You know I get the hell out of here at six."

"Yes," Mrs. L said. "That's right. You do."

Later, when Chic Bonner had come upstairs to the office, Virginia said to him, "Do you think we should keep Herb on?"

"I can't make up my mind," Chic said. "Maybe he's got another iron or so in the fire. He doesn't really take an interest."

"It wouldn't surprise me," Virginia said. "One day he'll tell us he's moved down the street or across the street. I have a feeling he wants to get out of retail entirely. Somebody told me he's been talking to Emerson. They need somebody to take over their Northern California office."

Chic put on his peevish look; she saw that a little bit of begging was on the way. "Why don't you ask Roger about doing the windows again? That wouldn't kill him. He's got plenty of time on his hands."

"He'd have to do it during the day." And both she and Chic knew Roger's reluctance to come into the store while it was open for business.

"Why not at night?"

"He can't see the colors," she said. "Except in daylight. Everybody who does windows holds to that."

"What about the weekends?"

"No," she said. And that's final, she said to herself. It was the arrangement between herself and Roger. The weekend was his. But of course Chic did not grasp that. For him, the world beyond the store had no substance. And for me, too, she thought. Except that I know about it; I understand it. Which is more than you can say for Mr. B.

"You decide about it," Chic said. He had spread order sheets out on his desk; with a pencil he began to make tentative marks. "I'd rather leave it up to you."

"There's no urgency," she said.

After he had worked on his order sheets for a time, Chic said to her, "Is it all right if I write Liz's check this month against the store account? Those hayfever shots I've been taking . . . I've had to dip into my checking account. I'll do what we've done in the past; I'll have the bookkeeper list it as part of my salary paid in advance."

"I don't care," Virginia said.

At his own desk, the bookkeeper heard and nodded.

"What is it?" Virginia asked. "Three hundred, isn't it?"

"Yes," Chic said.

"Maybe she'll remarry."

"That wouldn't help," Chic said. "It's child support; it's for the two boys." He stopped working and laid down his pencil in order to blow his nose. Then he tipped his head back and gave himself his nosedrops. "That man would have to legally adopt them."

"You take that off your income tax, don't you?"

"You bet," Chic said, sniffling.

"Do you miss her?"

Chic said, "I miss the boys. I haven't had time to miss her." He added, "The store, I mean."

"I think you did the right thing," Virginia said. But I really don't think that, she said to herself. I know that. There would have been no harmony here, with her banging around. I'm glad, she said to herself, that she could be persuaded.

"She's living up in Santa Barbara," Chic said.

"I know." She did not feel much like discussing it; she went on with her own work.

Chic said, "You always saw through her, didn't you? I give you credit for that."

"Okay," she said, knowing that he would go on and on.

"What did Roger think of her?" Chic said, turning his chair around so that he faced her, not his work. "Now there's something that frankly baffles me. There's a man I consider to have an innate ability to handle people and get along in the business world, but I'm convinced that when it comes to judging people on a personal level, he's almost as faulty as I am. Present company excepted, of course. But—I really think Roger had an idealized image of Liz. Not so much different from my own, originally. My God, it took me ten or eleven years to begin to realize how fundamentally—" Gesturing, he mulled about for the word. "How fundamentally one-dimensional her viewpoint was."

The phone rang downstairs. Then, at the bookkeeper's desk, a buzzer buzzed twice. "It's for you, Mrs. L," the bookkeeper said, passing her the upstairs phone.

"Hello," she said.

It was RCA, calling to report on some back-orders from the previous month. "No, they're not dropped," the distributor's office girl said. "Do you want them dropped?"

She said no. "Thanks," she said, and hung up.

During her phone conversation, Chic sat with his hands clasped together, meditating. "Before Liz decided to leave me," he said, "did she come to you and ask you your opinion?"

"Yes," Virginia said. In a sense, that could be said of it.

"What did you tell her?"

"I told her that I thought if she had no interest in your affairs then it was pretty ridiculous for her to hang around and pretend something she didn't feel."

Presently Chic said, "Sometimes I really do miss her."

"Not very much," Virginia said.

"No," he agreed. "I guess not." He continued to ponder, and then he picked up his pencil and returned to his order sheets. "I thought of visiting her one of these days," he said. "If for no other reason than to see the boys."

"She can send them down on the bus," Virginia said. "How old are they? Fourteen? That's old enough for them to come down here by themselves."

"True," Chic said. "She's probably got them so mollycoddled by now that they'd be afraid to. That's what bothers me, Virginia. Are they going to grow up to be sissy-like, and confused in their thinking, the way she is?"

Virginia said, "She only has them on weekends. As long as she keeps them in the school they're receiving a balanced environment."

With gloom, Chic said, "They only have the rest of this term. That's as high as the school goes."

"By then their minds will be formed," Virginia said. Getting up, she went to the file to see about a bad debt, one of a group that she was considering turning over to a collection agency. "You want to write Watt off?" she asked Chic. "Give it up and hope for fifty percent from the agency?"

"Suits me," he said, in his indifferent tone. At his orders he sat rubbing his forehead and breathing noisily. "This goddamn hay-fever. I get it every year at this time."

"It's common," Virginia said. "Allergies of one kind or another. Gregg's tests showed that he's allergic to string beans, potatoes, cat fur, wool, kapoc, house dust, and six or seven pollen-bearing plants. So consider yourself lucky."

"What do they feed him, then?"

"The regular meals, but he leaves the potatoes and string beans. He never did eat wool or cat fur."

"But he must have special blankets."

"Yes," she said. "He has had, for a year or so. It was the house dust that caused most of his asthma, not the smog. But on the smoggy days we kept the windows shut, and he usually played around in the house. That's where he picked it up. Up there, he gets pollens quite a bit, but it doesn't affect him anything like the house dust did."

Blowing his nose, Chic said, "It's a darn shame."

At six o'clock, Herb Tomford locked the front door, said good night, and departed, in his gray topcoat, with his newspaper rolled up under his arm. The salesmen followed him out, and then the two repairmen.

"Good night, Mrs. L," the bookkeeper said, taking down his coat from its hanger in the closet. "I'll see you tomorrow. Good night, Mr. B."

"Good night," Virginia said.

"Is it six?" Chic said. He had been comparing a replacement Zenith price list with an older one, changing the selling prices on their display tags. On his desk, representing an hour or so of work, was a heap of clean new tags. "I'll tie these on tomorrow," he said to Virginia.

All afternoon writing out new tags, she thought. Going downstairs to the front counter, she opened the register and began counting the money into two cloth bags. Then she marked the register tape, stuck a slip in with the money, and closed up the bags. At the other register, Chic did the same.

"Good enough day," Chic said.

"Yes," she said.

"We'll need dimes tomorrow."

"Okay," she said, examining the tags.

The front door opened, and Roger, key in hand, entered the store. "Hi," he said to his wife.

"Hi," she said. "How are you?" When she had left the house, that morning, he was still asleep.

"Fine. About ready?" He had come in with a cigarette in his hand, but now, as she glanced up at him, he dropped it into one of the ashtrays by the door and ground it out. Blinking, he wandered away. At sundown, getting off from work as he was, he had a gray spider-like quality; fatigue made him bend even more than usual, made him seem smaller and more dehydrated. His eyes, behind his glasses, were red-rimmed. Reaching up, he smoothed his hair back from his face.

"You look tired," she said

"Yeah." He nodded absently. He still had on his workclothes, his stained trousers and shirt and jacket, and his high-topped shoes. Rubbing his lip, he said, "You feel much like dinner? I don't. But I'll go with you."

"I'm hungry," she said.

His meanderings carried him toward the rear of the store. "I'll change," he said. He disappeared through the door into the service department.

"Well, Virginia," Chic said, in his hat and coat, "I'll see you. Take it easy."

"Good night," she said. Standing in the center of the store, she listened; she lifted her head to hear the various sounds. Anything left on? she asked herself.

No, she decided.

"Remind me to tag up those sets tomorrow first thing," Chic said. He unlocked the front door. "So we don't lose any money."

The door closed after him, and he walked across the parking lot to his Ford station wagon. As he backed from the lot onto the street he waved at her. She made a faint motion. Enough for him.

When Roger reappeared, he had on a stringy necktie and a pair of slacks. "Do I need my coat?" he said. "I guess not."

Virginia said, "How's the testing?"

At his job with Dunn, Inc. he tested switches along an assembly line; the switches became elements in circuits of computing apparatus, some of which eventually became missiles.

"About the same," Roger said.

"Wait," she said. "Before we go." Bending, she switched on the window lights. "Take a look at the windows, would you?"

"Why?"

"Because you know something about how they should look."

Not budging, he said, "They look okay."

"I wish you'd take them over again," she said.

"I don't have time for that."

"You only work five hours a day; you could do them in the mornings."

Roger said, "They're okay. Why do you keep picking on Herb? He's a good guy."

"Yes," she said, "but is he good at his job?"

"I don't see the difference."

"No, you don't," she agreed. And she thought to herself, That is why I am running our half of the store and you are not. That is why I am the L instead of you. It could have been you, my dear. But you would have wanted a store full of good guys.

And, she thought, you also wanted another good guy, a good pal, one with brown hair and bright, merry eyes, and a smile that never had anything in it except come and help yourself. She was a good guy, wasn't she? She loved and still loves her two boys; she probably loved and still loves you. And she was loyal to you, except that she was too stupid to act out her loyalty. And on your part, you were pretty stupid about it, too. You didn't do her much good, you who are another good guy.

Where is she now? Virginia said to herself. Off by herself in another town, living on child support money from Chic and on her salary as a clerical typist with a milk company. Is she happy? Who knows. Who cares. In her case, who can tell.

But at least she has her boys, Virginia said to herself. If Chic had found out about her and Roger, he would have divorced her and she would have lost her boys. That would not have been right. Nor, Virginia thought, would that have been fair to Roger. If Chic had found out he would have made trouble for everyone. There would be no store. There would be nothing for anyone. At least Liz had enough intelligence to see that.

In a way, she thought, you are lucky, Liz Bonner. Because you had such a dim consciousness, a sort of salamander-like view of the world, you were able to enjoy yourself. You had your short merry span of life. It had an element of purity; it was untainted by any alertness to the future, or to real consequences, or to facts such as your husband and children and the fact that Roger has a wife and a child and did have a store to manage. You carried it off in a flash, once you got started; you started it going, and enjoyed it, and then you were dismayed and astonished. But at least nobody can prove you didn't do it.

She thought, Nobody can prove you didn't get it for a while. And maybe, for your kind of mentality, it was a long while. Maybe, for your tiny lifespan, it was a long, long time. Perhaps even as long as you can remember. To the limit of your perspective.

Maybe, she thought, you got what you were after because that was all you were after. Maybe you could conceive nothing more.

I wish I could do that, she thought. I wish we all could get something like that.

"Anyhow," she said to Roger, "I wish you'd see if you could change the windows. You'd be doing Herb a favor. This window business is going to be a bone of contention, either until he gives in and humbles himself out in plain sight of everybody, or you do it, or the wholesalers do a better job of it."

"I hate those goddamn wholesalers," Roger said. "They walk into the store while you're busy and start gumming up posters on the walls. You look around and you've got RCA signs hanging all over the place. I used to rip them down while the guy was still there; I wanted him to see me rip them down." He lit another cigarette. His hands shook; she saw the match quiver.

"I'm ready," Virginia said.

Roger held the door for her and she stepped outside, onto the entrance way. "I'll lock it," he said, putting his key into the lock. "You turned everything off?"

"Yes," she said, "I listened. I can usually hear if any of the sets are on."

*   *   *

After dinner, Virginia drove on home. Roger returned to the store to make use of the repair bench and equipment.

He switched on the fluorescent lights over the bench, dragged the tall stool up onto the mat, and then put on the meters and test apparatus. The soldering iron had its own special switch and plug; it was always individually disconnected. He plugged it in and hoisted it, holding the extra-hot trigger to its *on* position in the handle.

His newfangled antenna had been mounted to the ceiling of the service department. Twin-lead trailed down the wall to the bench, and from there to a turret tuner of a TV chassis. The antenna formed a circle of thin aluminum tubing, within which was a network of even finer tubes, going in various directions like spokes and counter-spokes of a wheel. From the many tubes a meshed network of leads had been gathered and clamped into a single cable which led into a control box of terminals and lugs, and from there to the twin-lead.

It's not worth a fuck, Roger said to himself.

His idea was to provide an infinitely variable antenna controlled by the channel selector. As the selector was rotated, sections of the antenna were cut off and others were cut in. The idea was that ghosts could be eliminated, weak signals could be reinforced, static could be reduced, and so forth. In practice, however, the settings made no change in the quality of the picture.

With the soldering iron he changed some of the leads around, returned a few of the channel strips, and then gave up.

The hell with it, he decided. He turned off the chassis. The only thing that would affect the picture quality would be a raising of the antenna, and that would require a power source, such as a quarter horsepower electric motor. And that would price the system right out of the market.

So that's that, he said to himself. He coiled his legs into the rungs of the stool and then rocked the stool back as far as it would go without passing the balance point. Behind him was a concrete floor, and he thought to himself, Let's go all the way back. Let's see how it feels.

But he brought the stool upright.

Not for me, he said to himself. He uncoiled his legs and stepped from the stool to the rubber mat. The service room was cold and the fluorescent light made his head ache. Shutting off the service bench he walked through the open door into the main part of the store.

Most of the store—the extended single room filled by television sets and stoves and refrigerators and washing machines—was dark. The window lights flooded out onto the street and lit up the displays near the front of the store. He walked past the counter, in the direction of the Philco display. It had been in two weeks, and it had not been much good to start with.

Lousy-looking thing, he thought. Why is it there? Who put it in?

But, he thought, why should I change it? What have I got to do with it?

While he stood there, looking out at the window displays, a shape appeared on the sidewalk and flashed a light in his eyes. Blinded, he put up his hands. The shape motioned him toward the door, and as he peered to see, he realized that it was the cop whom the merchants had hired to go about after dark trying the doors of each of the shops to be certain they were locked. The cop, holding his light in Roger's eyes, brought out a pistol from his holster and held it pointed at him, still motioning him.

"Okay," Roger said, lifting his hands in a mock-gesture. He walked away from the counter, to the door. With his key he unlocked the door and swung it open.

"Who are you?" the cop said. "Let's see your identification."

The light glazed down on his hands as he tugged out his wallet. "I was working in the back," he said. "I came out front for a couple of seconds."

"Are you related to Mrs. L?"

"Yes." he said.

"You her husband?"

He nodded.

"Sorry I bothered you," the cop said. He lowered his flashlight and put his gun away. "I thought you were standing in there by the till waiting for me to go by—" He nudged Roger on the shoulder. "Then you were going to stick your hand into it."

"No," he said. "I was just taking a breather."

"Say, do you know anything about TV sets? I mean, you know what's the matter with them?"

"I guess so," he said.

The cop leaned near to him. "I got this Packard-Bell TV set; sometimes when I'm looking at it, like I'm looking at the Ed Sullivan show or something on Sunday night, the picture gets all grainy. What causes that?"

Roger said, "You mean a pattern on top of the picture?"

"No, I mean all grainy. You know."

"Probably interference."

"You mean some guy's interfering with the picture?"

"It's static," he said. "Only you see it instead of hearing it." He began to close the door; the cop noticed and immediately prepared to leave.

"Thanks a lot Mr. Lindahl. Say, if I keep on getting it, can I bring the set in and have you people look at it?"

"Sure," he said. "Bring it in any time."

"About how long does it take to have it worked on?"

"A couple of days." He shut the door and locked it. The cop waved through the glass, said something that he could not hear, and then passed on with his flashlight.

Christ, Roger said to himself. I might as well not be here. I'm not getting anything done.

He made sure that the soldering iron and the other equipment in the service department were off, and then he left the store.

Where now? he asked himself. Home. Where I've been going for ten years, except for a little period a couple of years back.

He thought about the Los Padres Valley School. Today was Wednesday, so in two more days, the day after tomorrow, he would make his weekly drive to pick up Gregg.

I wonder if I can hold out that long, he thought.

22

He lay in bed after Virginia had left the house. Outdoors, the red Ford station wagon started up and traveled down the street. He listened to the sound diminish. I'm glad she remembered to leave the Olds, he thought. I wouldn't get very far without it.

Getting out of the bed he padded barefoot to the telephone and called Dunn, Inc. to tell them that he would not be in. After that was done, he removed his pajamas and got into the shower. By nine-thirty in the morning he had shaved and put on a decent enough suit. He got the newspaper from the porch and tossed it on the kitchen table. Later, as he ate breakfast, he read the news and the comics and the various columns.

Plenty of time, he thought.

At ten-thirty he called Mrs. Alt up at the school.

"I thought I'd drive up early today," he said.

"Fine," Mrs. Alt said genially. "You want to have lunch up here? It's at one, today."

"Thanks," he said.

"You know what you might bring? You might stop at a stamp store and pick up some packets for Gregg. He's trying to build up his Austria collection. Yesterday he said he was going to ask you.

Just tell the stamp dealer you want a couple of dollars worth of Austrian stamps; he'll know what to do."

"What if Gregg already has some of them?"

Mrs. Alt said, "Then he'll trade them to the other boys."

"Have you heard from her this week?" He felt deep tenseness throughout his body: this was always the moment for it.

"Yes," Mrs. Alt said. "She called me on Tuesday."

"Will she be up?"

"I think so. You know how she talks."

"Good," he said. "I'll see you by one o'clock, then." He hung up, and then he wrote out a note to himself about the packet of Austrian stamps for Gregg.

Just before eleven o'clock he left the house, got into the Oldsmobile, and drove north along the highway until he passed a postage stamp store. Parking, he bought the Austrian stamps, and then he went on, following his regular route to the freeway that connected with Highway 99. He had driven it so often that he barely noticed the alternate cut-offs. His goal was to make the best possible time, and he figured that he would arrive in the Ojai Valley and the school in plenty of time for lunch.

The scenery did not interest him. I am going farther and farther from Los Angeles, he said to himself, and that's what matters. He watched only for obstacles.

At five minutes to one, he turned off the grade from Ojai, onto the school grounds. The closeness of the time gratified him. I really have it, he thought. Right down to the second. He shut off the engine and got out of the car, locking the doors after him.

No one saw him arrive.

He smelled the engine smell; the car gave off heat from beneath its hood, and waves of motion rose up from it, into the air. Here and there, trees responded to the mid-day wind, the autumn wind that he had heard as he drove through the range of mountains. It made a sound as if something were being poured from a height.

Looking up, he saw the tops of the fir trees whipping. It gave them a presence of violence. A group of birds were dislodged; the birds fluttered and tried to regain their positions. Now they're mad, he thought. The cheeping of the birds drifted down to him, where he stood. The birds thought that someone had dislodged them purposefully.

The smaller the birds, he thought, the angrier.

He started up the path towards the main building. When he reached the terrace he had to stop to let a gang of children go rushing by in the direction of the dining room. The children yelled and shoved; none of them noticed him. Off somewhere, the school bell rang, signifying lunch time. Split pea soup and bread sticks and milk and peaches. Coffee for the adults. After the children had squeezed by the glass doors into the dining room, he followed.

At a rear table, Edna Alt spied him and waved to him. He walked in that direction. "Hi," he said.

"You didn't forget the stamps, did you?" she said. With her at the table were Mr. Van Ecke and Mrs. McGivern. They both said hello to him.

"I left them in the car," he said. "In the glove compartment." Drawing back a chair, he seated himself and unfolded a paper napkin. "I smelled the soup," he said. "So I know what's coming."

"That's why we have a work-gang," Mr. Van Ecke said. "To give the bad boys something to do . . . we have them splitting the peas for half an hour every day."

From his pocket, Roger got out the weekly report that the school mailed him on the conduct and standing of his son. "Half hour on the work-gang," he read. "What did he do?"

"He made a bean shooter out of a curtain rod," Mrs. Alt said.

"The dirty little rascal," Mr. Van Ecke said, and they all laughed.

"The bigger boys have something that's a little more deadly," Mrs. McGivern said in her practical manner. "They've been making themselves match guns out of clothespins. The thing fires the match about eight feet, and ignites the head at the same time. The boys—

the bigger ones, not your boy—get out in a group of ten or fifteen, and shoot live matches at one another."

"But the unexplainable thing," Mrs. Alt said, "is that nobody ever seems to get burned or hurt or lose an eye. It's automatic suspension for a month, if they're caught. But they still do it. They sneak into the lavatories and load their match guns and carry them around in their pockets, sometimes all afternoon. Then when none of us is watching—" She made a firing motion. "Bang. Right in little Jimmy Morse's face."

Mr. Van Ecke said, "And little Jimmy Morse fires back, right into little Raleigh Hinkle's face. And then little Philip Adams gets both of them, with his pair of match guns."

The cook wheeled out the first metal cart carrying the split pea soup. The two Mexican girls began serving the tables; the children chattered away. At each table of children one teacher kept order and served his eight children from the main plates. Bowls of split pea soup were now being passed from hand to hand. The cook wheeled her cart toward the table of teachers. Mrs. Alt accepted their soup and began dipping it out with a ladle, into the smaller bowls. Roger's was presented to him by Mr. Van Ecke.

"You missed grace," Mrs. McGivern said to Roger. "So you can't have anything to eat."

"Say it now," Mr. Van Ecke said, starting to spoon up his soup.

"He doesn't have to say grace," Mrs. Alt said, as she served herself. "That's only for the little prisoners, as Liz calls them."

Roger said, "Is she here yet?"

"She showed up a little while ago," Mrs. Alt said, "but she drove her two boys down into Ojai. They wanted to see if they could buy a carbide lamp. I don't think they can. She'll have to get it for them in Santa Barbara."

"We're going on an overnight hike tonight," Mrs. McGivern said. "That's why they need the light today."

As she ate, Mrs. Alt said to Roger, "You ought to come along. You've gone hiking with us before, haven't you? We're not going far.

The forest has been closed during the summer, but now it's wet enough for people to go in. We have a place where they let us build a campfire. We cleared it ourselves."

"Maybe so," Roger said.

After lunch, he and Mrs. Alt searched out Gregg and gave him his packet of Austrian stamps.

"Hey!" Gregg yelled, leaping up and down. "Look at this! Can I go show them? I'll be right back; we're not going to leave right now anyhow, are we?" He ran about in a circle, clutching the stamps. "Can I take them with me to arithmetic class?"

Roger and Mrs. Alt let him go off to class with the packet of stamps. The one-forty bell rang, and gradually the children dispersed to their classrooms. Except for the boy operating the switchboard at the desk, the lobby was pretty much empty.

"How's Virginia?" Mrs. Alt said.

"Fine."

"How's Chic's hayfever?"

"About the same."

"He came up here, you know, about a month ago. To see the boys."

"She told me," Roger said. "Liz I mean. The boys mentioned it to her."

Mrs. Alt said, "You know, I wish you two could have got married."

"So do I," he said.

"Is there any chance Virginia would change her mind? Maybe when Gregg is older and she feels less concerned about him."

"It's possible," he said. But he did not really think so. "As long as she keeps looking out for my best interest," he said, "I doubt if she'll give me an uncontested divorce."

"Virginia is so moral," Mrs. Alt said. "What a blight it is. In her anyhow. For your sake, and Liz's sake. I suppose if you believe you're right you can do almost anything."

Roger said, "Even if I got a divorce and was able to marry Liz, I'd have to give up Gregg. And I'd have to raise Chic Bonner's two boys." He had never liked either of the boys. They reminded him too much of Chic, both of them so large, heavy, bullying, red-haired and freckle-faced. Both had that noisy, driving-quality. He could not see a real family coming out of them, out of himself and Liz and the two Bonner boys. Of course, he and Liz would have children of their own.

I keep telling myself that, he thought. But the fact is that Gregg is my son. And, when it comes down to it, Virginia is my wife. Even I—not just Virginia—recognize that.

Mrs. Alt said, "Liz would be a wonderful woman for you to have as your wife." She gave him a short, stern, sympathetic smile.

"This isn't too bad," he said. But both he and Mrs. Alt knew that it was bad. It was something, but it was lousy as hell. But it was all they could manage, as much as they knew to do. "Has Virginia ever called you or written to you about it?" he asked.

"No," Mrs. Alt said. "Except for business about Gregg, I never hear from her."

He and Mrs. Alt walked into the library. Through the window he made out the fir trees, and the path, and beyond that the parking lot and his car. "She should be back soon," he said, "shouldn't she?"

"Unless she gets tied up somewhere along the way. If you stayed overnight and went on the hike, she probably would, too. Why don't you?"

"Maybe so," he said. But he wanted to make sure that Liz would be along. That was what he cared about, and he had never made any pretense of anything else. Mrs. Alt had given them a place here at the school where they could stay; it was a room on the floor of the main building where the teachers' rooms were, and in it he and Liz felt themselves to be safe. Nothing could come and pry them out. Mrs. Alt's room was between theirs and the stairs to the main floor, and she had trained herself, because of her job, to wake up at any unusual sound.

Roger said, "You certainly have done a lot for Liz and me."

"I've always liked Liz. I've always considered her a friend of mine. I feel the same toward you."

"Thanks," he said.

At three o'clock, Liz and her two boys entered the building. Sitting in the library by himself, Roger heard their voices; he listened as the boys hurried off, and then he listened to the sound of Liz, in Mrs. Alt's office, putting down whatever she had bought in town and saying hello to Mrs. Alt.

". . . I knew you wouldn't find it there," Mrs. Alt said.

". . . Well, we had fun. You know what we saw? We went into the park and watched them practicing a play. I don't know what the play was. Something where there's a character who's a butterfly. What would that be?"

". . . I have no idea," Mrs Alt said. Then the voices diminished.

He continued sitting where he was, with his magazine on his lap. The nervousness crept through him, as it always did; his arms weakened and his skin got that cold, moist sensitivity. I'll never believe it's for me, he said to himself. I'll never really be able to accept it: I'm waiting for the loud steps on the porch and the front door flying open. I keep waiting to be destroyed.

But, he thought, I don't know why I'm waiting. That happened two years ago. Virginia got me, then. And the rest is nothing.

"Hi," Liz said, appearing.

"Hi," he said, standing up and putting aside his magazine.

She came over to him and kissed him. "Do you know anything about carbine lamps?"

"Carbide," he said.

"I smell like garlic," she said. "We had pizzas down at Sam's Oriental Pizza Palace or something like that." She had a proper bag full of stuff she had bought; supporting it against her with one arm she hugged him, breathing up into his face. She did smell of garlic, and of shampoo.

"You smell okay," he said. "What's in the bag?"

"Marshmallows and buns for the hike." Her face filled with delight. "This time we're not taking any tents; we're going to sleep on the ground, in sleeping bags only. And we're going to dig a trench in the ground and build the fire down in it, and put a grating over the fire, and cook on that. What do you say? If you don't want to go, I won't go either."

"Sounds fine to me," he said, sharing her excitement.

From the phone in Mrs. Alt's office he called Virginia at the store. A man, one of the salesmen, answered. "L & B Appliance Mart," the salesman said.

"Let me talk to Mrs. L," he said. At her desk, Mrs. Alt smiled a little.

"Hello," Virginia's voice said presently.

"I'm calling from the school," he said. "I'm going to stay overnight this time. We'll probably drive back tomorrow afternoon. If we decide to stay Saturday night, I'll call you."

Virginia said, "I hope you have a good time."

"We're going on an overnight hike," he said. "Up into the Los Padres. It's open again."

"Is Liz there, this time?"

He said, "What do you care?"

"All right," she said. "But if you're going hiking, be careful of your side."

After he had hung up the phone, Mrs. Alt said, "You have something to change into, don't you?"

"Yes," he said. "Upstairs."

He went upstairs to their room. In the closet he got out a pair of work trousers and shirt and heavy shoes. While he was lacing up the shoes, Liz slipped into the room and shut the door after her. He stopped lacing up the shoes.

At four-thirty the group started out toward the great forest, their packs on their backs. Mr. Van Ecke led the way. Seven or eight children, all boys and all of them older, followed him in a good-natured, confident gang. After them came Mrs. Alt and Mrs. McGivern and Liz and Roger, saying little, taking things easy.

"The rule here," Mrs. Alt said, "is no exertion. If we get tired, we'll stop for a while."

An argument began as to whether they could smoke.

"Absolutely not," Mrs. McGivern said.

"But the ground's wet," Liz said.

"That has nothing to do with it. You can't even bring cigarettes or matches across the line."

"We have matches for the fire," Liz said.

"Actually, we're breaking the law. We're camping by special dispensation."

To Roger, Liz said, "I'm going to smoke."

They entered the forest along the bank of a dried-up stream. The gully was filled with logs and boulders and broken sticks. Farther on, they passed the remains of a dam, and then a fire-watch tower that had fallen into decay. The trail cut upward, at an extreme incline, and then leveled off to follow a natural surface of earth. The soil was dry and light-colored. Except for one variety of plant, nothing grew. The area had a barren, windy quality. Halting, Roger looked back and saw the valley behind them, the squares that were separate fields and crops, the roads, the school itself on the side of the slope. From this point, the slope could be seen as a series of mounds, on which no trees, at least no living trees, were visible. A far-off region, a kind of plateau, had been burned several years ago; it was black, and from it stuck the dead trunks of trees.

Ahead of them the trail crossed to the other side of the dried stream, circled a higher knob, and then could be seen in the form of a spiral around the first peak. Haze had settled down to make the peak itself indistinct.

"Up there?" he said to Mrs. Alt.

"No," she said. "We take a cut-off."

They hiked on. Their trail, a smaller one, took them downward, into a wide gully in which trees grew. They crossed a narrow spillway of water and followed the stream eastward for a half hour. The ascent was mild. None of them became tired. At five-twenty their trail turned steeply away from the water, up over a crest. As they climbed, their view was cut off. Roger, helping Liz up, saw only the darkening evening sky and haze, and the elongated, exposed, weedy crest.

At the top, Mr. Van Ecke and the boys waited for them to catch up. The campsite was on the far side of the crest. The ground dropped in a series of levels. Here, there was no view of the valley. They were between hills. The air had become chill and thin, and it had a bitter smell. Sounds carried for miles. Somewhere far off an object rolled down a steep slope, probably a bundle of dirt-clods and roots. Birds flew among the clumps and plants, in a hopping motion. Bits of newspaper, left by earlier campers, rose up and swirled off, out of sight, carried into a ravine by the wind. Already, the lower places, the gullies and ravines, had become dark. Light remained in the hillsides, spread out over the higher slopes, but the colors were dimming away. Only a light brown and brownish green of foliage were left. The sky had turned from blue to gray.

They hiked on, down the slope and past rows of massive trees that cut off the wind and sunlight. The trail was vague; they stumbled among heaps of rock fragments that had broken loose and settled from the slope onto the flat places. A snake got out of their way. Mr. Van Ecke and the boys tramped on past the spot, but Mrs. McGivern and Liz halted.

"What kind of snake was that?" Mrs. McGivern said.

"A deadly nightshade," Mrs. Alt said, going on. Roger led Liz on, and she came, staring down at the ground.

The trail passed between two cliffs, into a slot. They had to climb rocks, holding onto roots. After a few minutes, Mr. Van Ecke appeared above them and declared that they had arrived at the campsite. The rest of them reached the top and found themselves at a level, smooth bowl between the rise of slopes. Here there was no wind. The spot seemed peaceful and protected.

Mrs. McGivern lit the gasoline lantern and stuck it up high so that its light bothered everyone. Roger took the short spade and began digging a hole for the fire. When he had finished, everyone brought firewood—their notion of the law varied according to their need—and crumpled newspapers. By seven o'clock dinner was cooking in skillets and pots over the grate, and the several sleeping bags had been laid out here and there. Now the sky was totally black. The only light came from the sizzling gasoline lantern.

Liz, circling the lantern, said, "Is there any chance it'll blow up?"

"No," Mr. Van Ecke said. "But somebody should keep their eye on it to pump it up when the pressure gets low."

A boy, one of Liz's, was assigned to watch the lantern.

For dinner they had lamb chops and baked potatoes and green beans, cake, milk from the thermos flask, coffee for the adults. Unopened cans of hash were put off to one side for breakfast in the morning.

The sky showed them stars in unending number, and for an hour different members of the hiking party pointed out constellations. Once, a meteor dropped like a stone the entire length and was lost to sight among the mountains to the north. No one saw it start; it seemed to come into existence out of nothing. And, they agreed, it did look as if it had come unattached. Gravity had yanked it down.

Beyond the light of their gasoline lantern, living creatures stirred and hooted. One sound repeated itself, a whirring, guttural and excited. "That's a ground squirrel," Mrs. Alt said.

Liz said, "You're sure it isn't a wildcat?"

"Ground squirrels are all around here," Mr. Van Ecke said.

Later in the evening, a frantic squabble broke out in the darkness. Screams and thrashings in the underbrush woke up all the sleeping boys.

Mr. Van Ecke said, "Something just now got something."

"Probably an owl," Mrs. Alt said. "It probably caught a field mouse or a squirrel."

She and Mrs. McGivern and Mr. Van Ecke and Liz and Roger sat around the fire, prodding it now and then with the sticks that had been used to toast marshmallows. The time was eleven-thirty.

"It's getting cold," Mrs. McGivern said.

Next to Roger, Liz sat with her knees drawn up and her arms wrapped about them. She wore rolled-up jeans, and in the firelight her calves shone dark-red, smooth, bare. As smooth, he thought, as bone. Reaching out his hand, he touched her on the ankle; he tugged at her sock and she put one hand down and closed her fingers over his. Her skin was hot from the closeness of the fire. The fire had become mostly coals, giving off a deep low current of heat. Liz had crouched forward so that her head was near. Her hair reflected the color of the fire, the reddish brown that came so close to being black. He saw that her neck was streaked with dampness, and it reminded him of the day, two years ago, when Virginia had burst into the house, and Liz had gone out of the bedroom, by herself, to meet her. In times of fear, and in times of excitement and exertion and even happiness, she seemed to become a little damp. She had leaped up in a kind of splash, as if she were rising to the surface.

But, he thought to himself, the texture, the substance in which she lived, had closed over for her. It had become calm and she had retired to that perfect core of unchangeability in which she was so much at home. Perhaps, he thought, she revolved slightly. But he saw no change in her. Nothing had happened to her. And, he thought, that was what he had sought out in the beginning. He saw that in her eyes; or rather, he saw within her eyes. Anybody could do that. The eye is not opaque. Looking straight at her, he had seen, revolving within, the utterly complete person. Nothing could alter her or affect her; Virginia had barged into the house, and Liz had leaped up and run from the bedroom, not so much to defend her house and honor but to protect him—and even that had passed over her and gone. And she was exactly the same as before.

Here she sits, he thought, with her head on her knees and her fingers closed over my own. Her legs are smooth and dark and shiny and warm. Her hair smells good, as it always has; she will always have that fine smile, and, beyond anything else, she will admit my gaze into her, all the way in, so that I can see, as I have never seen in anyone else before, what it is that I am really speaking to. And she will never be evasive. She will never lie. As long as I can hold her attention, I will see it as it really is. She is a kind of ultimate being, in so far as she goes. Within the bounds of her existence, she is absolute. And that, he thought, is because she has no real relationship to anything, except that she can be seen. But she can never be reached or taken over. Or acquired.

Her happiness, he thought, comes in this, in sitting by herself, next to me, doing nothing, needing nothing, going nowhere, and in a sense having been nowhere. Lacking memory, unable to anticipate, knowing nothing about death—as if, he thought, she had always been here, before the fire, with her fingers closed over his.

But as far as I go, he thought, I am finished. It was the end of me. Perhaps it failed to touch her, but it certainly touched me. Does she know that? She did her best, he thought, to get out of the room and between me and Virginia. She did everything she could. So she must have known what it would do to me. And Virginia did get by her, and did get into the room.

That goddamn Virginia, he thought. But eventually even Virginia would sicken and die. Her life would dwindle and she would creep about in a mid-world, knowing things only by their touch.

But I'll be long since gone by then, he thought. So it won't make much difference. I'll be the first to go. In a sense, I am already gone.

Beside him, Liz said, "If a wildcat jumps down in front of you, what do you do? Bang on a pan?"

"Yes," he said. "Or call on God."

Swinging her head, she fixed on him her earnest, hopeful gaze. "You don't believe in God; I know, you told me."

Roger said, "That's true."

"Shouldn't you?" she said.

"Maybe I should," he said. Leaning towards her, he kissed her on the mouth.

* * *

The next afternoon, Saturday afternoon, he and Gregg drove back to Los Angeles.

"Did they have stamps back in Roman times?" Gregg said.

"I don't think so," he said.

"I think I have a stamp from Rome."

"Maybe so," he said.

The glare bothered his eyes and he got his dark glasses from the glove compartment, the lenses that clipped over his regular glasses.

"I didn't feel like coming along on the hike," Gregg said. "I don't care for hikes."

"Why not?" he said.

"Well, once Billy Haag and I got lost. We were hiking by ourselves. We never told anybody. We were lost two hours."

"Better watch it," he said.

"We were using Billy's compass."

Ahead of the car, along the road, stood a bunch of Mexican farm workers, hitchhiking. They waved their hands at him, and he slowed the car a little.

She would stop, he said to himself.

But he speeded up. The Mexicans swiftly fell away behind. "I should have stopped," he said to Gregg.

"Look," Gregg said. "There's more."

Another bunch of Mexicans, some of them even out on the road, waited ahead, thumbing rides. This time he slowed more; the Mexicans began running frantically toward the car, and he knew that he had committed himself whether he liked it or not.

"Open the door," he said to Gregg.

Gregg opened the door, and the Mexicans bounded into the car, one after another. Behind them, the first group had begun to hurry; before he could start up the car they had reached it. By the time he had got them in, there was no room for Gregg. One of the Mexicans swept Gregg up and set him down on his lap.

"Where are you going?" Roger asked the Mexicans.

They conferred in Spanish. At last one of them said, "Santa Paula."

"Across the mountains," another said.

"Okay," Roger said. "That's where I'm going."

Later, after they had got up the steep curves to the top and were descending on the south side of the range, one of the Mexicans said to him, "This is your little boy?"

"Yes," he said.

The Mexican patted Gregg on the head.

"He goes to school," Roger said. "Back at Ojai."

All the Mexicans beamed at Gregg, and several more of them reached out and patted him.

"Where you going?" one of the Mexicans asked Roger. He was a dark young man with a hard, strong brow and nose. His lips were large but not fleshy; his teeth were huge.

"To Los Angeles," Roger said.

"You live there?"

"Yes," he said.

The young Mexican said, "We're going down to Imperial. Go down there in winter and work." They all agreed, those in front and in back and the one holding Gregg on his lap. "Crops all winter. Lettuce." He made a stooping-gesture, and all the Mexicans groaned. "Time to go down there," the Mexican said. "Getting to be late."

"I never been down in the Imperial Valley," Roger said.

For the balance of the trip to Santa Paula, the Mexicans told him about the Imperial Valley.

After he had let them off, Gregg said to him, "They sure all got in when you stopped."

"They wanted to get over the mountains," Roger said.

When he and Gregg reached Los Angeles he drove to the house and parked. The front door was open, so evidently Virginia or the colored maid was home. Probably the maid. He watched the house, and presently the maid, Kathy, came out on the porch and shook the dustmop. Seeing him and Gregg, she waved her hand.

"Let's go in," Gregg said, shifting around on the seat. "Come on, Dad."

"You go ahead on in," Roger said. His watch read five-thirty. Virginia would be home, soon. "Go ahead," he said. "I'm going to drive down to the store."

"Okay," Gregg said.

"Good-bye," Roger said, as his son hopped out onto the parking strip and started towards the path.

"Good-bye," Gregg called back.

He drove in the direction of the store. A block or so away he parked and sat smoking a cigarette. The sun had set. Lights appeared here and there. The various stores were shut up for the weekend. At six o'clock he got out, locked up the car, and walked until he came to a gas station. Inside the office the attendant was making out a lubrication tag; he did not pay any attention as Roger opened the office door and entered.

"You got any maps?" Roger said.

"What kind?" the attendant said. "Pirate maps?"

From the rack Roger took down a map of California. The other maps were all of Los Angeles. "Thanks," he said. He left the station and walked back to his car.

Within the car, he spread out the map. Highway 66, he thought to himself. Up to Barstow and then across the Mojave Desert to Needles, and then a long grade, across the Arizona border to Kingman. And then straight east, through New Mexico and then the Texas Panhandle, to western Oklahoma as far as Oklahoma City, and then north. All the way to Chicago.

The car was half his. He had a legal right to take it out of the state. Virginia would never make anything out of that; he was positive.

But, he realized, he needed money in addition. Once he got to Chicago he could get some kind of job as a repairman, an electrician or in a factory, the work he was doing now. But he needed at least three hundred dollars to get him there. Pulling out his wallet he counted the money he had. Twenty dollars. Not enough to get him out of Arizona.

There is no reason, he said to himself, why I shouldn't take them. In a sense, a very real sense, they are mine. Nobody will stop me, because they would recognize that I have a right to be there. The cop said that.

Starting up the engine, he drove along the street. The window lights of the store had been turned on and the interior was dark. The salesmen, the repairmen, Virginia and Chic and Herb had locked up and left.

He made a left turn and drove onto the parking lot beside the store. Parking at the loading dock in the rear, hidden from sight, he stepped out.

Then he walked around to the front and unlocked the front door.

The store was empty. Everyone had gone home.

He locked the door behind him and passed by the counter, through the rear door, to the stock room where the inventory of television sets and stoves and refrigerators, in their packing cartons, were stored. Table model TV sets, he decided, would be easiest to sell, especially in the towns through which he would be driving. He unlocked the back door to the outside loading dock, and then he picked out the television sets he wanted—those that had been stored behind the others, out of sight—and carried them, one by one, to the car. He filled up the trunk compartment and the backseat. The sets were heavy, and by the time he had finished, his side hurt like hell.

My goddamn side, he thought, gasping and trembling. But anyhow, the sets were in the car. At least seven hundred dollars worth, at dealer's cost. If he got less than one hundred dollars a set he would wind up with five hundred dollars.

Going upstairs to the office, he pulled out the inventory cards that represented the sets he had taken. He stuck the cards in his pocket and returned to the main floor. Making sure that he had turned off all the lights, he locked the store up and got into the front seat of his car, behind the wheel.

The car, when he drove out of the parking lot, seemed sluggish from the weight of the sets. It'll get lighter, he said to himself, by the time I get there.